PRAISE FOR *FIREWALL*
BOOK 1 IN THE FBI: HOUSTON SERIES

"Mills takes readers on an explosive ride. . . . A story as romantic as it is exciting, *Firewall* will appeal to fans of Dee Henderson's romantic suspense stories."

BOOKLIST

"With an intricate plot involving domestic terrorism that could have been ripped from the headlines, Mills's romantic thriller makes for compelling reading."

LIBRARY JOURNAL

"A fast-moving, intricately plotted thriller."

PUBLISHERS WEEKLY

"Mills once again demonstrates her spectacular writing skills in her latest action-packed work. . . . The story moves at a fast pace that will keep readers riveted until the climactic end."

ROMANTIC TIMES

"This book was so fast-paced that I almost got whiplash! . . . [H]eart-pounding action from the first page . . . didn't stop until nearly the end of the book. If you like romantic suspense, I highly recommend this one."

RADIANT LIT

"Fast-paced and action-packed. . . . DiAnn Mills gives us a real winner with *Firewall*, a captivating and intense story filled with a twisting plot that will have you on the edge of your seat."

FRESHFICTION.COM

"*Firewall* is exciting . . . thrilling. DiAnn Mills draws her readers in, holding them breathlessly hostage until the very last page. She is a master at her craft and her genre."

BOOKFUN.ORG

"Mills's writing is crisply transparent and filled with solid research and believable characters and a spark of romantic chemistry. The mystery-ridden maze of tumultuous twists and turns, suspects and evidence, difficult questions and half answers will rivet the reader's attention."

NOVELCROSSING.COM

"*Firewall* should come with a warning! Be prepared to lose your breath and a lot of sleep with this exhilarating read."

LYNETTE EASON, BESTSELLING AUTHOR OF THE DEADLY REUNIONS SERIES

"*Firewall* is an up-until-2 a.m. book. . . . I had no idea who the mastermind was until the last two or three pages. Mills keeps getting better and better. Can't wait for the next one!"

LAURAINE SNELLING, AUTHOR OF THE WILD WEST WIND SERIES AND *WAKE THE DAWN*

"*Firewall* is a gripping ride that will keep your blood pumping and your imagination in high gear."

DANI PETTREY, AUTHOR OF THE ALASKAN COURAGE SERIES

DOUBLE CROSS

FBI: HOUSTON

DiANN MILLS

Tyndale House Publishers, Inc.
Carol Stream, Illinois

Visit Tyndale online at www.tyndale.com.

Visit DiAnn Mills at www.diannmills.com.

TYNDALE and Tyndale's quill logo are registered trademarks of Tyndale House Publishers, Inc.

Double Cross

Designed by Nicole Grimes

Edited by Erin E. Smith

Published in association with the literary agency of Books & Such Literary Agency, 52 Mission Circle, Suite 122, PMB 170, Santa Rosa, CA 95409.

Double Cross is a work of fiction. Where real people, events, establishments, organizations, or locales appear, they are used fictitiously. All other elements of the novel are drawn from the author's imagination.

Library of Congress Cataloging-in-Publication Data

Mills, DiAnn.
    Double Cross / DiAnn Mills.
        pages cm. — (FBI: Houston ; #2)
    ISBN 978-1-4143-8994-3 (sc)
1. United States. Federal Bureau of Investigation—Officials and employees—
Fiction.   2. Houston (Tex.)—Fiction.   3. Suspense fiction.   4. Christian fiction.   I. Title.
    PS3613.I567D68 2015
    813'.6--dc23   2014046415

Printed in the United States of America

21   20   19   18   17   16   15
7   6   5   4   3   2   1

To Special Agent Shauna Dunlap, media coordinator,
FBI Houston Division.
Thank you for your friendship and your faithful attention to all
my questions while fulfilling your commitment to the FBI.

ACKNOWLEDGMENTS

I WANT TO THANK the following people for helping me with *Double Cross*. I appreciate you!

Cathy Barrett—Always grateful for your input.

Stephanie Broene and Erin Smith—Thank you for your patience and expertise. I'm lost without you!

Special Agent Shauna Dunlap, media coordinator, FBI Houston Division—I couldn't write a novel about the FBI without your valuable input and friendship. Thanks so much.

Cecilia Benningfield, Connie Brown, Barbara Gill, and Alycia Morales—So value your feedback.

Lynette Eason—What fun we had brainstorming this novel. Couldn't have done it without you!

Julie Garmon—Thank you for all the hours spent critiquing my story. I so appreciate you!

Guy Gourley—Thank you for helping me explore the inner workings of characters' minds.

Karl Haroff—Guns and ammunition. Thanks so much.

Christy Kennard—I so appreciate our brainstorming sessions at Panera.

Yvonne Lehman—Thanks for all your encouragement.

Dr. Richard Mabry—Thanks for the medical assistance about adult-onset asthma and poisons.

Dean Mills—Thank you for believing in me and challenging me to be a better writer.

Dane Money—Your experience as a Houston police officer helped me portray Daniel as real.

Roberta Morgan—Thank you for sharing with me how financial institutions work to protect the assets of the elderly.

Tom Morrisey—Your knowledge of weaponry helps keep my story credible!

Patrick Morrison—I appreciate the time spent helping me see how the health industry compiles patient and client information.

Stella Riley—Thanks for all the valuable feedback.

Lauraine Snelling—Thanks for helping me through a rough plot point.

PROLOGUE

Special Agent Laurel Evertson had done everything required of her and more to gain Morton Wilmington's affections. The gaudy diamond on her left hand proved it. She was prepared to end her undercover work tonight and walk away from this despicable role. All she had to do was find the flash drive that would send her fiancé to prison for life.

Morton reached into his closet and pulled out designer pants, a shirt, and a sports jacket. "Babe, I'm taking a shower. Thought we'd grab dinner downtown before the play."

"Perfect. I'm ready. So looking forward to tonight." She despised the lies and the counterfeit love.

"What are you going to do? Read here?"

"I am. A new romance novel." She pointed to a window seat that offered a scenic view of his condo's pool bathed in late-summer afternoon sun.

He chuckled, his deep-blue eyes smoldering. "As long as I'm your main man."

"None other." She kissed him lightly. "I'm turning on a little Andrea Bocelli to put me in the mood."

"For what?"

"The book, the play, dinner, and us."

"Another reason why I love you. Even if you did beat me last night in Monopoly." He disappeared into the shower.

The moment the sound of water met her ears, she confirmed

his location. Four times she'd found herself alone in his condo and attempted to access his safe, but each time she'd failed to hack into his computer, where he stored the safe combination that changed daily. Today she knew his password, and she quickly located the code on his laptop.

She placed the novel on the bed and removed a framed picture of a tank at Fort Knox from the wall to reveal the safe. Odd for a bedroom, but Morton had served four years in the Army. Probably the only thing he could be proud of. She rested the picture against the nightstand while the digital combination bannered across her mind. Squeezing her fingers into her palm to steady herself, she pressed in the code, hoping Andrea Bocelli's tenor voice drowned out the low click. If she was wrong, the alarm would blare throughout the condo, bringing Morton out of the shower along with his bodyguard from the kitchen.

Big business had made him one of the most powerful men in the country, and certainly in Texas. Murder, money laundering, and organized crime were his best friends—legitimacy his enemy. But he'd made one mistake, exposing it all on a flash drive. He'd bragged about where it was hidden one night after drinking too much. It had taken her months to locate the safe and figure out how to gain access.

Was she any better than he, using another person for her own agenda? She shook off the thought and concentrated on her commitment to stop Wilmington from breaking the law.

She secured the flash drive and replaced the picture. Stealing her way to the bathroom door, she confirmed Morton was still showering. His laptop sat on his desk as though beckoning her to prove the FBI's suspicions. She inserted the drive. Her heart pounded, ached.

"Babe, had an idea for our honeymoon," he called from the bathroom.

"Great." She breathed deeply to calm her scattered nerves. "Are you going to tell me?"

"Maybe."

"You know I love surprises." The details on the computer rose like rich cream: names, places, bank accounts. She ejected the device and slipped it into her shoe.

"I sent a check to MD Anderson this morning," he said.

"For the kids or in general?"

"The kids. The fund-raiser we attended hit me hard."

But you'd killed men who got in your way. "They stole my heart too." She texted the FBI and Jesse, her partner, providing the code to the condo's alarm system and telling them where the armed bodyguard was located. "Do you need anything?"

"That's a loaded offer, but I'm good."

He wouldn't be so good once the FBI arrived for the takedown. "What time are we leaving?" She moved back to the window seat and opened her novel.

He stepped from the bathroom, a towel wrapped around his waist. "Is six okay?"

She smiled. "Sure." Finally this charade would be over.

While discussing what Wilmington wanted to do for the children at MD Anderson, he dressed and she touched up her makeup. Her hands trembled.

"Are you okay?" he said. "You're shaking."

"Just hungry." She hated this game, made her feel as dirty as Morton.

"Want a glass of orange juice?"

"You're so sweet. Thanks, I'd love it."

He left the room and went down the hall to the kitchen. She checked her phone.

W r n place. Now

With a confident breath, she pulled her Glock from her purse and trailed after Wilmington. Only moments remained.

A crash sounded from the kitchen and seized her attention.

Morton swore. "Laurel, stay back. Call the bodyguards."

She rushed from the bedroom, her hand fused to her Glock.

Gunfire exploded. One. Two. Three shots.

A bodyguard sprawled facedown on the floor, blood seeping from beneath him.

Jesse hid in the back of the kitchen by the utility room, trapped but able to fire.

"Morton, drop the gun." She inched closer.

"You're part of this?" His eyes and gun stayed fixed on Jesse. "You set me up?"

"It was my job."

He called her vile names that would echo forever.

"FBI. Lower your weapon." She moved closer. "Morton Wilmington, you're under arrest. Agents are waiting."

"You know how I operate. No one gets the best of me."

"You can give orders to the prison guards."

"You have a choice," Morton said. "Put down your gun, or I'll blow a hole right through this guy."

"That works both ways."

Morton swung a seething look at Laurel, allowing just enough time for Jesse to move into position.

Morton whirled and fired, sending Jesse backward to the floor, a bullet in his neck. Blood seeped across his upper body. His eyes wide-open . . . The cost of her undercover work.

Agents poured through the door. Morton dropped the gun and glared at her. "I have people everywhere. You can't hide, Laurel. No matter how long it takes. You'll pay in blood."

CHAPTER 1

FIVE YEARS LATER
9:30 A.M. WEDNESDAY, SEPTEMBER 23
HOUSTON FBI

Special Agent Su-Min Phang stood in the doorway of Laurel's cubicle. "How's the progress on the elderly fraud?"

Laurel spun her chair to face her. "I don't see much in common with the crimes, but I'm not saying someone hasn't covered his tracks. If it's the same bad guys, they're smart to lay low, then strike again in a different way."

"What do you have? We need this handled."

Laurel hadn't worked in the field since the day her partner died. She'd paid the price of bringing a criminal to justice. The guilt refused to release its tentacles, and maybe it shouldn't.

Now she was investigating white-collar crime and its surplus of lying, stealing, and cheating. Made a few bad guys exchange their suits and offices for jumpsuits and six-by-eight cells. The responsibility filled part of the hole in her heart.

This morning she concentrated on a series of Houston scams targeting the elderly, specifically wealthy senior citizens who bore the weight of dementia. The latest operation used fraudulent life insurance to steal thousands of dollars from their victims. The case revved up anger and fueled her determination to stop the crimes. Abusing those who could no longer make good choices? That was low.

1

A dear woman who'd raised Laurel had suffered from Alzheimer's, and she'd been treated like an animal. For her, and for all the reported cases, Laurel would help stop those who preyed upon the elderly.

She mentally reviewed the initial reports. Eight years ago, an outbreak of counterfeit prescription drugs swept across Florida, north to Georgia, and along the Gulf states to Texas. An estimated two million dollars was reported lost by the elderly. Investigators suspected a money-laundering source in Miami. No doubt more money had been made, but victims were often embarrassed when they realized the truth and chose not to report the crime. No leads, and the bad guys went dark.

Six years ago, another deception hit the innocent. Funeral plans and caskets were sold to unsuspecting elderly. Again the crimes began in Miami and spread through the Gulf states, but this time Arkansas and Oklahoma were involved. More money than before vanished. An agent in Miami received a tip that a dozen elderly were gathered at a hotel to learn how to make economical funeral arrangements. When the agents arrived, the scammer had disappeared. The results were a paper trail that led to a computer housed in an empty office. The hard drive had been removed. A dead end with the criminals again going dark.

Four and a half years ago, wheelchairs and remodeling projects geared toward the elderly hit the scene, infiltrating Florida and the Gulf states. Five months into the scam, the team shut down. Investigators saw the pattern, but the bad guys were smart enough not to leave a paper trail and to stop when things got too hot.

Two years later, a real estate fraud sold condos for luxury retirement high-rises in Florida, Alabama, and both Carolinas. Four months and they closed up shop. An estimated $50 million was made on that scheme.

This latest scam against the elderly might be the biggest moneymaker yet. Although the operation worked the same range of states, different cities were targeted. How soon before greed caused them to make a mistake or the FBI exposed their methods?

Su-Min stepped into Laurel's cubicle. "I have info. A gentle-man in River Oaks stumbled onto an e-mail that his elderly father received regarding the purchase of a life insurance policy. It contained part of another e-mail in it and we found encryptions. Looks like the bad guys might have gotten a little sloppy. Since you worked cryptology, I wanted you to take a look."

"Did you locate the sender?"

"Bogus. I just forwarded it to you."

Laurel clicked on the e-mail attachment, read the message, and studied the text. A sickening fear twisted her stomach.

"What's wrong?" Su-Min said. "You're ghastly white."

If only she could mask her turmoil. "I recognize part of this code." Laurel faced her partner and friend. "Morton Wilmington used a similar encryption to text his men."

"The exact?"

"No, but similar enough for me to see a connection and decipher most of what's written."

"No wonder you're a mess. What does it say?"

Laurel moistened her lips. "'Same instructions. Contact me after. New leads.' That's all I can make out without spending time on it. But whoever wrote it didn't give specifics."

"Do you think Wilmington's operating from prison?"

"Why not? He doesn't fit the mold for rehabilitation." Memories rapid-fired through her mind, burning thoughts that stoked the flames of regret.

Su-Min crossed her arms over her small Korean frame as though holding back a tiger.

"What are you not telling me?" Laurel said.

"Two things." Her voice softened. "We need boots on the ground to question him."

"I agree. Needs to happen immediately."

"There's more," Su-Min said. "Word is Wilmington's found religion. Christianity. Lawyers are working on an appeal."

"No matter how long it takes. You'll pay in blood."

Laurel gazed into Su-Min's coffee-colored eyes. Admitting her deep, bloodcurdling fear of this man would make her look weak. "An appeal will take years, so I'm not the least bit concerned. Let's sort this out. I see a link between a fraud targeting the elderly and Wilmington's method of encoding messages."

"He's in the thick of Bible studies and donating money—"

Laurel waved away her concern. "He's always given to charities. Helps ease his miserable conscience."

"While advocating faith?"

"Su-Min, my findings cement the unlikelihood of him ever reaching parole. I'll get the truth out of him. After all, I put him there, and he's not getting out. He can spout Bible verses all day long, but crimes are to be paid for. No one has more of a stake in him staying put than I do."

"He's already gaining notoriety for his religious stand."

"Remember, Robin Hood loves the limelight. Our focus is the elderly fraud."

Su-Min shrugged. "Another agent can question him."

Laurel drew in courage. The only way she'd end the nightmares would be to face him. "I have to do this. And I'll nail him for the scam. Arrange the interview."

"Hope you're right. You know he hasn't forgotten the past. I'm surprised one of his men hasn't taken care of you." She tapped her foot. "Are you careful when riding Phantom?"

"Always." She refused to fall prey to her friend's caution. "Wilmington's too busy running his business to care about me. I'm not worth it."

"Or maybe one of the reasons he has a new platform is to walk out of prison free and kill you himself."

✳ ✳ ✳

11:00 A.M. WEDNESDAY

Houston Police Officer Daniel Hilton wove through the traffic of FM 1960 near Willowbrook Mall to a home invasion in progress, siren blaring and lights flashing, his version of parting the Red Sea. According to the call slip, a woman heard glass breaking at her back door and saw two men wearing ski masks and holding weapons. She hurried upstairs to grab her napping toddler and called 911. The operator kept the woman on the line. Other officers were on their way, but Daniel was the closest to the address.

Two minutes later, the dispatcher updated the call slip and repeated the victim's conversation while Daniel drove to the crime scene. The woman worked in the Galleria area but took the day off because her little girl was sick. If she hadn't been home, the alarm system would have alerted the police.

A red light stopped the car in front of him. Daniel slammed on the brakes while vehicles blocked him in on all sides. He alternated between the air horn and the siren. The driver ahead finally realized an HPD patrol car needed through and crept into the intersection far enough to let him pass. Where had this guy taken his driver's license test?

The home invasion address was in an upscale neighborhood, the intruders either high or stupid not to stake out a house before attempting entry. Did the woman have a weapon? And had she been trained to use it? She must be frantic . . . and with a child, too. He prayed they were safe and able to hide until help arrived.

Daniel braked next to the curb three houses back from the address as two hooded men hurriedly dumped armloads of goods into a late-model Ford parked in the driveway. They jumped inside, and the driver sped backward before the passenger door closed. Daniel sped his car to block them, but the driver jumped the curb and whipped around the front of the patrol car in the opposite direction.

"Don't think so," Daniel said and raced after them.

Fixed on the car's bumper, he tailed them toward State Highway 249 and radioed for backup. Another patrol car passed him from the opposite direction en route to the crime scene. Up ahead the burglars were slowed by a semitruck turning onto the feeder leading to the beltway. He anticipated them swinging their vehicle into a gas station, and he was right. The two men exited and ran, still in ski masks. Great.

No identity there. Daniel parked behind their car and chased the closest man, who disappeared around the corner of a storage facility. The second man pulled off his mask and headed into a residential area.

The pursuit through the storage facility reminded him of a TV script—down a narrow drive, then around a corner to hurdle a sleeping dog. The ski mask lay on the ground. He'd snatch it later. Probably some hair fibers on it. A fifteen-foot chain-link fence loomed in the distance, but unless the man held an Olympic track record, he wouldn't make it over before Daniel yanked him to the ground.

"Stop. HPD. You're under arrest."

The man continued toward the fence while reaching for his weapon, tucked into the back waist of his jeans. Daniel grabbed the perp's arm as he turned to fire, tossed him to the ground, and cuffed him.

"Hey, cop, don't you work in twos?" The man cursed. "If we'd known HPD sent just one, we'd have smoked you."

"No need for two officers when one works just fine."

"That woman invited us in. Wanted to give away some stuff," the man said.

"Tell that to the judge."

"I can explain. I have rights."

"Sure, buddy. Everyone has rights. Bet your story is real solid."

With the cuffed man in the back of the squad car, Daniel checked their vehicle. The rear seat and floorboard were filled with computer equipment, a large jewelry box, and a flat-screen TV. Big haul for such a short time. Recovering stolen goods was great news for the homeowner, making Daniel's job worth it. He radioed his location and where he saw the other intruder take off. The woman and child were fine, he was told, just shaken up.

"Meet you at the home," Daniel said. "Bring a K-9."

CHAPTER 2

Daniel opened the door to Silver Hospitality, the prestigious memory care facility that hosted his grandparents during the day, Monday through Saturday. Polished marble floors, white pillars that seemed to hold up the ceiling, and a three-foot-wide crystal chandelier gave the facility a five-star rating. This afternoon he didn't focus on the elite environment of Silver Hospitality or their state-of-the-art security system because he had a few hours of employee interviews to conduct here.

His grandparents had lost money to a fraudulent salesman who convinced Gramps to purchase a life insurance policy. An unexplained withdrawal of fifty thousand dollars from one of his grandparents' savings holdings to an overseas account alerted Gran, but nothing had been resolved. No receipt or paperwork. And his grandparents insisted the fraud occurred at the facility. Daniel had no idea how many clients had been affected.

Marsha Leonard, the director, greeted him in the foyer. The cavernous pits beneath her eyes told of sleepless nights. No one wanted to believe such an atrocity had happened. Since the clients suffered from dementia, asking them questions when they didn't know if a crime had even been committed made the going tough. The one reliable source was his grandmother—a mentally healthy woman. She'd witnessed a man persuading a client to purchase a

7

life insurance policy, not knowing Gramps had given the salesman access to their own financials.

"Daniel, I really appreciate your expertise in conducting these interviews." Perspiration beaded around Miss Leonard's mouth. "Notifying the caregivers and guardians of these precious people makes me ill."

Did she have reason to be nervous other than her job being at stake? "I want the situation rectified as badly as you do," he said. "We need to make an official announcement once the interviews are conducted. We have nearly twenty-five people to question. What we don't finish today, we'll continue tomorrow afternoon."

She drew in a deep breath. "I don't know what I'd do without your guidance. If this is true, our reputation is ruined." She hesitated. "That's callous. A crime might have been committed, and I'm worried about my job."

"A crime *has* been committed. The question is the source."

The lines between her brows deepened. "Let's get started."

"I'd like to speak to my grandparents first. Won't be long."

Daniel signed in and made his way to the recreation room, where Gran and Gramps spent most of their daytime hours. Gran had her nose in a Kindle, while Gramps played dominoes with a couple of other men. Daniel kissed the top of Gran's head.

Her gaze flew to his. "Hi, Daniel. You surprised me."

He chuckled. "What adventure are you in today?"

"Third novel in George R. R. Martin's Song of Ice and Fire saga, *A Storm of Swords*."

"Hope it's a good one." He glanced at Gramps. "How is he?"

She tilted her head. "Slipping."

"I'll say hello before talking to the staff."

"I don't want to think any of them are guilty, but there's no way that man got inside here without help."

"Right." He greeted Gramps, who paid no attention, and hurried to Marsha Leonard's office, where he'd be busy for a while.

For the next two hours, he talked to people who worked at the facility. Though he wasn't here in an official police capacity, he requested written permission to record the interview as a representative of Silver Hospitality and to verify the validity of their statements. The questions were the same. Were they satisfied with their position? How long had they been employed at Silver Hospitality? Had they allowed anyone to enter the premises without appropriate security measures? Had they ever been convicted of a misdemeanor or felony? All had undergone background checks prior to employment, but he repeated the questions in case their status had changed.

At seven o'clock, Liz Austin slid into a chair across from him. She'd applied a fresh coat of bright-red lipstick, and she'd pulled out her ponytail, allowing her blonde hair to fall in waves. Yep, a beauty right down to her light-blue eyes. No, he wasn't interested, no matter how many times she threw herself at him. Women who flaunted the obvious spelled trouble.

"Miss Austin, I see you've been with the facility for nearly ten months."

"Please, call me Liz. We're friends." She crossed her legs and leaned forward. Cleavage was her specialty. "Ten months is correct."

"Are you satisfied with your position?"

She laughed. "I'm in the kitchen with Chef Steven. I do grunt work. Seeing you is the highlight of my day."

He printed her response minus the personal comment. "Have you been arrested for anything since you began working here?"

"Not unless my thoughts about you can get me into trouble."

This time he gave her his best professional gaze. "The sooner we complete these questions, the sooner we can go home."

"Alone?"

"Absolutely."

"How sad. What are you doing later?"

"Have you ever allowed anyone inside Silver Hospitality without authorization?"

"No. Why? So they could slice limes and lemons for me?"

He smiled. "We're finished here. Thanks for your time."

"Later?"

"No, thank you." He stood and opened the door.

Once she left, he noted the list of staff was finished for the night. Good thing. Liz Austin tested his patience. Not exceptionally bright if she believed her body would get her through life.

None of the interviews indicated a problem. Body language and eye contact were good. He didn't really want any of them to be guilty, but it would make his life easier.

Daniel found his grandparents still in the recreation room and eased into a chair at a game table, where Gramps was winning at dominoes. His favorite pastime.

"Cleaned up on these old men." Gramps grinned. "Christmas has come early."

"But you cheat." Gran stood with her leather bag in hand.

"No, I don't."

She kissed his cheek. "You play with the same men. You know their habits and read their body language."

"That's playing smart."

"Call it what you want." She turned to Daniel. "We're ready."

"Sorry tonight's so late."

"It's all right." Gramps moved toward the foyer and out to the parking lot. "Had some great food tonight. Guess what we had?"

"Roast beef and mashed potatoes?"

"Even better. Pork tenderloin, and if I didn't know better, I'd bet Chef Steven marinated it in Jim Beam."

"Earl, the facility wouldn't permit alcohol even if it was cooked off," Gran said. "Interferes with some medicines."

"Maybe the cook used cider." Daniel ached with exhaustion.

Gramps blew out an exasperated breath. "I'm old, but my taste buds can tell the difference between Jim Beam and deluxe apple juice." He laughed. "It was cider."

Daniel patted him on the back. He relished these moments along with all the years spent with them. "Are you happy here?"

The older man stopped. "I see my friends every day. Abby is with me. Why wouldn't I be?"

"A change of pace might be nice."

"Are you kidding? Miss the chess tournament? Brownie and ice cream day? Watch those cute young girls make a fuss over us? No way am I missing a day here."

CHAPTER 3

Daniel set a bowl of popcorn on the kitchen table. Gran crossed the tile floor of the massive kitchen that looked like a feature from *Architectural Design*. With slow steps, she carried sweet decaf tea for her and Gramps. The telltale signs of fatigue swept over her, and rightfully so. Her low blood pressure had dipped below the normal level, but Gramps was hungry, and he always came first. Daniel remembered her playing G.I. Joe with him and climbing trees in their huge backyard. Days gone by, when his grandparents chose to put him above all things in their lives, except God.

She touched Gramps on the shoulder and pointed to the table. What good did seven thousand square feet of luxury do when Gran's health was deteriorating and his grandfather no longer had the sharp mind of yesterday? His snowcapped beard was his trademark, and his twinkling blue eyes still danced. But he often lived in the light of the past.

Once seated, Gran stroked Gramps's arm, but he ignored her, an indication his mind rested in the before.

"Daniel, she was a beauty. Don't you remember?" He bit into a handful of buttery popcorn.

"Gran?"

"No." Gramps leaned across the table. "The redhead in chemistry. She had lashes long enough to hide behind."

"That was Gran."

He slapped the table. "I knew my charm would win her. Where is she?"

Daniel studied the dear man, and a tear trickled down Gran's cheek. "She's sitting next to you, and she's still a redheaded beauty." Granted, the color had faded but was still vibrant, and she had a warrior's heart.

Gramps blinked, his mind obviously working to understand. He frowned. "You're wrong. . . . I . . . I . . ." He pressed his lips and took Gran's hand. "I love you, Abby."

"I love you too," she said. "We'll make it through this."

"You and I will share many good years together."

"Until death do us part," she whispered.

"Abby, promise me I won't be a problem to you."

"Love is giving, and with you it will always be easy." She dabbed beneath her eyes. "Have some more popcorn before we become the next Hallmark movie."

Daniel knew his grandfather wouldn't want to burden his wife with his care full-time. But Daniel had already promised himself that a permanent living arrangement outside their home for either of them would never happen. He'd move from his own home first. Silver Hospitality would be all either of them saw of institutionalized living.

"I told Tom and Emma not to dump their money there after we lost so much. Chased good money after bad."

Was this Gramps talking or the young man in his mind? Tom and Emma were friends from Silver Hospitality.

"I'm doing all I can to rectify this," Daniel said.

"Hey, I don't like that smart tone."

Gran patted his arm. "It's okay, Earl. I'm right here. He just wants to help."

Gramps blew out his exasperation. "I'm sorry, son. The big A's messing up my mind again. Anyway, my friends are losing money, and I don't know how to stop it."

"We're working on getting your money back. The lawyer says whoever withdrew the funds had the account number and proper transfer documentation. Now the bank won't allow a dime to be released without all three of our signatures."

Gramps shook his head. "Losing cash because a person makes a stupid decision is one thing. Take me to the FBI. Those folks will get the money returned to its rightful owners. Can't tell me Silver Hospitality was the only elderly care center hit by bad boys."

"I'd rather wait until I've had time to talk to Marsha Leonard again, and our lawyer."

"White-collar crimes are under the jurisdiction of the FBI. You're an excellent police officer, but we need more resources. The ones who stole the fifty grand still have our bank account number. You think we're safe, and maybe so. But those crooks need to be behind bars."

"I promise I'll get you answers."

Gramps pushed back his empty bowl. "Either you take me, or I'll get Abby to drive. Their office is on State Highway 290, big green windows. You choose."

"I need a receipt or a name." His grandparents had been swindled, but what could he do? Gramps's mind jumped from past to present to not remembering. The bank transaction had the appearance of his grandfather's conducting the business.

"Told you the receipt was to be sent e-mail."

"But you don't have e-mail."

Gramps shrugged. "I intended to set one up."

"Even the FBI requires evidence of a suspected crime."

Gramps drummed his fingers on the table. "I have the salesman's appointment on my calendar and his name. I also have a brochure from his company."

He disappeared and soon returned. He laid a brochure from Lifestyle Insurance on the table. No contact information was listed.

"Take this, and see what you can find out. The same guy who sold life insurance to Tom and Emma gave me his propaganda," he said. "The man convinced us that our families would benefit from our generosity." He spit the words. "The security camera at Silver Hospitality must have been down 'cause I know what happened."

"Give me a little more time."

"I'll handle this on my own."

"Daniel, I'll take him to the FBI." Gran hadn't said a word to this point. "This isn't your fight."

A dull ache persisted at the base of Daniel's head. "Okay, we'll go in the morning. I'll call into work now and tell them I'll be late."

His cell phone buzzed: Marsha Leonard.

"Daniel." Her voice trembled. "When Tom Hanson's son arrived to pick him up, we thought he was sleeping . . . but he'd died of a heart attack. Would you tell Earl and Abby? They were so close."

His gut twisted. "I saw him tonight, and he was fit, healthy. Gramps played dominoes with him. I can't believe this."

"Me too. But his time must have come. Tom's family has requested a memorial service tomorrow evening."

"We will be there. Please give our condolences to the family." The call ended, he glanced at his grandparents. Uneasiness dumped caution into his system. According to Gramps, Tom had purchased a fraudulent life insurance policy. And now he was dead.

CHAPTER 4

Laurel's stomach protested her lack of breakfast, and lunch was over three hours away. But she had a sure way to appease her stomach's growls. With her attention on the computer screen, she pulled open a drawer and wrapped her fingers around a Snickers bar. The luscious scent made her mouth water—the velvety milk chocolate and the crunch of peanuts. True nirvana.

Relishing each bite, she scrolled through the reports from state-wide agencies, reading the victims' accountings. Many were ashamed, robbed of their finances, and depressed. Instantly she sobered. These guys needed to be stopped. That meant following through in seeing Wilmington, proving he was behind the scams with his encoded communication. Did he think she wouldn't recognize it?

Acid rose in her throat. Wilmington was her prize criminal. She'd clip his wings for this and ensure he never hurt anyone again. The thought of meeting with him today made her skin crawl.

Her phone rang, interrupting her thoughts: Su-Min.

"Laurel, we have an interview. Thatcher Graves introduced me to an elderly couple and their grandson who need to talk to us." She indicated the interview room to meet them.

Thatcher worked violent crime. She and Su-Min worked white collar. Why the threesome on an interview when she had so much to do?

17

"I'll be right there." She popped the last bite of Snickers into her mouth and grabbed her iPad and cell phone. Curiosity filled her. But she didn't need another case to divert her time, only the one looming over her.

Laurel knocked on the interview door and waited for permission to enter. Five minutes later Su-Min joined her in the hall. The interview must be intense to make her wait.

"Won't take long," Su-Min said.

"Why Thatcher?"

She shook her head. "Random. He walked in with an elderly couple and their grandson. The older man told him his friend might have been murdered. That got Thatcher's attention, and he decided to take part in the interview."

"Okay. What's going on?"

"The intel we're receiving is indicative of similar cases involving elderly fraud. I think this complaint is worth pursuing." Su-Min gestured her inside.

An older couple and a younger man stood when Laurel and Su-Min entered the room.

Su-Min began the introductions. "Mr. and Mrs. Hilton, Officer Daniel Hilton, this is Special Agent Laurel Evertson. She and I work white collar crime together. I've called her in because she's been investigating a case that mirrors your concerns."

Laurel shook hands with the Hiltons, noting the white-haired man's Santa-type appeal and the younger man clad in jeans and a blue knit shirt. The woman trembled, perhaps fearful of the interview or an indication of a neurological problem. "It's a pleasure to meet you. Shall we get started?"

The Hiltons sat across the table from the agents.

Laurel opened her iPad. "How can I help?"

Su-Min cleared her throat. "Agent Evertson, the Hiltons are clients of Silver Hospitality, an elderly day care facility that provides assistance from 6 a.m. to 9 p.m. seven days a week. Their grandson, Officer Hilton, provides the transportation."

Laurel googled Silver Hospitality and learned it was a private facility off Memorial Drive that specialized in memory care, likely the reason the younger Hilton accompanied the older couple. How sad for him.

"I don't have dementia," Mrs. Hilton said, her brown eyes bright with intelligence. At one time, her hair must have been a vivid red, and the years had merely softened the color. "I accompany Earl to the facility six days a week as a companion. We've been together for seventy years, and I don't intend to stop because of a little mind blip. I spend most of the day with my husband, but sometimes I leave him alone with his friends to play games and talk." She straightened and revealed the sophistication of years gone by. "We're here because Earl was scammed and possibly a few others." She rested her hand atop her husband's.

Officer Hilton smiled at his grandmother, and she relaxed. Sweet sight.

"And you believe a crime has been committed?" Su-Min said to Mrs. Hilton.

"Yes, but I was not privy to any financial arrangements. Earl told me he had purchased a life insurance policy, and I ignored him. Then the savings account statement came in, and fifty thousand dollars was missing." She sighed. "We are financially secure, but the theft needs to be addressed."

"Abby, I'm so sorry," Earl said. "The FBI and Daniel will help us get our money back and find the answers."

The older man appeared lucid, but if this man had Alzheimer's or dementia, little of what he said in court would be valid.

"You're thinking I haven't a clue what I'm talking about." Earl folded his hands on the table. "Yes, I've been diagnosed with the big A. That means my mind jumps around from time to time, and it could happen during this conversation. So I need to say a few things now just in case."

The grandson stiffened. Yet his eyes emitted warmth and caring.

"My grandson here is a blessing. Daniel has his own home and responsibilities, but he's ready at a moment's notice to take care of Abby and me. Spends more time at our house than his. He was totally against the meeting today. In fact, he's helping Silver Hospitality conduct staff interviews to see if any of them bypassed the security system to let the salesman inside. But I threatened to come alone. One of our friends just passed, and I know he purchased something from the swindler. A woman at the facility bought sour goods too."

"What was your friend's name?" Su-Min said.

"Tom Hanson."

"What was the name of the company and the salesman?"

Mr. Hilton pulled a slip of paper from his shirt pocket. "I found this inside my Bible, the name of Russell Jergon. I think he represented a company called Lifestyle Insurance. As I said, my mind isn't what it used to be. I remember a gravelly voice."

Su-Min handed the piece of paper to Thatcher and on to Laurel, who did a quick search and found nothing listed for the business or the salesman. Neither did the slip of paper have the business's name. "Do you have an address or phone number?" Laurel said.

"No, ma'am. Jergon visited the center during the afternoon. Talked to Tom, Emma, and me." The lines in his face deepened. "Are you real agents or are you playing a game?"

Compassion poured through her. "No reason to feel deceived. We're here to help. Were you given a receipt?"

"All I remember is the man said he preferred to send an e-receipt. I didn't want to sound like a product of the Dark Ages, so I gave him the address Daniel had suggested I use for setting up an e-mail account." He shook his head. "Why I didn't give him Daniel's e-mail is ludicrous. Anyway, I intended to go home and have him get me online, but I forgot."

"It's all right, Gramps," Officer Hilton said.

A tear slipped from a clouded eye. "I'm aware of how ridiculous this sounds. But human dignity is involved here. A company scammed old folks whose minds are like light switches, and now a friend has died. Supposed to have been a heart attack. My Abby is the only mentally healthy client there."

"I'm surprised the facility allows her to join you." Laurel studied her for signs of dementia.

Abby Hilton smiled. "That's because our money is building a new wing. Get my own way a lot."

More of a reason for bad guys to get their fingers into the Hiltons' pie. Laurel mentally compared the other elderly scam cases, realizing the Hiltons' claims were nearly identical, except no one else had reported a death. The latter needed to be looked into.

"Technology can accomplish anything, and that scares me." Earl's shoulders rose and fell. Beaten and humiliated. "When we're logical, no one wants to admit they've been preyed on." He straightened. "The man came twice to talk to folks." He looked at his wife. "Right?"

"That's what you told me, dear. I saw the man talking to Earl, Tom, and Emma. I thought he was a visitor. Then I listened to the conversation and realized he was urging Emma to give him money. The rules state clients are supposed to keep personal belongings locked up in the safe, but there's always ways to get around the rules. I went after the director, but she was busy. By the time I convinced the security guard there was a problem, Jergon had left."

"Is the deceased's family aware of your claims?" Thatcher said.

"I have no idea," Abby said. "Tom's death is more my concern than losing money. He was a healthy man. Alzheimer's people usually die of pneumonia."

Laurel made notes on her iPad. "Did the salesman have anything unusual about his appearance?"

Abby nodded at Earl. "He was older than my grandson," he said. "Had streaks of gray in his hair. Dark brown. Possibly a little Hispanic blood, but no accent. He was under six foot. Muscular, like he worked out."

"Thank you, sir," Laurel said. "When did he visit?"

"A month ago. Like I said earlier, he came in the afternoons when some take naps."

"It's a perfect time," Abby said. "Half the staff is on break then. I often talk to the receptionist or director. Daniel, have I missed anything?"

"I don't think so."

What a gentle tone he used for his grandparents. "Mrs. Hilton, did you or any of the staff talk to the salesman?" Laurel said.

"Yes. I asked him what he was doing there. Later I checked but couldn't find where he'd signed in at the front desk."

Daniel nodded. "The facility has security cameras in place and no one is allowed past the receptionist area unless their name is on the client's list, they've produced identity, and they're electronically allowed inside the clients' area. I checked again before we came, and there's nothing indicating a man with his description." Daniel's voice was not the least condemning. Laurel's respect for the younger man rose several notches.

"The cameras could have been turned off. They're computer controlled," Earl said. "And you've been there in the afternoon, walked in without a question."

"In my uniform. They recognize me."

Earl clenched his fist. "Anything can happen if properly planned."

"My husband owned an accounting firm." Abby linked her arm with his. "He can spot a crime before it happens."

"That takes an intelligent man." Laurel smiled into the older man's face. "The FBI's work is useless without community support. Our job here is to sort through the facts and make an informed decision."

"Are you placating me, young lady?" Earl raised a brow. "How long have you been an agent?"

"Eleven years, sir."

"Because if you think a sweet smile will make me feel better, you're wrong. Dead wrong. I don't intend to give up until the truth surfaces."

Laurel liked Earl's spunky attitude, although irritability was an indication of Alzheimer's. She admired Abby's support of a man who was reverting to memories from the past to communicate in the present. "Not at all. You aren't the first person to complain about being cheated out of money. This could be a small operation or a large one working city to city. We have other reported cases similar to yours."

The older man turned to his grandson. "You'll follow up on this, right? We don't need any more suspicious deaths."

Normally Laurel would have smiled at Earl's attempt at manipulation, but not when the man had experienced a fraud.

"I'll keep in contact with the FBI," Daniel said. "Inform you of any new developments."

"I don't have any more questions," Thatcher said. "But we'll look into the matter. Special Agent Evertson may have a few questions."

Other than involving an artist for a sketch of Russell Jergon, she didn't have much to go on. The whole concept of coercing older people out of their hard-earned money frustrated her. What she needed to check was the mental and physical status of all the victims.

"What can I do to help? And who'd believe me?" Earl said. "I could pick out the man in a lineup, and that makes me a candidate to get hurt."

"I understand," Laurel said.

"Do you? Have you ever been afraid for your life?"

Laurel masked her fear. When Jesse died, she'd taken a six-week leave of absence to deal with the aftermath of her undercover work. "Since your caretaker is an HPD officer, I doubt anyone will bother you."

"Thanks, young lady. Jimmy, I'm ready to go. Your mom will have lunch on the table."

There went her idea to have Earl help compile a sketch of the salesman.

Daniel sighed. "We do need to leave. Gramps, I'm Daniel, not Jimmy."

Earl eyed him. "You aren't Jimmy?"

"He's my dad. I'm your grandson."

Earl stood. "Guess I'm confused." He peered at Gran. "Who are you?"

Abby took his hand. "I'm your favorite redhead."

Daniel nodded at the agents, obvious embarrassment creeping into his face. "Thank you very much for your time. You have my contact information. I apologize for any inconvenience."

"That's why we're here." Thatcher's words sounded professional with a twinge of sympathy.

"Wait a minute." Laurel wanted to soothe what the Hiltons might interpret as noncaring. "Here's my card, Officer Hilton. I promise I'll look further into this. Illegal activities involving the elderly are one of my personal projects." She moved around the table and took Earl's hand, pressing another card into his palm. His eyes no longer sparkled. "Sir, I do know what it's like to be afraid for your life. I'm here for whatever you need."

CHAPTER 5

Exiting the FBI building, Daniel glanced at the bureau's emblem etched in stone outside the glass doors. Many a press conference took place here, and he hoped the fool he'd made of himself today wouldn't be the subject of one of them.

He mulled over this conversation with Agent Evertson. He didn't need to act like she was the enemy. The whole matter could have been handled better. He tended to be hard on himself, demanding perfection in all aspects of his work. It was frustrating to feel shut out of an investigation, and he'd let his personal feelings for the big FBI and his grandparents' welfare get in the way of professionalism. The two law enforcement agencies needed to work together for the good of the people. Neither was superior to the other. His conclusions inched from irritated to logically thinking through what alienation from the FBI meant. If his grandparents had stumbled onto a viable crime—and he believed they had—then it must be stopped.

Gran was so loyal, but by her own admission, she hadn't witnessed all of Gramps's claims. But the money had disappeared from their account, and the problem originated at Silver Hospitality. Daniel had been adamant, insisting the facility had been lax in their security. With Miss Leonard's permission, he'd hoped to uncover some answers by conducting staff interviews.

Maybe he should pull his grandparents and find a new facility.

He assisted his grandparents through the security gate and on to the designated visitor parking area, where his Ford pickup awaited them, a dual cab deluxe he'd purchased for their added comfort. He couldn't get there fast enough. Humiliation sank to the soles of his feet. He scanned the FBI building and the towering windows. Just how many special agents were laughing at the HPD officer who brought in his Alzheimer's-stricken grandfather? Daniel should have stuck to his original stand and refused to take Gramps to the office. He still had the interviews at Silver Hospitality to finish this week.

His grandfather's problem began two years ago with a continuous inability to balance his checkbook. Then he couldn't remember if he'd taken his cholesterol and diabetes meds. Confusion. Frustration. Sudden bursts of anger so unlike Gramps. After several medical opinions and a consistent diagnosis of Alzheimer's, he accepted his condition. He expressed concern about Gran being able to care for him, since she had health issues of her own. Daniel found Silver Hospitality, where Gramps could stay while he worked. Gran insisted on accompanying him.

Gran scooted into the rear seat of the dual cab and buckled in. Gramps was quiet, probably revisiting another world where the past was kinder. He'd been coherent for most of the interview, giving the FBI his observations. It would help if Daniel had an idea where the fifty grand had gone—then he could investigate further. Gramps was convincing, persuading Daniel to look further into what might be going on at the senior care facility. Security was a selling point for Silver Hospitality, but the same technology designed to keep people safe could be reversed with a keystroke.

Torn between logic and his love for the two people who'd raised him, he gave Gramps a smile.

"Jimmy, don't drive too fast," Gramps said. "You just got out of jail, and I'd like to keep your record clean." He clicked his seat belt tight.

"I'm Daniel." How many times had he corrected Gramps?
"Who?"

"Never mind. I won't drive too fast. You're safe with me." Oh, the truth in those words. Right there with the sharp regret of his grandfather's illness.

He pulled onto State Highway 290 and drove into town, heading to the Memorial area of Houston and Silver Hospitality.

"Your mom hates for us to be late. She's made tuna melts and Jell-O."

"She's right here, Gramps. In the backseat."

The old man covered his face. Tears rolled down his cheeks. "No, Jimmy. What a horrible thing to say. I'm not blind."

Daniel swallowed the bitterness of Gramps's condition. Gran touched his shoulder. "We'll be home soon."

※　※　※

12:30 P.M. THURSDAY

Laurel believed in kindness. She'd learned it firsthand from Miss Kathryn, the most caring person who'd ever walked the earth, a dear foster mother. Su-Min, on the other hand, was irritated that Officer Hilton had brought his grandfather in for the interview. She'd called it a waste of taxpayers' time and resources.

Laurel felt differently. Investigating crimes was not a waste. She stared at her cell phone, her thoughts lingering on Earl Hilton's bright-blue eyes contrasted against his balding white hair and snow-colored full beard. He deserved better treatment.

Pressing in Daniel Hilton's number, she hesitated, not sure why. The call was prompted by her commitment to the elderly. Nothing more. He answered on the first ring.

"Mr. Hilton, this is Special Agent Laurel Evertson with Houston's FBI. Do you have a moment to talk?"

"I'm driving to work. Have a little time. I didn't expect you'd get back so quickly. Of course, the likelihood of the FBI considering my grandparents' case is nil."

"Quite the contrary. We're committed to going forward with the investigation. Would your grandmother be willing to help develop a composite of Russell Jergon?"

"I'm sure she'd agree. Would you take that same pic to Silver Hospitality for possible identification?"

"Yes, agents would handle that."

"I'm surprised the FBI is taking my grandparents' claims seriously."

She preferred not to give him details regarding the other cases. At this point, this was an FBI matter. If and when they joined forces with HPD as part of a task force, then he could learn more. "Whether they are related to other cases the FBI is investigating remains to be seen. Our concern is the scam and a death."

"Here in Houston, statewide, or national?"

"I'm not free to give more information. When the public can be informed, we'll provide a press release."

"I'm not the public or the community. I'm a police officer, and I will find the answers with or without your help."

"Officer Hilton, this is FBI jurisdiction. I'm sure your superiors will provide information on a need-to-know basis."

"My grandparents are my jurisdiction."

Stalemate. Yet she understood his stance. "I sincerely wish there was something you could do."

"I'll be the judge of my capabilities."

She didn't want a family member involved in the investigation. Those situations meant reactions from the heart instead of logic and training. It also led to mistakes resulting in death. "I strongly advise against your involvement, Officer Hilton."

"I understand you're not at liberty to report your findings, but these are my grandparents, and I will not sit idle. I'm committed to this investigation. Is that understood?"

CHAPTER 6

1:15 P.M. THURSDAY

Laurel glanced at the clock on her computer. The conversation with Officer Hilton still weighed on her. She understood how he felt, but the FBI were experienced in investigating white collar crime and murder, if that was the case.

Time she paid a visit to Morton Wilmington, without Su-Min. She'd explain to her later. Her friend had been distancing herself lately, and Laurel had no clue why . . . except Su-Min was anxious to climb the FBI ladder. Today's meeting with the Hiltons demonstrated a lack of compassion. No crime was a waste of time and resources. One day soon, Laurel would ask Su-Min if her career goals had stepped in the way of her commitment to protect the people and businesses of their community.

In reality, Su-Min would be right in objecting to what Laurel planned to do this afternoon. Interviewing a suspect alone went against FBI protocol, but Wilmington might lose his temper and tell her what she wanted to know. For her own peace of mind, she had to find out if he was working an elderly fraud. Too many unscrupulous people feasted on the older generation. They earned their trust and victimized them, but this group sought those with the minds of children. The victims who remembered the company's name or its representatives never matched. What bothered her the most was the sale of life insurance policies and what that could mean if the bad guys wanted to collect sooner than a natural death. And did that happen to Tom Hanson?

A smart operation, but not infallible.

She picked up a framed quote on her desk.

When I was young, I admired clever people. Now that I am old, I admire kind people.
ABRAHAM JOSHUA HESCHEL.

Earl Hilton's words bannered across her mind. *"Human dignity is involved here."*

Resolved, she drove toward the meeting. Chain-link fence and barbed wire surrounded Huntsville State Prison, home to a high percentage of repeat offenders and those who boasted of gang involvement. In years gone by, the prison hosted a rodeo for the surrounding community. Today it was only the local hotel for those who thought they were above the law.

Each time she deliberated Wilmington's model prisoner record and his allegation of finding God, she affirmed her conviction of why a huge chunk of the smartest people on the planet were criminals. The man was brilliant, but she had a few street smarts of her own, and the only way to get the edge on Wilmington was a face-off.

She left everything in the car except her ID and a copy of the e-mail with the encoded message. Her heart thudded, betraying her misgivings, but soon she faced a door opposite Plexiglas. She shivered, wishing she'd learned from textbooks what she'd experienced from life. With Morton Wilmington, her street smarts might need a refresher course.

Her nemesis appeared in the doorway. Smug. Full of confidence that came from those he'd crunched or eliminated while amassing money and power. She hadn't seen him since the day of his sentencing, after life took another ugly twist. Then he wore a contemptuous sneer and an imported silk suit worth more than her US-made car. Later he verbalized how she'd meet her demise.

The guard stood behind him, a young man who looked fresh out of the corrections academy.

She studied Wilmington in an attempt to see his soul, as if he had one. Still buff. Still carried his ego in his hip pocket. Still a lady's man from the way his gaze ravaged her. But now he resembled a painter wearing a white jumpsuit. He seated himself, his hands cuffed in front of him. She wouldn't let him intimidate her.

"Hello, Morton. Still playing Monopoly?"

"It's my favorite."

"How's the hotel business?"

"Did well on Boardwalk, but I misplaced my get-out-of-jail-free card."

Same wit. "Heard you were looking for it."

"I am, without a single bribe." He smiled, a lift of the right side of his mouth that didn't dispel the anger in his eyes. "I've achieved the game's objective—I'm still the richest player inside and out."

"I'm not bankrupt."

"Pretty lady, you didn't pay the rent, and the longer time passes, the more you owe."

She reached deep for the balance in her training and logic. "I recall the situation a little differently. The rent was more than paid."

He shook his head. Paused. Ah, the dramatics. "The past has a way of jumping into the present."

"Like the agent you murdered?"

He glanced down as though filled with regret, but the truth always surfaced. "Guilt is a flesh-eater."

She willed her emotions to stay stoic. "It was murder. Your so-called repentance doesn't change a thing."

His body language stayed intact. "Justice prevailed," he said. Did Laurel imagine the sneer in his tone?

"I'm sure his wife and kids think differently."

His face softened. "I've been tamed. My slate's clean according to my status with God."

Her stomach rolled. "You expect me to believe you?"

"*Your* opinion doesn't matter to me. Only God's."

"Your charade doesn't fool me."

"Doesn't have to." He smirked as though he'd uncovered every detail of her life. "I know your habits like you know mine. There's a big difference between us. While I'm in church on Sundays, you'll be riding Phantom, wishing you hadn't spent your childhood in a foster home, wondering why no one ever loved you. Hoping no one finds out you see a shrink. Trying to figure out what's wrong with you."

She glared at him, the words forming. But could she handle his response? "Do you still want me dead for sending you to prison? I'd like to hear where I stand before I talk about another matter. Total honesty."

"Do you still want me dead for shooting your partner?"

"I asked first."

"I'd like nothing more than to see you pay for what you did to betray me." The lines around his eyes deepened. "But until you make your peace with God, you'll spend every day of your life looking over your shoulder for who plans to end you. The sad part is you'll welcome it. I hope you find comfort soon. I found mine."

His words tore at her heart, frightening and bold, a combination that unnerved her. "I'm here to discuss an FBI matter."

"Alone?"

"I'm working on an elderly fraud case that implicates you."

"Impossible."

She unfolded the e-mail and pushed it to where he could read it. "The encoded message at the bottom is very much like the one you used with your men. Note the Greek numbers and Latin letters."

Not a muscle moved on his face.

"I know you recognize it, and your memory hasn't changed. What does it say?"

"Not today, sweetheart. Besides you've already figured most of it out. I have no idea about any elderly fraud case."

She swallowed her ire. "Are you working a scam while praising God?"

He pressed his lips together. "No."

"Why's the encryption so much like yours?"

He didn't blink. Only stared.

She kept her attention on him. Two could play this game.

"I can't help you," he said.

"Why? If you're serious about the faith thing, then wouldn't you want these innocent people protected? The victims are elderly with dementia. A man is dead, possibly because of this scam."

"I do care, but the situation's complicated."

"Like your bank account?"

He shook his head. "Some areas of my life are private."

"What can I say to convince you to cooperate?"

He sighed. "Nothing." He stood and nodded at the guard.

"I'm prepared to make an offer." Laurel was feeling desperate, grasping at straws.

"What kind?"

"Recommend parole."

He laughed. "And who will keep me alive? You? I've seen you in action, Laurel."

"You have my word. Help the FBI close in on the fraud case, and I promise to help shorten your sentence."

"You gave me your word when you said you'd marry me. What's the difference now?"

"This has nothing to do with back then. But if you won't assist in the case, I'll do everything in my power to block an attempt at parole." She paused for him to consider her offer.

"I'll think about it. This would be the deal—you don't pull the trigger on me, and I'll do my best not to pull one on you."

CHAPTER 7

Abby Hilton linked one arm with Earl's and the other through Daniel's before walking across the parking lot of the funeral home. All around her were old, blue-haired people wobbling in like it was their last day. A lot like her, though she'd never admit it. Seemed like they were attending more and more of these things, but then age had a way of catching up with you.

Hadn't she just talked to Tom earlier this week? He thought she was his sister, but that didn't matter. He laughed. Drank lemonade. Talked about living on a farm and milking cows.

Now he was in eternity, mind and body healed.

As they entered the funeral home, Abby squeezed Earl closer to her. Maybe she could prolong the inevitable, the passing from one life to the next, leaving her empty and alone. Memories were supposed to suffice.

Hogwash.

A woman couldn't cram seventy years into a thought that had no body. She couldn't spoon up to a warm husband and feel his love from every pore of his skin. Smiles were priceless, and a camera could never catch the special ones meant only for her since she was a girl.

Death. Who needs it? She lifted her chin. She and Earl would go together. Daniel shouldn't have to take care of them like

35

children when he needed his own wife and kids. She swallowed the emotion threatening to dissolve her. Life and death were a part of human existence. Birth came with joy, and most deaths were a celebration of life . . . when they occurred naturally. That ushered in again her fear that Tom's heart attack had assistance. Had Russell Jergon collected on a life insurance policy?

She shivered. If that were so, then who'd be next? Jerks. She might go after them herself. All her life, she'd faced challenges with faith and resolve, but this was different. She couldn't fight what she couldn't see.

Tom's daughter walked their way.

"So good to see you," Abby said and released Daniel but not Earl. "Why, Tom and I were talking just this week and he told me how you'd beat him at target practice when you were but ten years old."

The woman, a grandmother in her own right, dabbed at her eyes. "Daddy and I had a special relationship. We had a bond that made us closer than father and daughter, more like friends." She sighed. "Oh, Abby, I'm going to miss my friend."

"I understand," she whispered, unable to stop her quivering lips. "More than you know." Each time she lost a friend or loved one, a piece of her heart broke and fell onto her life's journey. What would she ever do without Earl? She kissed the woman's cheek and watched her walk away.

Daniel touched her shoulder. "I know what you're thinking. I promise to find out who's responsible for the fraud."

✳ ✳ ✳

8:45 P.M. THURSDAY

After leaving his grandparents at their home, Daniel remembered the days when his grandfather's opinion mattered to the businesses and city of Houston. No expansion project ever began without Earl Hilton's financial wisdom. He'd served in the Korean War and earned a Purple Heart. Had limped ever since. A hero in every sense of the word.

Gramps's mind was failing faster than the average stats for Alzheimer's sufferers. He wouldn't recover . . . only sink permanently into his own world.

Daniel's phone rang. The screen displayed Marsha Leonard's number.

"This is Officer Daniel Hilton."

"We have a problem at the facility."

"How can I help you?"

"Your grandfather has upset several of our clients with this scam business. I ignored it until tonight after the memorial service when clients' families approached me with their concerns. I have no idea what to do about the situation."

Daniel shoved aside the dramatics. "Gramps was a victim of fraud. We're trying to get to the bottom of it."

"My office has been flooded with calls and visits by family members. Discreetly questioning staff is one thing, but the gossip has to stop." Her voice rose, punctuating her words—and unleashing a load of anger in Daniel.

He counted to five. "What would you like for me to do?"

"How can you ask such a ridiculous question? You're his caregiver, and I need for you to take responsibility for your grandfather's actions."

"I'll talk to my grandparents."

"He claimed he was going to the FBI with his suspicions."

"He did. This morning."

Marsha Leonard gasped, and Daniel was certain the additional theatrics were for his benefit. "That must be why they plan to be at the facility tomorrow afternoon. Will the press be involved? Do you have any idea what this will do to our stellar reputation?"

"I have no idea how or if an investigation will proceed. Gramps told his story, and we left. Seems odd Tom was mentioned as being scammed and now he's gone."

"That's uncalled for. Was Earl of sound mind?"

"During most of the interview."

"Surely you understand the board of directors may request his dismissal."

"Not likely since he and Gran are paying for the entire west wing. Don't you think the best way to disprove my grandfather's suspicions is to reassure those concerned? Have you called a meeting of clients and families, or have you just threatened my grandfather's care if he doesn't comply with your demands?"

"I've decided to discontinue the staff interviews. The whole claim is preposterous."

"Are you censoring the conversations of every client there? Let me give you a word of advice. Removing an Alzheimer's victim from your facility because you don't like what he says makes you look guilty of neglect and is inconsistent with your mission statement."

"Removing your grandfather is not the purpose of this call."

"It isn't?"

"I'm asking you friend to friend."

"Yes, ma'am." He ended the call, stifling a frustrated sigh.

In the morning, he'd speak with Miss Leonard about his behavior and do his best to get back into her good graces.

But he'd messed up with Laurel Evertson by challenging her view of the situation. She was a skilled agent from the top of her golden head to her sensible heels. Yes, he'd noticed. She'd worn a black pantsuit with a white silk blouse, little gold hoop earrings, and just enough makeup to set off her nut-brown eyes. With a face that gorgeous, he hadn't expected her gentleness toward Gramps. He figured she'd discard an Alzheimer's patient's claims as a total waste.

After all, the only reason he'd taken his grandparents to the FBI was to avoid making them find a way to get there themselves—and because of Tom's death. Gran no longer drove . . . unless Gramps prodded her. Worse yet, Gramps might wander off in the car and get hurt. Soon Daniel must secure the locks on the front and back doors of their mammoth home. How he'd manage that feat when he didn't live there would be a huge undertaking. Gramps's independence meant a lot, but not as much as his grandparents' safety and well-being.

At the next light, Daniel picked up his iPhone and pressed in Agent Evertson's number. Apologizing wasn't his favorite conversation, but he needed to be on her side. He'd made her angry with his insistence upon conducting his own investigation. He hadn't changed his mind, but he didn't need to alienate her.

The agent's phone rang five times and rolled to voice mail. He left a brief message for her to call and offered an apology for his curt behavior earlier. Gramps would call his words "eating crow." Daniel thought it was being smart.

Agent Evertson looked familiar, but he couldn't figure out why. Once home, he googled her name and his recollection fell into place.

Special Agent Laurel Evertson's undercover work and testimony had put away Morton Wilmington five years ago. A drop for all the crimes assigned to him and his organization. Although many called him Robin Hood because of his generous contributions to charities, he was convicted of one murder and suspected of several others.

Daniel remembered the extensive media coverage. She and Wilmington were engaged, and she gained access to his computer files and aided in an FBI arrest. Upon his sentencing, he threatened to kill her.

Tough gal to stay in the game. Maybe Daniel was wrong about her.

CHAPTER 8

Daniel yawned and swung his pickup into Silver Hospitality's parking area with Gran in the rear and Gramps beside him. He'd stayed up until after midnight researching insurance fraud and rose before five this morning, pumping life into his body with espresso, to continue the same online probe. He found an FBI press release about the crimes involving the same kind of scam, which told him agents were investigating these.

Nothing online resembled the company, but complaints surfaced from those who claimed they or loved ones had been swindled out of large sums of money, all involving the elderly. Some comments indicated the victims had a form of dementia. But no other deaths.

He was onto something. The origin wasn't evident in every post, but Florida hit the radar in at least two. That made sense since it was the retirement capital of the US. The FBI had more information than he did, and for sure Gramps had uncovered a crime. Today's visit from the bureau might provide solid answers.

Reality hit hard. Whoever had planned an elaborate scheme to defraud the elderly would make sure their rears were covered. Daniel believed Gran and Gramps were in danger.

Were they safe at Silver Hospitality? The facility boasted cutting-edge care from safety technology to the full-time nutritionist. But someone had gotten inside. Or worked the inside. Would the FBI's interest in the case keep his grandparents from danger? Fear snaked up his spine.

"I was thinking, why don't you spend today at home?" he said. "We can turn around. I'll make a few calls and—"

"I'll keep an eye on Gramps," Gran said. "Won't let him out of my sight."

"My point is you shouldn't have to."

"The man who made money is too smart to return."

He swung around to see the lift of her chin. Oh, he recognized her stubborn stance. "Your safety is my number one priority."

"Don't be ridiculous. It's secure and—"

"We're going on a picnic today." Gramps unfastened his seat belt. Daniel would not challenge him. "With your lovely wife?"

Gramps hoisted his backpack, which held a journal and a framed picture of Gran on her eighteenth birthday. "She's not my wife yet. But I'm fixin' to pop the question today."

"Gee, thanks, Earl," Gran said. "Who am I? Or does it really matter?" She laughed, but her response didn't ease Daniel's stress. She faked it, and he knew it.

"Gran, I'm serious," Daniel said.

"I am too." She opened the truck door. "You do your job, and I'll handle Earl."

"Does Miss Leonard have a clue you carry an S&W in your purse?"

Gran frowned. "It's none of her business. We old people aren't frisked. Right now, I need to get Earl inside. Are you coming?"

"I'm right with you."

"Good," Gramps said. "I don't want to miss a minute of today."

"I'll be texting," Daniel said.

"I'll respond if I have time and the subject is important," she said. "Oh, here are your flowers." She handed him a bouquet of red roses that he planned to give to Marsha Leonard. The woman was a little odd—he never seemed to know if she was in a good mood. Charm and flowers should help his cause.

When his grandparents had settled into the multipurpose area to greet their friends, Daniel waited at the front desk to talk to Miss Leonard before leaving for work. She looked like she'd soon be eligible for a retirement center herself. He gave her his most dazzling smile and handed her the roses. "Are we friends again?"

She inhaled the roses. "I suppose, but you can be impossible sometimes. I was really angry last night."

"I'm sorry to have upset you." And he was.

"The roses cover a multitude of sins," she said.

"That makes me irresistible."

She pursed her mouth for a less-than-friendly look, then sighed. "Okay, Officer Irresistible, how can I help you?"

He showed her the brochure from Lifestyle Insurance. "Have you seen this before?"

She read it and handed it back to him. "I've never seen or heard of the company. There's no contact information."

Daniel nodded. "Gramps said a man gave it to him."

"While here?"

"Yes."

"The mysterious salesman who took their money and ran?"

"I'm simply trying to put what my grandparents have said in the right perspective. Learn the truth."

"I'd like that too. But I'm no help." She glanced at the security cameras. "These don't lie, and neither do our visitor ledgers."

No point in bringing up possible computer access to security cameras or the half-staff mode during the afternoon. "I would hate to find another center."

She paled, no doubt thinking about the wing his grandparents were funding. "That won't be necessary. The FBI's visit this afternoon has shaken our board of directors, and one of our staff members quit, probably because of your interview. I'd hate to lose more trained people when they fear for their jobs."

"People are nervous when they have something to hide. Law

enforcement are professionals who know how to be respectful. Did anyone complain about my questions?"

"No."

"My point, Miss Leonard. Who left?"

"Liz Austin."

Not much of a loss in his opinion. "Did she give a reason?"

Marsha shook her head. "Said she found a better position."

❊   ❊   ❊

8:30 A.M. FRIDAY

Abby Hilton closed her Kindle case and allowed her heavy eyelids to shut for just a moment. Silver Hospitality was quiet, and she hated it when her blood sugar dropped, dragging her down when she'd rather be doing a plethora of other things.

Shaking loose of the dream state, she reached into her pocket for a packet of almonds. Should have known better than to eat an apple turnover for breakfast. A little protein and she'd be back to finishing up the trilogy. She'd tried a couple of steampunk and vampire novels, but she preferred fantasy with strong symbolism that made sense in the real world. The stories kept her mind occupied while her heart broke for Earl.

Yesterday's meeting at the FBI weighed on her thoughts. If she believed for one minute those agents were making fun of Earl, she would have unloaded a box of shells on them. But she trusted Daniel, the light of her and Earl's life.

Time to exercise and walk off the stress while the other old folks played games. Glancing at Earl, she smiled at his setting up the domino board. Two women chatted and both were watching a John Wayne Western. Poor dears. Did either of them understand what was happening?

"Enjoy your movie," she said to the women. "Can I get you anything?"

"Coffee would be nice," one woman said. "Add a little rum, would you, honey?"

A staff member passed through and acknowledged the woman's request. "I'll get you a fresh cup, but we're out of rum."

Abby made her way to the front desk. Marsha Leonard hunched over her computer. "That frown will add years to your face."

Marsha glanced up and gave a half smile. "Abby, paperwork drives me insane. Compound that with the remote possibility of a staff member scamming a few of our clients, and I'm ready to take up full-time residence here."

"When I'm teetering between the overwhelmed zone and bring-me-medication, I do one of three things."

Marsha straightened. "I'm ready for suggestions."

"Head for the treadmill with a good book and jazz playing into my Skullcandy. Or walk and pretend I'm on my knees. Or go hunting. Not in that order."

Marsha laughed. "You never stop amazing me."

"When I do, I'm ready for the funeral home." Abby leaned over the counter. "How can I help you?"

"Not sure."

"Let's visit the new wing before I hit the treadmill."

"Are you stressed?"

Abby hesitated. Marsha was a friend, but not a sister type. "Like Earl, I'm concerned."

"The board of directors is screaming for answers."

Abby hooked her arm with Marsha's. "Hold your head high and tell the board what you know."

They walked outside into warm sunshine and on toward the new area. The hum and whine of saws along with the fresh scent of newly cut wood reminded Abby how soon Silver Hospitality would open their doors to eighteen more clients.

"How can I ever thank you for this?" Marsha said. "Larger rooms, the massage and hot tub area, a medical examining room. A dozen slots for new clients are already filled."

"Glad Earl and I could help."

"I'm sorry you're caught in the middle of this." She took Abby by the shoulders. "Those with Alzheimer's are easily confused, misunderstand reality. You live with it."

Abby heard the compassion. She wouldn't mention the trip to the FBI or how Special Agents Laurel Evertson and Thatcher Graves believed them. Or how Daniel promised solid answers. Or how she really felt about Tom's death. Or how she feared for Emma and Earl.

Sure wished she had a rifle and woods filled with wild boars to relieve her stress.

CHAPTER 9

Laurel drove to her apartment complex, yesterday's conversation with Morton Wilmington running on a constant replay in her mind, distracting her to no end. Where was her backbone? Seeing Wilmington was like looking into the face of the devil. And to think he claimed to be a Christian. If so, he'd forgotten to polish his crown, and his golden gate was doused in flaming tar. They'd spoken in terms of the board game Monopoly, a game he collected in various forms—and there were over 150 varieties. Trivia she'd like to forget. He said the game was in his blood. In the past, she'd played it to please him, to gain his confidence, and to influence him to fall in love with her.

The scene in the courtroom marched across her mind, when her testimony locked his prison cell. He'd called her Delilah. Media capitalized on it, and while her undercover work made her look like a heroine, she tried to rub the dirt from her skin. Didn't help he had the Robin Hood thing going, giving huge sums to charities.

Sleeping with a criminal. Pretending. Trash. A stigma of what she'd always been.

Miss Kathryn said one day Laurel would encounter a breaking point when she'd have to surrender to her need for God. For some it was admitting to an addiction, being tired of jail, or facing consequences for their behavior. Laurel long understood her god was

47

control. The God of Miss Kathryn had disappointed her years ago. Jesse had been a believer too, but God hadn't saved him.

"Wicked people behave like wicked people," Miss Kathryn had said. "Their choices are selfish, and other people get hurt."

Miss Kathryn didn't know the worst of it. Laurel had never told her the whole story of what happened the night burglars broke into her childhood home and murdered her parents. Law enforcement never found the two killers. God abandoned her that night, and she gave up on Him. It was her job now to stop those who preyed on the innocent. And she'd committed her life to stopping evil men like Wilmington.

Those who preyed on the elderly often used volunteers to infiltrate facilities and organizations where seasoned citizens congregated. Possibly representing a church or a charity. At Silver Hospitality she'd check that aspect as well as the other targeted victims. Agents were conducting investigations in the other cities, and she'd look into their findings tomorrow. Should have asked about volunteers during the Hilton interview.

An image of Daniel Hilton crept into her mind. He'd left a voice mail and asked her to return his call. Maybe new information had surfaced. Maybe she should acknowledge his message. The man was entirely too good-looking and kind to his grandparents. A distraction. One she didn't need. Laurel began her career single, and she'd end it single. Hopefully at retirement age unless Morton Wilmington made good on his threats. Or some other revenge seeker.

Sitting in her car, she listened again to Daniel's message, the sound of his voice strong.

"Agent Evertson, I'd like to apologize for my rudeness when we last spoke. Would you give me a call at your convenience?"

She honored his request.

"Officer Daniel Hilton here."

"This is Special Agent Laurel Evertson. I'm returning your call."

"I wanted to apologize for my rudeness."

"You did so in your message. Was there anything else?"

"Not at the moment, except I want to help in any way possible."

"Thanks for your concern. The FBI is investigating the situation at Silver Hospitality, so I'm sure we'll have this case solved before you feel the need to pursue your own findings."

"A nice thought, but I don't think it will happen. I've learned from the director that nothing has been found."

"The FBI doesn't dispose of an investigation until all sources of a case are handled."

"Good. I'm pleased."

She ended the conversation, irritated Daniel did not heed her instructions. She didn't want the elderly Hiltons hurt—or any of those threatened by the scam. Wilmington had orchestrated it, and she'd not rest until he was convicted of yet another crime.

A part of her feared for what little she held dear—Phantom, her home, and her career. What would she do if they were yanked away? How would she survive? How could she ever make it up to Jesse's family?

She climbed the steps to her apartment and unlocked the door. "Home," she whispered. "My friend." All around her were reminders of the things she treasured, antiques mixed with comfort. And yes, framed pictures of the dear foster mother who loved her despite the many times Laurel had pushed her away.

She closed the apartment door and secured it. Few visited her, but those who did were always surprised. Like Wilmington. They'd mistaken her for a contemporary gal—high-tech, vivid colors, and abstract art. How would they react to Laurel Evertson's need for the warmth of a traditional home, reminders of the ten-year-old who'd lost everything?

Sinking into a tufted steel-blue Victorian sofa, she drew air into her lungs and buried her face in her hands. Behind her crime-fighting veneer lived a woman who longed for so much more if only she could find it. Keep it. Hold it tighter than her antiques.

She glanced into the small dining area at her antique crystal chandelier, the most expensive piece she owned. An oak and mahogany library table rested beneath it with a green Depression glass bowl filled with wooden apples in a bed of apple spice–scented leaves. On the wall in her living area, a turn-of-the-century oak buffet held French opera glasses in dark and light mother-of-pearl. Beside it was a Chinese vase etched in greens with a pink dragon. On the other end of the buffet rested *Little Women*, a 1951 edition, a gift from Miss Kathryn. The rest of her two-bedroom apartment held the same items that appealed to her—old and intricately attractive. Eclectic but hers.

After closing all the drapes in the living room, she walked to her bedroom. There in soothing colors of vintage blue—delicate robin egg–blue wallpaper, a blue-and-white upholstered chair and headboard, and a white chenille bedspread—she changed into workout clothes.

How she hated the loneliness that fit like a tattered dress, but Wilmington had been right in his assessment. She'd go to her grave wondering what was wrong with her wretched soul. Why she'd let Jesse get killed. She'd never shared those dark parts of herself, yet a killer uncovered them. That's why she couldn't let anyone get close to her.

✳ ✳ ✳

4:00 P.M. FRIDAY

Abby chuckled. Dark suits and no smiles. Had to be the FBI. Now to see if they could find out who'd been scamming the elderly, maybe learn how Tom really died.

She wove through the staff scurrying about the front office toward Marsha, who was more nervous than a rabbit staring down a rifle barrel.

"Marsha, who are these visitors?" Abby said.

"Abby, I'm busy with these people. We can talk later."

"Are these gentlemen from the FBI?" Abby raised her voice. "You know Daniel took Earl and me to their office yesterday morning. If you haven't been there, it's off Highway 290. Lots of security. Anyway, we're so upset about the scam and Tom's death."

That worked. Abby jarred the attention of two special agents.

"Ma'am, can I have a word with you?" one of the young men said.

Actually 95 percent of the men in the world were young. "Yes, sir. I'd be glad to."

"We can talk in Miss Leonard's office."

Abby followed him down the hall to the small room. He settled behind the desk, and she eased onto a chair. He introduced himself as Jack something or other.

"I'm Abby Hilton, and I'm not a client here." She explained how she accompanied Earl six days a week to Silver Hospitality.

"Any relation to the new Hilton wing being added?" he said.

She smiled. "We thought the facility needed to expand. Now, sonny, you aren't here to talk about the new wing but what I know about the scam."

"Yes, ma'am. If you don't mind, I'd like to record our interview."

"Go right ahead. Listen carefully 'cause I hate to repeat myself." She drew in a breath. "I blame myself for this. Normally I spend the hours with Earl—that's my husband—and our friends. But they were in a domino match, and I was bored. I walked to the front desk to speak with Marsha, but she was busy. I took a walk outside, and when I returned, Marsha still wasn't free to chat." The truth was Marsha and Chef Steven were involved in a chess game against each other, and neither wanted to be bothered. She didn't want to see either of them fired, but their attention should be on their jobs, not on each other.

"What happened then?"

Abby snapped to attention. What was she doing slipping like that? She'd have to increase her ginkgo and green tea. "I returned to Earl, Tom, and Emma. A stranger was talking with them, and he introduced himself as Russell Jergon. He talked to Emma about life insurance. When he asked for money, my radar went nuts. I told him to leave. 'Where's your ID?' I said." She leaned closer to the agent. "Jergon had this rigor mortis smile going. Made some stupid comment about Emma wanting to make sure her family was taken care of after she was gone. Why, Emma doesn't recognize her family half the time. I stomped off to get Marsha. By the time I got her pried away from her work, the salesman was gone."

"Ever see this Jergon fellow again?"

"No, the slippery weasel. The next day I asked Earl if he'd bought life insurance from the man. He couldn't remember, so I checked our accounts. Sure enough, another thirty thousand dollars was missing. The bank had flags on our account, but a VP said they'd received an e-mail from Earl to have the money deposited to another bank." Abby snorted. "Now, do you think an old man with Alzheimer's would have e-mail?"

The thought of it again made her angrier at Marsha. While the woman had been engaged with a "knight," good people were scammed.

"Anything else?" the agent said.

"What have you learned today?"

"We haven't written our reports."

Abby frowned. "You've been here since one o'clock. What about the files, backgrounds on staff, glitches in the security cameras? Did you check out Liz Austin, a staff member who quit yesterday? She was a floozy, and I wouldn't put anything past her."

The agent jotted down something. "Mrs. Hilton, thank you for your statement." He rose from his chair.

Didn't the suit understand Earl might have made a dent in Daniel's inheritance . . . and their lives?

CHAPTER 10

Daniel settled into a recliner in his grandparents' media room. Before Gramps clicked the remote to watch the recorded news, he needed to make a request.

"Why don't you two stay here for a few days until this scam thing is settled. I can make arrangements for a nurse."

"Forget it," Gramps said. "Abby and I have friends there."

"Would you think about it?" Daniel said.

"Nope." He picked up the remote.

In silence, they watched the local news air a press statement from Houston's FBI media coordinator. He revealed four cases of elderly fraud involving false life insurance policies. Identical to his grandparents' case. The report warned the community that, if approached, they should contact the FBI. A phone number was displayed on-screen. Interested persons could obtain additional information on the FBI's website. Billboards would be up this weekend to assist in communicating the scam.

"Agent Evertson's a smart gal. I could tell," Gramps said. "I'd like to see the jerks who swindled us lined up in front of a firing squad. And if they killed Tom, I'd pull the trigger myself." He reached into a candy dish for a miniature Snickers bar, but Gran snatched it back. She guarded his sugar intake like a watchdog.

"Those are for guests, and you've already had two," she said.

Gramps didn't miss a beat. He reached for the candy with his other hand. "I'd share my Snickers with the good-looking gal from the FBI anytime."

"Earl!" Gran said. "You're a married man."

"Married, yes. In love with you, yes. Blind, no." He tossed her a grin that had won her over for seventy years.

Daniel chuckled. He adored their bantering, and tonight Gramps showed few signs of his disease. "Better watch it, or you'll be on the couch tonight."

"Aw, wouldn't be the first time. You know, Agent Evertson treated me with respect instead of like a worthless old man."

"She had some spunk, too." Gran didn't look up from her knitting, where her fingers flew at jet speed.

Daniel wouldn't reveal his conversations with her. "I'm glad you had a good experience."

Gramps chuckled and sat back in his recliner. "I read you better than a book, Daniel. You don't think much of the pretty agent."

"What?" Where was this headed?

"It's the same problem you have with every woman you meet. If she's intelligent—and Agent Evertson is definitely smart—you think she's out to use you up and spit you out. If she's drop-dead gorgeous, you think she's like your mom. Brains and beauty together throw you way out of your comfort zone. Especially when you're on a crusade to save the world."

This was not going as he anticipated. Last night Gramps talked about playing kick the can when he was a boy.

"I'm right, so admit it." Gramps crumpled the candy wrapper and tossed it back into the dish.

"I've dated pretty girls."

"How many times have you taken one of them out more than twice?"

Daniel had no plans of marrying, which fed into what Gramps believed was true. "You might be right."

His eyes twinkled. "I'd like to see you put a ring on a lady's finger before I'm completely senile."

"And I'd like to hold a great-grandbaby or two." Gran smiled. "A redheaded baby girl or boy."

"The right woman hasn't crossed my path." He shrugged. "Not sure if she ever will."

Gramps studied him, and Daniel feared he was slipping. Worse yet, a sermon might be on the tip of his tongue. "Son, open your heart to what God has for you. You're running from everything reminding you of your mother. I've said this before, but you've got to forgive her and not blame every female for one woman's mistakes."

Daniel picked up the glass of water and downed it, giving him time to form his response. "Every time I think I've grown and forgiven her, a reminder pops up and the bitterness nearly chokes me. I'm a grown man still acting like a kid." He'd visit her soon for his reasons. But he had no intention of setting himself up for a land mine relationship with any woman.

"Ask God to help you put your mother in the right perspective. Look at Abby. She's the best thing that ever happened to me."

"She's different, and she'll always be my best girl."

"Thank you, Daniel," she said. "I'm not the only different woman out there."

Gramps picked up the TV remote. "The right one will step into your life when you least expect it."

"Have you always been so irritatingly wise?"

"Ah, I push everyone to redemption, not just to cope with life's hard punches."

Daniel smiled at the white-haired wisdom. "Thanks. But it won't be Special Agent Laurel Evertson. She's not my type."

Gramps laughed. "Famous last words. I'll get off your case for now. I know they'd like for your gran and I to work with an artist about Russell Jergon. Should have done it when we were there, but I don't think they took us seriously."

"I could take you there on my day off."

Gramps waved his hand. "Daniel, my cooperation depends on where my mind is. I can tell you what I ate for breakfast when I was twelve, but this morning is another matter." He paused, tears filling his eyes. "Hate it when I can't remember or when you tell me I've done something stupid."

"We take one day at a time."

"By helping the artist, I can contribute to society instead of taking advantage of it."

"Gramps, you've given much to others, and you still are. I will find the answers you and Gran need." Daniel had already spoken to his superiors at HPD, but this was an FBI matter until a task force was formed. Didn't stop him from his own investigation.

CHAPTER 11

Abby walked outside Silver Hospitality toward the new wing's construction, her daily inspection. And that's exactly what she wanted everyone to think while she called Special Agent Laurel Evertson with an offer.

Slipping the business card from her pants pocket, she memorized the agent's number and pressed it in. She breathed in a mix of fresh air and a prayer.

Special Agent Evertson answered on the second ring.

"This is Abby Hilton. We met on Thursday."

"Yes, ma'am."

"I won't take up much of your time, but I wanted to talk about the case."

"Something new?"

"I'd like to work undercover."

"You what?"

"Hear me out. I'm at the facility six days a week. I have access to everything—files, gossip, visitor logs, the computer, and even the kitchen. I don't ask permission, just do what I want discreetly. I could do a little snooping and report to you."

"I'm not sure that's a good idea."

"Humor an old lady," Abby said. "But don't tell my grandson. He'd have a hissy fit."

"Mrs. Hilton—"

"Abby."

"And I'm Laurel. As innocent as what you're suggesting seems, it could be dangerous."

"I'm already packing."

"Whoa. They allow you to carry a weapon at Silver Hospitality?"

"Who's going to tell them?"

Laurel laughed. "I suppose you could keep your ears and eyes open."

"And my fingers. I'll report in when I find something suspicious."

"And you'll be careful?"

"Who's going to suspect an eccentric old lady?"

"Do you have anything to tell me now?"

Abby hesitated. "Observations maybe."

"I'm ready."

"A staff member quit after Daniel talked to her regarding the scam."

"What's her name?"

"Liz Austin. She helped in the kitchen. The job didn't fit her personality. I told the agent here yesterday, but he acted like I was a client." Abby drew in a breath. "Whatever I say is to be held in strict confidence. I overheard Liz talking to Chef Steven. She offered herself in exchange for the rear kitchen door to be unlocked. Said she needed to take smoke breaks."

"Why didn't you tell anyone?"

"None of my business, and Marsha Leonard, the director, is a longtime friend. Never married and very much in love for the first time. With the chef."

"So she's involved with a staff member."

"Yes."

"You didn't tell Daniel about the unlocked door?"

"I didn't want to bother him about one more thing. Now that I think about it, it was a stupid move on my part. But it's been locked since she left. And Russell Jergon hasn't returned either."

"I haven't heard a word that the security cameras exposed any-one smoking or entering the building through the rear entrance."

"The girl had an iPad in her purse. Used it constantly. I'm smart enough to understand the technology is there for her to temporarily disable the cameras."

"Wish I'd known this sooner. Thanks, I'll look into Liz Austin. Abby, your financial institutions are aware of the fraud, right? They have special procedures to protect clients from fraud."

"After the money went missing, Daniel went with Earl and me to the bank, and we spoke to a vice president. Earl had obviously given the salesman his account number, so nothing could be done but close out the account and open another one. We were told if the bank became aware of a client who might be suffering from Alzheimer's or any other physical or mental illness, they contact the Texas Health and Human Services Commission. The situation would be investigated to determine if the report was valid. Often, in the early stages of the disease, the client wouldn't be doing any-thing unusual for them to suspect a problem. Most everything is centralized and electronic."

Abby sighed before continuing. "Daniel is the brains behind keeping us old people safe. He made sure the new account and the others are flagged so nothing can be withdrawn without all three of our signatures. A child or family member can't waltz into the bank and announce a parent has Alzheimer's and demand to be added on the account. Only an owner can make those arrange-ments unless the courts direct it."

"I feel better that he's looking out for you."

"He's a good man. Needs a good woman to complement him." She wrapped up the call and pumped her fist into the air. Yes! About time she was useful again. And she already had her game day shirt on.

Abby processed what she'd learned and headed to Chef Steven's domain. Her first undercover assignment. She stood in the kitchen doorway and studied the bald, chubby man.

"What do you need, Miss Abby?"

"I'm bored. Is there something I could do? No need to tell the health department."

He waved a spatula like he was conducting a symphony. "I sure could use an assistant. I've got bananas and strawberries with a garnish of kiwi and mint ready for morning break, but the napkins, cups, and glasses haven't been arranged appropriately." He opened the oven to the delicious scent of fresh-baked pecan tarts. "I'm behind. Been that way since Liz quit."

She stacked china cups, crystal, and white linen napkins onto a wheeled serving cart. She'd already posed the question to Marsha about using items that could break or injure a client, but the facility's handbook expressly stated using the best.

"Great job," he said.

"I've done my share of cooking food for crowds, but not at your caliber. Just point me to what you want done."

"You're a sweet breath of fresh air."

"What were Liz's responsibilities?"

"Clean up, serve."

"And keep you company?"

"Not really. She had her own agenda." He paused, and his face reddened. "She liked spending time with the clients, which is not a bad thing."

"I agree. Earl loved her. Said she was 'hot.'"

He laughed. "I shouldn't have sounded critical. The one thing I valued were the afternoons. She gave me time to complete paperwork and visit with Miss Leonard." He shrugged. "It would have been nice if she'd cleaned things to my satisfaction or prepared the afternoon snack. But I'm being critical again."

"How long did she relieve you? I know Marsha cherished those times."

"Almost two hours. She and I have an ongoing chess tournament. We use the computer up front, and when the facility is quiet, we play viciously." He paused as though reflecting on the times with Marsha.

If the scammers had found a way inside the facility during the afternoons, jobs were on the line, and the chess games were on the computer. Abby stole a glance at the rear door. A camera panned the room. Could it be temporarily disconnected?

"I'm sorry Liz left you stranded." Abby swept strawberry stems into a dustpan. "Maybe I can do more."

"Thank you, Miss Abby. But I'm supposed to have new help on Monday. Maybe this one won't be texting her boyfriend or playing games on her iPad."

Interesting. "Did he ever show up here?"

"You sure are interested in the goings-on in my kitchen."

She smiled and placed Waterford pitchers of lemonade on the cart. "Oh, just chatting."

He handed her a tray of fruit. "And I'm picking on a precious lady. You can take these to the clients, and I'll bring the tarts."

He hadn't responded about seeing the boyfriend, which said he had . . . and the boyfriend being inside the building without signing in could cost him his job. If the cook confessed to how Russell Jergon might have gained access to the elderly, he and Miss Leonard could be charged with neglect.

Or be charged as accomplices.

＊　＊　＊

5:00 P.M. SATURDAY

Daniel parked his truck in Silver Hospitality's parking lot and focused on his grandparents' welfare. Tonight he'd talk to them again about safety precautions until this thing at the facility settled. When the Alzheimer's diagnosis threw them for a spin, Daniel assumed their health would be the most critical issue for the future, not someone stealing their money.

The scammer must have a database of wealthy elderly with

dementia. If he were looking to swindle defenseless people with dementia, what would he need to target them?

A medical database containing their health history, doctors' names, hospital records, prescriptions, or insurance company details.

A bank database with account numbers.

Addresses where the victims could be found.

More than one database would have to be merged to compile the scammer's targets.

After picking up his grandparents, Daniel listened to Gramps chatter while he drove home. He was a high school basketball star in love with a redheaded cheerleader.

Daniel glanced in his rearview mirror. A dark-green Dodge pickup had stayed on his bumper for the past several blocks. The driver wore a ball cap pulled down over his eyes. Daniel's sixth sense had always been suspicion. . . . For the next few minutes, the pickup tailed him through a series of left turns.

He merged into the left lane, squeezing between two cars.

The pickup inched in behind him. Horns blew.

A quarter mile later, Daniel eased back into the far right lane.

The pickup moved with him.

"Gran, Gramps, duck down. Now. The idiot on my bumper is up to no good."

Both must have heard the urgency in his voice, and they leaned down in their seats. The driver needed an attitude adjustment and a course in respect and courtesy.

That's when he saw the gun poking out the driver's window.

CHAPTER 12

A bullet destroyed Daniel's side mirror. Another pop burst the rear window.

"Stay down!" Daniel pulled his weapon from its holster and steered his truck to the right side, then whipped it ninety degrees toward the shooter's truck. "Gran, you okay?"

"Yes. I have my gun."

"Don't use it. Both of you get out and move toward the front. Now. The engine will protect you from gunfire."

The truck had stopped, which meant the shooter wasn't giving up easily, whoever he was.

"You're in his sights," Gramps said.

Thank God, he was lucid. "That's what he thinks. Go. Take care of Gran." Daniel switched off the engine and opened the door, firing at the dark-green truck. His grandparents exited, and another bullet sped past his head.

A shot from his grandparents' direction alerted him to Gran unloading her S&W. She always had his six. Daniel continued to pump bullets into the truck while moving around the open door to the front of his truck. Bending, he called for backup and glanced in the direction of Gran and Gramps.

That's when he saw the blood drops.

"Who's hit?" he whispered, adrenaline pumping through his veins, and returned fire again. Sirens sounded in the distance.

"Just some blowback shrapnel across my calf," Gramps said. "Looks like gravel or glass."

"Gran?" Daniel said. "Is—?"

The shooter backed up and raced in reverse to a hill leading down to a feeder, still shooting. The continuous fire stopped Daniel from sending a bullet into the tires or gas tank. The shooter bumped over the hill to the feeder. Vehicles slammed against each other to get out of the truck's path.

No front license plate.

White-hot revenge burned through his gut. No one endangered his grandparents and got away with it.

✳ ✳ ✳

11:15 A.M. SUNDAY

Sunday morning Laurel slept past eleven o'clock. Extremely late for her, but she attributed it to stress. It always knocked her out. Tossing off a quilt, she grabbed her laptop and brewed a cup of coffee, then crawled back into the comfort of her bed. With the thermostat in her apartment set at sixty-six degrees, she might stay there all day and snuggle. She spent over an hour working through her e-mails while drinking two more cups of coffee.

Next on her agenda were the latest reports on what was happening in the city, state, country, and around the globe. Before joining the FBI, media meant little to her. Now every event caught her eye. OCD and addicted.

Thirty minutes later, after another cup of coffee and a pair of brown sugar and cinnamon Pop-Tarts, her mind swung into work mode. She logged into the secure FBI site for updates. Normally she'd catch up on news, then head to the stables on Sunday. Perhaps in a few hours, she'd visit her valiant stallion.

When she spotted Officer Daniel Hilton's name on a report, she inhaled sharply and her chest burned. The driver of a dark-green Dodge pickup opened fire at him last evening while he was transporting his grandparents to their home in the Bunker Hill area.

Blinking, she focused on the news bulletin. The bullet shattered the rear window of his truck. An anonymous driver viewed the incident and reported the Dodge truck's rear license plate, but the vehicle had been reported stolen. No reason was given for the shooting.

Laurel leaned against the pillow. She feared Daniel's grandparents might be in the line of a scammer's fire.

She pressed in Su-Min's name on speed dial.

"Are you heading to the stables to see Phantom?" Su-Min said.

"I'm in bed. Haven't brushed my teeth or combed my hair."

"Doesn't sound like you, but you must have needed the sleep. Are we having our regular Sunday night dinner at six or six thirty? I have soup started."

Sweet friend. "Mandu?"

"Of course. Lots of dumplings. Can you pick up an apple pie for dessert? But you called me. What's up?"

"Officer Daniel Hilton, the younger of the two men—"

"The dreamy guy with those incredible brown eyes."

Laurel shook her head. "Yes, he's the one."

"He asked you out?"

"No. Would you hush and listen?" Laurel wished Su-Min would leave the dating thing alone.

Su-Min laughed. "I'm all ears."

"He was involved in a shooting yesterday evening, and his grandparents were with him."

"I read the report. They're okay or I would have called. No arrests, though. I thought we could discuss it tonight. I want to think through this business with Wilmington before we act on it."

"I don't think waiting is a good idea." An inkling told her not to reveal her unofficial meeting with him.

"I'm calling the shots on this one. You have too much animosity to deal rationally where he's concerned. Don't cross me on this, or I'll file a report."

Shock washed over her. The call ended, and Su-Min's threat repeated in Laurel's mind. During their friendship, Su-Min had chosen the religion of the agency and didn't care who got in the way. Laurel cared for her, but the warning flares looked like a bonfire.

She snuggled beneath the warm quilt. Glancing at her cell phone, she regretted the call to Su-Min. She should have called Daniel directly and bypassed her. His card lay on her nightstand, and she pressed in the number.

"Officer Daniel Hilton."

His voice sent warmth from her toes to the top of her head. "This is Laurel Evertson. I read about the shooting yesterday and wanted to make sure all of you are okay."

"Thanks for the call. We're all fine. My grandparents are a little shook up, that's all." He paused. "Gramps had three stitches in his left calf. We were lucky."

"Tell him I'm sorry. Any leads?"

"No."

She wasn't surprised. "Do you think the attack could be linked to the elderly scam?"

"Yep. We talked about the far end of this."

She wouldn't tell him about the eight-year history of supposedly the same operation or reveal any of the FBI's investigation unless HPD was pulled into the case.

Change the subject, Laurel. She heard country-western music. "You're off today?"

"Sunday. I attend church unless I'm called in. On my way home now."

One of those. *Forget it, Laurel.* He'd never be interested in her—even if the thought had occurred to her. His faith just answered her question. "Grandparents in church too?"

"Yep."

"I see."

"Hungry? We could catch a pizza."

Her stomach lurched, but not because of pizza. Was he asking her out? "To discuss yesterday's shooting?"

"No, to share lunch."

"I'd be poor company."

"Can I take a rain check?"

Laurel trembled. She couldn't handle the rejection sure to come when he learned about her past. "I . . . I don't think so. Not a good idea."

"Do you think I want to press you for FBI details regarding the case? Because that's the farthest thing from my mind."

"It's better to keep our relationship professional." She ended the call while her eyes pooled with tears. It was better this way.

CHAPTER 13

Sunday afternoons usually gave Daniel time to rest, work out, do yard work, or his favorite—take a long ride in the country on his Harley. Ah, the life of the suburban cowboy. But Gran had asked him to spend a few hours with her and Gramps. Not because it was National Grandparents' Day, but because she'd felt her blood pressure drop. He didn't refuse.

Today Gramps's mind slipped at church and hadn't returned to the present. He'd talked about Gran when she wore bobby socks and black-and-white saddle oxfords. She was the prettiest cheerleader, and he played center on the high school basketball team, yet again. Those were good memories, certainly better than the harshness of good against evil. The morning's sermon must have moved Daniel to philosophize.

No motorcycle ride today. Gran and Gramps wouldn't always be with him, and he'd promised himself a long time ago that they'd always come first.

Some days Gramps's stories wrenched Daniel's heart, especially when he recalled the vitality and respect his grandfather once held in the community.

His grandparents ended up napping, so Daniel googled elderly scams, not necessarily focusing on Texas, but all over the US. It was elementary compared to the FBI's realm of investigation, but it gave him a better snapshot of what was going on.

He pressed in the number for Silver Hospitality. Marsha Leonard normally worked during the afternoon. The facility was her home away from home. The only other staff person with the same commitment was Chef Steven.

"Miss Leonard, this is Daniel Hilton. Am I catching you at a bad time?"

"These are the quiet hours. But I'm a little preoccupied at the moment."

According to Gran, this was her time for online chess with Chef Steven. "When should I call back?"

"Goodness, I nearly forgot about y'all being chased by a crazy man. Are Abby and Earl okay? How can I help you?"

"They're fine. Napping actually. Does the FBI have a copy of your computer files?"

"Not yet. I asked for a subpoena. Have to be careful, you know."

Could he be wrong in his evaluation of Miss Leonard's sincerity? Far out there, but wouldn't she want to cooperate with law enforcement? "I'd like a copy of all who've visited my grandparents in the past year."

"I can have the list pulled and printed for you in the morning. Or do you want it e-mailed this afternoon?"

"Thanks. Electronically would be great. I have a few other questions. Do you mind?"

"What do you need, Daniel? This whole situation makes me physically ill. In fact I'm glad you're working aside from the FBI to find who's responsible."

"I'm on board with their investigation and will do anything to help."

"I have no doubt of your commitment. I'm simply upset with all that's happened."

"Do you purchase your supplies through a service?"

"Everything comes from Sysco, paper to food. The items

unique to our clients are purchased from a health service company." She gave him the name and number. "All prescription medications are furnished by the client. Daniel, those things are listed in the handbook."

He chuckled. "Fine investigator I am."

"You simply care about Abby and Earl and the other clients. Can't fault you for having a good heart. I'm not sure this is permissible, but whatever I learn from the FBI, I'll pass on to you. They probably have lots of red tape, and I could get it to you faster."

"I may have to take you to dinner."

She giggled like a young schoolgirl. "That might be bribery."

"Call it appreciation for putting up with my moods. Are you afraid people would talk?" At least he interested one woman, even if she was older than his mother.

She giggled again. Marsha Leonard had never been married. She'd spent twenty years as caregiver for her own parents, and now her life's work was directing the day-to-day activities at Silver Hospitality. He thanked her and ended the call.

More questions zipped through him. He started a spreadsheet using questions surrounding the scammers' operations. Where would they find trained men and women who could get in and out of the victims' homes or facilities undetected? How would the money be laundered through legitimate means that had nothing to do with the elderly? He knew the popular methods, and it would take time to investigate each one. Sophisticated hackers and people working on the inside of the crimes could pull it off. He could be standing in a Starbucks line, and the person next to him could download info from his smartphone. Scary, but true.

Miss Leonard forwarded the list of Gran's and Gramps's guests. Church people and old friends.

He studied the website of the church they attended. It mentioned Silver Hospitality as one of their outreach ministries. He googled Alzheimer's care and the church's name popped up.

That meant anyone looking for a way to gain access to the

facility could find information online. Serious predators could join the church and volunteer. He assumed other churches and charitable organizations offered similar opportunities. This was a common way to victimize the helpless, and it worked. The process took time to build trust and credibility and required people to infiltrate churches and charity organizations. Except establishing a large payroll wasn't a smart business practice, and it increased the risk of getting sold out to the law. The scammer must have a few people who worked a city, then moved on.

Liz Austin struck his thoughts. Was he fishing, or could she be a part of the scam? She'd given him her phone number many times. He pulled out his cell and pressed in her number. Disconnected.

Giving Laurel Evertson information on Liz Austin was a step forward. He texted Laurel with Liz's name, employment status, and a possible FBI query.

CHAPTER 14

Abby finished her workout, showered, and grabbed a bottle of ice-cold water. Time to do a little snooping before lunch while Marsha cheered on the TTT: table tennis tournament. Abby had seen Earl lose enough of them, and they were utterly boring.

She walked to Marsha's office, where the director kept her files, both paper and computer. Abby wanted to take a look. After all, the FBI team could have missed something important on Friday. Her first job would be a walk-through of employee files. They were alphabetically listed, one drawer with current staff and a lower drawer with previous employees. Abby made a list of every person. She leafed through the current ones, noting Marsha hadn't made any derogatory notations. Next she searched through the older staff. Liz Austin's file was missing. Neither was it on the desk or in another drawer. She finished the files with none of the others arousing suspicion. Had the FBI taken Austin's information?

If Abby could figure out how to access the computer-based visitor logs, she might find something. Visitors keyed in their info and obtained a stick-on badge to wear while on-site. Daniel claimed she was computer savvy, but how fast could she find the information and not get caught?

"Abby, what are you doing?"

73

She swung around and plastered on a smile for Marsha. "Looking for you and going to leave a note."

"Oh, the TTT had my attention until I realized the FBI would be back again this afternoon." She shook her head. "I want to make sure everything is in order."

"I don't blame you. Those federal guys would scare me."

"Amen. Hey, did you see the flowers for you at the front?"

"No. Are you sure they're for me? I'm not the flower type. Rather have something more lasting like a book."

"Your name is on them."

Abby left the office to check on the mystery flowers. On the desk was a basket of orange and white roses with a green vine woven around the handle. How very sweet, but what was the occasion? A card held her name. She opened it. What kind of sick joke was this?

Abby, life insurance policies are no good to the beneficiary until Earl is dead. Either stop cooperating with the FBI, or the next funeral arrangement will be for Earl. Your choice.

✳ ✳ ✳

10:00 A.M. MONDAY

Laurel scrolled through her e-mails at work, responding to the most critical issues. Her cell phone buzzed, and she glanced at the caller—Supervisory Special Agent Alan Preston.

"Yes, sir."

"Good morning, Agent Evertson. I'd like to discuss the elderly fraud case in my office. Are you available?"

"I'm on my way." Had another scam been uncovered? A death? Evidence? She grabbed her iPad, wishing the fraud against dementia sufferers were over.

Laurel sat across from the SSA's desk. Even the walls oozed with wisdom and experience, and she stared into his dark-blue eyes. "Is Agent Phang coming?"

"No. This is between us. She is not to know about our conversation."

A jolt of apprehension had her senses on alert. "Yes, sir."

"For eight years we've investigated various elderly-related frauds, believing there is a connection but not finding substantial evidence."

She nodded. "I've examined the files and read the theories."

He steepled his fingers. "Your past experience with Morton Wilmington left a scar on all of us who care about you and Jesse's family. None of us will ever forget the sacrifice. We owe you for Wilmington's takedown and the end of his nefarious activities."

She blinked and held her breath, knowing the question that was coming.

"Why did you see him alone?"

"I had to talk to him personally, to pose questions which needed to stay between us."

"There's a reason why the FBI has policies and procedures."

"Yes, sir."

He captured her gaze long enough to show his displeasure. "Morton Wilmington's lawyer contacted us early this morning indicating his client's willingness to cooperate in ending the elderly fraud. Later we spoke with Wilmington. He decoded the message on the e-mail you showed him last week. His decryption has been verified."

"What did he claim it said?" She understood most of it: *Same instructions. Contact me after. New leads.*

"In addition to what you'd discovered, he gave us the next memory care facility to be victimized. The director there stated a wealthy woman had been visited by a man already this morning. We have no idea at this point if the woman gave him money, but the man gave a fictitious name and avoided security cameras. Granted, Wilmington could have set this up, or he could be sincere."

"Why are you telling me this?"

"He claims to know who's behind the elderly frauds. He's

agreed to help us with the investigation, contingent on his immediate release."

"But this is all staged, right?"

"If he's sincere, we'll make permanent arrangements." He cleared his throat. "We have a few terms we need you to consider before moving forward."

Acid slammed against her stomach. "Terms, sir?"

"If you agree, you'll be working closely with him. The two of you will be a couple in appearances only."

Laurel held up her hand. "Who packaged this deal?"

SSA Preston stared her down. "We did."

The acid crawled up her throat. "I'm sure Wilmington is real excited to be working with me."

"Trust me, he's not, but the flip side of the deal makes our proposal attractive."

A killer set free because he snitches on one of his buds. What a lowlife. "What are the rest of the terms?"

"We know you and your partner are also friends, but communication with Special Agent Phang regarding this case must cease. She's not to be told anything. It would be better if there's no communication, period."

Su-Min? They'd had their disagreements, but no contact? "How do you know he's telling the truth and not covering up his own crimes? Especially since his info about the new scam came after the fact."

"We're working the case from all angles, and this is just one of them. You proved your ability to secure evidence from him five years ago, and we're confident you can again."

Bitterness and dread settled on her shoulders. "Sir, I'm not convinced this is a good idea. Why would anyone believe we were together since I put him in jail?"

"He's tossing the faith card—"

"I was with him constantly for six months. I learned how his mind works, his choice of friends, his manipulative nature, things you don't want to hear, and what matters most to him. And believe me, it's not a Bible study or God."

"We'll be providing history to make the relationship look legitimate."

She dug her fingers into her palms. "Forgive and forget in the name of love?"

"Exactly. He needs to gain the confidence of the person he claims is responsible and make contact. Get what we need. Work the game. And we need to keep him under close watch."

Like she'd done to him. "Can you expand?"

He nodded. "Tomorrow he'll be released. The press will play up his rehabilitation."

"As in his faith."

"Right. For this assignment, you'll be relieved of your FBI position for undisclosed reasons, but the rumor will be a conflict of interests. You chose Wilmington over your career, and you're furious about the dismissal. No one is to know about our arrangement."

"Sir, he threatened to kill me. And now you want me to work with him?"

SSA Preston stared at her for several seconds. "We have confidence this will work. We think we can trust Wilmington. If not, he'll take permanent residence in the penal system."

"Think? So you'll know who to prosecute for my murder?"

"Agent Evertson, this is your choice."

More like a snapshot from a nightmare. "Sir, can I keep my badge and weapon?"

"Yes. Send all correspondence directly to me. Call or text me with any updates or problems. You'll be seen with Wilmington while he's working to gain the confidence of the one he claims is behind the scams."

Her head swam with the danger and the unlikelihood of success. "Won't I discourage the operation? I'm not convinced of his newfound faith. For all I know he's playing us and is orchestrating the whole scam from the inside." She paused. "How would my partnering with him aid the case?"

"With your career ruined, your desire for revenge against the FBI will be a solid cover." He drew in a breath. "Your contribution will be an asset to your career. You may need to prove you're on his side. Whether Wilmington is once again involved with a crime, or he can lead us to the criminal, remains to be seen."

"How long would I play the role?"

"For as long as it takes. Dress the part."

Did she have a choice when he'd killed Jesse? Images of Earl and Abby were fixed in her mind, as well as the other elderly who'd been victimized. "All right. I'll do it. When do I get started?"

"After our meeting, you'll return to your desk. Call Special Agent Phang to your office to discuss the scam. There I'll confront you in front of her about your unauthorized visit to Morton Wilmington and call you into my office. Afterward you'll clear out your desk and be escorted from the building."

She nodded. There went the only friend she had.

"Wilmington will contact you later this week. We're calling the scammer Leopard. He knows how to pick and approach the victims, change his habits, and when to go dark."

A whirl of apprehension mixed with determination filled her. She'd never trust Wilmington, and when this was over, he'd be behind bars for good. He'd never hurt good people again.

CHAPTER 15

Laurel drove home from the FBI office with a boxful of belongings. The looks she received from other agents when she was escorted off the property were that of disgust, especially from Su-Min. Laurel expected it, needed it for credibility with her assignment. Her personal mission was twofold—stop the elderly fraud and prove Wilmington should stay behind bars.

She was honored to go undercover again, but working with Wilmington would take all of her acting skills.

Her cell phone rang, and she recognized the caller as Abby Hilton.

"Laurel, I have critical information for you." Her voice quivered.

"What's going on?"

"I received a basket of funeral flowers. . . ."

When Abby finished, Laurel wanted to turn her car around and drive to Silver Hospitality, but she couldn't. Not with most of the FBI office believing she had been dismissed. "Did you see the deliveryman?"

"No. The flower shop is local and confirmed the order. They said a woman walked in and paid cash. Wore a baseball cap. Nothing on their security cameras."

"No one's that slick. We'll end this. Did you call the police?"

"Not yet. Wanted to tell you first since we have an arrangement."

"I'm no longer with the FBI."

Abby gasped. "What happened?"

"I've been dismissed. Driving home now." Wish she could have told her in a more gracious manner. "Anyway, call HPD and your grandson. The FBI are scheduled to be there again this afternoon, and you'll want to give them the note and tell them what you learned about the origin of the flowers."

"Got it. Call HPD and Daniel, and then make sure the FBI has all the info too. I'm really sorry about what happened."

"I should have been more careful." Laurel hated lying to a sweet lady. Part of the job description. Abby had enough on her plate. Too frail to be taking care of a husband whose mind worked like a light switch. Her thoughts sounded condescending, and she didn't feel those emotions at all. The situation made her angry. Bad guys victimizing the defenseless needed to be locked away permanently.

"I have confidence in you. My grandson pretends he doesn't like you," the older woman whispered. "But I know better."

"Abby, we don't have a thing in common, and I'm not interested, nor do I have the time."

"He's a man and you're a woman. Both independent. Neither looking for a relationship. Works for me," Abby said. "I wasn't sure how I felt about Earl, afraid of a relationship. Then one day he smiled just the right way, and it's been heaven ever since. We've weathered bad times and rejoiced in the good ones. Even here with all of us inching toward our coffins, I see the boy, the man, who stole my heart."

Laurel searched for the right words, but there weren't any. If only she could meet a man who treasured her as much as Abby treasured her husband.

"No need to answer," Abby said. "One day soon we need to have a nice chat. I learned something today that I'm not sure the FBI is aware of."

"Which is?"

"Liz Austin's personnel file is missing."

"Can you find a discreet way to tell the FBI?"

"I'll think on it. I could tell them I didn't trust her and hope they look for her file."

"Sounds good."

"I also talked to Chef Steven. He told me Liz has a boyfriend and spent a lot of time texting him and playing games on her iPad. He also avoided a question about whether he'd ever seen her boyfriend. I believe she could have used her iPad to disarm the security camera at the rear of the kitchen."

Great observation. "You should call SSA Preston with what you've learned." Laurel gave Abby the phone number.

Liz Austin's name had come up on more than one occasion.

✳ ✳ ✳

2:15 P.M. MONDAY

Daniel had made a decision. Once he picked up his grandparents from Silver Hospitality, they wouldn't be returning. He'd arranged for off-duty policemen to work 24-7 and nurses to do the same. Gramps could kick all the fuss he wanted. Didn't matter.

What he didn't understand was why Laurel no longer worked for the FBI. Did he dare call her? That thought lasted ten seconds. Fifteen minutes were left on his lunch break, and he'd use them. She responded on the third ring.

"Officer Hilton, are you at Silver Hospitality?"

"Not yet. Gran told me you're no longer with the FBI."

"True."

His gut told him something else was happening. "Is there anything I can do?"

She sighed. "If you uncover anything about your grandparents, don't hesitate to contact the FBI. I'm taking a little time to look for a job."

"Who's taking over the elderly fraud case?"

"I don't know who's been assigned. SSA Preston is your go-to agent at this point." She paused. "Don't really care either after what they did to me."

"All right. Once I have my grandparents safe at home with a police officer, I'm checking on Emma Dockson, the woman who gave money to Russell Jergon."

"Call me later?"

"Sure."

Daniel smiled. Laurel was still on the case.

CHAPTER 16

Daniel introduced his grandparents to the bodyguard at their home and promised to be back by six thirty. Gramps didn't know why they'd left the facility early or why a stranger sat on their front porch, and the confusion upset him. Once he was calmed, Gran coaxed him with a favorite TV show. She was on board with Daniel's plan. Although frail-looking, she had the inner strength of a bulldog.

Daniel had left directly from his precinct office, not taking time to change, and headed toward Houston Methodist to check on Emma Dockson. According to Gran, this was Mrs. Dockson's second hospitalization due to a bleeding ulcer, but she'd progressed well. How wonderful if she had good recall. Her testimony likely wouldn't hold up in court, but she could provide vital information.

Emma's niece transported her to Silver Hospitality every weekday. The elderly woman's deceased husband had owned a lucrative commercial construction business, plenty for predators to scam. But how were the thieves gaining access to victims? Any suspicions regarding Marsha Leonard had dissipated when he saw her twelve-year-old Honda, and he figured the board of directors had undergone an extensive background check. For certain the FBI was on it.

While traffic inched ahead, his mind wandered to his grandparents' safety.

The idea of keeping up-to-date with the latest findings through the media agitated him. HPD and the FBI worked together on task forces, but unless something happened on his beat, he was clueless. And where did Laurel fit?

At the hospital, Daniel greeted the receptionist. "I'd like to see Emma Dockson. She's a patient in geriatrics."

The woman checked her computer. Lines etched across her forehead. "I'm so sorry, but Mrs. Dockson passed this afternoon."

Doubts soared through him. "What happened? I called at noon, and she was fine."

"Are you family, sir? Or is this police business?"

"Both. I've known this woman long enough to be considered family." He stretched the truth a little, but he needed answers and access to those who had them.

The receptionist picked up the phone and explained Daniel's visit. "The head nurse on Mrs. Dockson's floor will speak to you."

Daniel nodded his appreciation and took the phone. "Thank you for talking to me. What happened to Mrs. Dockson?"

"She went to sleep this afternoon and never woke up. Poor thing. From all indications, her heart simply gave out."

His pulse sped at the unlikelihood of a heart attack when she'd been hospitalized for a bleeding ulcer. "Is her niece here?"

"She's with me now."

"I'm on my way." Daniel took the elevator to the sixth floor. How would he recognize the woman? The one crying? A familiar face from Silver Hospitality?

A sixtysomething woman stood at the nurses' station, red-eyed, tissue in hand.

"Are you Emma Dockson's niece?" he said.

When she affirmed it, he reached out his hand. "I'm Officer Daniel Hilton. So sorry for your loss."

She grasped his hand as though he were a lifeline, then released it. "Lila Dockson. Why are the police involved?" Uncertainty edged her words. "Are you a friend of my aunt's?"

"My grandparents are clients at Silver Hospitality. I provide transportation for them. I just got off duty, ma'am."

She relaxed. "You look familiar. I'm sorry if I sounded rude."

He gave her a sincere smile. How would he handle the same moment when his grandparents passed? "I understand the challenges of loving an Alzheimer's sufferer. My grandparents are concerned about your aunt, so I wanted to check on her."

The woman's shoulders slumped. "Emma is my husband's aunt, and we're her caretakers. She's lived with us for over ten years. Her days were numbered, but today was still a shock. She had pneumonia twice last summer, and her body must have succumbed to it with a heart attack. Such a dear lady. Even when she didn't recognize us, she was kind."

"Gramps is the same way. Did your aunt have a history of heart problems?"

"No, but I gather it's not uncommon for her age." She took another tissue from the box on the nurses' counter. "I really wish my husband were here. Unfortunately he's out of town."

"Can we talk for a few minutes?"

Her gaze darted. "I suppose. Nothing I can do while they take care of Aunt Emma. The funeral home has been contacted, and our pastor will be here soon."

Daniel pointed to a waiting area. "We could sit there. Do you mind answering a few questions for me?"

She raised a brow over reddened eyes. "What about?"

He sighed. "My grandparents have made a few comments concerning unusual happenings at Silver Hospitality, and I'm looking for answers. Both are clients, as I stated earlier. However Gramps has Alzheimer's, and Gran spends her day with him."

She blinked. "The facility is so highly rated."

"I agree. I'm more than pleased with the care, and the staff is amazing."

They seated themselves on a leatherette sofa in the corner away from the others. "I appreciate your time, considering the trauma of the afternoon. Did your aunt ever mention someone selling her a life insurance policy?"

Lila Dockson startled. "Why?"

"So she did." When the woman glanced out the window, he continued. "It's all right. I'm facing the same questions. Money missing from my grandparents' savings account. We're uncertain exactly how it happened."

She dabbed her eyes. "Aunt Emma talked a few times about doing something special for us. We had no idea what she was talking about. We thanked her and changed the subject."

"Does the name Lifestyle Insurance sound familiar?"

She shook her head. "Like I said, Aunt Emma babbled a lot. Can't say if the name is familiar, but I can ask my husband. He'll be home late this evening. Since you're a police officer, is the facility under investigation?"

"I'm looking into a possible elderly fraud case involving a couple of people at Silver Hospitality because of my grandparents' experience. The FBI is making inquiries. My grandfather said your aunt had given a salesman money."

Her eyes widened. "Someone took money from an Alzheimer's patient?" Indignation rose in her voice. "Why did the facility permit it?"

"They have no record of anyone visiting other than family, friends, and clergy. Nothing on the security cameras or the sign-in register." He paused for her to consider the lack of evidence to substantiate claims. "No receipts either. All I have is a brochure from Lifestyle Insurance, which has no contact information."

"How odd people with dementia have similar stories. One always hears reports of scams and such, but I find it hard to believe someone could have gotten past the front desk."

"That part has me baffled too. But elderly fraud is not uncommon." Another thought occurred to him, one he'd need to investigate further. "How often has your aunt been hospitalized?"

"Several times, actually."

The right keystrokes into a hospital's medical records would offer valuable data from Social Security numbers to diagnosis codes. He wouldn't reveal his suspicions—a link to dementia patients who were financially secure. "Have you noted a substantial withdrawal from your aunt's accounts?"

She touched her heart. "We take care of Aunt Emma's financials."

"All someone would need is a routing or Social Security number to hack into her accounts."

Lila pulled her cell phone from her purse. A few moments later, she dropped her cell into her lap. "The account we use to pay bills is fine. But her savings shows two extremely large withdrawals, the latest from this afternoon. I can't believe this."

"You need to file a report immediately. I can help you with that."

She rubbed her arms. "Of course. I need to call my husband before he boards a plane in New Hampshire."

Daniel wanted to ask one more question, one the family might meet with resistance. "Would you and your husband consider an autopsy?"

She paled. "Surely you're not suggesting—"

"It's a possibility."

"I'm not sure. Maybe we should, under the circumstances. What do you suggest?"

"I only know what my grandparents have stated, and I could be way out of line."

"But you could have stumbled onto something horrible."

✳ ✳ ✳

5:50 P.M. MONDAY

Daniel left Lila Dockson at the hospital in the capable hands of a pastor friend. He'd love to be the one to break the elderly fraud case, but with the FBI's investigation, his chances looked slim. His motives were selfish, and he retracted his thinking. The ones preying on innocent people needed to be behind bars, no matter who broke the case. Law enforcement was a team project. Period.

He phoned Marsha Leonard about Emma Dockson's death. The director of Silver Hospitality had always been the epitome of caring. Not once had he seen her act in an unkind way toward the clients or staff. For that matter, he'd not experienced her being rude to anyone. Except when he got under her skin. Still wanted to believe she was innocent of any wrongdoing.

"Miss Leonard, this is Daniel Hilton. Do you have a minute? I have some bad news."

"Are Abby and Earl okay?"

"They're fine. Emma Dockson passed this afternoon. I visited the hospital and learned what happened. Spoke with her niece. Told her I'd make the call to you."

"Daniel, I'm never ready for our clients to pass. What happened?"

"A heart attack. But Lila made a discovery. Money from Mrs. Dockson's savings account was missing. A sizable withdrawal this afternoon."

Miss Leonard broke into sobs. "When will this end?"

"I don't know how the criminals are operating, but I'm committed to finding out just like the FBI."

"I'd expect nothing less of you," she whispered. "I've gone over and over the security cameras, and nothing is amiss. The FBI's investigation is a comfort, but you have more at stake in seeing arrests made."

Daniel noted her trembling voice. "Whoever is responsible is organized, precise in what they're doing."

"It's frightening," Miss Leonard said.

"I promise you, answers will be found. Do you use volunteers from a specific organization?"

"Only from my church and those I can trust. We conduct rigid background checks. You and I have our differences, but we both care about the people here. I . . . I think you've made a wise decision regarding Abby and Earl."

"Thank you. Keep your eyes open, Miss Leonard. I'm convinced the situation is part of a sophisticated operation."

Daniel's next call was to Laurel. "Hope I'm not intruding on your privacy. But I have new information. A woman from Silver Hospitality died at Methodist early this afternoon, one who Gramps claimed gave Russell Jergon money. Although I'm not sure if she purchased a life insurance policy, her savings account took a huge hit."

"I don't like the sound of that. A scammer collecting both ways. But we knew this was probably where the crime was headed."

"My thoughts too. This is random, but Emma's hospitalization was for bleeding ulcers, and she died of a heart attack. Probably just my cop nature, but I asked her niece if she'd consider an autopsy."

"The scammers are not infallible. Officer Hilton, be careful. You're a great cop, and I don't want to read your name in the obits." The concern in her voice confirmed she had additional information.

"What have you discovered?"

"I'm no longer with the FBI, remember? They fired me."

CHAPTER 17

Once dinner was cleared—Gran's homemade firehouse chili and jalapeño corn bread—Daniel paced his grandparents' media room searching for the right words to explain the dangerous situation at Silver Hospitality. He prayed Gramps was coherent enough to understand. A headache hammered his skull: Emma's death, Gran's threat, and Laurel's dismissal from the FBI.

Daniel stared at his grandfather's mammoth grand piano, the focal point of the floor-to-ceiling windowed room. He could make those ivories sing with the expertise of a concert pianist, and yet his mind hovered over the past and present.

"Why don't you spit it out and tell us what's going on?" Gramps said, his eyes clear.

"You're in danger, and it's my responsibility to surround you with those who are trained to guard innocent people. Gran received a threatening note today."

"How?"

Gran took his hand and explained the flower delivery. "Whoever is involved thinks I'm feeding investigators information. But you were threatened. Staying home will protect both of us until arrests are made."

"You mean protect old and senile people?" Gramps said. "Told you earlier, I'm not deserting my friends."

Daniel took a deep breath and planned a new tack. "Gramps, I already made the arrangements. I've hired around-the-clock nurses and officers. The police officer outside will guard you until the officer who takes the first shift arrives at eight."

"Bodyguards?" Gramps frowned. "I have an arsenal to protect Abby and me. Who taught you how to shoot?"

Gran touched his arm. "What if your mind slips, Earl? You and I've done a lot of hunting together, from deer to big game in Africa. The truth is I don't know if I can shoot a man. I'm afraid I'd be too nervous, and he'd take away my gun. Use it on us."

Gramps buried his face in his hands. "I hate getting old. Losing what once made me a respected man. Can't even take care of my own wife."

"Earl, you've protected me since I was fourteen years old. Seventy years of loving you. Let me return the favor."

"Abby, girl, no matter how far the big A takes me, I promise you this—I'll always recognize you and know your name."

Gran kissed his cheek. "What more could I ask?"

Daniel swallowed the thickening in his throat. "When I couldn't take care of myself, you stepped in and showed me real love and how to be a man. You helped me see I needed God in my life. The arrangement away from the facility won't be too long. Only until arrests are made. A nurse will be here at eight o'clock tonight and she'll begin an eight-hour shift. The nurses' shifts will overlap thirty minutes, and I'll visit whenever I can."

"Will the officers be inside our home?" Gran said.

"Only if you want them."

She nodded. "I'll sleep better." She walked across the room and hugged him. "Thanks. You have a good heart, Daniel."

He focused on Gramps. "Will you let me do this for you?"

"Yes and no. Yes, I agree to your arrangements, but we'll pay for it. We have more money than we can ever spend—minus eighty grand." He lifted a brow. "Most all we have goes to you, not some swindler."

"Thanks. Now I have some sad news for you. Emma Dockson passed this afternoon. She had a heart attack."

Gran touched her chest. "Such a sweet lady."

Daniel explained the missing money. "Another reason for you to stay here."

"I'll do all I can to cooperate," Gran said.

Daniel smiled. "Thanks. How about a song tonight? Joplin?"

"You got it," Gramps said. "Abby, prepare to dance."

Daniel's phone rang. He didn't recognize the caller's number, but with all that was going on, it could be important. "Officer Daniel Hilton," he said.

"Back off from this case," a distorted voice said.

Daniel left the room and walked into the kitchen. "What case?"

"You know what I mean."

"I have no clue what you're talking about."

The voice cursed. "Yes, you do. This is over your head, cop. You got the wrong person's attention. Now he's upset with your interference."

"When it comes to my grandparents, I'm not backing off. Tell your boss that."

"Then you're more stupid than we thought. Your grandparents aren't in good health. Be a shame to lose them in an accident. Only a matter of time." The caller disconnected.

He'd notify the officers protecting Gran and Gramps of the potential danger. Double the men on each shift. If the caller thought Daniel would leave the case alone, he was wrong. Dead wrong. He'd call Laurel in the morning for her input.

He walked into the media room and plastered fake enthusiasm on his face. "The police officer will be here in a few minutes. Good man. I'm anxious for you to meet him."

"Let's hope I can remember his name from one day to the next." Gramps's dry tone indicated depression. "Some days I can laugh at myself. This is not one of them. I'm praying for a miracle drug. Dying and meeting Jesus is one thing, but I want to recognize

Him." He shrugged. "I'm being foolish. I'll be healed then and none of this will matter."

Daniel considered how much to tell them. Did they really comprehend the danger? "Promise me you won't leave the house without protection or let any strangers inside."

Gran slipped her arm around Gramps's waist. "Whatever it takes, right, Earl? I'm ready to dance if this old man can make a little music."

An hour later, Daniel left his grandparents, glad he'd made the arrangements for their care and yet fearful for their safety. They liked the officer, who held several commendations and needed a little extra money for his daughter's college fund. Daniel privately explained the call. The other two officers were good men too, men of faith and courage.

He phoned HPD to check the number used to call him earlier. As he expected, a burner phone.

Tomorrow he wanted to talk to Laurel. Perhaps she'd open up. But he had to curb the impulse to phone her too often when she had personal issues with her career. Made him look selfish, as if he were interested.

CHAPTER 18

Laurel learned from SSA Preston that Liz Austin was an alias. Her missing file had contained a photo, and her online file had been deleted. She was the insider. They'd hit a temporary dead end until she surfaced again.

No man was an island in the investigation business. Teamwork solved crimes and put bracelets on the bad guys. Then she remembered.

Wilmington made his exit today. Media would video his walk back into society with a recap of what sent him to prison. An interview too, and most likely at his lawyer's request. Chances were her role in his takedown would hit the radar. They'd post photos from the past, the kind she'd pay to have destroyed. The whole city and state would hear about his conversion, his remorse, and his future plans of living for God.

Media speculated on why she'd been dismissed from the FBI, most of it derogatory. That aspect helped lend credibility to what would happen later on in the week.

Su-Min sent a text: Do not contact me ever.

The finality hurt and yet Laurel had expected it. Didn't make the news any easier even if it played into SSA Preston's plan.

The clock inched toward ten, when Wilmington would be released from prison. No doubt some of his fans who hailed him as Robin Hood would be on hand to cheer, along with media coverage.

She brought up a live feed on her laptop.

Wilmington stepped out of prison wearing designer jeans and a button-down shirt. He smiled and waved at the onlookers. She sickened. Those blue eyes might fool others, but she knew the evil behind them.

This man killed Jesse, and now he wanted to look like he'd paid his price to society. Laurel's nerves leaped in time to her heartbeat. How could she even bear to speak to him?

An older, serious reporter spoke into the mic. "In less than five minutes, Morton Wilmington will speak to the press. His lawyer states he has a special message regarding his recent conversion to Christianity. From here he's meeting with Pastor Emerson McKee of Community Evangelical Church, Houston."

Who would believe his trash? Had they forgotten the murderer who steamrolled his opposition? Could she really follow through with this assignment?

❋   ❋   ❋

12:10 P.M. TUESDAY

Daniel clicked off the radio in his patrol car. Morton Wilmington's release wasn't a coincidence. Laurel had worked undercover to secure the evidence leading to his arrest, and now she no longer had a job. He took his lunch break to phone his best source for word on the streets, a woman of many talents.

"Hey, Coco. This is Daniel."

"I don't work for free, sweet man."

Daniel laughed. "No one does. I need info."

"Hold on. Let me get something to write on."

"That could be dangerous if you're caught."

"I have a code."

Another one who worked encryption. "Hope it's a good one."

"Personally developed it myself," she said. "I use words from my line of work."

Not sure he wanted to hear what they were. "Ready?"

"Fire away."

"Are you charging by the minute?"

"Business is business, and you never see me professionally."

And he wouldn't. "All right—two things. Somebody tailed and fired at me the other evening. Had my grandparents with me. Then last night a caller threatened them. Have you heard anything?"

"Not a word. Your chosen career isn't safe. That could have been anybody trying to get to you by threatening them."

She was right, but the sophistication of the elderly fraud wouldn't hit the streets. "What's the word on Morton Wilmington's release?"

"How quick do you need this?"

"An hour ago."

"This will cost you a little more."

"But you're the best."

"Right. I have many talents."

"Cut the hype, Coco. This is important."

"Okay, I heard Wilmington's men are laying low. They heard Monday about his release. Confused. He's called a meeting with them late tonight. With all the religious talk from inside the prison, they're either questioning their jobs or waiting to hear how business will play out."

"Job security in today's economy is critical."

Coco laughed, a rough crackling sound that spoke of her addiction, booze, and cigarettes. "My rates have gone up."

"Last I checked, a warrant was out for your arrest. One of your associates turned you in."

"Since when?"

"Do you want to take the chance? Some of those girls in jail aren't happy with your success. Your pimp can't help you there."

Coco swore in Spanish. "Oh, be glad you're so good-looking. I'll call you tonight. Same price as always. Leave it with the girl at the McDonald's inside Walmart."

CHAPTER 19

Daniel wanted to see Laurel or talk to her. Her dismissal bothered him, especially when the FBI had given the media a conflict-of-interest reason. Paper-thin. What did he have to lose with a phone call, since he had no idea who'd threatened his grandparents?

She responded on the second ring. "Officer Hilton," she said.

"It is. Are you busy?"

"I'm supposed to be updating my résumé for a headhunter, but my heart's not in it."

Not a job he'd want to tackle. But he detested paperwork too. "Need some help?"

"I got it. Thanks."

"I have a blunt question."

"No, I don't want pizza."

He chuckled. "Good one. This is another matter. Are you going to tell me why you're no longer with the bureau? I realize it's none of my business, but you did take an interest in my grandparents' case."

"I can't. The circumstances are raw. Maybe in the future."

"Fair enough."

She sighed. "I care about your grandparents and all the others who've been abused by a scammer. The FBI's following up on all leads."

"So I direct everything to SSA Preston?"

"Yes. What happened?"

"Got a call last night, ordering me to back off the case or my grandparents might have an accident. Burner phone. What have you found as the typical way to scam the elderly?" Daniel said. "If you'd rather I talk to SSA Preston, just say so."

"I don't mind. The typical victim is an older person who lives alone with no family or the family is not attentive. Too many times, the victim meets a couple, husband and wife, at the person's church or a reputable charity organization. The scammers start out taking care of little things for the person, doing more than the family. When the couple establishes trust, they persuade the elderly person to add them to various accounts." Laurel sighed. "But that's not true of all the victims. We're looking at an out-of-the-box scam."

"How do you think Russell Jergon weaseled inside Silver Hospitality?"

"Found a way to avoid the security cameras. The FBI is constantly pouring inquiries into the FIG—Field Intelligence Group."

"I know the FIG's function." He swallowed his irritation. "This is an operation with nationwide potential. They're using a computer database that gives them a list of specific victims. I found out a few things about health insurance databases from a friend of mine. You probably have the info, but I'm being the good guy and sharing."

"I'm sorry. The situation with my job and Morton Wilmington has me distracted."

"And I'm probing you. My apologies."

Laurel hesitated before continuing. "One of the reasons I want the scam ended is because of my growing-up years. A dear woman raised me, a foster mother. Ten years ago, she was diagnosed with Alzheimer's, and her husband put her in a filthy nursing home. I saw her every chance I could until she passed."

"So you understand my protective nature with Gran and Gramps."

"When your grandfather mentioned dignity, I was transported

back to her suffering." She paused. "Fat lot of good it does me now that I'm no longer working for the system. I have to ask you not to contact me until this is over. Please. This has gotten dangerous." She ended the call.

He didn't believe she no longer worked for the FBI. She specifically said, *"No longer working for the system."* Wilmington had been released from prison. She'd supposedly been dismissed from her responsibilities. Neither was a coincidence. Even with her abrupt end to the conversation, her mood didn't match that of a woman whose career had just been flushed down the toilet.

＊ ＊ ＊

8:30 P.M. TUESDAY

Laurel finished the laundry while her mind spun with Morton Wilmington's release and how she loathed the man. Washing, drying, and folding clothes hit the no-brainer level, making it impossible to push the man away from her thoughts. Partnering with him collided against everything she believed in. Yet, the end justified the ugliness. At least that's what she told herself.

SSA Preston had promised they'd watch her back, but that meant a device inserted in her phone, a chip implant, or a wire. She'd refused them when she worked undercover with Wilmington before because of his security methods, and she did so again. Today's sophistication meant she could lose her cover, and she'd rather risk her own life to find the truth. Her reasons sounded heroic, but they only reflected her low self-esteem. She had nothing to live for except justice for Jesse. His death could have been prevented if she hadn't hesitated in shooting Wilmington. It was only one of many areas where she'd failed.

Taking a deep breath, she shoved aside the piercing fragments of her past. Being alone brought it all on, and she despised the memories. If—

Her cell phone rang, and she didn't recognize the number. Laurel answered with a simple hello.

"This is Morton."

Chills numbed her. "I thought you weren't contacting me until later."

"We have a new development."

No surprise there. "What is it?"

"My contact called. Wasn't expecting him to get in touch this soon. Wanted to know my plans. I dropped the bomb and told him we were back together since I became a Christian. Gave him the scenario about the FBI giving you the ultimatum of your career or me. You chose me and they fired you. Stated both of us were bitter. Told him I wasn't sure what the future held, but trusting in God wasn't exactly working out."

"His reaction?"

"Has a business proposition for me. Not sure those with him will approve of you. I told him we'd discuss it and get back to him. But we were a team and I had plenty of contacts of my own."

"Faster progress than SSA Preston expected. Did this guy contact you in prison?"

"Yes. Offered me a partnership in an elderly scam. At the time I wasn't interested. He asked why I hadn't eliminated you. Told him I still cared."

"Sounds like overkill."

"He and I go back a long way. Were in the Army together. He went on to serve in Delta Force. He was the first person I told about asking you to marry me. I made myself believable."

She shivered. "When we have a face-to-face, I want to know everything."

"Got it. We need to move dinner to tomorrow night. The longer we wait, the more victims."

Still using his control tactics. "Okay. When do you think he'll get back to you?"

"Hard to tell. I've arranged for a leak to the media. That will show him we're together."

"Wonderful." She didn't hold back the sarcasm.

"Laurel, you despise me. That's a given. You don't trust me. That's a given. I'm not happy about this charade either. But I'm ready to see it through to the end. Staying out of prison is at the top of my list of priorities."

"How noble."

"Watch how it plays out."

"I don't see how your *friend* will ever believe I'm on the wrong side of the law."

"We might need to stage a crime. With FBI clearance, of course."

"That's the only way, Morton. They're heading up this project."

"I'm working with the law on this whether you believe me or not. My driver will pick you up at seven thirty Wednesday night. Bodyguards are watching you. These people tend to leave bodies in their wake."

"How big's his operation?"

"Haven't figured it out yet."

"Does SSA Preston have this information?"

"I just learned about a few specifics tonight. I'll give you more tomorrow at dinner."

"Why not now?"

"Because I want to verify it first."

Laurel set her phone on the counter when the call ended. Fear spiraled through her, but courage took over. She'd see this through. What more could she lose? Her former partner and best friend had cast her aside, and the one man outside the FBI she could trust could get himself killed along with his dear grandparents.

CHAPTER 20

Laurel wriggled into a short red dress and slipped on six-inch red glittery heels. Dress the part. Photographers would focus on every inch of her. She wore the color of passion from her nails to her toes. Her makeup would make a cosmetic artist proud—lined eyes and four shades of color complete with two applications of mascara. Her lipstick was called Blood. The implication caused her stomach to churn. She thought the days of placating Wilmington were over. His information and connections had better be worth it.

You're a strong woman, Special Agent Laurel Evertson.

Morton Wilmington cannot hurt you any more than he already has.

She added diamond drop earrings to her streetwalker ensemble, while a sense of professional escort swept through her. She excused her actions tonight with a reminder of her commitment to the FBI. Sacrifices came with the territory. To put Wilmington away for good, she'd do this. She dreaded the photos sure to hit the *Chronicle* and far too many online sites tomorrow.

She'd rather spend the evening devouring pizza with Officer Hilton—dressed in jeans.

She spritzed on perfume, a brand she'd not worn before. Wilmington preferred Jean Patou Joy perfume, which she'd poured down the drain years ago. For a moment, Laurel feared she'd be truly ill. Every tick of the antique mantel clock on her dresser brought her closer to him . . . enduring dinner, talking through the case, searching for evidence to nail him. Easing onto a bench in her bedroom, she drew in a deep breath and held a protective arm over her middle. The girl who shunned boundaries had died when Jesse bled out. She hadn't undergone any religious conversion. After all, the prayers for Jesse went to his grave. But morals and truth became more important, the only thing she could hold on to. Or control. She and Wilmington both had the big C going on.

Now she was being tested by the man who brought out the worst in her.

I can do this and find out what he's planning.

She closed her closet door and grabbed her bag, complete with her Springfield 9mm. Bodyguards, agents, and cameras waited in the shadows, yet if her life was in danger, she'd use it. Thoughts of previous dates with him . . . things she'd said and done. Shivering, she left her apartment. One more mission with Morton Wilmington.

Morton's driver picked her up on time and drove to Damian's, an upscale Italian restaurant. Morton wanted media coverage to show he'd forgiven the woman who'd betrayed him. What about her forgiveness for his shooting an agent? Of course, he'd state her good works for the FBI helped him to find the error of his ways. Trash talk.

She clenched her fist to control the shaking. The time had come to think like an agent and not a wounded woman. She'd been assigned to this mission for a reason, and she'd not let anyone down.

Within the hour, Laurel sat across from Wilmington at a rear corner table at Damian's. A place they'd frequented five years ago. No one had searched her, which was a surprise. Or did he assume she'd be wired and packing? Judging by the empty tables around them, Wilmington must have paid well for their privacy. He'd cleaned up. Haircut. New suit. Same smug look. Memories stabbed at her like a knife twisting in an open wound.

"You're tempting a man who hasn't been close to a woman in five years. I like your hair longer." His full lips turned upward. "Forbidden fruit."

She might throw up. "I remember how you liked red."

"And you wear it well. We have much to discuss tonight, so I appreciate your moving the date up."

Smile, Laurel. It won't break your face. "We have a job to do, and success means your permanent parole and an elderly scam ended."

"You rehearsed those lines well considering your feelings about me." He raised a hand before she could speak. "You look lovely, my dear."

Should she blush and act coy? She bit her tongue to keep from blasting him with the scathing details of how Jesse died.

The waiter handed them the wine list.

"No thank you." Morton returned it. He gestured to Laurel. "The lady may want a glass of chardonnay."

To keep up appearances, he was no longer drinking. Interesting, considering how much he once spent on alcohol. "Sparkling water will be fine."

"The same for me."

The waiter, complete with a bow tie, left them alone, and she could feel Morton's eyes boring into her. What should she expect when she was dressed like a high-class hooker?

"What else is on your mind?" she said.

"You have a new perfume. I like it."

She hated the charade. "You're welcome. You didn't answer my question."

"SSA Preston said you refused to wear a wire." He leaned back in his chair. "I have a proposition for you."

"Is this personal?" Laurel danced her red fingernails on the tabletop.

"I have an addendum."

The waiter returned with their beverages and asked if they were ready to order.

"What will it be for you tonight, Laurel? Are you still fond of Chilean bass?"

The low timbre of his voice annoyed her. "The bass is fine."

Morton ordered the house steak, medium, and again they were alone. Soft piano music kept the silence from driving her crazy.

Control.

"Once the public sees us together, we'll have more credibility. In every sense of the word. It'll go viral on Facebook and Twitter. In return, I will give the FBI names of key persons from my former life."

"What if one of your old buds gets wind of what you're doing?"

He grinned. "The FBI will have them all dead or locked up unless you plan to tell my old business partners."

"Don't tempt me."

"Just look at the great service I'll have done for society."

"Doesn't matter what color of the spectrum you paint your words. They're still a lie."

"So you don't believe I'll provide the information."

She forced a smile. "Prove me wrong. If you want to do the turnaround thing, then why don't you pull out the millions of dollars you have stashed in undisclosed accounts. Give it back to those you robbed. Print business cards with the sign of a fish."

He took a sip of water, his face red. She hadn't said anything to make him so furious. "You're selfish, Laurel."

"And you?"

"Tell me, did you think you'd get away with it?" The muscles in his face tightened.

This was the Morton Wilmington she knew. "Get away with what? Sending you to prison?"

"Embezzling $4 million from me."

She startled. "You've got to be kidding."

"My sources tell me otherwise. A welcome-home present with your signature."

"If I found a way to access your funds, it would be in the FBI's hands. I don't have a death wish. Your source is full of it. Look somewhere else for your missing money." While anger wanted to take over, she defused it and reached for logic.

His eyes narrowed. "The account was hacked a few hours ago and traced to you." He pulled his phone from inside his jacket and handed it to her.

She recognized the account number. Saw her name. Whoever was working hard at discrediting her did a good job. She gave him eye contact. "I have no idea how the money got there. If I'd stolen from you, I would have put it in a good place, not my own savings account."

"Point taken."

"Since you hacked in, you pulled it out?"

"No."

"Reported it to the FBI?"

He nodded.

"I will make sure this is handled. I'm not a thief."

"I had to ask. I think someone arranged it to discredit you."

She analyzed his body language: softened features, relaxed. "What can you tell me?"

"First off, I'll confirm the person behind this." He took another sip of water. Perspiration dotted his brow. "I liked you better when you were working undercover."

"I didn't," she said.

The server returned with salads. Wilmington bowed his head. How long would he keep up the act?

"I'd like to hear your history with this friend of yours," Laurel said when he raised his head again.

He nodded. "We met in the Army and served in Afghanistan. I'd already dabbled in lawbreaking and enlisted before getting caught. In the heat of a firefight, he saved my life. I finished my time and came home. He went on to serve in Delta Force, got married, and had a daughter. His career ended when he was diagnosed with adult-onset asthma. He was furious with the medical discharge. Then his mother died, and his brother received most of her estate. He found a way to hack into the funds and transfer them to an overseas account. His brother figured out what he'd done, so my friend eliminated him. He realized there was money to be made by scamming the elderly. Been downhill ever since."

Laurel filed these details away. It'd be easy enough to figure out an identity with military records and all these clues. "But you hadn't kept in contact?"

"He visited me in prison as my cousin. I don't have a cousin, but I played along and accepted his request. He showed up and talked about his scam. He'd heard my lawyers were working on an appeal. Thought I might need a job. I declined."

"Are you thinking he'll understand my fury with the FBI because of his discontent with Delta Force?"

"Exactly. His partner is another matter."

"In what way?"

"She taught him the art of disguise. While he has military skills, she has the brains behind the operation. Both are cunning. Neither can be trusted."

"What do you know about her?"

"We all served in the Army together. She has a record, but so far nothing leads to the elderly scam."

"Does Preston know her name?"

"I contacted him this afternoon."

"Got a pic of her?"

"Depends on who she is at the time."

Laurel hated dealing with him. "I'd like whatever you have. And for the record, I asked nicely."

He took a sip of water, but she saw his ploy. Delaying an answer made him look like he was in control. Fat chance.

"I'll see what I can do," he said. "I might have it."

"You can get me this woman's name and pic. How many others are in the operation?"

"I don't know at this point. Hope to hear by the weekend. Not much we can do until then except be seen together."

"Did you ever reciprocate after he saved your life?"

Wilmington shook his head. "I'm using my indebtedness as an excuse to team up with him."

She understood his approach, if only she could believe him. "Okay. I know my job. Sit tight and wait until I hear from you." She considered what he'd told her. "I'm assuming I'll be followed until your friend believes he can trust me."

"His favorite method is to meet you face-to-face. If you're seeing someone, I caution you to avoid him until this is over."

There went any hope of a friendship with Daniel.

CHAPTER 21

Laurel tightened the girth on her white Arabian stallion, Phantom. Best friend a girl ever had. She told him about the past, the present, and her goals for the future. Never a fear her words might appear on Facebook or as the subject of online chatter. He heard details concerning FBI cases, her victories, her regrets, and her discouragements. Lots of the latter. Her stallion's demands were simple—good food, a clean stall, and a brush-down after a vigorous run. Controlling his sometimes-unpredictable nature fit her personality, but he was the perfect stress reliever and a good substitute for a boyfriend—without complicated demands.

North of Houston near Pinehurst, where the earth rolled gently toward Dallas with tall pines and oaks, she could race Phantom across the open pastures and release all the tension the world threw her way. The city was her home, where she worked and lived, but here she breathed escape.

Slipping her foot into the stirrup, she hoisted herself into the saddle. Such joy, wild and free, like the wind until she became the wind. She should have been born a century earlier, when technology didn't consist of instant communication from anywhere in the world. Her Samsung Galaxy S 5 rested in her jacket pocket for those who needed immediate attention—and her Glock within inches of her fingers.

She patted Phantom's neck and laughed when he tossed his head. A gusty breeze added to his friskiness. They both wanted this run. Dusk would fall in two hours, which gave them a little time to enjoy the somewhat-cooler temperatures of fall combined with green pastures and full ponds. Goldenrods sprang up like nature's final hold on color, proud of their fall beauty, and deep-yellow daisies held court around a huge rock.

"I need to unload," she whispered to the stallion. "Just when I thought I'd never have to be concerned about Morton Wilmington, life throws a curve. I'm afraid, Phantom. He has motive to see me dead."

Last night she'd dug into Wilmington's Army records and confirmed the names of Geoff Cayden and Josie Fields. With the names, she texted SSA Preston for the FIG to run a complete background. Fingerprints would be in military records for future reference. Now to wait for the report.

Who'd gotten into his offshore account and helped themselves to $4 million just before his release? A poor sport of a business associate? One of his bodyguards? If the purpose had been to discredit her, what would happen next? And why make it so obvious by depositing it into her account?

She raced the stallion over familiar landmarks, her mind whirling with issues biting her heels. Slowly her muscles relaxed, and the latest FBI case was pushed to a remote corner of her mind. Inhaling the crisp air, she admired the landscape not chewed and spit out like the city—natural, peaceful, and flowing. Not like her job and the mounting danger from it.

Phantom's coat dampened beneath her jean-clad legs, and the sun descended in streaks of gold and orange. Time to head back to the stables, where a group of riders had completed their day too. Someday she'd have her own acreage and take care of Phantom herself, a ranch in the hill country with a facility like Silver Hospitality. An idea she'd held on to for years. She dug her heels into Phantom's sides for one more race.

Movement to her left, behind a huge live oak, grabbed her attention.

Her shoulder stung as though a swarm of bees had taken revenge on her flesh. She grabbed her burning shoulder. Blood oozed between her fingers. Her head spun, and she bent low over Phantom.

✳ ✳ ✳

8:35 P.M. THURSDAY

Daniel drove home from his grandparents'. The article and photo of Laurel and Wilmington's reunion in the *Chronicle* threatened to put him in a bad mood.

Green inched up his spine. He was beginning to despise the color.

Stupid for a grown man.

He turned up the volume on the radio for an update of the local news.

"A former Houston FBI agent was shot this evening near Pinehurst. Laurel Evertson met a sniper's bullet while riding at Lone Star Stables. No arrests have been made, and there's no information at this time about her condition. She'd been relieved of her official duties at the bureau on Monday. Sources didn't indicate a motive for the shooting."

Alarm rattled him. He was convinced she was still working the case with the FBI. Why else would someone take a shot at her? Old enemy? He contacted a dispatcher at the station.

"Hey, Mike. This is Daniel. Can you pull up a report for me? Just heard a former FBI special agent by the name of Laurel Evertson was involved in a shooting."

"Sure. Give me a minute while I get the information." He made small talk for a moment before apparently finding the report. "Okay, here goes. No arrests have been made. Evertson has a horse at Lone Star Stables. Usually rides on Sunday afternoons. Tonight she wasn't so lucky because someone took a shot at her. She rode to the stables for help."

"How serious?"

"Treated and released. What's your interest?"

"I've met her. Surprised, that's all. What kind of bullet?"

"A .45."

"Any leads?"

"Speculation. She's hit the news a lot this week regarding her relationship with Morton Wilmington, the FBI giving her the boot, and now this."

It all seemed highly suspicious to him. "The FBI isn't going to release information on one of their own, past or present, if it jeopardizes a case," Daniel said.

"They're working with us at the crime scene, which leads me to wonder why she was fired. The media's running with all of it."

Daniel turned his truck toward Pinehurst. He knew the location of Lone Star Stables.

CHAPTER 22

After the emergency room trip, Laurel drove back to the stable with her right shoulder bandaged and in a sling. So lucky the bullet hadn't penetrated the bone. She masked the apprehension stalking her with an agent persona while her insides cratered. Floodlights lit up the night sky, illuminating the crime scene and those seeking evidence related to her shooting. Too many Montgomery County cops, FBI agents, and media types combed the area. She avoided the FBI. No point getting into a shouting match. The shooter could be among any of them, and she'd never know. She slipped among the law enforcement, looking for a clue.

This morning she'd texted SSA Preston about Josie Fields to ensure Wilmington had told the truth.

Had Geoff Cayden or Josie Fields called the hit? Had Morton Wilmington? Was it a threat? Had the shooter missed on purpose, or had Laurel gotten lucky?

Laurel observed the investigation. Most of the items retrieved were collected in plastic and leakproof containers. She'd bet next month's paycheck on nothing incriminating being found. Thank goodness she'd seen the movement and Phantom jumped—and not tossed her off.

Miss Kathryn would have called it a God-thing.

"Agent Evertson."

She recognized the voice and slowly turned. "Officer Hilton."

"Daniel."

"Okay. I'm Laurel. What brings you here?"

He frowned in the shadows. "The obvious. Are you okay? Looks like you should be home in bed."

Fresh blood seeped through the sterile wrappings. As soon as she finished here, she'd get some rest. "The hospital fixed me up. Got the bullet."

"I see your red badge of courage. Did you drive yourself there?"

"It wasn't that bad." Actually she'd fought to keep her car on the road, and her shoulder stung horribly.

"Which means you drove back to the crime site. Why am I not surprised?" He pointed to reporters taking pics and videos. "You're the focus of every camera."

She cringed. "I'm trying to avoid them. A good investigator has to check out the crime scene."

"Who are you working for?"

"Myself." *Think, Laurel, before you're exposed.* "I'm done here. Hard to retrace a shooter's path in the dark."

"What did the doctor give you?"

"Intravenous antibiotics and a shot of morphine."

"Now I understand your lack of common sense. Couldn't have been much more than an hour ago. You could have killed yourself driving here. What are you doing, setting yourself up for another close-range bullet?"

Laurel swallowed a response, noting the pain and morphine would be talking. She and Daniel barely knew each other, but she sensed an unspoken attraction between them, or maybe that was wishful thinking on her part. "I wanted to make sure my horse was okay, brushed down."

"Really? Aren't there people in the stables to take care of that?"

She stiffened, more with the pain than his question. "This is none of your concern. I'm the victim here, and I wanted to check for evidence."

"As if it's not bagged and marked. What else did they give you for pain?"

"Prescription meds."

"Have you filled it?"

"When I leave here, I'll find a 24-7 pharmacy. I want the shooter found, and I want the motive. The guy fired to my left, making it weird my right shoulder caught the bullet." She drew in a weary breath. "If Phantom hadn't bolted, law enforcement would be investigating a murder." She paused, allowing reality to settle to the bottom of her stomach. "Can't figure out why he didn't shoot again. What ran him off?" Looking back at the stables, she remembered the crowd of people. "He was afraid of being seen."

She was talking too much. Must be the drugs flowing through her veins. She and Daniel walked toward a section of the pasture beneath the canopy of the live oak where the shooter had been positioned. A police officer carrying a flashlight greeted them. Another officer searched through the leaves with his K-9's nose to the ground.

"I saw movement here, but it could have been an animal. Then again, the wind could have affected the bullet's trajectory," she said.

"The shooter had to be aware of your schedule," Daniel said. "Followed you and didn't leave a trace."

"A pro doesn't leave a calling card." Laurel moved toward the area where others sifted through pine needles and brush. "I looked there too. Clean." She blew out her exasperation. "I seem to attract the volatile ones on both sides of the law." The fire in her shoulder marred her good sense. "You mean well, Daniel, and I appreciate your being here. But you're stepping on treacherous ground. It's best you leave here now. I—"

"Ma'am, can I have a word with you?"

Laurel whirled toward the male voice. She hadn't heard anyone approach. In the dim light it was difficult to make out his features. He had light hair swept back to his collar and wore jeans, a cowboy hat, and a University of Texas sweatshirt. "What can I do for you?"

"I work at the stables, and I'd like to brush down your horse.

Don't look like you're up to the job. Can't remember your horse's name." He drew out his words, a good ole boy.

"It's a he, a stallion, and his name is Phantom. I'd really appreciate it. Your name?"

"Alex Lockhart."

"Thanks."

He nodded and turned toward the stables. She studied his back . . . hadn't seen him before. Could he be Geoff Cayden, or was she being paranoid? She shivered. Rest would clear her mind. She called to the man. "Alex, can I see your ID?"

He returned to her side and pulled out his wallet—Texas DL. Matched up. "Thanks." She handed it back to him. Her thoughts ran crazy. Geoff Cayden wouldn't be stupid enough to not have ID. "Thanks for the offer, but I'm good."

"Sure, ma'am. Just wanted to offer my assistance." He tipped his hat and walked away.

"Laurel, like the stable hand, I want to help." Daniel's words were gentle. "You can't solve what happened tonight in your condition, and I agree the likelihood of a shooter leaving anything behind is slim. Be glad the doctor yanked the bullet from your shoulder because it's all you have."

"Laurel." She recognized Wilmington's voice. He touched her shoulder and she cringed. Would this night ever end? "Sweetheart, are you all right? I just heard you were shot. Why didn't you call?"

Oh, the things she'd like to spit at him. Instead she forced a smile and kissed his cheek. "I didn't want to worry you."

He glanced at Daniel and stuck out his arm. "I'm Morton Wilmington."

"Officer Daniel Hilton."

"Looks like you were taking care of my girl. I have the situation under control now."

Laurel gazed into Daniel's face, wishing for the impossible. "Thank you for your help. Be safe."

CHAPTER 23

12:02 A.M. FRIDAY

Laurel sat in her car, seeking energy to climb the stairs to her apartment. But Wilmington had followed her, and he would stay parked until she disappeared up the stairs. She'd held her own in hand-to-hand combat, even knocked out two of Wilmington's bodyguards when the FBI surrounded his condo five years ago. Bruises and sore muscles were part of the game, but not the steady throb of taking a bullet to the shoulder, even if it wasn't serious. Every time her heart beat, a surge of white-hot pain tore across her flesh, leaving her angry in one breath and wanting to cry in the next.

She was such a girl.

Grabbing her purse, she exited her car and waved at Wilmington. Exhaustion pelted every inch of her flesh, and her wound hurt worse than when the doctor did his probing and numbed her. As she took the last flight, she bumped her shoulder rounding the turn and cried out. Now she was bleeding. Tears welled her eyes, not just for her injury but for the regrets stalking her. Tomorrow she'd feel better.

Glad none of her neighbors were out at this hour. They'd see the blood oozing from the bandage and call 911. She unlocked the door to her haven, the sights and smells of spiced apple greeting her. Tonight her fragile spirit required comfort that came only from her private domain.

Standing in the tiny kitchen of her apartment, she grabbed a glass. Oops. She laid the pain relievers on the counter and searched her pantry for peanut butter. No way would she take those babies on an empty stomach. After washing down the peanut butter with a swallow of orange juice, she reached for the pills and the antibiotic, the size of one of Phantom's pills.

Her phone rang, and she grabbed it. "I'm inside and good," she said.

"I'll get to the bottom of this." Wilmington's voice ground with determination. "Cayden or his sidekick is responsible."

"Okay. I'm going to bed. Uh, Morton, we're supposed to catch them, not kill them."

He chuckled. "Thanks for the reminder."

She was hit with a burst of pain from her shoulder. Yep, she was taking two of the prescription pain meds. If someone with murder on their mind got inside her apartment, he'd have an easy kill. "I gotta go." And ended the call.

She crawled into bed and snapped off the lamp. Officer Daniel Hilton popped back into her mind. Correction: far-too-good-looking Officer Daniel Hilton.

※ ※ ※

11:35 A.M. FRIDAY

Daniel never knew what to expect when he worked Fridays. Usually crazy. People not at work or in school were in a hurry to get an early start on the weekend and didn't appreciate anyone or anything getting in their way. They were testy, rude, and careless. And those were the good guys.

So far, it was a typical Friday, not giving him a free moment to think about the situation with his grandparents or Laurel. He'd left the crime scene last night when Morton Wilmington apparently took over things. Laurel had thanked him. . . . She didn't seem too pleased to see the ex-con. Strange, the two were supposed to be cozy.

Late morning he responded to a 911 call. Another possible home invasion. A frantic woman was concerned about her friend. Blood droplets outside the door alarmed her. The friend's car was parked in the designated area, but when the woman rang the doorbell to check on her, no one responded. Neither did the friend answer her phone. The blood indicated a possible crime. He turned on his lights and sped to the address. A long time ago, he realized God would have him respond to the cases where he could do the most good. Potentially finding a woman's bloody body made him question that resolve.

The brick complex sat behind an iron fence. Attractive, well-kept, and encased behind a security gate. He hated those things when responding to a call. He showed his creds and parked in front of the address before hurrying up the stairs to the second floor. Sure enough, blood drops spattered the cement steps and the floor outside the door. Pulling his Glock, he patted his Springfield XD on his vest—his own backup.

When the resident didn't answer the doorbell, he knocked and identified his purpose. Nothing. He turned the knob. Locked.

"Open the door. This is Houston Police Department."

No sound came from inside. He located the manager's office, but it was empty. Didn't give him much choice.

Daniel returned to the woman's apartment. When she didn't respond to another knock, he mule-kicked the door. Gun drawn, he peered inside. A darkened room meant someone had something to hide.

Silence greeted him. Spiced apples met his nostrils.

He peered into dark corners, his eyes adjusting to the lack of light. On the left he cleared a kitchen and dining room. Dark spots on the floor indicated more blood. To the right an open living area. From the looks of the furnishings, an older woman lived here. Down the hall he pushed in a bathroom door. Why did the woman live in a cave?

A gun jammed into his back.

"Drop it now," a woman said. "Or I'll blow a hole through you."

"Ma'am, I—"

"Who are you?" She pressed the gun deeper. "And why are you breaking into my home?"

"I'm a police officer."

"Right. And I'm Sherlock Holmes."

Great. This wacko lady planned to shoot him for breaking and entering. "If you'd turn on a light, you'd see my uniform, badge, and ID."

"Testy, aren't you? I have a mind to search you."

A wacko and a pervert.

"Don't turn around."

Furious best described him. "Look, lady, I'm responding to a call that a woman was in distress, a possible home invasion. When you didn't answer the door, I assumed you needed help."

She flipped on the bathroom light and groaned. "I know who called you—my overprotective neighbor. Turn around, Officer. I owe you an apology."

She gasped.

Special Agent Laurel Evertson held him at gunpoint.

CHAPTER 24

Laurel had nearly put a bullet into Daniel, thinking he worked for whoever had shot her. Didn't help at all that she stood there in flannel Mickey Mouse pajamas.

"I'm so sorry." She stepped back. "The lady who lives downstairs is the motherly type, and I'm her special project. I imagine she panicked when I didn't answer the door." She ran her fingers through tousled hair. "I took a few pain meds before I went to bed last night."

A hint of amusement sparkled in his brown eyes. "It's all right, really. Glad you're not hurt." He radioed in the all clear.

He looked good in his uniform, while she resembled a castoff from a Disney cartoon.

She moved from the bathroom door down the hall to the living area. When she pulled back the drapes, golden sunshine illuminated the room. Normally it thrilled her, filling her with peace. Now it highlighted the warmth rising from her cheeks.

She groped for words. "Would you like a cup of coffee? I have a Keurig."

"Sure. How's the shoulder?"

"It'll be fine." Actually it throbbed, but she wouldn't admit it. Walking into the kitchen, she snapped on a light. At least she'd cleaned this week, as if it mattered. Great. Dried blood spotted the floor. She wet a paper towel and bent to clean the stain.

"I can handle that," he said.

Dizziness hit her hard, and she wobbled like a drunk. Strong hands steadied her, his touch increasing her discomfort. Taking in a long breath, she regained her balance. "I'm fine. Thanks."

"Sure?"

"Yeah." She forced a smile.

Blood spots dripped all the way to the doorway. She moaned. "Can't believe I missed this before I went to bed."

"My guess is you were exhausted. There's more telltale signs outside your door."

She swung toward him. "No wonder my neighbor thought a crime had been committed."

"I thought the worst too." Daniel ripped a paper towel, dampened it, and proceeded to clean her bloody trail.

"Odd you were the officer to respond." Perhaps it was better he responded than an officer she didn't recognize. Yet her reasoning seemed muddled.

"This is my beat. No coincidence."

When he opened the door, she peered over his shoulder at the blood. "Really, I'm sorry. You shouldn't be doing this." What was she thinking? Her neighbors might see her standing in her pajamas talking to a police officer.

He grinned and headed back to the kitchen. "Won't take a second. I'll clean right outside your door and no one will ever suspect you prompted a 911 call." He tore off more paper towels.

"Thanks." His eyes were like a love potion, milk-chocolate pools. Must be a side effect of the pain meds. She kept the door open so they could talk. "I'll fix your coffee. What kind do you like?"

"Breakfast blend, if you have it. And a spoonful of sugar."

"I'm on it. How are your grandparents?"

"The same. Gran's feisty, and Gramps is stubborn." He scrubbed the spots on the floor.

She smiled. "I like them. Where do your parents live?"

"They're both out of the picture."

She startled. Her first impression of the handsome officer was a product of total function. "I'm sorry."

"About my parents or how you almost shot me?" He grinned.

"Both, I guess."

"You've said 'sorry' three times, and there's no reason." He stepped inside with the red-tinted paper towels in his hand. "Don't look so shocked. I figured you'd already run a background on me."

"I hadn't thought of it." She opened the cabinet beneath the sink and pointed to the trash can. They had at least one thing in common, but she wouldn't vocalize it. "Then your grandparents raised you?"

"Yep. They took over when I was two."

"From what I've seen, they did a good job."

He leaned against the refrigerator, inches away. "I'll pass that on."

"You were telling me about them."

"They're doing fine with round-the-clock bodyguards and nurses. Both grumble, but it's working."

"They were comfortable at the facility. Feeling accepted and loved often overrides other challenges."

"Gramps would agree, and Alzheimer's patients need lots of understanding. I don't like his claim to have purchased a life insurance policy for him and Gran. Whoever sold it now has both Social Security numbers along with financials." He shook his head. "More money's missing from one of their accounts."

"I'm sure law enforcement are on it." She wished she could tell him more. "Guess that sounds lame."

"The elephant in the room is the likelihood of the scammers collecting big-time in the event he has an accident. As in the note Gran received with the funeral flowers."

"Wish I could help." Lying to a friend, who'd just cleaned up a bloody mess, made her feel disgusting.

"But you're working undercover."

She scrunched her forehead. "I was fired."

"Your Glock and badge are behind the toaster."

Her gaze flew to where she'd left her tools of the trade. She hadn't expected visitors, least of all Daniel.

"Laurel, what is going on?"

Could she trust him? "Sit down, Daniel." She reached for a mug beside the single-cup dispenser and pressed the On button. "I promised you coffee." She avoided his stare, still feeling uncomfortable about her pajamas and, worse yet, his discovery about her work.

"I'll be patient," he said. "Good-looking apartment. I like your collection of antiques, especially the library table. Works great with the ladder-back chairs."

"Thanks." He made number four who'd been inside her private domain.

He pointed to the framed photos of Miss Kathryn. "A grandmother?"

"No, but a dear lady. Are you an antique collector?"

He shook his head. "My little house is a mix of whatever was on sale when I needed it. My grandparents have a houseful of antiques blended with contemporary. Reminds them of the past and present. They reminisce about the old days, when life was simpler. Not easier, but when they were in better health."

"Do you live far from them?" She handed him the coffee.

"Twelve minutes, give or take. They live inside the beltway in Bunker Hill, and I'm outside. It's just a few minutes' drive to Silver Hospitality."

"Your grandmother looks frail."

He nodded. "Degenerative heart disease." He took a gulp of coffee. "This tastes wonderful. Thanks. I'm rattling on like an old man. I need to spend more time with those my own age." He glanced up. "I'm ready for the truth."

"Not quite yet. Thanks for cleaning up my messes."

"And thank you for not blowing a hole through me." He laughed and she joined him.

Change the subject, Laurel, before he thinks you're attracted to him. "Hey, do you like Snickers?"

"Now you're talking like Gramps," he said. "Can't keep him away from them. And don't get me started on his diabetes."

She opened the freezer and handed him one. "Dip it in your coffee. It's heavenly."

He tore off the wrapper and tried her suggestion. "Pretty good."

"My dad got me hooked on eating them like this when I was six. Back then, it was hot chocolate. He'd give me math problems to solve, and when I mastered them, we celebrated."

"Sounds like a great dad." He glanced at his watch. "I have fifteen minutes left."

She couldn't think of a lie to explain why she had her badge and Glock. She liked Daniel, and her judgment of character had always been solid. "I need your word you will keep this to yourself."

"You got it. So you're relieved from the FBI, and the next day Wilmington is released from prison. I don't buy the love affair that went beyond your undercover work or the media's take on your heading to the dark side."

"Let's hope a few people do."

"So I'm right. My guess is Wilmington has made a deal to give the FBI information about the elderly fraud case in exchange for his freedom."

She scooted into a chair across from him. "Pretty close."

"Meaning . . . ?"

"Nothing else. Do you see how innocent people can get killed if this leaks out? The scammer will go dark until he comes up with another scheme."

"I do see. My grandparents are directly in their path." He peered into her eyes, and her stomach knotted. "I need to get back to work. Thanks for the coffee, Snickers, conversation, and a good scare."

"Anytime."

"Don't forget to call your neighbor and tell her you're okay."

"Will do, right now."

He left and she leaned back against the door. How did a girl like her find a decent guy? Impossible. She'd have to lie or settle for a loser. Like herself. At least then she stood in familiar territory.

All the lights were flashing, telling her not to fall for Officer Daniel Hilton, but the warnings didn't stop her heart. Her phone alerted her to a call. She grabbed it: Wilmington.

"Officer Hilton stayed there quite a while," he said coldly.

She trembled just knowing he had someone watching her every move. "One of my neighbors saw blood on the steps and . . ." Easing onto the sofa, she anticipated his response. He'd once broken a bodyguard's nose for looking at her.

"We already know my friend has eyes on you."

"I learned a few other details about Mr. Cayden that you could have already shared."

"Good for you. Want to fill me in?" His dry tone unnerved her.

"He works for Almet Pharmaceuticals in Miami, a company that manufactures drugs for those suffering from dementia. No priors. Outstanding work record. Stay-at-home wife and young daughter. Recently he took a medical leave of absence and is here in Houston being treated at the VA hospital. Staying at an extended-stay property. We confirmed the doctor's diagnosis of a heart problem related to stress."

"He covers his tracks, one step ahead of you all the way. I've already told Preston—don't tail him or haul him in for questioning. He'll bolt."

"What about Josie Fields? She's wanted for numerous crimes."

"Same thing. I really don't think these two are the masterminds behind this scam. Josie is a maniac, and she has disappearing down to an art."

"Yes, sir." She gritted her teeth.

"Hey, you need me to pull this off and don't forget it."

"I'm sure you won't let me."

"You'd better hope his people saw the blood and discounted

your relationship with Hilton, since he was in uniform. I'm meeting with Geoff tonight, see what I can learn."

"Call me. I don't care what time."

"Okay. You and I are having dinner tomorrow night. I'll pick you up."

Her head and shoulder ached. "I suppose."

"Listen, Laurel, I saw the way you looked at Hilton last night, and if I detected it, then others will too. Keep him safe. Cool off until this is over. Neither of us wants anyone else hurt."

Were his words a threat or a warning?

CHAPTER 25

Daniel drove through a green light and past Willowbrook Mall. He couldn't keep Laurel out of his mind. Even tumbling out of bed in Mickey Mouse pajamas and carrying a weapon, she looked pretty good—golden hair and nut-brown eyes filled with mystery. If he were looking for a woman, she'd be a candidate.

What was he thinking? She was FBI. Used to giving orders. Independent. They'd kill each other. He'd tasted the stormy side of her and didn't enjoy a moment of it. Then the trust factor rolled in about women. The only thing he and Laurel had in common were their weapons, a series of crimes involving the elderly, and frozen Snickers dipped in hot coffee.

Nope. Bad idea. *Give it a rest, Officer Hilton.*

Before he committed himself to any relationship, he needed to settle things with his mother. Should have seen her a long time ago. Sometimes he thought his grandparents' urging was what kept him from driving to the prison.

He activated his hands-free on his iPhone and requested Siri to "note" what had happened since he realized his grandparents had been victims of an elderly fraud.

1. Gramps supposedly bought life insurance policies for him and Gran from a man who went by the name of Russell

133

Jergon. The salesman obtained enough information to get
into an account.

2. Tom Hanson died of a heart attack, but Gramps claimed
   he'd purchased a life insurance policy from Jergon
   too. Tom's daughter had been unavailable to question
   regarding her father's financials.

Daniel added a reminder to later phone the woman.

3. While driving Gran and Gramps home from the facility,
   someone shot at them. No lead there, just a green Dodge
   pickup. Then Gran's threatening note.

They were under the care of trained professionals, but it didn't
stop his queasiness.

4. Emma Dockson passed while in the hospital. Another
   victim of the phony salesman. Her nephew refused
   an autopsy, stating he had no reason to suspect foul
   play. However several thousand dollars mysteriously
   disappeared from Emma's account before and after her
   death. Daniel heard the nephew had filed a case with
   the FBI.
5. Laurel is dismissed from the FBI, and the next day
   Wilmington walks the street. She warns Daniel to stay
   away from her.
6. Laurel's shot, and when Daniel follows up on a 911 call, he
   sees her badge and weapon on the kitchen counter. She and
   Wilmington are working undercover. Strange alliance.
7. What's next?

Wish Laurel would confide in me. . . . If Daniel faced the truth,
he'd admit her spending time with Morton Wilmington made him
a bit jealous. Ridiculous.

He told Siri good-bye and listened to the familiar voice respond with "It's been a pleasure." If only others could be as courteous.

He finished his shift and drove to his grandparents'. Every day the same routine. Every day he looked for signs of someone watching their home. Every day he wondered what would be left of his life without them, despite all he was doing to protect them. What if he failed?

His iPhone alerted him to a call, a number he didn't recognize. "This is Officer Hilton."

"Morton Wilmington. Did you file a report with HPD regarding the 911 call to Laurel's apartment?"

What was this about? "Excuse me?"

"Look, I'm trying to keep both of you alive. She's being watched, and I'm gambling on the bad guy not recognizing you from the stables."

Daniel understood that undercover work meant taking precautions, and Laurel winding up dead looked dismal for a man seeking parole. "I did my job."

"Good. Thanks. I'll be talking to you." Wilmington ended the call before Daniel could ask more questions.

No way would he sit back and do nothing while people he cared about were in danger. He might not have the latest technology, but he'd learned a few things as a cop.

❋ ❋ ❋

11:40 P.M. FRIDAY

Daniel continued his nighttime online search for those preying on the elderly and for bogus websites. He understood why people responded to fraud and scams. He received e-mails constantly, worded to tug at the heartstrings or some get-rich scheme shot with the arrow of greed.

Tonight he looked at the realm of fake websites. They were illegal, but it didn't stop the developers who wanted to make money on goods that didn't exist—wheelchairs, insurance policies,

services never rendered . . . the list continued. One site targeting the elderly claimed to represent the Red Cross, eager to take
contributions for the latest disaster relief. The FBI warned and
prosecuted, but the owners of the sites just looked for better ways
to hide their activities.

Daniel massaged tense neck muscles. He was a police officer
who worked a job that satisfied his deep-seated hunger to keep
people safe. This case stretched him beyond his comfort zone.

He yawned and returned to the computer screen. Where was
Liz Austin hiding out, if that was even her real name?

A scraping sound outside the kitchen door leading into the
garage alerted him to an intruder. It sounded again. Granted, he
was working in the dark, and an intruder might think he was in
bed. An animal? Unlikely.

Wrapping his fingers around his Glock and grabbing his
phone, he moved toward the door. Surprise was one of his favorite tactics. The exterior door of the garage had a dead bolt but was
not hooked up to his alarm system. He moved closer to where the
sound had originated. Silence.

Gun poised, Daniel stood in the dark for over two minutes.
Slowly he released the kitchen door lock and twisted the knob,
pushing it open with his foot to avoid a possible bullet. He
snapped on the light.

Nothing.

The rear door leading to the backyard stood open about three
inches. He distinctly remembered locking it. He turned the garage
light off and inched toward the exterior door, then flipped the
outside light on. Quiet shadows failed to light the right side of
the area. He grabbed an old bandanna from a nail and wrapped it
around the handle of a rake. With the rake in his left hand and his
gun in his right, he poked the rake outside. A bullet ripped off the
cloth and lodged into the garage wall. A figure loomed to his right.

Daniel returned fire.

Someone groaned.

The gate squeaked open. A smaller man or teen rushed toward the front of the house and the curb. Daniel raced after him. The intruder jumped onto a Yamaha and took off down the street. Daniel sped back to the garage and turned on the exterior lights. No footprints or tire marks to photograph for evidence.

Before he called HPD, he wanted to check his garage and truck. Nothing appeared out of place, and Daniel memorized where every tool and piece of equipment was stashed.

He stared at his truck. A bomb? Wired to explode when he turned on the engine or with a cell phone trigger?

One way to find out. He crawled under his truck and used the flashlight on his phone to examine the undercarriage.

Very clever. Why did it look like the bad guys were winning?

He walked back inside and out to the street before pressing in a number. "This is Officer Daniel Hilton. I need a bomb squad at my home."

CHAPTER 26

Laurel woke to pounding at her door. The clock on her nightstand blared the time: after midnight. Who wanted to see her at this hour? Her heart thudded. This couldn't be good.

She flung off the quilt, grabbed her firearm, and raced to the door. "Who's there?"

"Su-Min."

She confirmed through her peephole, laid down the weapon on a nearby table, and opened the door. "Isn't it a little late for a visit?"

Su-Min staggered, and her breath smelled of alcohol. "It's a perfect time." She pushed herself inside and pointed her finger into Laurel's face. "Because of you, I've been denied a promotion. You ruined my career."

"I'm sure you managed that all by yourself." Laurel crossed her arms over her chest. She'd seen Su-Min drunk before, and it wasn't pretty.

"I have no choice but to ask for a transfer."

"Go for it."

The finger continued to wag in Laurel's face. "You chose a killer over the mission statement of the FBI. All those times you called me crying about your nightmares of Jesse's death. Lies. One after another, and I fell for it."

Laurel needed to get rid of Su-Min. Cayden's men had seen

her, and this late-night call could ruin the mission. "Get out. It's none of your business who I love or want to spend the rest of my life with." Her voice rose. "What do you want from me anyway?"

Su-Min raised her chin. "Nothing. Just want you to know that you're a stupid—"

"And you have." She shoved Su-Min out the door and stood with her on the landing. "I'll call a taxi."

"No thanks. I'll drive. One day you'll pay for what you've done." Su-Min wobbled down the steps until she disappeared.

Laurel listened for a car to start up and leave. Her shoulder throbbed along with the heartache of losing a friend . . . even if their relationship had been superficial.

Hopefully Cayden's men heard it all. Wilmington's men too. A tear slipped down her cheek. She hated this ruse. Once this was over, she'd still have nothing but miserable regrets.

Just as she drifted off to sleep, Wilmington called.

"You sound like you're not doing well," he said.

"Sort of."

"Heard your ex-partner came by."

Cayden must know too. "Fun times. Ran her off."

"I'm sorry. Won't take much of your time. Hilton found a bomb under his truck tonight. HPD disarmed it."

Daniel targeted? Had Cayden seen them together . . . ? Or could it have been Josie? "Is he all right?"

"Yes."

She closed her eyes. "I assume Cayden's responsible?"

"One of his people. Since I didn't see Josie tonight, it might have been her. Hilton thought he shot the intruder but no blood spatters. We'll see if anyone shows up at the hospitals or all-night clinics."

"Thanks. We should get his DNA, see if we can link him to any other crimes. This has been going on for eight years, and the man's not that bright."

"I'll get it."

"What else do you know?"

"Dinner with Cayden brought us one step closer. I used his hatred of the Army, actually with all forms of law enforcement, to talk up your bitterness with the FBI."

"Did he buy it?"

"Not yet. SSA Preston and I've talked about a way to prove our loyalty to Cayden. He'll call us in the morning to confirm."

"Like what? A drug buy?"

"Has to be more substantial."

She bolted alert. "Are we going to stage a murder?"

"Yes. He's bringing in a special agent from violent crime."

"Who?"

"Thatcher Graves."

"Great. I graduated from Quantico with him."

"Get some rest. Preston will conference us in on a call mid-morning. We'll stage this on Sunday night."

After hanging up, Laurel made her way to the kitchen for a pain pill. Now she'd be labeled as a killer.

CHAPTER 27

Abby treasured being in her own home even under the dire circumstances. If she lost her vision to the macular degeneration creeping into her eyes, she could still roam from one room to another and not get lost. Every piece of furniture, plant, doorway, and bend in the winding stairway were sealed in memory.

She loved the life she and Earl had built. Good times. Tough times. But always with God as the head of their marriage. Too many people failed to notice His hand in the events of life, thinking being a Christian made them free of heartache and trouble. Quite the opposite. The more she trusted, the more the devil tossed her way. Daniel was their blessing when Jimmy chose selfishness. They'd dealt with years of guilt before realizing Jimmy was responsible for his own poor choices. She and Earl had done all they could.

Gracious, she was getting old. Only an old woman tried to make sense of life.

Nameless faces stalked Earl and her. Who was behind selling the life insurance policies that named a scammer as beneficiary? Neither Tom's nor Emma's families wanted autopsies, so it looked like the killer had gotten away with it. What if the killer was a friend, a person whom they trusted? What turned a man to murder and a lack of respect for others? What if the man was hungry and had children to feed? But the scammer wasn't stealing to provide for the needy—he was greedy for what he could not get legally. She rubbed her arms. Jimmy's addiction had caused him to do the unthinkable. She shouldn't be surprised that others had evil intentions.

The person who'd planted a bomb under Daniel's truck made her see red—blood red. The bomb had been wired to his ignition. The thought of losing him was more than she could bear. *God, what are You thinking with this mess?*

She knew in her head that He was in the business of handling unseen evil. But fear still riddled her. She'd had her bags packed to meet Jesus for years, but what about Earl, Daniel, Laurel, and all the elderly victims?

Abby didn't believe for one minute that Laurel had chosen a life with a criminal over her dedication to the FBI. Laurel had goodness stamped into her heart. Something was going on behind the scenes, and Abby prayed the good guys stayed safe.

She stood at the wall of windows in the sunroom and watched her beloved husband. He rocked on the patio in the warm morning and stared ahead, an indication his mind dwelled beyond the here and now. He held a dog collar. They'd had a collie for sixteen years, but he passed just before Earl was diagnosed with Alzheimer's. The dog had been not only a constant companion, but also a member of the family.

Earl's disease progressed far too quickly. Some days she wanted to believe the medications had successfully stopped its advance, especially when he spoke with the wisdom of days gone by, like the insight into Daniel's problem with his mother.

A tear trickled down her cheek, and she whisked it away. This old woman needed to help find the scammers in some way. And sitting in her home with a bodyguard made her feel worthless. But right now bringing Earl a tall glass of ginger-peach iced tea would have to suffice.

Abby stepped onto the patio with Earl's drink. "Brought you something."

He smiled and reached for it, his hands shaking until she took the dog collar and wrapped his other hand around the glass too.

"Thank you, Abby girl. I've been thinking."

She sat in a rocker beside him. "About what?"

"Jimmy. There's got to be a way to reach him. He's been in jail. We've paid for three rehabilitation centers, and still he persists in breaking the law. I tried to persuade him to join the military, thinking the discipline would help. But that went nowhere." He took a gulp of the iced tea. "There's a Benedictine monastery in Switzerland known for treating addictions. What do you think?"

They'd sent Jimmy there when he was nineteen. Hadn't helped because Jimmy fought the program and walked out. "Do you think he'd go willingly?"

"I really don't know. I wish I could help him. Wish even more I could figure out what I'd done wrong."

"We didn't do anything wrong. So stop belittling yourself." She patted his shoulder. "You take action however you think is best. Right now I'm going to bake something for Officer Pete. Glad he's working the day shift. Gives me someone to talk to."

"Who am I?" His clouded eyes whispered confusion.

"You're my sweet husband."

"Brownies with pecans and a chocolate glaze?"

"Always." She kissed his cheek and set the dog collar in his lap.

Twenty minutes later, with the goodies in the oven, she checked on Earl. He'd disappeared from the back porch. She stepped outside and searched the yard.

"Earl? Where are you?"

She looked behind several old oaks, calling his name. The rear gate leading to a small grove of trees stood open. Normally it was locked, the key hidden under a flowerpot on the back porch. A path through those woods ended near Memorial Drive. Panic rose like a bubbling pot.

She clutched her heart and raced to the house, calling Pete's name.

✳ ✳ ✳

10:30 A.M. SATURDAY

Daniel received the call from Pete that Gramps had wandered off. Too many scenarios slammed against Daniel's brain. Gramps's confused mind could be the cause, but would those who wanted him dead take advantage of the situation?

Gramps was in excellent physical health. Another concern was how far he'd walk. After calming Gran, he checked with one of the officers searching the area.

"Do you have any idea where your grandfather could have gone?"

"There's a Starbucks less than a mile from where the path empties onto Memorial. In the same shopping strip is a yogurt shop."

"What about the bus stop?"

"Never gave that a thought." Daniel had a good idea where Gramps had gone. "How close are you to Memorial Trace Cemetery?"

"On my way," the officer said. "You're on your beat?"

"Right. You'll get there long before I do. My dad's buried there on the southwest side—James Earl Hilton."

Daniel's next call was to Marsha Leonard in case Gramps had taken the bus to Silver Hospitality. Nothing there.

When his phone rang, he answered it without recognizing the caller.

"Daniel, this is Morton Wilmington. Have you found your grandfather?"

Did anything get by this man? "I have an idea. HPD's on it."

"I'm concerned he could get nabbed."

"By the scammer who wants to collect on his life insurance?"

"Let's hope not. I'm thinking you should be aware of what's going on with the investigation. You've got big stakes in this, and I need a man I can trust."

But whose side was Wilmington on? "Talk to me when my grandfather's found." Daniel ended the call. Wilmington might trust Daniel, but that didn't work both ways. Right now finding Gramps alive held his attention.

His radio buzzed. "Officer Hilton, we've found your grandfather at Memorial Trace Cemetery. He's shaken and bruised, but okay. I called an ambulance. Probably should have him checked out."

Thank You, Lord. "Were you able to find out what happened? Did he fall?"

"He's confused. All I've learned is a woman wanted him to get into her car, and he ran, hid behind tombstones. He claims the woman threatened Abby if he didn't go with her. We pulled up as a woman drove away."

"Did you see what she was driving?"

"A pickup. We didn't get the license plate number."

"Have the ambulance take him to the Methodist Hospital. I'll meet you there."

Daniel let Gran know what was happening while speeding to check on Gramps. "Have Pete bring you to the hospital."

He wanted to know about the woman who approached Gramps, and he was ready to get on the inside with this scam. Frightening an old man and threatening an old woman hit his fury button.

CHAPTER 28

Daniel hesitated leaving his grandparents tonight. Gramps had suffered a few bruises, and his mind hadn't surfaced to the present. Gran wouldn't take her eyes off him. Two police officers were on duty per shift this weekend as well as two nurses. The back gate had a new lock, and only Gran and Daniel knew the key's hiding place. They'd be fine. Had to trust God with all this.

The one positive for his grandparents was their deaths would have to look natural. He didn't want to think about Gramps getting into the woman's car at the cemetery.

"Go home and get some rest," Gran said. "We're good, and I have my S&W with me all the time."

"I'll record tomorrow's church service. Have an errand to run in the morning, so it will be midafternoon before I arrive. I'll call on the hour once you're up."

"Yes, Father Superior."

"Humor me. Makes me feel good."

Their doorbell rang. With the problem earlier today, Daniel wasn't taking any chances. Picking up his gun from the kitchen table, he ventured into the foyer. The officers all used the side door, so who'd gotten past them tonight?

Morton Wilmington, dressed in jeans and a button-down shirt. Light-brown hair touched his collar. Hands in front of him.

Daniel snapped on the porch light and opened the door. An

officer waved from his car at the curb. Obviously he didn't think the man before him posed a threat. They'd have a talk later.

Wilmington stuck out his hand. "Daniel, I realize today's been hectic, but I'd like a word with you."

Daniel eyed him. Not a trace of malice on the man's face, but charm and charisma often masked motive. Maybe Wilmington had no conscience. Daniel shook his hand and checked for any padded pockets indicating a weapon. "Are you packing?"

"It's in my car. Illegal, but some habits are hard to break."

Was this a twist of honesty? "You know I could arrest you for that."

Wilmington chuckled. "But you won't because I'm working to help end the elderly scam."

Irritation dug into him. "What can I do for you, Mr. Wilmington?"

"I'd like to talk to you privately."

"More of our conversation today?"

He nodded.

"Is Laurel aware of this visit?"

"No." Wilmington's voice deepened. "She's familiar with my unpredictable behavior."

Great. A dose of baseless jealousy poured through him. Laurel hadn't chosen Wilmington—her undercover work made the alliance. "Okay. We can do this outside."

"Can't blame you. My reputation precedes me."

Daniel joined him on the front porch, and they sat in a pair of rockers.

"Real comfortable. Homey." Wilmington looked relaxed, as if he belonged there. "Beautiful home. Looks like your grandparents have an acre here."

"Yes."

"Nice night."

"For what?"

Wilmington chuckled. "Suspicious, aren't you?"

"Can you blame me?"

"Not at all."

First forthright thing he'd heard since Wilmington arrived. "I'd like to know who's behind the elderly scam."

"You could have offered me an iced tea."

"My grandmother's better at hospitality."

"I see." He rocked a few more seconds. "You've figured out that Laurel and I are working undercover in the scam case."

Confirmation. "Thought so. Not sure it's believable."

"It will be after tomorrow night."

"A name?"

Wilmington glanced into the night. "I prayed about this. Sure hope I heard right."

Faith had to be shown, not spoken like a cliché. "I'm listening."

"The FBI sprang me to help end the elderly scam. I know the person in charge from a long time ago. I needed an agent to work with me, and we worked out Laurel's dismissal from the FBI."

"Why would anyone swallow that, considering your past with Laurel?"

"This man saved my life. I owe him."

"He'd never think you'd betray him?"

"Not at all."

"You're trading an old friend for life outside prison."

"Not exactly. He's breaking the law and killing people. My faith doesn't support that."

"Does he have a record?"

"No. Nothing to even bring him in for questioning."

"Where does that put me?"

"I'd like to hire you as a bodyguard."

Daniel shook his head. "They'd recognize me."

"Not if you wore a disguise."

He'd gone undercover a few times. Knew how it was done. "I'd need the FBI's approval. And Laurel's."

Wilmington leaned forward. "Despite what you think, I'm a changed man. I'll cooperate with any law enforcement. I want the days ahead of me to speak more than the ones I left in prison."

"Tell me why you're really here."

Wilmington stared at the street and waved at the officer, who was observing from a distance. "The best thing I can do to prove my case is help the FBI."

"Did your crusade begin at your release?"

"Not exactly. Geoff Cayden visited me in prison. Wanted to go into business together."

Pieces were beginning to fit with what he'd gathered from Laurel. "So you know how the scam works?"

"Cayden may look at me as his old Army bud, but he's not about to reveal the whole operation."

Daniel couldn't argue with that. "If this new position is agreeable with the FBI, when would I start?"

"Early next week." Wilmington stopped rocking and studied him. "I know your trust isn't there. Can't blame you. When you realize the life forward means more to God than the past, then what you do doesn't have to make sense."

Daniel heard the sincerity, but those skills could be learned. He wouldn't be anyone's marionette. He'd seen too much of that in his line of work. "Show me your faith."

"I will."

"Where are your bodyguards?"

He gestured into the darkness. "They're here."

"Do you trust all of them?"

"Depends on the day. Are you reliable, Daniel?"

"My grandmother told me something when I complained about her driving. She said, 'If you can't trust me, trust God.'"

"Fair enough." Wilmington stood and stuck out his hand. "I'll have someone from the FBI contact you."

CHAPTER 29

Daniel had a crucial task, and the nearly three-hour drive to a prison in Gatesville gave him miles to think. The urgency to see the woman who'd given birth to him and get out what he needed to say pounded against his brain. He'd put off the task for too many years, a mission of sorts to clear his mind and heart. Months ago, without telling anyone, he requested his name be added to her visitors' list. Even when the permission was approved, he failed to follow through. Didn't have the guts to see her until now. How many times had he judged others for not facing what they feared most?

Strange how protecting his grandparents and potentially working with Laurel and Wilmington pushed him to see his mother. In many ways, the urgency made little sense. Yet he felt God telling him to make the journey. In another hour he'd be at Gatesville. He'd rather face the scammers without a weapon.

After his mother's many years of street living and a meth addiction, Daniel wasn't sure he'd recognize her. Amazing he hadn't been born with a weakness for alcohol or drugs. He stayed away from both just in case.

The only photo of the two of them was taken on his first birthday. Back then she'd had huge brown eyes and long dark-brown hair. A beauty, as Gramps had said, with a smile that melted ice. Daniel had been told he looked like her.

How many times had he given the speech about choices, thinking of all the wrong ones his parents had made? He used to teach Sunday school for eighth grade boys when Gran and Gramps were in better health, and he played the good role model to the hilt. What a self-righteous hypocrite. He couldn't forgive his own mother.

How often had Gramps said that if Daniel couldn't forgive her, the hatred would eventually consume him? His inability to trust a woman stemmed from those emotions. What kind of woman chose meth over her husband and child? Daniel's attitude toward her was not one of honor or respect. Laurel's face appeared in his mind. She'd waltzed into his life, stirring a longing that scared him, but without a cleansing of his charcoal heart, he'd soon push her away. And botch up the proposed undercover work.

In a way, he hoped his mother refused to see him. Sure would make the day easier to manage. He could shake his head and claim he tried reconciliation.

Once at the prison and out of his truck, he studied the surroundings: cold and lonely. He grasped the door handle of the women's prison unit and hesitated. Gramps called indecision a wrestling of the spirit. Daniel swallowed what he termed the "little-boy fear of rejection" and waited his turn at the counter. He completed the visitor form and prayed for guts. The conversation he'd rehearsed earlier seemed sorry. Canned.

Female inmates filed into the visitation area, looking as hard as the concrete walls. No matter their age, many had eyes that told the harsh story of mistakes, and the only regrets were those of being caught. One woman scanned the room while the others took seats in chairs at white painted picnic-style tables across from friends or relatives. Daniel caught her eye, and she stepped forward with a slight limp, an injury resulting from trying to outrun a police officer. How ironic.

His heart dropped to his toes. Brittle gray hair. Dull eyes. No teeth, a product of meth addiction. Sad. A waste of a life.

"Mom?" He moved closer, willing his feet to begin the communication.

She inhaled sharply. "Daniel," she whispered. "You're so grown-up, handsome. Married? Any children?"

"Not yet. Haven't found a woman to put up with me yet."

"Be picky."

"Sit down so we can talk." He surprised himself with kindness. "Thanks for seeing me."

"I'm shocked you'd want to come." She folded thin hands on the table. Veins pushed up through transparent skin like blue limbs from a withered tree. Not much older than fifty-five, yet one would guess a decade or more older.

"Should have done this a long time ago. I'm sorry I took so long."

She narrowed her gaze. "To gloat?"

"Of course not."

"Cop has meth mama doing time for murder."

Her change in attitude didn't surprise him. "No, to check on you."

"I don't need you. Never did. That's why I dumped your sorry—"

Daniel waved his hand in front of her face. So much he could say about her behavior. But lowering his standards to look like he had all the answers didn't solve a thing. Respect was something she never saw, and he could offer it. But he didn't want to. He wanted to walk away. "I'm not here to argue."

"Then why?"

She jutted her jaw, a stubborn response he'd seen many times from the women he arrested. All scared little girls covering up their insecurities, and this was his mother. She'd toss his compassion back with words meant to slice him raw.

"I came to say I forgive you."

For a moment, her eyes softened. Then the look threw fiery daggers. "Your grandparents put you up to this. Pious freaks. Always turned their noses up at me and Jimmy. You're a Bible-thumper too, aren't you? Get out of here, you no-good—"

Daniel tensed as the curses flew from her mouth. Old issues surfaced. Hurting. Slamming into his heart with torment. The years he questioned why. Not anymore. "They have no idea I'm here or applied for visitation. No one sent me. I'm a grown man."

A guard approached them. "Keep your voice down, or you'll be escorted back to your cell."

She smirked and sat back in the plastic chair. "Those tougher than you have tried to convert me, Danny boy. Never worked. The only thing I ever needed to lean on is the next high. If you can't bring me something to help me forget the hand I've been dealt, I don't need you."

All these years Daniel had harbored guilt for not being good enough. But now the truth calmed him. He pitied the woman before him, a woman battered by her own choices. He'd been dealt the ace—been blessed by two people who believed they'd failed as parents the first time around.

"I forgive you, Mom, for killing my father and abandoning me. But I thank you for allowing Gran and Gramps to raise me."

She slammed the tabletop with her fist. "You sound like a twelve-year-old kid instead of a man."

"My idea of a man and yours aren't the same. If you change your mind about wanting to see me, I can arrange another visit. I'd like for us to be friends, but the decision is yours."

"Don't ever come here again. You disgusting piece—"

He walked out the way he came in. The burden had lifted, but sadness for his mother brought a few unbidden tears.

✳ ✳ ✳

3:46 P.M. SUNDAY

Hours later, Daniel joined his grandparents in the living room. Gramps had entertained them with Scott Joplin while Gran danced. Now they chatted, Gramps sneaking a Snickers and Gran knitting and pretending not to see.

"I visited Mom today," he said.

Gran dropped her knitting. "You did what?"

"I saw her, talked to her."

Gramps shuffled to his feet and headed to the kitchen.

"Earl, where are you going? Our grandson has just made an incredible announcement and you leave the room. Haven't I taught you better than that?"

Daniel swallowed a chuckle at her exasperation, guessing what Gramps had in mind.

"I'm breaking into the sparkling grape juice." Glasses rattled in the kitchen. "This is cause for a celebration."

"You haven't heard what happened." She wiggled her shoulders. "I'd better help him before he breaks one of my crystal glasses." She glared at Daniel. "Don't say a word until we're all back in here together."

"Not a word until I have my sparkling grape juice."

A few minutes later, the three sat in the living room. "A toast," Daniel said. "For two people who raised me with morals and a respect for God and country."

Gran swiped at her eye. "Thank you, dear boy. But you were easy. Much easier than your father."

"Amen to that," Gramps said. "Tell us everything. Don't leave out a single detail."

Daniel told them about his actions months ago and believing today was the right day to visit her. Gran winked. No doubt she saw through what he didn't say: Laurel. He'd not confess his deep need to have a clear conscience. He explained how Mom looked and reacted.

"You're the man." Gramps slapped his knee. "You forgave her. That makes you ten feet tall."

"I expected this music from heaven or a 'Well done' booming." Daniel took a long drink of grape juice. "Better than those illusions, I simply feel good—like I did a five-mile run and took a long shower."

"And changed your clothes." Gramps grinned.

"Mercy, forgiveness is healing," Gran said. "Let's finish the bottle. I think I'll write my poor daughter-in-law a letter, see if she'd like a visit."

Daniel raised his glass and toasted them. Today proved to him how much he loved his grandparents. If protecting them meant working alongside a criminal, then he'd do it.

CHAPTER 30

Laurel had memorized her shooting of Thatcher Graves to the second. He wore a Kevlar vest with an ample supply of fake blood. She carried a cloth bag containing a dozen eggs and a loaf of whole wheat bread and exited through the automatic doors of Kroger. Her Charger was parked at the far end of the lot, away from other vehicles and innocent people. No one could get hurt tonight.

Her heels clipped across the pavement.

Timing.

One.

Two.

Three.

Thatcher appeared at the driver's side of her car. "Laurel, I need to talk to you." His voice rose across the night just loud enough for Cayden's men to hear, in a truck parked on the edge of the lot.

She moved faster. Shoulders rigid. Head high. "I told you to leave me alone."

"You're making a terrible mistake with Morton Wilmington. It's not too late to save us and your career."

She laughed. "I'm right where I want to be. The FBI got rid of me." She sneered. "You and I were never together."

"What kind of future do you have with him?"

"He's a Christian now."

"Right. That's what he used to get out of prison."

"Get away from my car or you'll regret it."

"Not until I talk some sense into you."

One-minute conversation over. She dropped the cloth bag onto the pavement and reached for the revolver in her purse, a Ruger that SSA Preston supplied. "You're jealous. That's all. I'm tired of your stupid calls." She pulled the trigger.

He fell backward, blood spurting from his chest. She chirped her alarm, slid inside, backed over her groceries, and drove away.

Her attention flew to her rearview mirror. The truck she suspected followed at a safe distance. Her heart wasn't racing, nor were her hands shaking. This was her job.

"Done," she spoke into her phone to SSA Preston.

One murder closer to nailing Wilmington and Cayden.

✳ ✳ ✳

10:30 P.M. SUNDAY

Daniel's phone rang, and the number wasn't familiar. Lately that meant bad news. He walked into the kitchen to take the call.

"Officer Daniel Hilton here."

"This is FBI Supervisory Special Agent Alan Preston regarding Morton Wilmington's request."

As if Daniel would believe a voice on the other end of the phone. "Excuse me? I have no idea who you are."

"You've been cleared and will be working with Houston FBI until the case is ended."

"I'm an HPD officer."

"On temporary loan. Can you be at the FBI office tomorrow during your lunch hour to discuss your new responsibilities?"

Maybe this was legit. He'd call HPD headquarters to find out. "I can be there around eleven."

"This is not to be discussed with anyone."

"Yes, sir."

Let the games begin.

CHAPTER 31

Daniel started his beat for the day, while his mind spun with the case and what it meant to work with Wilmington and Laurel. Sounded like a bad triangle to him. He responded to an assault at a bakery and coffee shop, his first call of the day. He turned on his siren and cautiously sped through a red light.

When he walked into the bakery, the Asian owner looked like he'd gotten the knuckle end of a beating—swollen face, broken tooth, and two black eyes. His wife wept while washing blood from the counter, and the owner locked the door behind Daniel.

"Please, leave the blood there," he said as he called for backup. "Investigators can determine DNA and fingerprints."

The small woman shook her head. "I'm sorry. Should have known that. Makes me feel better to be cleaning. Without something to do, I'm afraid I'll fall apart." She stared at the red-tinged cloth. "The blood is my husband's. The men wore gloves."

Great. "Work type or plastic?"

"The kind medical people use."

Her husband, a thin man with glasses, gestured to her. "Sit with me. We'll talk to the officer together."

"Sir, can I call an ambulance?" Daniel said. "Your injuries should be looked at by medical personnel."

"I'll take care of it." He dabbed at the blood around his mouth.

"I need to ask a few questions," Daniel said. "How did this get started?"

He dragged his tongue over his lips. "We opened at six and the day was just normal. A man and a woman walked in and asked for coffee and donuts. They smelled like they'd been drinking all night. Hadn't showered either. The man asked for eight buttermilk chocolate glazed, but all I had were six because of a regular pickup order. Told him I'd have more in thirty minutes. He pounded his fist on the counter and called me a liar." The owner took a long breath, and his wife leaned on his shoulder. "I'm a little more shaken than I thought. Before you arrived, I was mad. Paced the floor before calling 911. Now I keep thinking what could have happened."

"I'll get you some coffee," his wife said. "You too, Officer?"

"Yes, ma'am. That would be good." Daniel offered encouragement in his smile. The couple's business was in a good neighborhood where crime was at a minimum. "I understand telling me what happened is hard. But everything you remember will help us arrest these guys."

The man nodded. "He gave me two minutes to find the rest of his order. I told him if he didn't leave, I'd call the police." He touched a purple bruise on his face. "Wrong thing to say. He grabbed me, and I tossed a cup of coffee onto his shirt. You see the result. He said he'd kill me. Pulled a gun out, but the woman told him to calm down. They had a job waiting that was more important than donuts. The two argued, then left."

"Was it about leaving or settling things with you?"

"Leaving. Whatever they were supposed to do had them riled."

"Did you recognize the gun?"

"No, sir. I don't own one."

"Any identifying marks on the two?"

"The man and woman both had dark hair. Hers was long. They wore jeans. The man had a black T-shirt with a cobra on the front. And a tattoo."

His wife called to Daniel. "The woman called him Crow."

Daniel circled the name on his report. "What were they driving?"

"A dark-green Dodge pickup. It was beat up too. Full of holes."

Sounded like the truck that followed him and his grandparents. He nixed the similarities, viewing it as too coincidental. "Did you happen to get the license plate?"

"No. I'm sorry."

"Please, find them." The woman set two Styrofoam cups on the table and wrung her hands. "The man who did this to my husband threatened to come back and finish the job." She flushed. "What he planned to do to us is unthinkable."

Daniel clenched his fist. Sometimes it was hard not to get personally involved. His job: find those two and make an arrest. If they'd bullied this couple, then they probably had a string of other crimes too. "I promise I'll do everything I can to ensure these men are apprehended."

"Thank you." The owner sipped his coffee. "What can we do for you? Donuts or a muffin sounds pitiful, but I don't have anything else to offer."

"I'm fine." Daniel shook his hand "Sir, make sure you get those injuries checked out. Your wife wants you healthy." He glanced to a corner facing the door. "You have a security camera."

"Yes. It feeds into my computer. I should have pointed it out earlier. Nervous, I guess. Want to see the footage?"

The man retrieved a laptop from the back of his bakery and pulled up the security camera footage. Clear images of the man and woman. The woman received a call. Less than ten seconds later, she grabbed Crow's arm.

A siren alerted Daniel to another patrol car. He needed to work fast and e-mailed the camera footage to himself before finishing up the report. Call it his suspicious nature, but he wondered if these two had gotten hungry after surveilling Laurel . . . less than half a mile from her apartment.

✳ ✳ ✳

10:30 A.M. MONDAY

Daniel wore his uniform to his appointment with SSA Preston. After all, if the call had been legitimate, they didn't call the shots until Tuesday. He'd woven through back streets to the FBI office. Taking chances often left bodies in the wake.

Once at the FBI office, SSA Preston confirmed the previous night's call. He escorted Daniel to an office where he was introduced to the assistant special-agent-in-charge, David Stearns, and Special Agent Thatcher Graves, whom he'd met previously. Preston explained the undercover operation, noting Laurel's position, Wilmington, and now Daniel.

"Your records indicate success in undercover operations, and you have a personal stake. We respect your discretion," Preston said. "We need to infiltrate the operation and secure evidence to make arrests. Wilmington claims Geoff Cayden is part of the scam, and he has a partner."

"Do you have any reason to believe Wilmington is telling the truth other than the claims?" Daniel said.

"We've verified what he's given us."

Daniel had worked with informers who'd slit his throat for the right price. Wilmington didn't strike him as any different. "I'm ready to see this to the end. My grandparents have been threatened, and two of their friends are dead."

"The scammers understand natural deaths rarely lead to an investigation. Family members have no reason to request an autopsy."

The problem with Tom Hanson and Emma Dockson.

"We can handle a disguise," Preston said.

Daniel shook his head. "I'll take care of it."

"Special Agent Evertson and Wilmington are taking the necessary steps to prove themselves to Cayden," Preston continued.

Thatcher gestured for Daniel's attention. "The FBI agent killed last night in the Kroger parking lot? None other than yours truly."

Daniel smiled. More pieces slid into place. A reason for the FBI not to release the victim's name. "Who supposedly fired the shot? Laurel or Wilmington?"

"Laurel."

"That cements whose side she's working for. Are either of them wearing a wire or recording device?"

"Too dangerous. It's your job," Preston said. "We'll equip you with a few before you leave."

He nodded. Too dangerous for Laurel and Wilmington to be wired, but not for him. At least ASAC Stearns, SSA Preston, and Agent Graves hadn't asked if he had personal feelings for Laurel. But all of this was about justice, and he was on board with whatever it took.

"We want to bring you up to date on the latest findings. Wilmington says a woman by the name of Josie Fields is supposedly working with Cayden. You know her as Liz Austin, one of her many aliases."

Daniel absorbed this news without reacting. Now he understood why the woman had been interested in him. Who'd suspect someone involved in a scam who dated a cop?

"We have addresses for her in Seattle, Dallas, Denver, Phoenix, and last placed in Miami. Ten years ago she worked alone. She likes wealthy, married men. None issued a complaint until she hooked up with a man in Phoenix. She claimed to be pregnant, and he discovered her game. He was sterile, demanded to see the pregnancy test. She threatened to go to his wife with their affair, but he reported her to local law enforcement. She stabbed him. Left him for dead. Then skipped town. Looks like missing credit cards were in the mix. We haven't heard from her in all these years, which feeds into the scam. She served with Wilmington and Cayden in Delta Force. Same unit. Her specialty is disguises."

"Silver Hospitality does extensive background checks. She covered her tracks." Daniel mentally placed what a relationship with Austin could have cost him. "I had her phone number at one time.

Suspected her involvement in the scam and called her, but it was disconnected." He jotted down the number from his contacts and handed it to Preston.

"Looks like she's gone from rich, married men to preying on the elderly with Cayden."

"Maybe Wilmington too. If he's involved, you're about to bust a huge case."

"*We're* about to." Preston pressed his lips together. "Another reason why we want you on the inside. This afternoon our media coordinator will hold a press conference, alert the public again before anyone else is victimized.

"One more thing," Preston said. "You begin tonight. Before you leave here, we have three burner phones. The three of you are to use them for all communications regarding the case. I can't force you to leave your other phone at home, but the scammers could trace you."

CHAPTER 32

Laurel whipped across two lanes of traffic. Late for a hair appointment, and her locks had taken on the look of a drenched golden retriever. A dark-green pickup shadowed her rearview mirror, resembling the one that had tailed Daniel and his grandparents and the one from the Kroger parking lot when she and Thatcher did their acting stint. If this was the same person, then why was she being tailed after she'd murdered an FBI agent? A crystal ball would help. She picked up her phone from the console and called Daniel. By now he'd been briefed.

"Got a truck on my rear. Matches the description of the pickup that blasted the rear windows out of your truck." She rattled off the license plate number. "Check on it, would you? Maybe this one isn't stolen."

"Give me a minute. Do you have a visual?"

"Looks like only the driver. Hard to tell with the tinted glass."

"Be careful, Laurel. Remember Josie Fields might not want you as a part of Cayden's operation. Where are you?"

"Just past the railroad tracks heading east on 1960." She changed lanes. "They must have been watching my apartment, and that says Cayden or Wilmington. Except . . ."

"Except what?"

"Seems too soon for Wilmington to turn on us. Wish I

could see the driver." The pickup tailed inches from her bumper. She registered every detail. "I'm getting off this busy street, turning left onto Champion Forest Drive." The truck turned with her.

Stepping on the gas, she raced down the street. A bullet pierced her trunk. Two more pelted the bumper. She whipped into the right lane past a retail center with a popular breakfast restaurant. Couldn't stop there. A half mile later, a huge church loomed behind a massive parking lot. Empty, and just what she needed to get rid of the green monster and its gun-totin' driver.

In the middle of the parking lot, she whirled her car around and skidded to a halt. She exited and crouched low, her breath coming in spurts. No place to run in the parking lot. The pickup sped toward her.

She fired repeatedly into the pickup's windshield. It headed straight toward her, its speed failing to diminish. She stepped to the rear and rolled over the trunk. Her feet hit the pavement as the vehicle roared toward her. She stumbled and ran to her right, clearing the truck's path just as it pounded her car and pushed it into a light pole.

A dark-haired man stepped out and aimed. Laurel cut him down.

Daniel swung into the parking lot and hurried to her side. "I called Preston. He said for you to get out of here now. They'll handle it."

She glanced at the body sprawled out on the parking lot, lifeless open eyes. Who was he? Why?

"Laurel, I left my car running. Yours isn't drivable. Get out of here. Not sure what's happening, but this isn't the first time this guy has struck today. I've already called for backup."

She nodded and headed to his patrol car. "All right. Find out who he is. Call me. I'm heading home." She stopped. "Is this the same truck that chased you?"

"Yes. Now get out of here."

✳ ✳ ✳

12:55 P.M. MONDAY

Daniel snapped a pic of the dead man with his burner phone and sent it to SSA Preston. It was the same man who'd assaulted the owners of the bakery. His hardened features spoke of a rough life, and the tats were typical tough guy but not gang related. The man lifted weights and had needle marks on his arm. He wore latex gloves, increasing the unlikelihood of fingerprint detection, but his right knuckle held blood. The Asian bakery owner's? Once the gloves were turned in to the FBI, they'd undergo a thorough search.

Daniel wanted facial recognition done on the woman from the bakery. Where had she gone? Wilmington's men were typically more high class than these two. He took another pic of the man's P220 Sig. Grim reality hit him. The gun used was a .45, the same caliber that had taken a chunk out of Laurel's shoulder. He'd find out if ballistics matched today.

Bits and pieces slowly rolled together.

If the man had been out to kill Laurel, why didn't they take her out one of the many times she came and left from her apartment? Knowing who fired the shot would help. He'd investigated enough crimes not to put a hasty conclusion into a report until all the evidence lined up, but this tempted him.

Climbing inside the man's pickup soured his stomach. The interior reeked of spoiled food and stale beer. A few to-go bags from McDonald's and a boatload of empty beer cans littered the truck. A party gone south.

A black SUV arrived behind an ambulance. Special Agent Thatcher Graves emerged from the vehicle and walked his way while his partner, a man Daniel didn't recognize, spoke to the paramedics.

"You started sooner than you expected," Thatcher said. "Got a call this truck was chasing Laurel."

"Whoa." Daniel didn't attempt to cover his anger. "Why are you here? You might have blown Laurel's and my cover."

"Relax, Hilton. I know what I'm doing."

"I have my doubts. I suggest you leave the scene, since you're supposed to be dead." His insides burned. Thatcher's arrogance could get good people killed.

"Don't worry about me. For the record, Laurel and I were at Quantico together, training you haven't had." Thatcher made his way to the body. "One of Wilmington's or Cayden's men?"

"Good guess."

The other agent snapped pics, a steady clicking. Thatcher bent to the dead man. "I want everything on him—records, his buds, underwear size, blood analysis on the glove. Now."

So the case now had a hero.

Thatcher stood and studied the surroundings. "This parking lot is about the safest place for a shoot-out with a minimum of casualties."

Daniel pointed to the church. "The staff would appreciate your comments, especially since they have a preschool on the other side."

Thatcher groaned. "Good call."

Thatcher's cell alerted him to a text. "Have an ID already." He scrolled through the message. "The name's Trey Messner. He went off the grid from 2010 to 2012. Wanted in British Columbia for questioning in a suspected murder. A year ago he appeared in Miami. Pending further investigation."

"Is Wilmington mentioned?"

"I'll find out. And if Messner visited Wilmington before he was released from prison."

"Check on the reported elderly scams in Miami. See if Messner was there then."

"I'm also requesting Messner's pic be sent to the offices in other states and law enforcement where elderly scams are reported," Thatcher said. "Wilmington claims to be innocent, but that's hard for me to swallow."

"Possibly. Why jeopardize his freedom to scam innocent people who don't know what day it is? His style was drugs, bank fraud, prostitution, and gambling. Then give to charities. Check the bullets that the FBI pulled from my truck to see if they match Messner's gun."

Thatcher grinned. "Might recruit you yet, Mr. HPD. Keep your eyes open and your head down."

If Preston wanted Daniel risking his life, he'd better give Special Agent Thatcher Graves a few guidelines.

CHAPTER 33

Abby picked a burnt-orange mum from her flower garden, stuck it in her hair, and yanked on a weed. A clod of dirt dumped on her favorite boots, the same ones she'd worn with Earl to hunt big game in Africa and bear in Alaska, the same boots from her trek along the Amazon and her hike to the top of Mount Kilimanjaro. A chuckle rose deep in her throat. The trip to the Amazon had almost been her last encounter with nature when she nearly stepped on an anaconda. Same boots. Still fit like a glove, better than her house slippers.

She stood and stretched her back. Getting old was for those who were finished living. Not Abby Hilton. Too much of this earth yet to experience.

Reveling in the spectacular display of fall color in her backyard, she spotted a cropping of weeds near a bottlebrush.

"Like life," she said. "Just when the days ahead look blessed, some jerk gets money hungry and goes on a scammin' and killin' spree."

"Gran, who are you talking to?" Daniel said behind her.

"What are you doing sneaking up behind an old, defenseless woman?"

"Old, maybe."

"Watch it." She adjusted her baseball cap over her eyes and

admired the second love of her life. "Did you finish your shift to help me pull weeds?" She startled. "Where's your uniform?"

"I'm taking some time off until the scammer's arrested." He scratched his left shoulder.

She'd read him for years, and he was keeping something from her. "How long?"

"I have a few weeks' vacation coming."

She wagged a gloved finger at him. "Daniel, when you're ready to tell me the truth, I'm ready to listen."

His face held a trace of a smile, but his body language told a different story. "The nurse said you didn't eat much lunch, and squash casserole and meat loaf are your favorite."

"I'm out here because I need to think. You know my best thoughts come when I'm working with my hands."

"Let me help." He pulled a handful of weeds. "I'd be upset too if my friends were dying and I didn't know if it were natural."

"What if you were afraid someone you loved was next?"

"I won't let that happen, Gran."

"Nearly did. My fault. I should have changed the lock on the gate."

"If anyone is to blame for Gramps walking off, it's me. And I never considered the gate."

"Wish I could do something besides pull weeds." In truth, she wanted to go hunting for two-legged animals who preyed on old people.

"I'm on it with a team of others."

"How are you going to stop them? By taking vacation time?"

"Now, Gran. I haven't taken time off in a long while."

"Hogwash. What's the FBI saying?"

"Hasn't been enough time to complete an investigation."

"They were working on this before we met with them." She grabbed a weed. "Why was Laurel fired?"

"I'm not exactly in the loop."

Abby fumed. "How sad if an HPD officer made the arrest."

Her temper rose with sarcasm, not against him but at the unfairness of it all. "And the stupid excuse to release Laurel from the FBI is a black lie."

Daniel touched her shoulder. "It doesn't matter who finds the most evidence or makes the arrest. When I can, I'll tell you about Laurel."

She narrowed her gaze. "That's what I thought. You're keeping information from me."

Sadness swept over his rugged features. "Gran, I'm keeping you and Gramps safe."

"You're right." She glanced around them, drinking in the peace her garden offered. "I simply want it stopped. Earl is eighty-five, and I'm eighty-four. In all the years we've been together, I've never been more afraid. Not with Jimmy's death. Not with your mother's trial or the insurmountable task of raising you and praying I didn't make the same mistakes twice." She swallowed her melted emotion. "Don't let anything happen to you or Earl. Please."

✳ ✳ ✳

7:05 P.M. MONDAY

Laurel watched the clock, nervous and filled with anticipation. Wilmington would call by eight if Cayden agreed to a face-to-face with her. She blew out her irritation. Dinnertime came and left, her appetite lost in the heat of this morning's firefight.

The silence rang deafening around her, her apartment like a tomb. She shivered.

A knock at her door caused her to jump. Great undercover agent. She made it to the door and stood to one side of it. "Who's there?"

"Your friendly HPD officer, a real crime fighter."

Laughter bubbled from deep inside her. Just the man her heart wanted to see—not her logic. She opened the door. The man before her had combed his brown-and-chrome hair back, sported a gold earring, green eyes, a tattoo, and wore a black knit shirt that showed every muscle. "You must have eaten ego cereal for breakfast."

"With tiger's milk."

She gestured him inside and closed the door. "What's your name?"

"C. W. Krestle. Driving a black BMW." He looked around. "Don't you ever turn on the lights?"

"Not when I'm in a mood. Believe me, after this morning, I refuse to be pried or peeled. Just dark and sour."

"Sounds like vampire candy."

She laughed again. "Where do you get these?"

"Just being my charming self."

She tilted her head to study him, really see him. "Thank you. Even if you are dressed as Wilmington's bodyguard."

"Are you doing okay?"

"I'm a friendly FBI special agent, a real crime fighter."

The rumble of laughter deep in his throat warmed her. "Good one."

"I'm all right. Hate the idea of a life wasted."

"Can I help? I'm an Eagle Scout."

"Be my friend."

"That's easy. I would like coffee and a frozen Snickers."

"Coming right up. Wilmington's supposed to call at eight. He's arranging a meeting with Cayden. See if I passed inspection."

"What about the punk who attempted to run you down?"

She hadn't shaken it off yet. "I learned a few things from SSA Preston. Have a seat. This case gets muddier and muddier." She pressed the button on the coffeemaker and pulled out a pod.

Daniel eased onto a chair. "Same gun that pumped a bullet into your shoulder?"

"No." She frowned at him. "But the bullets matched the ones fired into your truck. So I may still be dodging fire if Wilmington isn't successful."

"Josie Fields?"

She nodded and allowed his cup to fill. "She came on to you.

You refused. She's seen us together with you in your police uniform and doesn't trust me."

"I was her alibi, but I made her mad when I didn't play her game." He smiled. "Maybe you should have shot me?"

"Then I'd have to deal with Abby." She pulled a Snickers from the freezer and handed it to him with his coffee.

"You're not indulging?" he said.

"Stomach is queasy. Comes with the territory." She'd been lucky. Daniel had been lucky. But that could change in a flash. "Here's what I learned. Trey Messner, the shooter from this morning, was with Josie Fields at the bakery."

"Lovers?"

"Worse. Half brother and sister. If she wanted me dead before I killed her brother, imagine her vendetta now."

Daniel unwrapped the candy and set it beside the coffee. "No wonder your stomach isn't cooperating. Not sure Wilmington can buy you credibility with that history." He peered into her face. "I care for you, Laurel. I'd do anything to keep you alive."

Her eyes moistened. "You have no idea about my past."

"Let me be the judge of who you are."

If only she could change the filth. "You're good and kind, Daniel. You deserve better."

"I'd like to tell you something. Got another minute?"

"Fire away." She cringed. "Poor choice of words there."

"This is personal. Do you mind taking a seat?"

"Okay." Her pulse sped. Could she handle this?

When she sat, he took her hand and gave a thin-lipped smile.

"Daniel, what's wrong?"

"I hope everything's right."

She'd not overreact. "Go ahead and spill your guts."

"Is this how you handle an interrogation?" His eyes sparkled, and she wanted to melt into them.

"Depends on what I want to know." Great. She was flirting. "Me as an interrogator? I can get real nasty."

"We all can be unlovable."

Her thoughts bolted to what she'd done with Wilmington. "What made you decide to be a cop?"

"I wanted to be in law enforcement ever since I can remember. My idea of a career meant keeping people safe, fighting crime."

"Were you a superhero fan?"

"Even wore a Superman cape. Had the neighborhood convinced I was a hero."

He hadn't changed, but she wouldn't tell him. She tossed a smile his way. Her heart raced like Phantom when she loosened the reins. "What did you want to talk about?" Relationships cratered when truth surfaced. She should end any hope for both of them.

"I visited my mother in prison yesterday. First time since I was a toddler."

She inwardly startled. "That must have been hard. Why now after all these years?" His body language was open.

"I needed to square things with her." Daniel told her about the woman serving a life sentence for murdering his father.

How could a woman abandon her son? Or refuse his forgiveness after pulling the trigger on his father?

"Not sure I'd have the same courage," Laurel said. "Honestly, I'd be bitter. She'd be the last person I'd ever want to see." She paused, thinking over the last few days.

"Gramps says we should never say never because then we'll be forced into walking through our fears. Ready for a family story?"

How ironic. He was about to spill his guts, and his history couldn't be any worse than hers.

"My dad grew up doing everything opposite of what his parents wanted or instructed. According to Gramps, he showed remorse only when caught. When he was ten, he vandalized a neighbor's house. The judge determined Dad was the victim of poor parenting and ordered Gramps to spend three days in jail." Daniel shrugged. "So untrue. Dad went on to brutalize animals, steal, bully, and break the law every chance he could find. He quit school his senior year after beating up a teacher and went to work at a fast-food restaurant. His rebellion grew from using drugs to selling them. In and out of jail. He hooked up with my mother, and together they made and sold meth. Then I came along. When I was eighteen months old, my parents got into an argument. Both were high. Mom shot Dad and pleaded self-defense, but the courts didn't buy it. She received a life sentence, and Gran and Gramps raised me."

"Why did you want to tell me this?"

"I realized I'd never be free of Mom's influence until I forgave her."

Laurel studied the man before her. He'd stated his mother wasn't in the picture, but she had believed it was a small hitch in an otherwise-pristine life. Perhaps she hadn't wanted to consider anything else. "And you wanted to do this?"

"Want had nothing to do with it. I had to. The hate was eating me up, a barrier to my faith. I claimed to be a Christian, and yet I couldn't forgive. And then there's you."

She grew warm. *Here it comes. The end before the flame is snuffed out. End it, Laurel. Do him a favor. You're selfish to lead him on. It's—*

"Laurel, I've seen the odds of a cop and an FBI agent succeeding in a relationship. We've only known each other a short time, but I want to get to know you more. I want to put my past behind me and give my best to a relationship with you. The case needs to be solved first, but I wanted you to know how I feel."

Confusion soared through her. She heard the words, dream words, and stared at the strong hand wrapped around hers. "I don't understand."

"In the past, when I dated a girl, it lasted at most three weeks. Then I broke it off before she rejected me. Got myself quite a reputation as a player in college." He hesitated. "Afraid to trust. Afraid to take a chance on me or her. I don't want the same thing to happen with us."

A relationship? It couldn't happen. "No," she said, pulling back her hand. "You don't have a clue about who I am. I've done things you've never dreamed of. My faith is zilch. You know exactly what I did for Wilmington to propose. We lived together. You need a woman who's in church, a good woman who doesn't have history."

Not a muscle moved on his face, but the warmth in his eyes unnerved her. "Yes, faith must be mutual, but we can explore your questions together."

"I'm not interested. My list of sins is far too long. Your God isn't interested."

"There's no such thing as God not wanting anyone. No matter what they've done." He stroked her arm. "Your eyes tell me so much more. I have no idea who or what has hurt you, but I'm not those things. And neither is God."

Laurel failed to control the tears slipping over her cheeks. "This has to stop. Now. I'm glad you have resolution with your childhood and—"

"I'm not giving up."

"Daniel, I . . . Please go." Her heart threatened to shatter, but she held her resolve. "We're two people dealing with a criminal case. That's all."

"When you're ready, I'm right here." He startled and rose from the chair. "Someone's coming up the stairs."

CHAPTER 34

Abby listened to Earl's steady breathing. The TV blared a rerun of *Perry Mason*, but she refused to snatch the remote and turn it off. Lack of sound would wake Earl, and she enjoyed the alone time.

She dropped a stitch in her knitting, reworked the piece, and continued to let the needles fly through her fingers. Arthritis still evaded her as well as mind glitches, but her heart failed to join forces with her mind to live to one hundred. She must outlive Earl so Daniel wouldn't have to bear the burden of his grandfather's care alone.

Please, Lord. Daniel's been through enough.

He'd stopped over earlier. Seemed preoccupied. No doubt whatever he planned to do over his presumed vacation wound him up like a top.

Putting her knitting aside, she reached for today's mail. Not much ever there but sales circulars and funeral-planning dinners. She covered her mouth to stifle a laugh. Earl had received a coupon good for forty-five dollars off his next Botox treatment. A greeting card–size envelope lay in the mix with her name and address stamped in black ink. Who'd mailed a feel-good message? She opened it gingerly. The green-leafed *Thinking of you* embossed lettering touched her. How kind. Marsha must miss her at Silver Hospitality. She opened the card, one of those in which the sender writes her own message. It too was stamped in black ink.

Hi Abby,

The big day's coming. Are you looking over your shoulder?
How sad Daniel has you locked inside your own home.
He must care for you very much to have police officers around
the clock. Ah, he forgets you and Earl must die naturally.
Did you enjoy the flowers? Remember our deal.

Thinking of you.

Abby flipped the envelope to check for a return address and where and when the postage had been canceled. Only the downtown post office insignia gave any indication of the sender. Could Daniel trace this? Probably not. The scammer hadn't been successful without being smart. She tucked the card back into the envelope.

Instead of letting the card frighten her, she felt anger swell. Much like the time in Africa when a lioness charged her and Earl. All she'd done then was pull the trigger. And the big cat didn't die naturally.

Tomorrow, when Daniel stopped by, she'd share the card. Her gaze flew to the foyer. Best she let the officer on duty be aware of a potential problem.

Abby shook her head. The danger had arrived wearing a cloak of heart attacks and natural deaths.

✳ ✳ ✳

7:55 P.M. MONDAY

Daniel slipped to Laurel's apartment door, gun in hand. Heavy steps moved closer and stopped.

He motioned for her to speak.

She grabbed her Glock from the kitchen counter. "Identify yourself."

Nothing.

Daniel pointed at Laurel to repeat her question to whoever stood outside her door.

"Identify yourself?" she said.

"Morton here."

Daniel lowered his gun, and Laurel placed hers on the table. He looked through the peephole before opening the door. "You nearly got yourself full of holes."

"Good to see you too. Guess I should have called to alert you." He walked inside. "Glad both of you are here. We need to strategize." He made his way to the kitchen table and eased down, his forehead a mass of lines.

"Since you were to call me, I take it tonight's meeting took a nasty twist." Laurel sat across from him, and Daniel seated himself beside her.

If the look on Wilmington's face was an indication of a failed mission, they were starting at ground zero.

"Give me a moment to regroup." He buried his face in his hands. Was he praying—or just giving the impression to deceive him and Laurel? "I'm sure Cayden had someone follow me." Daniel thought he heard Wilmington swear under his breath. "And I'm glad Daniel is dressed as my bodyguard." He focused on Laurel. "Do you have a Starbucks pod?"

She nodded. "I'll get you a cup, but first tell me if this is over."

"Not yet. Depends on who Cayden believes."

She pulled a mug from the cabinet and proceeded to brew the coffee. "Believes what? I killed an FBI agent."

"Solidifies your position with Cayden but not Josie."

Daniel leaned back in his chair. "What are we dealing with?"

"Two highly intelligent people. Cayden's intelligence propelled him through Delta Force. His medical resignation has made him angry and greedy. Josie is brilliant but a psychopath. If she has any reason to dislike you, then she'll send you on to the next life."

"The hitch is her," Daniel said.

He nodded. "You hurt her pride when you refused her as Liz Austin. She followed you enough times to see you take your grandparents to the FBI and then later visit Laurel. A cop who isn't interested is one mark against you, strike two is your grandparents purchased two life insurance policies and that's money in her pocket, and strike three is you've been seen with my girlfriend."

Laurel set the cup in front of Wilmington with a spoon and a carton of half-and-half. "So she doesn't trust me."

"Josie and Cayden got into it tonight, and I'm not sure who will win out. Cayden calls the shots and yet he has this love/hate relationship with her."

"Then I killed her half brother."

He poured the creamer. "Another point of contention between her and Cayden. Josie ordered the hit on you without Cayden's knowledge." He paused. "She also sent Mrs. Hilton the flowers and note. Not sure who shot you with Phantom, but I'll find out."

"Thanks."

"Cayden says he's the boss. It's his account in Switzerland, and he holds the money over her head. I learned about the financials when Cayden visited me in prison." He paused. "Had to be Cayden who took the four mil. It was a means to get my attention."

"How can you be sure?" Laurel said. "Why not Josie? Or any of the other enemies you've made?"

"Calm down, Laurel. It's all money with him—how I used to be. Green does the talking. It's power and he used it."

She closed her eyes. "You're right. I knew that. What about Messner?"

"His death was no loss to Cayden. From what I gathered, Josie and Messner might have been trying to double-cross him."

Daniel analyzed the information. "Is there proof she and Messner were working against him?"

"No. Cayden accused her of it. He understands taking me on as a partner includes Laurel. He might agree just to make Josie mad."

"And I'd have to sleep with an assault rifle," Laurel said.

Wilmington sighed. "I made it clear that after my release from prison I lost a few bodyguards, but I'd recently enlisted one— C. W. Krestle. Your ID is intact, so we're good there."

Daniel regretted the danger for Laurel. "I keep thinking you should have shot me instead of Thatcher. Might be easier for Fields to digest Laurel's role." He forced a smile at her. "Want to get rid of a cop?"

"Too coincidental," she said. "Don't cross me, though."

He chuckled. "Wondering how I could keep low as Officer Hilton on vacation and Krestle the bodyguard."

"Why not stay at my condo in the Woodlands?" Wilmington said. "I can put a couple of men on your grandparents. Daylight hours you can check on them and in between be Krestle. Like the silver, by the way."

Could he be walking into a death trap by living with him? "SSA Preston has men watching them, but I appreciate the offer. The sooner we're working with Cayden, the better. So if staying at your place helps cement my role, I'm game. When will he make a decision?"

"We have a meeting tomorrow at one o'clock. I'd like for you to go with me. Something big has to be in the works for him to move this fast."

"You could ask him," she said.

Wilmington drummed his fingers on the table. "I need to find out if October 15 means anything."

"Why?" she said.

"Heard it mentioned tonight on a call Cayden received. He indicated invitations had been sent for the fifteenth." He shrugged. "Something's in the works. That's in a little over three weeks." He sighed. "I tried to get my hands on something for his DNA, but it didn't happen."

"I'll see what I can do tomorrow," Daniel said. "It takes a while for the lab to process it, and time is something we're lacking."

"Even if we get a DNA sample, that doesn't mean the FBI has what it needs to arrest him." Wilmington said.

Daniel looked at Laurel for a response. "If Cayden isn't calling all the shots, then we need the partner."

Wilmington blew out obvious exasperation. "It's not Josie Fields. She can't be trusted, and Cayden has no use for a hothead."

CHAPTER 35

Daniel reached for a slice of Gran's banana nut bread, doing his best to appear normal. Rain beat steadily on the roof, the sky a mass of angry clouds.

"Why are you spending your vacation days with a couple of old people?" Gran said. "Why not go hunting or catch a plane to Hawaii?"

He wished it were all that simple. "Soon, Gran." He pulled up a pic of Trey Messner taken from the bakery's security camera footage and showed it to her. "Not exactly a pretty sight, but do you recognize this man?"

She shook her head.

He scrolled to a second picture of him taken in Miami. This one had been computer treated with gray woven in dark-brown hair to resemble the description of the salesman who'd swindled Silver Hospitality guests.

"I know the jerk. He's the salesman from Silver Hospitality."

Bingo.

"Let me take a look." Gramps was in a good place this morning. He pointed to the man. "Sure, it's Russell Jergon, the dirty, no-good scoundrel who took our money."

"Are you taking this to Silver Hospitality to confirm?" Gran said.

"Someone will. I'm on vacation."

"Right. An arrest would make us all feel better," she said.

"Not exactly. The man's dead."

"I hope it was done by a senior citizen," Gramps said.

"Earl! Shame on you."

Gramps waved her away. "Saved taxpayer money to have him housed and executed."

"Is this from the man who opposes the death penalty?" Gran said.

"Abby girl, some no-goods can't be rehabilitated."

Daniel had heard this discussion before, and he'd better stop it now. "The man chased Laurel, fired at her, and she shot him. Drove the same truck that fired at us. Both times stolen license plates were used."

Gramps held up a finger. "You ought to hold on to her. Never know when you might need an extra gun."

"You have a point." Daniel had no desire to discuss Laurel when everything was on hold until the scammers were arrested.

"I received a card in the mail yesterday," Gran said.

"You didn't tell me." Gramps swallowed half a piece of banana bread.

"What's the occasion?"

Gran disappeared and returned a few moments later. She placed the card before him, her fingers shaking. "Maybe your friends at the FBI can analyze this."

Daniel opened the thinking-of-you card and read the message. He masked the fear swirling through him with a calm demeanor. "Those guys don't give up."

"Apparently not," she said.

Gramps took the card. "Sniveling coward! Just let him come near my Abby."

Daniel touched his arm. "Good men are guarding the house. You're safe. We both know Gran is a better shot than we are." He focused on her. "Can I take this to the FBI?"

"Sure. I wanted to burn it but thought better of it." She lifted her stubborn chin. "Don't think I won't unload on whoever's doing this."

"Promise me you won't go anywhere. Not even with a bodyguard."

"Staying here is boring," Gran said. "I can't experience the world."

"Please. You asked my help in this."

"All right. You have my word."

✳ ✳ ✳

11:00 A.M. TUESDAY

Daniel dropped off the greeting card to SSA Preston before driving to meet with Laurel at a park near her apartment. Being dressed as C. W. Krestle allowed him time alone with her. He had questions from his online searching, ones he preferred to have answered without Wilmington present.

The scammers were becoming more aggressive. SSA Preston reported two more cases in which the elderly claimed to have purchased life insurance policies and their bank accounts were minus several thousand dollars. Fortunately no more deaths. And with that information, Daniel renewed his commitment to find who was behind what the FBI referred to as the Leopard case. Wilmington? Cayden? Fields? Or all three?

Wilmington played into the unanswered questions. But how? Trusting him seemed like offering shelter to a psychopath.

Although the woman with Trey Messner at the bakery attempted to hide from the security camera, she'd been identified as Fields. Looked like she was more influenced by her half brother than the man holding on to the money. Or maybe that was the problem.

Daniel requested a complete psychological profile of Fields's and Cayden's personalities. Previous behavior would help predict how they interacted in the present. Laurel had access to all the information at her fingertips, but he'd rather request it from SSA Preston.

At the park, he found a bench where he could watch those

who entered the wooded area. Using the burner, he texted Laurel where to find him and that he had Sonic burgers and fries for lunch. Drawn into the world of treachery through a massive puzzle, he pushed aside everything else in his life to concentrate. With every moment that passed, another victim was exposed to a killer.

Five minutes later, Laurel walked his way in jeans, boots, and a blue sweater that made her golden hair sparkle. She waved and he stood. A hug would have been nice, but he'd spotted a man near a clump of trees reading. Highly unlikely. Instead he handed her the bag of food and pointed to her drink beneath the bench.

She sat and reached for a fry. "What's up, Krestle?"

"Lots of questions and no one to answer them but you."

"Are you going to drive me nuts? Be irritating?" She smiled. Perfectly white teeth.

"Marsha Leonard said the same thing numerous times. She prefers Gramps."

"She might be right." She glanced around.

"To the right. Reading."

"Thanks," she whispered. "What's first?"

"Almet Pharmaceuticals. Among other drugs, they manufacture medications for those with dementia and Alzheimer's. Gramps has tried them all."

"Which are?"

"I'll text them, but the list is Aricept, Namenda, Exelon, Razadyne, and Cognex. I'm sure you've been briefed with this, but I need to voice my thoughts."

She popped a fry into her mouth. "Yes, I'll humor you."

"We know Cayden works for Almet, and we've heard about his medical leave of absence. But why hasn't the FBI here brought him in for questioning?"

"Daniel, there's no evidence. The Miami office is interviewing everyone there. He was one of the first ones they talked to before he left Miami."

"You're right. It would be Cayden's word against Wilmington's, and the testimony of a convicted criminal isn't worth much in court. When will the FBI have the results from the others?"

"Soon. I could check again with SSA Preston."

He shook his head. "I'll ask him. If I'm a player, I don't want to use you as a source for all my information. I need to look smart."

"You're challenging an FBI agent?" Her tone was teasing, and he'd already learned she covered emotion by skirting around what she really meant.

"Yes, ma'am. Whoever figures this out owes the other a steak dinner and two dozen Snickers bars."

"A bet? You're on. But I prefer sea bass. Hope you're not a bad loser."

He was, but she didn't need to gloat over it. He winced, his emotions kicking into gear. *Push aside your feelings for her until later.* "Ready for topic number two?"

"There's more than two?"

She was flirting, and he enjoyed every second. "What's Morton Wilmington's background?"

"Other than the man's a genius?" She took a bite of her burger, and he did the same. "He was in and out of trouble as a teen, then supposedly got on the right track in college. Received his master's in business management. Sometime after that he went to work for a well-off family in Chicago. Taught him how to launder money—basically lie, cheat, and steal. Sort of a *Godfather* scenario. Wilmington slipped away before facing arrest and joined the Army."

"What about his growing-up years?"

"His parents were hardworking, blue-collar people. According to him, they were good and moral. He simply wanted what others had and didn't care how he got it. In fact, he didn't believe he had a conscience. Go figure with his new supposed stand on God."

Daniel mentally stored the man's background. No conscience meant anything goes. If he was behind the scam, Daniel would tear him apart. There wouldn't be anything left for law enforcement to cuff.

"A penny for your thoughts?"

Her voice broke into his vendetta. "I just want justice."

"And I want revenge. We're a strange pair."

"For the agent killed in Wilmington's takedown?"

"The agent was my partner, a good man with a family."

Daniel wanted to take her hand, enclose her fingers in his. Cayden's man would report it for sure. "How many people have told you his death wasn't your fault?"

"Too many."

"God works in ways we'll never understand."

She glanced away. "I'm not on His dance card."

"Yes, you are. All He wants is an opportunity to lead."

"That's why God and I don't dance. I have to be in control to survive."

"I figured out your method of doing life during our first meeting. You're a strong woman, Laurel, but I see the pain in your eyes."

"Don't even try to get near me. Might get you killed."

"I've never done well taking orders from the FBI."

"Daniel," she whispered, pushing back. "I don't need more blood on my hands."

"I'll take my chances. We can't do a thing about our relationship until this is over, and don't try to deny it."

"I'm not looking for or wanting a relationship. I'm not exactly dating material. Baggage, remember?"

"I have a railcar full myself."

"We're both stubborn, independent. Probably kill each other," she said.

Hadn't he said the same to Gramps? "We could try to leave our firearms in our holsters."

She laughed, a real one. "To see who could inflict the most damage? You have this Christian thing going. Doesn't your Bible warn you about being unequally yoked?"

She was right. "You must have read a lot of the Bible."

"Daniel, I like you. I really do. Your Christian beliefs are principles I'm familiar with but have never been able to accept. We can be friends, and that's exactly what I need. All I need or want."

"I know better, but I'll not press you." He could have corrected her principled beliefs regarding a relationship with the God of the universe. Except he didn't feel his convictions were what she should hear right now. Kindness, yes. Miscommunication as in condemnation, no. He'd show her what his faith meant to him.

"Thanks." Her wistful tone told him the truth. If he wanted this to work, then he had a job to do before approaching her again about his faith or a relationship.

She glanced away. "You have plans for us?" Not a trace of emotion touched her face. He was sure she carried some heavy baggage. Beginning with her deceased parents, a foster home, and a killed partner. But that would be another time.

"It takes two."

She peered at two children on swings. "Is the man still reading?"

"Yes. Should I kiss you and give him something to report to Cayden and Wilmington?"

"It would make Fields ecstatic. But we could wind up dead." She stood. "Talk to you later. You have a date with Wilmington and Cayden?"

"Right. Then moving into Wilmington's condo."

She laughed. "Better you than me. I've been there. Views are great but the company's deplorable."

He figured before the afternoon was over, she'd contact SSA Preston herself for the Miami information. Loved how she operated.

Oops. The *L* word had slipped into his thoughts without warning. Crazy.

CHAPTER 36

Daniel met with Wilmington outside a popular Cajun restaurant near the Galleria. They had some things to discuss before Cayden joined them, especially if Cayden refused Wilmington and Laurel as part of his operation.

Wilmington laughed at Daniel's appearance as Krestle the bodyguard. "You clean up pretty good. I'm the only one of us having lunch who looks like my real self."

"I'm up for an Academy Award." Daniel enjoyed this part of law enforcement.

"Did you know a nonprofit organization dedicated to finding a cure for Alzheimer's and dementia has booked a fund-raiser dinner on October 15 at the Junior League?" He glanced around. "Been on the calendar for eight months. SSA Preston texted me on the way here. Laurel was copied."

"I'm low guy here. Last to find out."

"We'll see if Cayden brings the date up."

"You mean if we've passed his scrutiny."

"Here he comes now."

A broad-shouldered man walked into the restaurant and stuck out his hand to Wilmington. "Glad you could make it, Mort."

Wilmington shook his hand. "I've been looking forward to our conversation." He pointed to Daniel. "This is my bodyguard, C. W. Krestle."

"I wasn't expecting anyone but the two of us." Cayden smiled, but his eyes emitted displeasure in a cold stare. "A table for three." His face tightened.

Once seated, they gave the server their food and beverage orders.

Wilmington leaned onto the table. "What's the stand? Laurel and I have plans on hold while waiting for your decision."

"Josie is opposed, but I expected that. She sent her errand-boy brother out on a job and lost."

"Why?"

Cayden shrugged. "A female thing about Laurel being seen with some guy she wanted to date."

"Hardly. My Laurel's loyal."

Daniel cringed internally.

"Do you run the operation or does Josie?" Wilmington's words raised a challenge.

"I do. And I say you and Laurel are in. But if I suspect anything from her, then I'll personally take her out of the game."

"You indicated a female partner, and I assumed she was it."

"Got to cover my bases, Morton," Cayden said.

"So no partner?"

"A silent one. For now."

Wilmington snorted. "Glad it isn't Josie. She was wacko years ago, and from her record, she's wanted all over."

"Yes, but her IQ makes up for it. As long as she behaves herself, she stays alive."

The server set their beverages on the table and disappeared.

"What happens from here?" Wilmington said.

"What we discussed in prison. Did I mention my nonprofit? It was formed to aid those suffering with Alzheimer's and dementia. In fact I'm hosting a fund-raiser on October 15 right here in Houston."

Daniel bit back his thoughts about Cayden's nonprofit and fund-raiser. The man just thought he had the good-guy facade.

"Who's invited?"

"A select group of four hundred men and women from the Southeast and Gulf States who share our ideals. Wealthy, highly respected."

They were talking in circles. Then it hit him. Cayden feared one of them might be recording the conversation. Nothing he'd said could be used against him. Wilmington played into it too. Daniel had now hit the big dogs, and he wasn't sure he could outsmart them.

"Your input, support, and encouragement with the nonprofit is what we need."

"Laurel and I are in."

"Excellent. We appreciate your participation. All that we went over a few months ago is still intact. Our website has a tab for online donations."

"When do Laurel and I meet with you again?"

"Friday night. I'll let you know where." He sneered at Daniel. "Without your bodyguard. If you can't trust me after what we went through in the military, who can you trust?"

Wilmington leaned back. "No one. I owe you, and this is how I can repay what you did for me."

How much of this was real for Wilmington? Daniel chose not to go there—his facade might crack.

Cayden pulled an inhaler from inside his jacket and drew in the medicine. Didn't look like it was for show.

The server approached their table and asked for Geoff Cayden. "Sir, there's a woman who wants a word with you."

"Who is it?"

"Says it's a personal matter about your daughter."

Cayden swore. "My wife would have called." He turned to Wilmington. "Excuse me while I see what this is about. Be right back."

Daniel watched them walk away and used his cloth napkin to retrieve the inhaler and drop it into his jacket pocket. He swiped a napkin from another table and stuck it by Cayden's plate.

"You might be in the wrong business," Wilmington whispered.

"Don't think so."

In less than three minutes, Cayden returned. He took his seat swearing, face red.

"Is your daughter all right?" Wilmington said.

"Wasn't my wife at all, but a woman I met last night. Said she followed me today from my hotel. I blew up and she ducked into a car. She won't live past the day."

Coco had come through for him. The FBI had arranged transportation for her to the airport and she was off to a Hawaiian vacation, courtesy of a dip into Daniel's savings account. Worth every dollar to have Cayden's DNA.

✳ ✳ ✳

2:35 P.M. TUESDAY

Laurel had never been one to wait for information, and finding out the results of FBI interviews in Miami meant contacting SSA Preston. She'd win the dinner with Daniel—sharing a meal with him sounded better than all those with Wilmington. Once home, she checked e-mail and saw a Google alert about her and Wilmington.

Her stomach rolled, and she almost wished she hadn't set up a way to keep tabs on him.

Laurel and I are planning a February 14 wedding. I'd like sooner, but Valentine's Day makes it special.

Beneath the post was a photo of the two of them at Damian's for dinner. She couldn't remember smiling at him. Must have been Photoshopped. For a moment she despised herself as much as she had five years ago.

Why did he give someone a quote? Then it hit her like a punch in the gut. This told Cayden and Fields they were committed to the relationship. Smart but irritating.

She read through the comments. Well-wishes from those she didn't know. Probably criminals like him.

Where was the woman who once worked violent crime? She reached deep down to regain her composure. The Facebook post played into the ruse with Wilmington. She simply needed to stay on top of it.

The task at hand was to call SSA Preston on her burner. "Good afternoon, sir. Can you tell me if the employee interviews from Almet Pharmaceuticals are completed?"

"Received them earlier. I'll forward the report to you."

"Thanks."

"You and Wilmington are receiving a lot of attention."

"I saw. Hope it works."

"Just sent the reports your way. Interesting, as I'm sure you'll find. We think Cayden is our man, but we still have nothing for prosecution. From his history, if we bring him in for questioning, he'll go dark."

The call ended, and she read through Miami's findings. The employee interviews revealed information about thirteen males and females who had military backgrounds. That pinpointed her concentration and the FBI's. Ten of the ex-military passed FBI radar. Two men held possibilities for a strong cover.

The first suspect was a former Navy man who was less than honorably discharged for admitting use of a controlled substance. The incident occurred eleven years ago. Vendettas could easily fester. The Miami FBI office was in the process of an investigation. His ex-wife claimed his drug addiction led to their divorce. Police record for assault. Currently in a court-ordered rehab.

The second man, Geoff Cayden, managed a team of salesmen. He was married with a daughter. Described as intelligent and reliable. He'd been a part of Army Delta Force until adult-onset asthma forced his early retirement. Commendable. Highly decorated. FBI was investigating his unconventional missions. No flags there except Wilmington's claims. Delta Force knew how to plan and execute missions. Trained to beat a polygraph test. But she didn't think he'd offer to take one. Preston sent her the information regarding Cayden's nonprofit, which he'd formed eighteen months ago. The board of directors were influential people across the US, a blend of clergy and politicians. Nothing on this guy but the American hero who wanted to help the elderly.

Laurel texted SSA Preston for more information from the FIG. Did Cayden travel with his job? She received a positive response. He had trained salesmen all over the country prior to his medical leave. She posed four additional requests: Did the FBI have his travel log? What was his work attendance for the past year, along with his sick days? Did his travel and sick days line up with any of the elderly scams? Had the doctor who wrote the work release and past medical slips been questioned again?

A text came in from Daniel.

They always say time changes things, but u actually have 2 change them urself - andy warhol

She laughed. So Daniel. She loved it and texted him back.

Thanx

Got the DNA

Yes! I have the employee interviews you wanted

Why am I not surprised?

Sending now

What am I to do with a partner who always seems 2 b one step ahead of me?

Change the music.

She held her breath as reality paralyzed her. She cared for him, and it frightened her. He could be taken in an instant, and she'd be alone. Selfish . . . but life had always thrown her a curve when it came to her heart.

She'd gladly step into the line of fire to keep him safe. Inhaling sharply, she felt chilled at the gravity of her thoughts. Would she give her life for Daniel? Had her feelings for him gone too far?

She needed to talk to someone who could help her make sense of what was happening.

CHAPTER 37

Abby believed the secret to longevity was a positive outlook on life. Other things were important too, like eating healthy and exercising, which meant doing sit-ups . . . *Forty-one, forty-two, take a breath, then forty-three.* She stood and admired her flat stomach.

Girl, you still have it. A few things might not look like a Barbie doll's, but the rest of you is in place. At least she didn't need a walker.

The doorbell rang, and she made her way to the door with Earl emerging from the living room. Pete escorted Laurel. Abby swung the door open and gave the young woman a huge hug.

"So glad you came to see us. Earl and I are bored to tears," she said.

Earl wrapped his arm around Laurel's waist. "Now I have two beautiful women to keep me company. Come on in."

How dear to see him like the man he used to be.

Laurel stepped inside the foyer. "Hope I'm not interrupting anything."

"Please do." Earl's blue eyes twinkled.

Once all three of them were seated on the living room sofa with iced tea, Abby sensed Laurel wasn't making a business call. "Is everything okay?"

"The best it can be while I look for a job. Won't be long, though."

"What can I do for you?"

"Oh, just talk."

Earl excused himself. "You girls have a nice chat. Laurel and I will have plenty of time to catch up in the future."

"I hope I'm not running you off," Laurel said.

"The History channel is calling my name. Time I generated some brain cells instead of wasting them." He disappeared into the next room.

"How can I be a friend?" Abby studied her. Why did Laurel want to visit with an old woman?

"I'm in a reflection mode." Laurel's lips turned upward but quivered slightly. "I want to tell you about my foster mother."

Abby listened to the heartbreaking story of a little girl abandoned except for an older woman who loved her unconditionally. She believed Laurel held back, but Abby wouldn't question. Not at this point anyway.

"Joining the FBI helped me deal with the ups and downs of life while helping others."

"But you're still with them, right?"

Laurel blinked. "The FBI released me."

Abby reached for Laurel's hand. "Oh, I know. Just calling it like I see it."

"Abby, I think you could handle anything."

"Not always. Life can be a formidable taskmaster. Jimmy, Daniel's dad, nearly destroyed us, but Daniel is our joy."

"Have you ever made choices you regret?"

Abby pressed her lips together. The question was more about Laurel than herself. "Choices can be forced on us or made voluntarily. In either case, we can have regrets."

"Do you mind telling me how you met Earl?"

Abby laughed. "How much of it? I'm a cross between eccentric and quirky."

"I respect the woman you are now. So tell me about the beginnings."

Abby stared into the depths of the young woman before her.

Daniel could easily fall in love with her. Laurel could feel the same for him. Love was like that. People spent their lives looking for the perfect fit, but did they always recognize it? Hopefully both of them would see the gift before life passed them by.

"All right." Abby kept Laurel's hand firmly in hers. "I was born on a farm in east Texas, deep in the Piney Woods, where time still seems to take a step back. I was one of eight children, right in the middle with three older and four younger brothers. My mother and I had a hard road working the fields beside the men, then cooking and taking care of them. I hated it. When I was fourteen, I ran off with a man who swore he loved me. He said he had a ranch in west Texas and we'd go there. But that isn't what happened at all. He sold me into slavery. Law enforcement types now call it human trafficking. I couldn't figure out how to get away. Couldn't trust anyone.

"Once a month, the man who owned the business took three of us into town for a treat at the Dairy Queen. Called us his DQ girls. Earl and his father had stopped there on their way home from a hunting trip." Abby closed her eyes. "He was the most handsome boy I'd ever seen. I could see the man he'd grow into. He approached me at the booth and started talking. The man who owned me told him to get away."

"What happened?"

"Earl's dad must have suspected something. He leaned over the table and asked me if I was all right or if he should call the police. I couldn't go back home after the things I'd been forced to do. But living on my own had to be better than what I'd experienced. I asked him to contact the police. My owner was furious. Earl's father wouldn't let me leave with the man. So my captor took the other two girls and left. When the police arrived, I explained how I'd been tricked. The officer contacted my parents, but they didn't want me back. No surprise there. Earl's dad made a few phone calls and found a place for me to stay with a family from his church. From then on, Earl and I were inseparable. He showed me faith

204 II DOUBLE CROSS

and helped me find my way to heaven." Abby swiped at a tear. "Jesus and Earl, in that order."

Tears streamed down Laurel's face. "Oh, Abby, you are an inspiration. Maybe I can walk through this nightmare, see it through to the end. All I have to do is remember your strength."

✳ ✳ ✳

11:20 P.M. TUESDAY

Laurel drove to meet Wilmington in the bar near downtown. Finding answers often meant looking into dark and angry places. Laurel understood associating with Morton Wilmington brought those things and more. She'd been there, a survivor on the outside, a fragile soul on the inside. The one thing she hated about her job was the exposure to the worst of evil. The one thing she valued was contributing to the end of that evil.

The seclusion of night fit their conversation. She needed to pose a few questions without Daniel. If the situation got hot, she didn't want him killed.

She watched her mirrors and didn't detect anyone. Agents were there, hidden in the unknown, like the ones who'd followed her on the other occasion. Then there were Cayden's people. He'd approved her as part of the team, but Fields wasn't pleased. Cayden and Fields were good at accidents.

When she arrived, Wilmington sat at a small table in a corner. The shadows of the bar hid far too many people. Her gaze swept the room before she joined him. Two bodyguards faced the entrance at one table, and a third nursed a beer at the bar, all looking like businessmen enjoying a drink. Their hands rested close to their concealed weapons, and their scrutiny was fixed on her the moment she stepped in. She understood they didn't trust her any more than she trusted their boss.

The others didn't appear as threats. A woman with more cleavage than Laurel owned eyed the bartender. A couple clasped hands and shared a drink. Another couple brushed past her.

Wilmington stood when he saw her. She knew his leather jacket held a weapon in the left pocket. Possibly two. He was fond of wallet guns.

"We made it through tonight and it worked."

She reached for his hand and noted the cold fingers. "I'm assuming we're being photographed."

"We are." He ordered water and lime for them.

Anger bubbled inside her. The new info regarding him made her want to pull her Glock. "Why didn't you tell me Messner had been on your payroll?"

"He left my business while I was in prison." He paused and smiled. "We kept tabs on him."

"I'm sure you did. Who'd he go to work for?"

"Mostly himself."

"Can you be clearer?"

"Flew low until he connected with his half sister."

She held on to his hand, but her thoughts were murderous. Wilmington *had* kept information from the FBI and her. "You've not held up your end of the deal."

"I'm not the man from five years ago, so wipe that image out of your mind."

She kept her emotions intact, playing the role of the agent, not the woman concerned about a bullet piercing her skull. "Explain why you kept valuable information from me and the FBI."

"We lost him until he turned up dead."

One more reason why she'd never trust him.

"Why isn't Daniel with you?" Wilmington said.

"I wanted this private."

"He can't work undercover, help his grandparents, and babysit you. I like the man, what I know of him. Wouldn't want to see him dead either."

"I don't need a babysitter. Neither am I protecting him. He's your bodyguard."

"Look, babe—"

The sound of his voice made her skin prickle. "Don't call me that."

"Laurel, back when we were together, I loved you the best way a man like me could. When I saw you at the prison, the old anger and bitterness surfaced. I thought the issues of betrayal were resolved, but I was wrong. Those things won't vanish overnight, but I'm working on it."

He took a deep breath. A look of tenderness swept over him, and it frightened her more than his anger did.

"I'm following God and I'm committed to ending the elderly scam. When this is over, I'll leave you alone. But I'll continue to assist the FBI in fighting crime."

"I'm afraid for Daniel."

Wilmington chuckled. "At least I'm aware of one allegiance."

"It's not like that. We're all a part of a team." Dare she play into the emotion she'd just seen? "Please, Morton, don't keep information from me."

He finished his water and set the glass on the side of the table for a refill. "I could use a good epitaph on my tombstone."

"I'll do my best."

CHAPTER 38

Abby replaced the crackers in the pantry and opened the dish-washer to stow away the soup bowls from lunch. Earl loved home-made chicken noodle soup with a kick of jalapeño. He wanted corn bread, but he'd had butter and apple jelly on biscuits for breakfast, raising his cholesterol and sugar. Since he'd had bacon, eggs, and hash browns too, she'd taken a nutritional stand. After all, she was the head dietitian in the house.

Melodious sounds from the piano took her back in time to when Earl played for churches and weddings. Even though his mind might not be onstage, music still flowed from his fingertips.

The doorbell diverted her. She hurried to the foyer. Ah, Pete and a young woman. She disarmed the security system and opened the door to greet them.

Pete smiled. "Miss Abby, you and Earl have a pizza."

"Oh, my. But I didn't order one."

"Looks like Daniel sent it." Pete picked up the note on the box. Strange, since Abby didn't care for pizza. "How nice of him."

The young woman laughed. "I wish someone would surprise me with lunch. When he called it in, he asked that I set it on your table."

"Impossible, ma'am," Pete said and took the box.

"Let me get you a tip." The smell of pepperoni and tomato sauce filled Abby's nose. If only she enjoyed it.

"Not necessary." The young woman smiled. "Your grandson took care of me nicely." She left, turning to wave when she got to her car.

"Mercy, Earl and I just ate." She glanced at Pete. "But you haven't. Why not enjoy this, our treat?"

"Are you sure?" He lifted the lid on the box and stared hungrily. "Mushrooms aren't my favorite, but I'm hungry."

"You could pick them off. Come on in."

"No, Miss Abby. The front porch is fine."

Abby retrieved a few napkins and a tall glass of iced tea for him, then returned to tidy up the kitchen. One thing about being at home meant she could cook a decent meal instead of eating on the fly. While the officers guarded their home, she could fix plenty and it would be eaten. Another reason she didn't understand the delivery.

She made her way to the front porch to see if Pete needed a refill on his tea. Pizza could be messy, and she'd given him only a couple napkins. Opening the door, she gasped. He lay facedown beside the rocker.

"Pete!" She bent to his side. He was breathing but she couldn't wake him. She grabbed his phone sticking from his shirt pocket and dialed 911. "I have an unconscious man. Possibly a heart attack." Abby listened to the instructions. "Yes, sir. I'm right here until help arrives."

Pizza littered the porch floor. She counted two pieces missing. Her mind flew to the young woman who'd delivered it. Neither her ball cap nor her car had advertised a pizza company.

She pressed in Daniel's number. He responded on the first ring.

"Hey, Pete. Everything okay?"

"This is Gran. We have an emergency. I called 911 for Pete. He's unconscious on our porch."

"What happened?"

She drew in a heavy breath. "I'm not sure. But I have an idea."

"Is he breathing?"

"Yes."

"Did he arrive sick?"

"No. Earl and I ate lunch early, and then your pizza arrived."

"Gran, I didn't order pizza."

She touched her heart. "A young woman delivered it. Said you'd sent lunch. I gave it to Pete since we'd eaten. I should have known you wouldn't have ordered it. Where is my common sense?"

"Calm down. Did he eat it all?"

"Two pieces."

"Tell the paramedics there's a good chance Pete's been poisoned."

"My thoughts too. How awful. Daniel, it was supposed to be us. When will the tragedies end?"

"Soon. I promise. Many people are working on stopping the scammers. Pray for Pete and for those responsible to get caught."

A siren blared in the distance. "The ambulance is almost here. I'll text you with the hospital. Earl and I will follow in the Lexus."

"Gran, I don't like you driving."

"Get over it."

"Okay. Be careful. I'll call Pete's wife. He's a strong, healthy man and can pull through this."

She studied Pete's pale face. "I hope so. I'm ready to fight back. Unload on them."

"Gran—"

"Remember when I said I couldn't shoot someone? The rules have changed."

CHAPTER 39

1:45 P.M. WEDNESDAY

Daniel swapped out the BMW for his truck and hurriedly changed his clothes from "Krestle" to jeans and a pullover. He doused his hair with a bottle of water and sped to the hospital. The doctors were taking care of Pete, and a few minutes for Daniel to change his disguise meant staying on the case.

Attempting to poison his grandparents would have worked if not for Gran despising pizza and not allowing Gramps to have it. Plus they always ate lunch at eleven thirty.

He pulled into the visitor parking area of Houston Methodist Hospital and pressed in Laurel's burner number on his burner phone.

"Laurel, I have a problem."

"What's happened?"

He explained the pizza poisoning.

"I'll be right there."

"Think about it. Cayden's people are tailing both of us. I've changed clothes and have my truck."

"I'll lose them and change up my looks."

"This is beginning to feel like a bad movie."

"It's what we do, Daniel. Don't worry. Pete will be okay, and I won't give myself away. I promise."

✳ ✳ ✳

2:40 P.M. WEDNESDAY

As afternoon lowered its shawl over the city, Laurel hurried into Methodist Hospital. Temps dipped into the fifties, unusually chilly and yet befitting her mood. Why couldn't they catch these guys?

She exited a rented vehicle wearing a long dark wig and a cap, a dark-brown tunic, leggings, and boots with four-inch heels.

She and Daniel had their differences—more like oceans dividing them with the faith issue—but the officer's serious condition was a result of someone wanting his grandparents dead. She cared about Abby and Earl, and that brought her and Daniel together in many ways. She loathed that older people were losing thousands of dollars and others were dying of supposedly natural causes. Yet she was convinced Wilmington had a part in it.

October 15 loomed like a savage beast. Nine days until the fund-raising dinner. So many agents were on the case. The FBI needed a list of the guests. The obvious ploy would be the scammers having their hands on credit card information. The next step would be identifying how the money would be laundered. And what about all the money stolen from the elderly? How had it been laundered? If the victims hadn't taken steps to ensure the safety of their funds, then more would be drawn from their financials.

Inside the hospital, Daniel and his grandparents sat in a waiting area. Whom did she approach first? So much for the confident agent who managed her life according to textbook principles. She made her way to them and spoke before Daniel recognized her. He rose and gave her a hug, then directed her away from his grandparents. The strength in his arms flooded her senses. She refused to get used to this.

"Thanks for coming. Good job with the getup." A slight smile from him met her. "Pete's holding his own. He's conscious."

"Stomach pumped?"

"Yes, and they're filling him with IV fluids. His wife is with him."

"I bet he's miserable. What's the word on the poison?"

"Poisonous mushrooms," Daniel said. "We have a report from a restaurant near them about a young woman dressed in jeans and a baseball cap who picked up the pizza matching what was delivered to my grandparents. She avoided the security camera but appears to be the same size as Fields."

"She's persistent. Getting bolder."

"More like desperate. She's pressed me a little too far. Not sure poisoning would hold up for a life insurance policy, but she obviously thought so. She altered her appearance from her stint at Silver Hospitality and the bakery."

Laurel had spent hours analyzing this woman. "Feeds into her behavior."

"Fields is working to eliminate as many people as possible who bought life insurance policies."

"Would she think your grandparents had any incriminating information other than the life insurance policies?"

"Only the brochure." He paused. "They could possibly have something else, but Gran or Gramps would have told me."

"Daniel, with your grandfather's health . . ."

"I'm well aware of what he does and doesn't remember." He glanced away as though thinking. "I'm going through every inch of their house tonight. Don't want to assume anything without looking into every angle."

Abby walked to their side and took Laurel's hand. "Took me a minute until I saw your pretty brown eyes. I appreciate your coming. We're concerned about Pete, but he's better. I admit he had me shaken before the paramedics arrived."

Laurel glanced at Earl. "Is your husband okay?"

"Not his mind. Skipping, as he calls it."

"I'm so sorry."

Abby smiled. "His places are often better than the real ones. Days like this I envy him."

When Laurel pondered the blackness of her own life, an escape into oblivion sounded appealing. As a teen, she'd used sex and whatever else to smother reality. Nothing helped. She gave up. The only temporary satisfaction came from doing her job.

Daniel suddenly took fast steps toward the hospital elevators.

Laurel saw the woman leaving too, dressed in hospital scrubs—Josie Fields.

"Stop, HPD!" he said and pulled his gun.

Fields raced toward the entrance doors, turned, and fired, narrowly missing Daniel and sending a bullet back through the hospital reception area. Screams erupted. People bolted and sought refuge. Fields sprinted outside and into the parking lot with Daniel and Laurel in pursuit.

Laurel held her breath. Had she already gotten to Pete?

Daniel fired.

Fields grabbed her right thigh and shot at him again. Blood seeped down the leg of her scrubs.

"I need her alive!" Daniel shouted.

Fields turned and took dead aim at Daniel.

Laurel pressed the trigger. Fields staggered, and blood gushed from her upper left shoulder. A black Escalade sped to her side. The driver yanked her onto the front seat. It sped away before Fields's feet left the ground.

Laurel and Daniel pumped rounds into the vehicle's rear. It wove through the parking lot in a squeal of tires and with a host of holes, including a shattered rear window.

"Run-flat tires," Daniel said. "What haven't they done to cover their rears?"

"Blood spatters will help prove her identity." Laurel's frustration at not stopping the Escalade burst into her words. "The best we can hope for is her need for medical assistance."

"I have the license plate number." Daniel sounded strange.

Laurel whirled around. Blood poured from his left lower arm, near his wrist. She swallowed, remembering Jesse bleeding out. Already her feelings were getting in the way of her job.

He set his jaw. "Got me one more reason to find that woman. She'd better not have hurt Pete."

"At least we're at a hospital."

"Can you get her blood sample?"

She reached for her phone. "I need to call the Evidence Response Team for one of them to collect it." She made the request while concern for Daniel's wound mounted, competing with the urgency to keep the blood sample safe from contamination until the ERT arrived.

"I'm calling Preston," Daniel said, his face pinched with the pain.

"With the shots, HPD will be here soon. They'll be checking all the hospitals and clinics."

A security guard hurried to their side.

Daniel flipped his HPD creds. "Stay here until authorities arrive. HPD and the FBI are on their way. I'll be inside the hospital."

"Don't touch the crime scene," she said. "Guard this blood spatter until it's photographed and gathered."

Supporting his wounded wrist while blood seeped between his fingers, Daniel moved toward the hospital entrance. "Guess it could have been my right arm."

And Daniel might have ended up like Jesse. "I should have seen her before you."

"Why? So the FBI could have credit for saving a lowly cop?"

He hurt and she understood where the cutting words came from. "No, you idiot. My awareness might have prevented your injury."

"Heroic."

"The ER is around the corner," she said.

Abby met them outside the hospital door. She covered her mouth and stepped forward.

"I'm checking on Pete first. Not now, Gran. The bullet grazed me, more blood than anything else."

"You can't help Pete like this. You can't even help yourself." Abby sounded harsh, but fear didn't have a fixed vocabulary.

"Daniel," Laurel said. "I'll see about Pete. You're losing more blood than you realize."

Lines raked across his forehead. "I'm heading up the elevator. I don't give a rip about what some medical professional says. Gran, stay with Gramps. Laurel, you can go with me or do whatever. Your choice."

Gran removed her sweater and wrapped it around Daniel's wrist.

"You are the most stubborn man I've ever met." Laurel wanted to shake her fist at him.

He glared at her. "I'm in good company."

CHAPTER 40

Daniel managed to endure Laurel's lecture in the elevator and find Pete's room. The pain in his wrist thumped in time to his heartbeat. When had he become such a wuss? He'd never been shot by a female until today. It hurt just like the time he'd been shot by a drunk a few years ago.

But first things first.

Pete's wife, an attractive redhead, sat at her husband's bedside. She rested one hand on his shoulder. Daniel greeted her, then focused on Pete. He opened his eyes and frowned.

Daniel bent over the bed. "Hey, Pete. How are you doing? Heard you liked pizza."

"Very funny. Looks like I'm doing better than you are. You must have tangled with the gal who serves up tasty mushrooms with pepperoni and extra cheese."

"Was she here?"

"Yeah. Tried to stick something in my IV, but I recognized her. Took off real fast. The little wife tore after her too. My kind of woman." He blew a kiss at her. "I pushed the call button, but she got away." He squinted. "Who's with you?"

Daniel chuckled. "Laurel."

"Makes me wonder what's going on with you two." He shook his head. "Aren't you with Morton Wilmington? And why the disguise?"

217

"Yes. But Abby and Earl are special people."

His grin told Daniel that Pete understood exactly what was going on. "This stays right here. You can trust me."

Laurel stepped closer. "Thanks, Pete. Daniel recognized your delivery gal leaving the hospital and chased her outside."

Pete positioned his fingers like a gun. "She must have fired her pleasure at being chased."

"He left a bullet in her thigh," she said.

Daniel forced a chuckle. "Laurel's aim did more damage to her shoulder. Somebody was waiting for her to exit and picked her up. Or rather, dragged her into an SUV." He reached deep for pain control. "I wanted her alive for questioning." Great, he was whining.

She shrugged. "Admit it, we're a sick team. All three of us nursing our wounds. And the bad guys are on the loose."

Pete closed his eyes. "I'm on the mend. Batman and Batgirl need therapy."

Daniel snorted at Pete's remark and eased onto a chair, noting the blood staining Gran's sweater, a new one that he'd bought her. He'd replace it. "You're the officer of concern here. What's the diagnosis?"

"After the stomach pump and taking enough blood to start my own bank, the doc announced an overnighter."

"Good call. Bet you won't be eating pizza for a long time."

Pete lifted a brow. "The thought of even smelling it makes me want to puke. Let's cut the chitchat. You need a doctor."

"I'll get to it." The overprotective virus was killing him worse than the gunshot. "What can you tell me about the gal who delivered the pizza? I want to make sure it's the same person we just shot."

"Dressed like a teen. Perky and sweet." He responded with the same story Gran had told. "The moment I started feeling sick, I suspected what happened. At least it was me and not your grandparents. Some bodyguard I am. The gal said you ordered it hand-delivered on their kitchen table, but that didn't fly with me."

The situation raised Daniel's fury. His earlier commitment to search through every inch of their home now became urgent. "I'm putting Gran and Gramps in a hotel tonight. Sending them home bothers me. The shooter might not be moving too fast right now, if she's even alive, but she's not the only one involved."

"Who is she?"

"She uses several aliases."

"I agree your grandparents need to be moved. What about keeping an officer posted at their home in case someone shows?" Laurel said.

Why did every comment make him mad? "I'm getting this arm bandaged up, and I'll handle protective detail myself."

Laurel planted her hands on her hips. "I don't think so, Officer Hilton. You can't be alone in your condition. You'll be given pain meds, and those things knock you out. Better to hire someone."

"Says who?"

"Hold on," Pete said. "Do you two always get along like this?"

"Always," Laurel huffed. "No wonder he doesn't have a partner with HPD."

"Don't get me started," Daniel said. "No one knows the real Laurel."

Pete's wife laughed. She hadn't spoken two words since they walked in to check on her husband. "Let me point out the obvious—both of you have injuries and that sets the stage for bickering. I suggest you lock up your weapons."

"Then we'll take care of each other." Laurel rubbed Daniel's back, then caught herself and stopped. "After a doctor looks at his arm."

"Wrist."

"Lower arm."

"Okay, Batgirl," Daniel said. "Let's get Batman fixed up. We have a cave to investigate."

✳ ✳ ✳

7:00 P.M. WEDNESDAY

Daniel's grandparents' home lit up the darkness with the highest quality landscaping lights and motion detectors on the market. They were so sensitive, squirrels could occasionally trigger them. But all the precautions he'd put in place for his grandparents' safety, including the bodyguards, were useless if someone wanted inside badly enough.

He pulled his truck into the driveway, and Laurel hugged the curb with her rented vehicle. At least the long night ahead gave him time to persuade her about looking to the future. His conscience slammed against his heart. They had an unsolved case. Hadn't he decided his first concern should be his grandparents and all the victimized elderly's welfare? And what about the condition of her soul? But to reach that area, he needed to understand her past. Anything else was selfish.

Before exiting his truck, he reached into his glove box and swallowed three Tylenol dry. The prescription meds would have to wait. He stepped out and chirped the truck alarm system. A moment later Laurel joined him. Her incredible nut-brown eyes still stole his breath.

"Are you sure you feel up to this?" she said.

He chuckled. What a loaded question. "How did you respond to that when you were shot? I recall a concern for Phantom while you looked for clues in the dark."

"Touché. You could nap while I stand guard. Then we can do the searching."

"Batman and Batgirl work together. Beside, you're recovering from a bullet too."

"Not by the same gun."

"More of a reason for us to stay alert. Let's park our vehicles in the garage." He pointed to the driveway winding around the home. "If someone shows up, I want the element of surprise on our side."

"Sure. With the lights on, it'll look like your grandparents are at home."

They drove to the rear of the house and parked inside the four-car garage.

"Look at the tools." She ran her fingers over a locked chest. "Why two enormous tool chests?"

"One for Gran and one for Gramps."

"After spending time with your grandmother, I'm not surprised."

"Until five years ago, she changed the oil on their vehicles."

Laurel shook her head. After ensuring the house was clear, a task in which she let him lead the room-to-room search, she touched his arm.

"I want to see the trophy room again," she said. "The one with the animals."

He laughed. "We call it the game room."

"More like big game room. Did your grandfather shoot the bear, lion, jackal, and I think the mounting was a crocodile?"

"Nope."

"So he collected them?"

"Nope."

"Then why are they there?"

"Gran shot them."

She shook her head. "Is there anything she hasn't done?"

"She has a bucket list."

"What's left?"

"Crocheting a blanket for my child."

She drew in a breath. "I see."

Sometimes the thought of parenthood gave him hope of doing better than his own parents. Other times it shook him worse than facing bad guys without a weapon.

They entered the kitchen.

"Wow." She surveyed the room, and her eyes sparkled. "This kitchen is amazing. Stainless steel appliances, and I'd trade my stash of Snickers for these copper pans. Cupboards to the ceiling too." She whirled around. "Two gas ovens. Yet it's comfortable. Like your grandparents . . . and you."

"Did I hear a compliment?"

"If you think being compared to a kitchen the size of my apartment is a compliment, go for it."

"Why not? Don't know about you, but I'm hungry."

"Me too."

"Great. I'll put on coffee," he said. "We could have omelets before we dive into the night's search."

"Perfect." She tore off the wig and washed her hands. "Lots of veggies would be great. Did you ask permission to look through your grandparents' personal possessions?"

"Will a verbal suffice?"

"I suppose." She grabbed the refrigerator door. "Got any bacon?"

Daniel assessed the woman before him, figure perfect and yet she loved Snickers and bacon. "Yep. May find a few buttermilk biscuits too."

She offered a high five, and they both winced with their gunshot wounds. He liked spending time with her. Very much.

"How many people cook this time of night with firearms tucked in their waistbands?" she said.

"Few, Agent Evertson." He faced her. "Kinda cool, though."

She opened the fridge. "We need apple jelly."

"Get the dairy-free butter, too," Daniel said.

"Lactose intolerant?"

"Another one of my dark secrets."

She stood with his butter substitute in one hand and apple jelly in the other. "So am I."

"You mean we finally have something in common?"

"That and slugs."

Daniel whipped up omelets while she fried bacon and warmed biscuits.

She set silverware, napkins, and large glasses of orange juice on the table. "This smells so good."

"Then let's eat." He filled two plates with their feast. "Mind if I pray first?"

Her face went blank.

"It'll be short."

"Sure, why not?" Her terse tone indicated she wasn't on board, but her disapproval didn't stop him.

His prayer lasted all of twenty seconds, but they still ate in silence and cleaned up the kitchen with only a few words exchanged between them. Daniel left her to her thoughts and rummaged through the upper cabinets for anything Gramps might have hidden away.

Laurel paced the kitchen floor, reminding him of a caged cat.

"I'm not apologizing for praying before we ate."

She opened a cabinet filled with cookbooks. "Give me some hints about where your grandparents might hide this thing, whatever it is."

"Avoiding a subject doesn't make it go away."

"A business card or a phone number that seems obscure?"

"Laurel, being a Christian doesn't mean you've entered enemy territory."

She kept her back turned to him. "As if you're going to influence me. Morton Wilmington already tried, and both of you struck out."

"Is God the problem here?"

"Something like that."

"How about an open mind?"

"No, Daniel. I'm not interested."

"Why?"

"Because of who I am."

"You're not making sense. We're both in law enforcement. My past and my beliefs are why I'm committed to the police department."

"My past is why I have no choice but to avoid God. Conversation ended."

He took her shoulders and turned her to face him, gazing into the depths of her smoldering eyes. "If you can't trust me after what we've been through, who can you trust?"

She trembled. "I don't think there's anyone alive who fits the bill."

He released her shoulders and planted a kiss on her cheek. "We have time to find something or nothing. Tell me what's tearing you apart. I care too much to see you upset."

"You faced your demons and mastered them." She stepped back, releasing his hold on her. "I am a demon."

CHAPTER 41

Laurel fought her staggering emotions as Daniel's face softened. "Don't pity me." She meant the words to be harsh. Instead they choked out, sounding like the frightened little girl inside her.

"This is not about pity. I see a beautiful woman who's hurting. All I want is to help."

Her stomach tightened. "I'm the kind your grandmother warned you about, the kind who hung out with your mother. Name it, and I've probably done it."

"Who are you running from? Yourself? God? Or me? Actually, I'm not the real issue. I know from experience it's God."

She frowned, doubting he had any clue how she felt. "You think because you visited your mother in prison that everything's right in your world."

"She told me never to come back. My point is I know life is hard. When we keep the junk bottled up inside, we end up like those who hurt us."

She crossed her arms, realizing her body language indicated what she wanted to hide. Coming here was a bad idea. Daniel seemed to look straight through her, but he didn't see the ugliness. She avoided his gaze while wrestling for control. "My story is a nightmare. Wilmington learned most of it through his sources. Su-Min heard bits and pieces."

"I don't judge. I read media reports about what you had to do regarding Wilmington. I have a good ear. You could start at the beginning and finish at the end."

If only she could make all the nightmares disappear. "You make it sound simple."

"I know better. Every word and memory will be tough." He nodded at the coffeemaker. "We have plenty of coffee and lots of time."

She hated her inability to stay strong. Why not unload so he'd stop pursuing her? "All right."

He gestured to a kitchen chair, and she lowered herself onto it. Her gentle giant seated himself across the table and took her hand. He smiled, and she clawed for courage. Could she tell him about the night her world collapsed and how it hadn't made sense for far too many years?

"What if we're interrupted?"

"We'll pick up where we left off. If it's easier, close your eyes."

She obeyed and was immediately transported back to a peaceful time, when her world danced and sang to a little girl's whim—the days when she and Mom baked cookies and visited the art museum, and Dad showed her how to ride a horse and play math games. "When I was ten years old, while I slept in my canopy bed in a room painted pink, with my dolls and stuffed animals in perfect order, burglars broke into our home. I heard two shots and rushed out of bed and down the stairs, surprising two masked thieves. They must have thought shooting a child was beneath them because they left through the back door." How many times had she wished they'd killed her, too? She opened her eyes.

"My mother had collapsed on the floor near the sofa with a hole in her chest, and Dad made it as far as the kitchen. A shot in the head. Blood everywhere. The walls, furniture. I called 911, but my parents bled out before the ambulance arrived. Mom struggled for breath and whispered my name. I cried for God to save them, but He refused." Memories sliced through her heart.

How many times had Miss Kathryn begged her to talk about that night?

"The police never found the killers. My whereabouts were kept secret because law enforcement feared my life could be in danger. Social services placed me in a foster home—a little girl overcome with bitterness, hurt, and incredible loneliness. Rebellion became my middle name. My foster parents tried to reach me, and Miss Kathryn never gave up. No one could take my parents' place, and I refused to let anyone into my hellish world. Miss Kathryn showed me unconditional love. She showed me in every way what it meant to love with no stipulations." She drew in a breath that hurt.

"Don't stop now." He lightly squeezed her hand.

She'd come this far, but her heart seemed cold, like the little girl in her nightmares never existed. Laurel tried to smile, but it refused to grace her lips. "In the past, I worked as a cryptologist, where I decoded puzzles, even though I can't make the jagged pieces of my own life fit. So that's why I'm on a crusade to stop anyone who threatens others." She stood from the chair, not willing to look at him, and walked into the mammoth living room. Her energy depleted, she sank into the cushions of the sofa. Daniel followed her into the dark room and eased down beside her.

"Miss Kathryn was a Christian. I had no clue what she meant. Neither was I interested. Her husband tolerated me because of her. He had no use for a little girl who swore like a sailor and later drank like one. I attended church with her, but I couldn't trust a God who'd allowed the horror in my life." She paused, reining in the tears. "Miss Kathryn was my lifeline."

"Love works that way," Daniel said. "It's a glimpse of how life is supposed to be."

His tender words swirled through her. "As a teen, I grew tired of feeling invisible and wanted someone to notice me. My method was sexual promiscuity." She caught his chocolate gaze. "Except I refused Miss Kathryn's husband, and he hated me for it. I locked in a scholarship at Stanford and later earned my master's. Went to work for the FBI, and here I am." She rubbed her arms. "Daniel, there's more. The agent who was killed the night of Wilmington's arrest? I thought I could talk Wilmington down and hesitated. That's when he was shot." She swiped at a tear. "Jesse had a family, a dear wife and children. He was a Christian. A lot of good his faith did for him or his loved ones."

"Laurel, his death was not your fault. The agent made the choice when he planted his feet at the scene."

If only she could believe him, maybe the blackness covering her heart would vanish. "I transferred from undercover to cryptology after Wilmington was sent to prison. Tried to put it all behind me. Thatcher Graves had been my partner before Jesse, and he suggested we work together again, but I couldn't. I stopped sleeping around and placed my heart in a cocoon. Then I learned Miss Kathryn had dementia and her husband had shoved her into a nursing home that barely met state requirements. I'm sure his reason for not allowing me to see her was because I refused to sleep with him. Being alone at my desk was worse. So I transferred to white collar."

She was thankful for the shadows so she couldn't see his condemnation. "You heard it all. Junk my counselor has been trying to pry out of me. You should consider hanging a shingle, 'Police Officer and Psychologist.'" Now for the inevitable question. "Where's your interest in me now?"

"The same place it's always been. You haven't said a thing to change my mind. You heard my story, and now I've heard yours."

Shock trickled through her. "Didn't you listen?"

"I heard a story about a beautiful woman who's smart, compassionate, and loves my gran and gramps." His fingers brushed against her cheek, and his gaze captured hers. His lips met hers gently like she'd imagined. She wanted to stop him, but one time shouldn't be a problem.

When the kiss ended, he drew her closer to him. "When this case is over, will you give me a chance?"

"I can't promise." She sensed an urgency to fall into the warmth of his words, but he deserved so much more. The sharp edges of regret cut deep, but someday the shattered pieces would all come together. At least she could cling to a dream. But not tonight. "I can help look for what might have your grandparents in danger."

CHAPTER 42

At midnight, Daniel wanted to end the search. He'd checked Gramps's hard files for past business dealings and gone through each one. Nothing indicated a potential threat. His wrist pounded like a war drum, and his efforts to find an unknown item among his grandparents' belongings produced nothing. Each time he attempted to use his injured wrist, pain shot up his arm, adding frustration with it.

His current project was to sort through Gramps's desk, the place where the brochure from Lifestyle Insurance had been found. But nothing obvious or hidden surfaced. He needed to stretch his legs and dump energy into his body.

"You're pale," Laurel said. "Why not take a nap, and I'll keep looking?"

"When I find something substantial, I'll call it a night."

"More like a day. Okay, how about a break? We can analyze your grandparents' habits."

His agony won. "Short break."

She pointed down the hall to the living room. "Stretch out on the sofa, and we can talk."

"Keep the lights on, and don't let me sleep." Once he rested his head on a pillow, and she curled up in Gramps's chair, he explored his brain for a hiding place. "I'm fresh out of ideas. Beginning to wonder if this is a wild-goose chase. A smart man would see the life insurance policy is what the scammer values. I imagine it's a chunk of change."

"What is your grandparents' schedule?"

"Up early, take their meds, shower, and dress. Until recently, on to Silver Hospitality for six out of seven days."

"Where do they keep their meds?"

"Some are at the facility. A supply is with them at the hotel, but extras are kept in their bathroom. Why?"

"Great place to hide something small." She wagged a finger at him. "Stay right there. I'm going to take a look."

"For what?"

"Not sure. Remember I found a flash drive in Wilmington's hidden safe."

"I'm right there with you." Daniel forced his aching body off the sofa. Crazy, useless wrist.

In the master bathroom, which was larger than his bedroom and contained more marble than he'd ever own, Daniel opened the cabinet containing the prescription meds. "It looks like the back room of Walgreens," he said.

"Or CVS." She pulled the lid off each one. "Agents are working on your theory, the idea that Cayden and Wilmington are preying on the elderly with health issues by hacking into a pharmaceutical database, most likely Almet. But that might be too obvious."

"My grandparents' prescriptions come from the same pharmacy, one of the most reputable in the country." Daniel picked up a bottle of antidepressants with Gran's name on it. But she refused to use them.

She reached for her phone. "I'm sure agents have looked into that." She typed a text message. "I'll find out for sure."

"To see if Preston has researched it?"

"Yep. I'd like to see a comparison of the victims and the pharmacies they used." She laid her burner on the counter. "Take a deep breath, Officer Hilton. You could use a little color."

"You're as tired as I am. I'll look through the top shelf while you wait for a reply." He pointed. "It's Gramps's storehouse."

She stepped back, a little colorless herself in Daniel's opinion, but he wouldn't go there. Two type A personalities could inflict a lot of damage. A multitude of reasons lined up for her less-than-stellar appearance, from her shoulder, to lack of rest, to her confession. He'd process it later. All he could see was a little blonde girl with sorrowful eyes who needed someone to love her. If his images were pity, then he was guilty. Not the kind of sympathy and compassion some men ran from, but the kind survivors were made from. Laurel had fought and won—she simply didn't understand victory came with sacrifices, and the One who'd given her stamina had already saved her.

Her phone buzzed and she snatched it. "Yeah, individual pharmacies have been cleared."

One by one, he opened Gramps's prescriptions, not without a struggle, everything from liquid cough syrup to old meds once used for his Alzheimer's. Nothing out of the ordinary. In the far back, he noticed a ballpoint pen. Grabbing a tissue, he draped his fingers around it and made a path through the bottles. He slid the pen to the front and read the advertisement on the barrel. "Are you ready for this?"

"Only if it's good."

"The pen is from Almet Pharmaceuticals in Miami. Where did he get this? A lead? Wonder if Gramps will remember where he got the pen. Send SSA Preston the info."

She grinned. "On it, Officer Hilton. This can't be what they're looking for, though."

"You're right. My wrist has gotten in the way of my better judgment. Those guys want my grandparents dead to collect on the life insurance. Not a ballpoint pen. I'm sure Preston appreciates the late-night texts."

She scrunched her forehead. "Daniel, I'm not sure what to think. But this needs to be investiga—"

The piercing crash of broken glass snatched his nerves on alert. A siren burst through the house. Daniel rounded the corner to his grandparents' bedroom, where a red light flashed on the alarm system, an indicator that someone had attempted access through a bedroom window on the second story.

CHAPTER 43

Daniel whipped out his Glock and cut the lights, then glanced at the alarm panel in the master bedroom. "We have a visitor in the rear, west side of the house. There's a balcony right outside it. Easy for someone to scale. I'm heading upstairs."

"Right behind you."

He frowned. "You could get hurt."

"Batgirl has your back."

"Are you pulling the FBI card?"

"Naturally."

"Rather have you than anyone else. The alarm system is tied to the police station, so we'll have help soon. I'm not disarming it."

She didn't respond, but he didn't expect her to. He crept through the house to the stairway, Laurel behind him, her presence strangely comforting. Not the time to label it caring. It was her training with the FBI or simply a body with a weapon. He climbed the winding staircase and reached the landing. The construction gave the intruder an opportunity to bring them down on the turn.

Daniel reached behind and stopped her. No sounds, only the knowledge someone lurked upstairs. Messner was dead. With the hospital shootout, Fields was out of commission tonight. Who'd yanked her into the black Escalade? Cayden? One of his men? How many roamed the upstairs, and were they looking to eliminate his grandparents? Were the orders to get rid of Laurel and him?

The third step from the top always creaked. He whispered the potential giveaway and motioned for her to follow. He aimed his gun. He'd been in better condition, not the best physique for a shootout. The upper level held thirty-five hundred square feet of bedrooms, baths, a library, and a sitting room—all rarely used. Each area contained corners and closets to hide.

A flashbang to flush out the intruder would help, but those were in his truck. In the hallway, he and Laurel slid into the first room on the right, a bath. A quick search revealed they were alone.

Risking revealing their whereabouts, he ventured forward. "Hey, you're trapped up here. Come on out before this gets bloody."

When only silence greeted them, he and Laurel moved into an adjoining bedroom and cleared it just as gunfire broke out in the hall. From the sound of the weapon, Daniel guessed it was a Tactical 12. The pistol grip and strap would make it easy to carry, and the glass-break attachment got the intruder inside. The direction confirmed he and Laurel were dealing with at least one trained shooter.

Across the hallway was Gramps's library. It had an adjoining bath with an exit closer to the shooter. "Cover me," Daniel whispered.

Laurel opened fire into the hallway, allowing him cover to the library. He cleared the room and bath, searching for whoever was after them.

"Hey, scum," Laurel said. "You don't scare me."

Nothing. Had the shooter figured out he and Laurel had separated? The walls wouldn't withstand a barrage of bullets, and neither could Daniel risk her getting hurt.

She laughed. "Fields must have a new puppy. Her other dogs have gotten themselves killed."

A rattle sharpened Daniel's awareness. The shooter had bumped into Gran's shelf of breakable giraffes, and Daniel knew exactly where the person stood. He must not be wearing night goggles.

Laurel shot three more times down the hallway, and a faint

grunt met his ears. A barrage of fire from the injured man stopped Daniel from bursting into the hallway to take him down. She continued to fire, blocking the shooter's advance and forcing him to remain in the west section of the house.

The shooter released another round.

The firefight stopped.

Daniel slipped toward the bedroom where the shooter had gained access to the house. At the balcony, he spotted a figure darting out from shrubbery below, then rushing into the wooded area. Daniel inserted a fresh magazine.

"I'm going after him."

"Right here. Go."

If he'd been a swearing man, he'd have twisted a few phrases about the condition of his wrist, especially when he encountered the thorns on Gran's climbing roses. He jumped to the ground and followed the shooter's path into the woods separating his grandparents' property from a narrow creek. The trees lifted branches into a starless night where light sensors didn't cover. He stood and listened. To his right, a single limb cracked. He didn't move a muscle. The intruder had solid training, and that awareness put every nerve on alert. Stealing closer toward the sound, he heard the distinct whine of a motorcycle engine drown out the night sounds. Daniel rushed ahead in time to hear the engine escape into the night. Had to be Cayden.

* * *

7:35 A.M. THURSDAY

After the long night's vigil with Daniel at the Hilton home, Laurel arrived at her apartment shortly after seven thirty, ready for a hot shower. Her shoulder ached too. Hungry—and furious that the shooter had escaped—she wanted relief from the weariness pelting her body. The time spent at the Hilton home had uncovered only a ballpoint pen from Almet Pharmaceuticals.

The early morning shootout attracted cops and the FBI to an

otherwise-quiet community, and she'd yanked on the wig. Within twenty minutes, the property swarmed with law enforcement types—questions and more questions. Media joined the mix, and she slipped back to avoid the cameras, even with her change of appearance. Life seemed to throw one wrench after another.

The massive home would take a fortune to repair. Bullet holes peppered the upstairs walls along with broken glass and destroyed expensive collectibles.

"My grandparents care more about us finding who's committing the crimes than the cost of their valuables," Daniel had said.

She doubted a fingerprint sweep would reveal a thing. Not a trace of blood dripped on the hardwood there, which seemed unusual since they heard the intruder grunt. Whoever broke into the Hilton home had training and skills above her pay grade. Which said Delta Force and Geoff Cayden.

She desperately needed a diversion and time to think. Her beloved Phantom crossed her mind. After a long nap, she'd visit him, hopefully take a ride if just for an hour. Stress had her on overload, although SSA Preston would frown on her taking the afternoon off. Daniel wanted to pick her up at two thirty in his bodyguard mode.

Laurel pushed her thoughts aside and turned on the shower. She grabbed her comfy Mickey Mouse pj's and a pair of thick socks.

No sooner was law enforcement notified about the crime than a text from Wilmington came through for her and Daniel wanting to know if they were okay. Never mind how she felt about the felon. How did he learn so quickly about the incident?

She and the dark-haired police officer were drawn to each other, but why? They disagreed constantly, sharing a pigheaded streak wide enough to scatter the strongest of fighters. Yet their playful bantering while they prepared last night's omelets, bacon, and biscuits had been . . . easy.

Before the prayer thing.

Before she confessed her past.

"You haven't said a thing to change my mind," he'd said.

She believed codes and puzzles went together like ice cream and cake, law and order. This time, the situation had escalated to hurting others she cared about. She needed to harness her personal feelings, but her normal methods of control weren't working. And she was running out of options.

Laurel let the hot water massage her aching muscles. She grabbed the shampoo and closed her eyes. Only her bed would feel better. As she allowed the steam to fill her senses, a nudging at her spirit blindsided her.

More than her strange preoccupation with Daniel, thoughts of tomorrow and the next day wouldn't leave her alone. How many times had she faced death and escaped its clutches? How many lucky breaks were left?

Miss Kathryn's words echoed in her mind. One day Laurel would be faced with a decision, a choice of living either the world's way or God's. She said every person encountered a breaking point when their need for a relationship with God became real and they had a choice to make.

The confession to Daniel hadn't been the only thing bothering her. During the afternoon when she met him and his grandparents at the hospital, the love and unity the small family shared was more than blood or the same last name. She recognized it. Craved it. Hope. Something she didn't have of life beyond the grave.

In the past, she wasn't interested in what she couldn't see or touch. The world offered more: Love when she needed companionship. A career to give her purpose and boost her ego by making the world safe. Friends who accepted what they saw in her. But nothing filled the emptiness, a hollow black hole where no one cared.

Maybe someday she'd find the answers.

CHAPTER 44

After informing his grandparents about the condition of their home, Daniel persuaded them to change hotels again with police protection and an exchange of nursing staff. Exhaustion punched his body, and his wrist stung. In his twenties, he'd have barreled through the day. Fat chance of making it through the next few hours with any logic before taking some downtime. Maybe he needed to increase his workout, build up his endurance.

His thoughts drifted to Laurel. For the first time, he understood why she pushed him away. She believed she was unworthy of love—from God or him—stemming back to when her parents were killed and she'd been powerless to save them. Sad. She had so much to offer, but she didn't see it. Her past only made him more determined to show his caring, fast growing into something more. After all, she didn't refuse his offer to escort her to the stables as Krestle the bodyguard.

When Daniel reached his temporary home in last night's disguise, Wilmington was leaving in his Mercedes with his driver. No surprise there. The man kept strange hours. Daniel waved and waited for him to pull out of the driveway. Wilmington parked and stepped out.

"Morning." Daniel exited and walked his way.

"Need anything beside a good night's sleep?"

He laughed. "World peace."

"I'll second that. She didn't get hurt, right?"

Daniel shook his head. The man had feelings for Laurel, maybe even loved her. It was evident in the way his tone changed when he spoke of her. Hard to understand, considering their history. "She's at home resting, and we're taking a ride out to the stables later."

"That horse is like your Harley."

"So your men have been inside my garage?" *And are they responsible for the bomb in my truck?*

He shrugged. "I believe in being thorough."

Daniel was too tired to argue. "It's my way to escape the pressures of life. Are you playing golf?"

"Breakfast. Want to come along?"

"Not this morning. I need sleep." Daniel studied the man neither he nor Laurel could trust. Manipulation? Deceit? He smiled. "I'll cook tomorrow. I can do mean waffles."

"Sounds good. Why is a bright man like you working a beat instead of a detective's desk?"

"First of all, I'm not bright. Just an average police officer on loan to the FBI." He drew in a breath. "Right now this is what God wants me to do. It's not about how many crimes I prevent or how many people I help. My significance is in being available for whatever's needed."

"I see you one day as Houston's police chief."

"We'll see."

"Get some rest. Need you carrying the flag. Two minds are always better than one," Wilmington said. "And when God's in charge and minds have the same goal, how can we lose?"

He climbed back into his car, and the driver sped away.

Daniel had an errand to finish before resting—running the fingerprints on the ballpoint pen in his pocket. He'd gotten permission from SSA Preston to take it to the police lab. Even if the original holder of the pen wore latex, leather, or fabric gloves, forensics had ways of detecting the print by matching friction ridges, the butt of a palm, the body's natural oils, or telltale ID on the object. Criminals often preferred the tight fit of a latex glove, which over time offered more identification possibilities. If a print belonged to Messner, Cayden, or Fields, evidence piled against the threesome and made for a solid reason to bring Cayden in. He startled. Banking on a ballpoint pen for evidence and recalling experience in law enforcement revealed his lack of sleep.

The early morning intruder had pro written all over him. Anyone who could bounce back from a bullet that fast was wearing something stronger than Kevlar. He'd read about various new fibers stronger than the department-issued body armor. Possibly Zylon. Transparent and flexible, making it easier for the wearer to move. Expensive, which meant the scammers were backed by high dollars.

He reached into his truck for a bottle of water and three Tylenol. Where was this all leading? Doubts about Wilmington assaulted him like bullets.

CHAPTER 45

1:30 P.M. THURSDAY

Daniel slept hard for three hours until his phone alarm jarred his peaceful world. He had one hour before picking up Laurel, and although he didn't want to crawl out of bed to shower, he wanted to be with her more.

As he forced himself awake, the thought of someone getting to her by doing damage to her horse crossed his mind. Worked in *The Godfather*. Pretty low blow, but Daniel would suggest housing her horse at another stable. In the middle of brushing his teeth, he texted Wilmington. If the bad guy had access to Laurel's personal life, he'd target her horse.

Do u have a man on phantom?

Should have thought of that. on it

One of Wilmington's men would be watching Laurel and him this afternoon. Better one armed man on their side than a shooter with a nervous trigger finger. Of course, that implied he trusted Wilmington, and he didn't.

Laurel met Daniel at the door looking far more rested than he felt. Dressed to ride, she put purpose into gorgeous. How this woman could make it through a shootout and look this good amazed him.

"Mr. Krestle, you look more tired than I am."

"I've been busy. The FBI lab couldn't lift any prints other than Gramps's from the pen."

"But we're keeping at it, and it is a source of evidence."

"Thanks. I needed a boost to my ego."

They climbed into his BMW and headed out of town.

"I checked just before you got here, and the FBI sweep hasn't found a thing on the hospital shooter," she said. "The blood sample will take a few days even with a rush. And the DNA tests won't be available until the end of next week. Do these people ever slip?"

"You and I are a pitiful case, gunshots and sleep-deprived. Yes, they slip, and we'll find them."

"We're battle scarred, Daniel. Have you talked to Wilmington today?"

He laughed. "Have you been spying on me?"

"I'm a good FBI agent. So you did."

Daniel told her about Wilmington this morning. "He's putting a man on Phantom."

She whipped her attention to him. "Hadn't thought about my stallion."

"Want to move him?"

"I'll make the arrangements this afternoon."

"Wilmington's man will be watching."

She nodded. "I have to do what I can. The FBI doesn't have an animal protection division. Wilmington never had a problem killing a man. He wouldn't think twice about harming a horse."

Daniel reached for her hand in the car. "We'll ride this out to see what side of the fence he falls on. My vote's for a life sentence." He refused to mention Wilmington's feelings for her.

The countryside welcomed them, but Daniel had a difficult time enjoying nature. "Are you meeting with Cayden tonight?"

She nodded. "Wilmington says we'll find out about the fundraiser. I want to know how the money's being laundered. Fields is supposed to be there too, but I don't see how."

"I expect to learn she's dead. No one could survive those wounds without medical care." He paused. "Doctors can be forced to treat someone at gunpoint. But we don't have any reports of missing or dead doctors either."

At the stables, the aroma of fresh hay and horse pulled Daniel back to the days when he and his grandparents rode horses. They walked down the long row of stalls, admiring the splendid display of horseflesh.

"I should have asked if you rode," she said.

"I'm a Texas boy. Until six years ago, Gran and Gramps had a small ranch near San Antonio. Beautiful rolling acres—a lazy creek, a few longhorn cattle, a half-dozen quarter horses, and a huge log cabin. We spent many weekends and summers there. Gran and Gramps taught me how to fish, shoot, and use a bow and arrow."

"You learned how to hunt too? I should have guessed that with your game room."

"Gran can bring a deer down and grill a mean venison steak."

"Make sausage too?"

"Of course. We've done it all. When I was four, they had a leather jacket made for me from one of our hunting trips."

"You had such a wonderful life." She paused. "So did I until the tragedy. I must keep the good memories intact. Without them, I'll grow into a bitter old woman." She drew in a breath. "At least I'm telling myself that now."

At Phantom's stall, she wrapped her arms around the horse's neck, whispering to the animal like Daniel wished she'd do to him.

"He's a beautiful stallion," he said. "No wonder you're devoted to him. But I'll keep my distance until he's okay with me."

"I'll convince him you're a good guy." She patted the stallion's neck. "I've always called him my boyfriend."

"How can a guy measure up to a white stallion who can do no wrong?"

"That's the point." She laughed.

Daniel helped her saddle Phantom the best he could. Between his wrist, her shoulder, and an awareness of a stallion's temperament—they were clients for a nursing home.

"I need a horse to ride," he said.

"Phantom is buddies with a gelding."

"Perfect. No repeats of the last time you rode alone."

"As if you could stop a sniper."

"We have an extra pair of eyes, remember?"

She nodded. "True. Let's get one of the hands to saddle you up. I don't want to attempt it again." She disappeared to the office.

When a mount was ready, the two rode out into the pasture. Dazzling sunshine met them, along with trees still green. But the cooler temps marked Daniel's favorite time of the year. He pointed to a couple of squirrels scampering over branches but saw her distraction. "What happened back there?"

"I'm thinking before I spill my guts." She tucked a strand of hair behind her ear.

"We can work through it together."

"Okay." Her gaze stayed fixed ahead. "Probably need to record that. Might never hear it from me again."

"Yes, ma'am."

"The stable hand told me a man stopped by last week and requested information about Phantom. Said he wanted to make an offer on him."

Daniel wasn't surprised and didn't think she was either. "Did he leave contact information?"

"No. Asked for mine and got it."

"Description?"

"Bald and muscular."

"Not good, and no one meeting his description has crossed my path," Daniel said. "Glad you're having Phantom transferred until this is over."

"Me too. This has gotten way too personal."

"Would you like to take a walk around the pond?"

They dismounted and made their way through thick grass. "I do fish," she said. "Miss Kathryn used to take me. Never mind how I felt about slimy bait and cleaning guts. She gave me her favorite cornmeal breading, forced me to fry 'em up."

"You're kidding. I see a fishing trip in our future."

She stopped. "Are you sure?"

He understood exactly what simmered beneath her words. "Any girl who can clean and fry fish hits the top of my list, especially one who can also use a gun."

Her cheeks flushed, or was the color due to the afternoon sun? Whatever the reason, he enjoyed it very much. Daniel stepped closer, his attention on her nut-brown eyes, her flawless skin. He wanted to kiss her. But that would risk a bullet in both of them. Instead he backed up.

"Thanks," she whispered. "Daniel, I need time to think about us. Too much too soon."

Her words sparked reality. "I understand. Forcing a relationship will push you away and distract us from what we need to do."

"One of us could make a mistake while worrying about the other. I couldn't survive losing another partner."

He smiled. "You're one smart woman. Ready to head back? Being alone with you is tempting. All this nature stuff is driving me nuts."

At the stables, Laurel frowned at Phantom. "He's missed me. I can tell by the way he keeps nudging me. I'm going to brush him down the best I can." She pointed to the end of the stables, where Daniel had seen a vending machine earlier. "If you'll get us a couple bottles of water, I'll get started. May take a while with one hand."

"Ah, the horse over me. I know where I rank." He left her alone to search for cold water. A driver unloaded feed from a pickup, and the young stable hand stacked it in a corner. Daniel listened to the conversation.

"You're new to the delivery service," said the hand, who couldn't be much more than eighteen. "Early too. Wasn't expecting the feed until Tuesday."

"Just following orders."

"Don't I know it." The hand spit a wad of tobacco juice, then examined one of the bags. "The feed's a different brand."

Daniel's ears perked. The conversation continued about the weather. When the driver said his good-byes, Daniel typed in the license plate number on his phone. He approached the young hand.

"Yes, sir," the hand said. "How can I help you?"

He stuck out his hand. "C. W. Krestle. I have a few questions concerning the delivery you just received."

"Why?"

"I'm part of an investigative team who's looking for an operation that poisons horses."

The hand's eyes widened. "The boss isn't here, and I don't want to get into trouble."

"I agree. Taking chances can mean a mistake."

He grinned, reminding Daniel of a fence post–thin cowboy from the Old West. "Craziest thing," the young man said. "I don't have feed on this week's order, and it's a brand we don't use. Not even delivered on the right day." He bent to read the label. "Not a good blend for our horses either."

"I'd like to have this tested before you use it. Why take the chance?"

The young hand paled. "Really."

"Can I take a bag with me? Don't let anyone use these others. In fact, do you have your boss's number? I'll call him."

He produced a card. "What kind of lowlife poisons horses?"

Daniel lifted a brow. "Read the news. They're all over the place. Sometimes they add people to their list of victims."

"What if the delivery guy returns?"

"Be friendly and call 911."

Daniel phoned in the license plate number and hoisted a bag of feed to his shoulder, gritting his teeth with the pain in his wrist. Between the man inquiring about purchasing Phantom and the possibility of tainted feed, Laurel would be ready to take her horse home.

"You were gone a long time," she said, brushing Phantom's mane. "Thanks for the water. What are you doing with that sack of feed?"

He explained what happened. "Once Phantom is in a temporary hiding place, I'll get the feed tested."

"License plate number?"

"Already called it in."

She leaned against the stallion. "I understand the old psychology thing about getting to me via those things that matter." She frowned. "I'm ready to unload my Glock on whoever's responsible."

Daniel hated not knowing the scammer's plan. "We just need to find out who is responsible."

CHAPTER 46

Laurel and Wilmington walked into a small Greek restaurant on the southwest side of Houston. Wilmington escorted her to a single man at a booth. No other persons were around.

The man, about Wilmington's age with a muscular build, stood. "Good to see you, Mort." He smiled at Laurel, but in the dim lighting she couldn't see his eyes. "I'm Geoff Cayden." He took her hand. "It's a pleasure, Laurel, and congratulations on your engagement."

"Thank you." She'd remembered the ring. Felt as heavy as the burden to end the scam.

"How's the shoulder?"

How very nice. "Better. Keeps me sharp."

With the pleasantries ended, they took their places in the booth and ordered drinks and food.

"Only a Coke Zero?" Cayden said. "You don't have to hold back. Share a bottle of wine with me."

Wilmington waved his hand. "Keeps my head clear. Laurel and I prefer to keep the alcohol behind closed doors."

For the next several minutes until their food arrived, Cayden and Wilmington talked about old days in the military. Stunts they'd pulled and how good it felt to be together again. Cayden's wife and daughter, who were clueless to his operation, never learned any of it.

"Where's Josie? I thought she'd be ready to come out of the closet," Wilmington said.

"She couldn't be with us," Cayden said. "Had other things going on."

"Why's that?" Wilmington said. "Is she still opposed to us joining the operation?"

"Not anymore." Cayden lifted a glass of Bordeaux to his lips.

Was Fields even alive? "I want to meet her," Laurel said. "To prove I'm on your side." No need to claim revenge. She'd already shown it.

Cayden laughed. "I'll pass on your comments. For your information, the fund-raiser will be my last gig of the year. Oh, the FBI questioned me with all the Almet people. Got nowhere. My wife was interviewed too. Got someone following her. Did they think I was stupid?" He laughed again.

Wilmington snorted. "They tail me everywhere I go. What's our cut?"

"Ten percent."

Wilmington seemed to ponder the situation. "Was that your decision or the silent partner's?"

"Always me."

Wilmington took a long drink of his Coke Zero. Laurel sensed he didn't believe Cayden.

"What do you want from us?" Wilmington said.

Cayden set his glass on the table. "The fund-raiser is the key here. We have live entertainment, a well-known Christian singer who will perform during the meal. You'll give your testimony and talk about how an elderly volunteer at the prison helped turn your life around. Then I'll speak—the favorite grandparent story—and encourage donations. Every guest will have an envelope with a form for them to donate with their credit card. Typical stuff. Except the security cameras will have a glitch. The donations will be gathered by servers, and Laurel will collect them in a basket. During a video with the lights down, Laurel will switch the basket and give the original one to a man who'll be stationed outside the door. When the lights come up, you and Laurel will still be with the basket. The singer will perform two more songs, giving my man time to get away. I'll close by asking you to pray before leaving. All three of us will be in plain sight."

"Later on, you cash in on the credit cards. Wait until the money clears, then send it offshore before we're paid?"

Cayden chuckled. "Something along those lines. I'll work on getting the money due me through several life insurance policies transferred to my silent partner. And then we'll all be paid."

"You said you were in charge," Wilmington said. "Why is it I've risked Laurel's and my future and dealt just with you when someone else is calling the shots?"

"I have it handled."

For a former Delta Force soldier, Cayden didn't lie well. Laurel touched Wilmington's arm. "I like the plan," she said. "Old friends are the ones to be trusted. Geoff is the victim. Someone hacked into the nonprofit's account and took off with thousands of dollars."

"We lay low," Cayden said. "Keep up appearances until the funds are available."

"Seems simple for 10 percent." Wilmington pushed back his grilled lamb. "Who stole my four mil?"

"Bro, I have no clue. I have feelers out there if it makes you feel any better."

"Appreciate it. What else is on the list for Laurel and me?"

"You two will take a trip to Paris and then a train to Switzerland using stored-value cards. A lovers' getaway. Then both of you will travel to Cairo, where I'll give you the name of a *hawala* there and the code. This will be one big explosion." Cayden's razor smile rested on Wilmington. "You've wanted a way to repay me."

Finally she'd learned how the money would be laundered. Neither the stored-value cards nor using a *hawala* were illegal. But absconding with credit card information would get Cayden solid time.

Now they needed rock-hard evidence before the night of the fund-raiser to make an arrest. She hoped SSA Preston was awake when she called him, because now they had the method.

CHAPTER 47

Daniel sat at his computer in Wilmington's kitchen. Weird . . . this was where the man had been arrested and Laurel's partner killed. Wilmington said the condo had been through a complete renovation. The blood had to have been splattered everywhere.

Last night Wilmington had relayed the meeting with Cayden and how October 15 was supposed to play out. Since Daniel didn't trust either of the men, he cemented the meeting with Laurel. Very easy to blame the crime on Wilmington and Laurel or just Laurel since she'd be passing the credit card envelopes to the driver. But that didn't put money in the operation's pocket, just framed someone else. Wilmington's revenge against Laurel bannered across his mind. Sure . . . a way to get even with her for sending him to prison. Then he changes his tune, acts like a great guy, offers to help the FBI, and asks for Laurel's support.

How did he plan to incriminate Daniel? Bore a hole into the public's view of the FBI? Good question. Maybe he'd figure it out later.

He scrolled through his burner phone for texts. SSA Preston reported that Marsha Leonard and Chef Steven remained mute. Probably afraid for their jobs. Gran indicated they both had evidence. Maybe he should talk to them. Daniel texted Preston and copied Laurel about a visit this afternoon to Silver Hospitality.

Daniel's mind swept from the fund-raiser on October 15 to his grandparents' safety to his growing feelings for Laurel. He understood the performance issues to prove her worth and still feeling undeserving. Add to that a heavy dose of control. What would it take for her to reach out to God?

Daniel refused to give up.

He poured another cup of coffee, adding an extra spoonful of sugar. Tylenol sat beside his computer, and he downed three. The clock alerted him to thirty minutes before calling to check on his grandparents. He grimaced with his own issues of concern for them, which he masked with an appropriate trait of responsibility. Who didn't have issues?

Wilmington walked into the kitchen, dressed for a run.

"Do you need a bodyguard?" Daniel said.

Wilmington grinned. "With the mood I'm in, my run will be up and down the stairs. I smell coffee."

"Second pot of the morning. Haven't checked my latest list of duties. Do bodyguards pour coffee?"

He chuckled. "Not unless I think a bomb's in it. The good Lord might take me home before I'm ready."

Daniel hesitated. "How much of this conversion business is bunk?"

"None. I'm simply new at it and rough around the edges."

Rough—or still in the other zone?

"How's the wrist?" Wilmington said.

"Hurts enough to make me mad."

"Revenge can be a good thing."

Daniel would remember that statement. "I have the latest on the horse feed."

"Poison?"

"Poisonous mushrooms again. The driver who delivered feed to the stables has a clean record. Stated he was paid to make the delivery. Everything on him checks out. Cayden or one of his men?"

"I'm sure Cayden ordered it."

"So what are your thoughts about last night?"

"A few things don't add up, but I'm working on it." Wilmington poured half a pot of coffee into a huge mug with a cross that said, *Jesus Loves the Ex-Con*.

"Where did you get the mug?"

Wilmington grinned. "Custom-made. A constant reminder of where I came from." He took a long drink of the coffee. "Nothing like the first drink in the morning. I was up all night thinking through this, and I'm beat." He took another gulp. "Among other things, I'm a coffee snob. Prison coffee was the worst, and now I'm making up for lost time."

"Right there with you. Have you figured out if Cayden told you the truth last night?"

"Sorry. Tired and distracted. He might be the Leopard, but his spots are true when it comes to me. Living through life and death bonds men." He set the mug on the counter. "Daniel, what if I'm wrong?"

This wasn't the time to debate honor among thieves. "Why would a man spend eight years finalizing an elaborate scam to give away 10 percent of a huge chunk of money?"

"That 10 percent is only from the fund-raising part."

"Okay. Where's Josie Fields?"

Wilmington eased onto a stool. "My guess is she's dead. Outlived her usefulness. She tugged at her leash too many times. Ran free rein with her own vendetta. Think about it. With her out of the picture, part of her cut goes to us minus the silent partner. Cayden's still making money."

"If by some chance she's alive, would she testify against him?"

"With all the charges against her? She'd plea-bargain her mother."

"Another reason why she's probably dead." Daniel reached for a Snickers he'd placed in the freezer.

Wilmington walked to the kitchen window overlooking the golf course. "I'm surprised Cayden allowed her to pull in her brother.

He must have done a decent job posing as the life insurance sales-man. They worked as a team. But anyone can be replaced."

"Did Fields shoot Laurel?"

Wilmington whirled around. "Sure did. Told Laurel last night on the way back to her apartment. Fields's miscalculation made the boss very unhappy. She had a vision problem and refused to wear glasses or contacts."

He was referring to Fields in the past tense. "Did he give you the name of the silent partner?"

"Not yet."

"Any ideas?"

"No. But I'll find out." Wilmington grabbed a banana and peeled it. "The doc tells me I need more potassium. Doesn't seem all that important right now, given all of us are flirting with death." He studied Daniel. "Laurel comes out of this alive. Understand?"

"I feel the same." Jealousy coiled up his spine, but he yanked it back.

"She'll get herself killed protecting you if it comes down to it."

Daniel had attempted to put ice on his feelings until the case was solved. But he'd failed. What he liked about her was her dogged determination for justice. It also scared him. The relationship had started out of concern for his grandparents, and that commitment had to be maintained. "Ever teamed up with a cop before?"

"Not legally. But you and I work good together, Daniel. For as long as it lasts."

"More like an unlikely alliance."

"I'm programmed for teetering on the edge of a cliff. It's a high that keeps me going. That and Jesus."

Where did Wilmington fit into all of this? For him and Cayden to outsmart the FBI and end up very rich men? Strange circumstances. Laurel called him last night after being dropped off at her apartment and hadn't said a word about Fields being the one who shot her.

He hoped this wild alliance didn't send him to the morgue or put him in a cell next to Wilmington. At least he'd never be bored.

✳ ✳ ✳

"We've made it through thirty minutes of lunch without an argument." Wilmington smiled, one that charmed the ladies. But not her.

Laurel had recognized a reporter from the *Chronicle* earlier. Their pic would hit the next issue.

All she could think about was Daniel. She longed to be with him, as though she were betraying him by seeing Wilmington. How insane was that? The gal who refused a relationship. She swung into agent mode. "Thoughts about last night?"

"Dessert? I remember you favored key lime pie. We could split it?"

Sharing dessert hit the intimate level. "No, thanks. All these meetings with food will make me too fat for my wedding dress."

He lifted a brow, and she saw it again. How could the man have feelings for her when she'd sent him to prison? And did he possibly think in all his wild dreams that she'd ever want to be with him?

Today he'd been his charming self. They'd discussed Phantom, her wounded arm, her past position as a cryptologist, and some of the things he'd learned in prison.

"Since I can't tempt you with dessert, how about coffee?"

"That works."

He summoned the server and ordered for them. "Aren't you curious about my conversion?"

"A little." She didn't believe it, choosing instead to think he'd acquired new manipulation skills. "How did a man like you make the decision to humble yourself? Turn your life over to a deity? I remember a few discussions that ruled out any mention of God." Her thoughts swirled through the night he got drunk and informed his bodyguards who was in control of the universe.

He seemed to contemplate his words. "I'll tell you, but I imagine you'll doubt everything I say. I would, in your shoes."

"Fair enough."

He took a deep breath. "A fight went down in the yard. Saw a man die in front of me. Gang related." He paused as though reflecting on his words. "I realized I could be the next one bleeding out. I walked away from the killing with a resolve to find a better way to live. My choices in life had brought me to a cell, facing consequences from the law and revenge from those I'd hurt. I studied Islam, Middle-Eastern religions, scientology, and anything else that seemed to have the answers to this dung-infestation we call life. Last of all, I picked up the Bible. Read it cover to cover. Became obsessed with every word. Found myself drawn to God's promises. Took nine months for me to give up my stubborn pride." Their coffee arrived. "Like giving birth."

Her insides tossed. Believing him was an impossibility. No future in it. "Do you feel different?"

He sighed and traced the rim of his coffee cup, an old habit. "It's easier to give up the anger and the entitlement cravings. Every day is a new one, and it's usually another vice for me to put away, overcome. Lots of guilt. Even more regret. Sometimes my thinking reverts to the old Morton, but not to the point of before. I call those poison thoughts."

Those in-between times were what bothered Laurel. "I'm not a believer, and I'm not totally convinced you are either."

He smiled. "You're right. No reason to believe me. Got to see it for yourself. I admire your tenacity, Laurel."

She glanced away, looking for an excuse to leave, but every conversation brought her closer to the needed evidence.

"Laurel, are you having a hard time finding my angle?"

"Mildly put."

"Quit looking. It's a situation between me and the Lord. Right now we need to find the proof before the fund-raiser." He sobered.

"What did Cayden mean by 'explosion'?"

"I hope he meant how the scam would affect the FBI." He

waved at the reporter snapping photos. "Four hundred hand-selected guests, known for their generosity to causes like this. They'll be tossing plastic like beads at Mardi Gras. And that doesn't include kitchen staff and servers. If he means a real explosion, the body count would be horrendous."

She swallowed hard. "You'll probe him about it?"

"For sure." He shook his head. "If he's planning to bomb the event, then the fund-raiser has to be cancelled. But I really think Cayden is in this for the money. No reason to cause mass chaos or an international manhunt."

She stared at him, wishing for telepathic abilities. "We have to find out. Isn't Cayden coming by your place tomorrow?"

"It's on the calendar. Daniel will be there, but Cayden won't like it. Might bring his own bodyguard. Did you receive the list of the fund-raiser guests?"

"Yes. Thanks. Surprised Cayden handed it over."

"I needed confirmation of the potential income. What did you make of it?"

"Some of the names are impressive. I forwarded it on to SSA Preston."

"So did I." He summoned the server for the check. "Laurel, there've been bad times between us. All my fault. The old Morton Wilmington would have gotten even, and you know it. And he'd have covered his tracks. I don't want to lose my freedom, but my biggest reason for helping the FBI was to prove my credibility to you and fulfill my vow to God."

"What?" She clenched her fist in her lap. "I don't understand."

"I want you to find God and hold on as tightly as you can."

"I have no reason to trust you."

"Rough edges can be filed down."

"Metaphorically speaking?"

"You'll find out soon enough."

An alert on her phone prompted her.

Josie Fields's body was found in a wooded rural area east of the Woodlands. Died of bullet wounds.

Laurel shook her head. The woman hadn't walked into those woods.

CHAPTER 48

An hour before the scheduled meeting at Wilmington's condo, Cayden changed the location to a bar at an airport hotel.

"Daniel, go with me on this one."

"I thought you trusted your old military bud."

"I do. But not necessarily his men."

"Which one?"

"Bulked-up Mexican. Bald. Mustache. Name's Ignacio Vega. He gave Messner the name of Crow."

"Why haven't I heard about him before?"

"Calm down, Daniel. I can't remember everything."

Daniel attempted to swallow his anger. "Vega worked for you too?"

Wilmington cringed. "Okay, I should have told you sooner."

"That would have kept eyes on one more man." Daniel thought twice about tearing into him. That could get him tossed out of the condo, and the end result was worth more than a shouting match—or a hole in his chest.

"I wish I had an insider," Wilmington said. "Instead, all I have is a man to whom I owe my life, a man who's too smart to implicate himself. Trying to outthink him and trust him at the same time is tough." He stared into Daniel's face. "I've been a fool. I can't trust Cayden."

"What about his wife and daughter in Miami?"

"They're innocent. Live on a tight budget from Almet Pharmaceuticals and whatever compensation he receives from the Army. They believe every word he says." Wilmington paused. "Here's a thought for SSA Preston. Cayden loves his daughter. She's eight years old. My guess is he calls her often while on his so-called medical leave of absence. He uses a burner, but the wife's phone could be traced."

Daniel texted Preston and copied Laurel with the new information. "Thanks."

"How are your grandparents?"

"Seems strange not to see them every day. But I don't want to risk being followed, so I'm using my burner to check in with them and their bodyguards."

"I have a man watching their hotel."

"Appreciate it."

"Those are two life insurance policies that Cayden won't cash in."

Wilmington chose to drive them to the airport hotel. Inside, Cayden already had a table. "Glad you're here." He lifted a glass of amber liquid. "I'm hungry. I see you have Mr. Krestle with you." His eyes flashed. "My man's seated behind us. Hey, Krestle, looks like you fell down. What happened?"

"I got back up," Daniel said. "Who's your man?"

"Vega," Wilmington said.

The man turned and nodded. No emotion. No body language.

Daniel smiled at Wilmington's food selection: fried alligator and jalapeño grits. It set the stage for devouring the scammer. All during the meal, Cayden and Wilmington talked about the old days, while Daniel listened. Vega wasn't much of a conversationalist.

"Any prenups between you and Laurel?" Cayden said.

Wilmington studied his longtime friend. "Our marriage will be based on trust."

"Just like mine. The way it's supposed to be."

"I'm about to be a married man and start a family." Wilmington laid his knife and fork across his plate. "The idea of spending the rest of my life in prison doesn't sit well. So I have a question for you. Are you planning on bombing the fund-raiser?"

Cayden swore. "Are you kidding? I want to enjoy my life too. Living the good life, not looking over my shoulder for a bullet."

"Then what did you mean by an explosion?"

He laughed. "A little distraction while we pull the operation together." He glanced at his watch. "Hey, I've got to catch a flight. Moved it up on me. I won't be back until Monday afternoon, and I'll have Natalie and Erin with me. We'll be staying at the Galleria Marriott. Helps to have family at a fund-raiser."

Daniel breathed relief. Having Cayden's wife and child at the fund-raiser somewhat ensured the safety of the guests.

"A man needs to enjoy his family," Wilmington said. "Looking forward to kids with Laurel. One more question." Wilmington's voice was low. "Who tried to poison Laurel's horse?"

Cayden lifted his hands. "My guess? Josie or Messner. Both are dead."

"If you hear different, I want to hack that person into little pieces."

"Don't blame you." Cayden shook Wilmington's hand and left the restaurant.

A few moments later, Wilmington and Daniel rode the elevator down to the lobby. The two walked outside and across the street to the parking lot where Wilmington's Mercedes was parked. Uneasiness crept through Daniel, that extra sense he always attributed to God.

"Humor me for a moment." Daniel stopped. "If you were dead, how would that fit into Cayden's scheme?"

Wilmington stared at the pavement. "If he proved I had plans to scam the fund-raiser and was the mastermind behind the life insurance sales, he'd be in good shape. And it would be easy to blame crimes on a dead man with a record. Are you thinking he's going to wipe me out of the picture?"

"He could have planted a bomb in your car."

Wilmington swung a look at his car. "I should have brought my driver." He walked toward it.

"Wait," Daniel said. "What if it's cell phone detonated or attached to the door opening or ignition switch? Cayden could be watching. I'll make a call to the bomb squad."

Wilmington glared at his vehicle. "Doesn't make sense to call a bomb squad for nothing."

"I'd rather we make the call than meet my Maker prematurely. Let's move back in case we have company."

"More and more it's looking like Cayden might double-cross me." He pulled out his keys and hit Unlock.

The explosion rocked the parking lot. Daniel pushed Wilmington down hard. Metal flew around them, the smell of gasoline assaulting them. A second explosion and Wilmington groaned. A trickle of blood flowed from his back. A piece of glass had pierced him just left of his spine.

"What hit me?" Wilmington said, his face pale and drawn.

"I'll get help. Don't move." Daniel phoned 911. Couldn't tell how deep the glass penetrated—very little blood around it, but if he pulled it out and caused a gusher, the man would bleed out. Best wait for the paramedics.

"Got shot once," Wilmington said. "Feels the same."

"Mort! Krestle!"

Was that Cayden? Daniel stared at the man running their way, wanting to strangle him.

"What can I do to help?" Cayden said.

"Ambulance is on its way."

He grimaced and bent to Wilmington's side. "Hold on, buddy. Don't you think you should yank out that glass? It's ten inches high."

Daniel hadn't wanted Wilmington to know the source of the problem. Shock had crossed his mind. "Paramedics will handle it. My job is to keep him from moving."

"Daniel, if there's glass in my back, get it out of there." Wilmington's breathing grew ragged.

"Trust me on this."

Cayden whistled. "You must have made someone really mad to blow up your Mercedes."

Reality bulldozed Daniel, and he sucked in his rage. This was a game. Cayden was gambling on Wilmington and Daniel suspecting a car bomb.

An insane game.

CHAPTER 49

Laurel had read through FBI reports and Cayden's dossier until her eyes were crossed. She glanced at the showy diamond on her left hand. Reminded her of what she wanted to forget. Looked too much like the one Wilmington had slipped on her finger five years ago. Both times, the engagement meant she was one step closer to nailing him.

She picked up Miss Kathryn's photo on the buffet. The dear woman would have advised her to pray. That didn't solve a thing.

Agents had zeroed in on another scam operation in northwest Houston. Before victimizing Silver Hospitality, Fields and Messner were identified as scamming two of the wealthier residents who had some form of dementia. One had passed recently of a heart attack. No sign of foul play. Laurel read through the report. The scammers had used brochures with other fictitious business names. There had to be a slipup. They hadn't dug deep enough.

The decision to work smart regarding Wilmington needled her. She never dreamed it would be this difficult. Seemed like she was running on fumes. Nothing falling into place.

A call came in from Daniel. Wonderful distraction.

"Wilmington's been hurt. Someone planted a car bomb, and he was in the path of flying glass."

"Where? How bad?"

271

"Glass shards embedded in his back. He'll be okay. We're at Cypress Creek Hospital in the ER. Doc said it'll need a few stitches."

"I'm on my way. Need to look like the caring fiancée. Daniel, did Cayden do this?"

"What do you think? He has a man who used to work for Wilmington."

"When did you find this out?"

"Today."

She sighed. "Okay, we can talk about that later. Hey, are you hurt?"

"I'm fine. Nice to know you care." His teasing eased her concern.

"Can't have my partner down. Makes too much work for me. See you in a few minutes."

The moment she ended the call, questions bombarded her. The car bomb didn't make sense. Wilmington had done a lot of damage before he went to prison. Could be a contract out on him. But she doubted it.

She grabbed her purse while her head pounded from trying to outsmart the bad guys.

In the hospital waiting area, Cayden sat with an over-the-top bruiser type. She nodded hello and hurried to the nurses' station to find Wilmington and Daniel. Wilmington lay on his stomach while a doctor stitched him up. His wound looked raw and nasty.

"Honey, are you in much pain?" she said, bending to his side.

"Fifteen stitches and counting," he said.

"I got here as quickly as I could." She took his hand.

"Somebody decided to blow up my Mercedes."

"Where was Krestle?" She glared at Daniel as if he were at fault.

"Not as close as I was to the explosion," Wilmington said. "Sweetheart, don't be angry with him. His gut told him something was wrong, or I would have been blown to pieces."

She lifted her chin. "Thank you, Krestle. I apologize for sounding harsh."

"No problem, ma'am."

This ruse had to end soon.

"Cayden and a friend are in the waiting room," she said.

"He was flying home to Florida, but postponed it until tomorrow," Daniel said.

"Wait until the doctor's finished and I'll talk to him."

"I'm right here." Cayden stepped in. "Mort, you have a problem of not listening."

Laurel stored his comment.

"I know. Nearly got me killed in Afghanistan and today. Now I owe Krestle. He had this sixth sense that my car was rigged."

"Are you going to be okay?"

"Yeah. As soon as the doc is finished, I'm out of here. I ordered a rental and Krestle will see me home."

"Will Laurel be your nurse?"

"No need," Wilmington said.

"I'll check on him in the morning." She smiled. "He'll sleep like a baby tonight."

Cayden gave her a smug look. Laurel read the body language, and a shiver raced through her. A man who lied to his family and killed helpless people was capable of anything.

CHAPTER 50

Laurel responded to a call from SSA Preston. "Wanted to give you a heads-up on the case," he said.

"I'm all ready for good news."

"This is a small break. A judge approved an order to tap Natalie Cayden's cell phone."

"How did you manage that in so short a time?"

"The judge's father suffers from Alzheimer's."

"Wonderful. Does she have a landline?"

"No. She and the daughter use Skype to stay connected with Cayden. We're monitoring the account."

"Did you learn anything during the interview with her?"

"She's either ignorant or a good liar. Said her husband was seeking medical care at the VA hospital here in Houston. And he is. Everything about this guy says all-American husband and dad—clean, hardworking, ex-military."

"He's not that bright. I'll tell Daniel. Not anything I want to share with Wilmington. Is his wife being followed?"

"Yes, for now. Honestly, I think that's a dead end. We've watched her since Cayden's name was brought into the case. She has a master's in accounting but works part-time at home. Active in community and volunteer projects."

275

"You're right. Cayden's using her."

"How's Wilmington?"

"Checked with Daniel, and he was still sleeping."

"Lucky man."

"Depends on how you look at the situation." She scrambled to avoid any more cynicism. "I'm headed over there now. Maybe he'll slip into delirium and tell us what we need to know."

"Have a meeting with the ASAC this morning. I'll call later. Keep your eyes open, Laurel."

As if he had to warn her.

* * *

10:45 A.M. SUNDAY

Laurel held her breath, willing stamina to fill her body. She hadn't been in Wilmington's condo since the night of the takedown. Daniel said he'd remodeled the entire thirty-two hundred square feet, but the nightmares were still there.

She parked her rental, an inexpensive Chevy with little power. Messner had totaled her Charger, and she hadn't taken the time to look for a new car. She grabbed her purse and forced herself inside and to the elevator. Memories bombarded her. The things she'd done and said to seek evidence. At least this time they didn't share the same bedroom. The thought twisted her stomach.

She knocked in case Wilmington was still asleep, and Daniel answered.

"Hey, gorgeous," he whispered.

She stepped inside. "Be careful. I'm engaged to a powerful man."

"He's asleep." Daniel shut the door, then whirled her around. "Been wanting to do this again since the night at my grandparents' house."

Before she could protest, he drew her to him, kissing her lightly, then deepening the embrace. She pulled back. "Daniel, I thought we were putting this aside until the case was over."

He grinned. "We are. Just wanted to make sure you don't change your mind."

She feigned annoyance while her lips tingled. "You can be so unpredictable."

"Good. Keeps life lively."

"Good morning, you two." Wilmington, dressed in a white robe, hobbled into the living area. "Tell me I didn't see you kissing."

"A hallucination," Daniel said. "I'm your trusted bodyguard."

"Who's in love with my fiancée." He shook his head. "I won't tell a soul. Just keep it private."

Laurel sensed the heat rising up her neck. "I'll go make a fresh pot of coffee. Do you two want breakfast?"

CHAPTER 51

Abby snapped off the TV and narrowed her gaze at the books and knitting she'd brought to the hotel. The suite held the grandeur of a five-star-plus property, but as a vacation spot, not a cell. Which was exactly how she viewed the hotel room. Just when she'd gotten settled in the last one, they'd been detected.

Oh, to feel the sunshine, hear the noises of the city, walk through a park. Anyplace outside of uniformed maids and room service swamped by off-duty police officers. She closed her eyes and transported herself down the Amazon in a boat with only three other people and Earl. Staring into the thick growth of the tropical forest, beaming with colorful birds and hidden animals. The bulging eyes above the wicked-looking teeth of a twelve-foot crocodile. That was life, not this day-after-day boredom.

Couldn't garden.

Couldn't tinker with her jigsaw, and she'd designed a new birdhouse.

The riding lawn mower needed an oil change, and the lawn guys were sloppy.

Didn't want to bother Daniel, although he'd given her a burner phone.

She didn't mind heading home to Jesus. But she'd rather stand up and fight whoever wanted her and Earl dead. Daniel

279

risked his life every minute of the day, and she'd called his supervisor. Wouldn't tell her a thing. All that bunk about him taking a vacation. She knew better. He was working the case, most likely with the FBI, and so was Laurel. What part did Morton Wilmington play?

"Abby, what time is it?" Earl said from the couch.

"Too early to go to bed. Want me to find you a detective show on TV?"

"*Perry Mason* sounds good."

Earl's mind rested in the past. "I'll see what's on, honey."

"Jimmy's late again, isn't he?"

She blew out her misery. "I suppose." Nope, this wasn't living at all.

The officer stationed outside their door stepped inside. "I'm going to order dinner. Have it delivered. Do you want anything?"

"Order me something chocolate," Abby said. "Sinfully delicious. Hot. And a scoop of ice cream." She held up a finger. "The last time I ordered a hot dessert, the ice cream was melted by the time it arrived. Why don't you pick up one for all three of us?"

The officer shook his head. "Bad idea. I'd better stick to room service."

Abby narrowed her eyes at him. "What can happen with the door locked? I'd go get it myself if I could."

He studied her.

"You have my word. I won't open the door to anyone but you."

"Are you sure?"

"Get going. Probably will take just a few minutes, so I'll shower while you're gone."

"Yes, Miss Abby."

The door closed and she double-bolted it. "Enjoy your show, Earl." She retrieved her pajamas and robe, then headed into the bathroom and turned on the hot water, letting the steam fill her lungs. Thoughts of rich chocolate with ice cream helped make up for the boredom.

A knock on the bathroom door stopped her from undressing. "What is it?"

"Just got a call on your cell from Morton Wilmington. Daniel needs us."

"The burner or the other one?"

"Your regular phone."

Puzzled, Abby turned off the water and opened the door. She could better read Earl's frame of mind. "What's going on?"

He bounced the car keys in his hand. "The two were having dinner at the Cafe Express at Uptown Park when Daniel got sick. Can't drive home."

"Why didn't Mr. Wilmington drive him or call a taxi?"

"You know Daniel. He's too stubborn. Wilmington has an appointment and can't take Daniel."

Something didn't seem right. "It's not like Daniel to call us for help."

"My point. So are you driving, or do I go alone?"

Abby stiffened. "You aren't driving anywhere." She snatched the keys. "First I'm calling Daniel on my burner."

"We need to hurry. The boy needs us."

Annoyance with a twinge of alarm settled on her. She pressed in Daniel's number. No response. Although he'd called her on her iPhone, she'd keep her promise not to use it. "Okay, let me leave a note for the officer when he returns. We ought to wait for him. He could go with us—"

"Abby, you can stay here if you want to, but this may be Jimmy's turning point." He walked toward the door. "I'm not turning my back on my only child."

"Hold on, Earl. We must leave a note."

She scribbled it and hurried with Earl to the elevator to ride to the first floor. Thank goodness their Lexus was valet parked. She'd insisted upon their own car when all this hotel business started. Glad she'd refused to leave home without it.

Abby drove south toward Uptown Park. Driving at night made

her nervous. Her vision just wasn't what it used to be. Daniel had called this afternoon to check on them, and he seemed okay. He must be really sick not to answer his burner.

Finally she was doing something to help instead of rocking away her life like an old woman.

CHAPTER 52

Daniel regretted not seeing his grandparents, but it was for their safety. He understood the need to quiet his mind in order to focus on what had to be completed and keep others safe. For him, sometimes all it took was soft music or a good speech on how to handle stress. Exercise and prayer took him to a calm level where his mental state lowered his blood pressure. Tonight he'd done the whole gamut. His wrist ached, and that added to his list of frustrations. Laurel left around seven after Wilmington had gone to sleep. The tiny lines around her eyes spoke of her exhaustion, and he'd encouraged her to go home.

He reached for more Tylenol in Wilmington's kitchen and walked upstairs to his bedroom. He peered out the window. A vehicle entered the driveway. No headlights. Not a car he recognized. He snapped off the lights and picked up his Glock, tucking it into the back of his waistband while watching the happenings on the driveway.

A figure emerged from the car, a frame accented by the streetlight. Tall. Unrecognizable. Daniel walked downstairs to the living area and waited in the dark with his firearm. His gut told him this wasn't a group from church wondering why he hadn't attended this morning.

The doorbell rang. He expected the man to shoot his way inside. "Who's there?"

"Special Agent Thatcher Graves."

He looked through the security hole for confirmation. "Little late for office hours."

"I'd like to talk to you."

He opened the door and faced Thatcher. This couldn't be good. "What's going on?"

"We have new developments."

His thoughts raced to a nightmare situation. His grandparents? Laurel? He gestured Thatcher inside. "Are my grandparents okay?"

"To our knowledge they're okay," he said. "Where is Mr. Wilmington?"

"Asleep. Heavily sedated after the explosion."

"Is he able to ride with us to a meeting?"

"I suppose. I need an explanation. Is Laurel okay?"

"She's fine. In fact she's waiting for us there."

"A meeting at this hour? Has the case escalated?"

"We're being pressured to end the scam."

Daniel understood the clock ticked toward the fund-raiser. "I'm glad to accompany you, and if Wilmington is up to it, he'll cooperate too." He excused himself to check on Wilmington. Seemed a little cruel when the man had been injured.

Daniel turned on a lamp and woke the man. He explained Thatcher's request.

"Can you give me a hand with a shirt, or does your wrist hurt?" Wilmington said.

"Sure. What about your pants?"

"I'm not that bad off." He slowly brought his legs to the floor. A moan escaped his lips. "I'm not the in-shape guy I used to be."

Daniel chuckled. "We're just wounded old men."

In a few minutes they met Thatcher at the door. Questions flooded Daniel's mind while he grabbed his wallet and keys.

"You don't need your Glock." Thatcher pointed to his firearm still tucked in the waist of his jeans.

"If you weren't concerned about being followed, you wouldn't have pulled into the drive with your lights off. I'm taking it. And I need to get my burner phone upstairs." He hurried to his bedroom while Thatcher complained about time being important. Daniel disconnected his phone from the charger and dropped it into his jeans pocket.

Fifteen minutes later, Daniel sat in an enclosed waterway taxi at the Woodlands Town Center. Thatcher drove it—the man apparently had many talents. SSA Preston, Thatcher, Wilmington, and Laurel were the only ones on board. Only in terrorism and espionage cases was information classified, so Daniel intended to get answers. The aroma of fresh coffee filled the taxi, courtesy of the FBI. Good thing because he needed the caffeine kick to his system.

He snuck a glimpse of Laurel while she talked to Preston. The rock on her left hand put to shame anything he could ever purchase on his salary. He'd like to think it was fake, but he knew better. Wilmington was living out his true feelings for her. As if she'd guessed Daniel's thoughts, she covered her ring finger.

"Let's get started," Preston said. "We need solid answers about the elderly scam case. The fund-raiser is this Thursday, in case you haven't checked your calendar. Which is why we're having this meeting tonight. We're not shutting it down until we can ID the silent partner." He had a laptop in front of him, but he didn't look at the screen. "Although we can't seem to pinpoint any specifics, as a precaution, we'll have a thorough bomb check prior to the event and agents in place monitoring the evening.

"Regarding the investigation—the only thing incriminating on Silver Hospitality's computers was a lapse in security on the part the chef and director. The chef, Steven Thomas, confessed to an affair with Josie Fields, who posed there as Liz Austin." He glanced at his computer.

"Apparently Fields bribed Thomas with sexual favors to allow her 'boyfriend' to visit while Thomas and the director, Marsha Leonard, played online chess. He claimed not to have compromised the security system. We believe Fields hacked into the system and handled Messner's entrance and exit when Thomas was unavailable. Leonard denies any knowledge of what was going on. Both have been questioned and released. The two other memory care facilities here in Houston don't have as rigid security as Silver Hospitality."

Daniel pitied Chef Steven and Miss Leonard, although they shouldered some of the blame.

Preston scrolled down his laptop. "About the $4 million withdrawn from your account in the Cayman Islands and deposited into Agent Evertson's account—we traced it to Switzerland."

"Name?" Wilmington's face reddened. Pain or anger?

"Working on it. At this point it's linked to Natalie Ashton, Cayden's wife's maiden name."

Laurel swiped her iPad screen. "Sir, you indicated she was innocent in the scam. Have you revised your conclusion?"

Preston pressed his lips together. "He could have opened the account in any name."

"She's an accountant," Laurel said. "I'd like to request investigating her further."

"Natalie Cayden's on the back burner at this point. Cayden has our concentration with the fund-raiser on the fifteenth. He's brilliant and capable of spearheading this scam. With his exemplary military career, we have no doubt of his extraordinary abilities to deceive. He has the MO of the intruder at the elder Hilton residence.

"Officer Hilton, we learned your grandmother contacted Emma Dockson's nephew and persuaded him to have an autopsy on his aunt's body." Preston shook his head with a slight smile. "Maybe we need to hire this lady, because he agreed. We've learned Mrs. Dockson died of a drug-induced heart attack. The hospital indicated a thirty-second gap in their video surveillance system, which gave someone time to administer the drug. We're working to rebuild the time segment. An additional three hundred thousand dollars is missing from the deceased's account."

He steepled his fingers. "Officer Hilton, we appreciate all the work you've done with this investigation. Mr. Wilmington, you've been a tremendous asset. You and Laurel are playing a critical role in drawing out the players. Earlier this evening, we received an encrypted message identical to the one Mr. Wilmington decoded for us. We'll get to that later."

Preston eyed each of the participants. "We need to nail this operation before Thursday. With the crimes that have been committed against the elderly and our own people, I don't want to think what could happen that evening. We've dug further and learned Cayden's mother died three years ago of pneumonia. However, she suffered from dementia. Left her estate to her eldest son, who earned well over six figures. Our suspect received only five thousand dollars. The money disappeared from the older brother's account six months later and restitution hasn't been made. Two months later, the brother and his wife and children were tragically killed in a car accident."

Daniel gestured to SSA Preston for his attention. "So he's suspected of embezzling his so-called inheritance and then moving on to exploit the elderly. Murdering along the way. Currently he has the bank account numbers of several elderly people. If he was telling Mr. Wilmington and me the truth, he has more than one way to launder money."

"Granted, you've learned a significant amount of information. But without the name of the silent partner, a sharp attorney could get the whole case thrown out of court based on Cayden's impeccable record. By the way, Cayden's inhaler revealed he removed his fingerprints."

"He could have burned them off while overseas on a special-ops mission," Wilmington said. "Or removed them later to avoid being ID'd."

"We didn't find anything in his medical other than the asthma and the stress-related problems bringing him to the VA hospital," Preston said. "The doctor checks out."

Preston secured the whole group's attention. "We've put together a good composite using the past eight years of elderly fraud, thanks to a combined task force. Almet manufactures and distributes various drugs used for treating dementia patients. Their database lists health insurers that store information in codes—like the patient's diagnosis, address, and medical data. Cayden apparently identified the victims through the medication and accessed hospital records, which list financial information about every patient. The perfect database to scam dementia sufferers would merge health info with financials, including bank records pointing to the patients' income. The dementia sufferer has the potential to be scammed on many levels. Our man would have all he needed to scam them with false charities, investments, claims of long-lost grandchildren, home repairs, health care–like prescription fraud, and life insurance policies."

Preston brought up something else on his laptop. "Which brings us to the message decoded earlier today. 'Congratulations on deciphering my code. Unfortunately by the time the pathetic FBI figures out who's responsible, it will be too late.'" He glanced at the group. "For him to take the defensive, something has to have been exposed."

"He's always been a little arrogant," Wilmington said. "Someone drove the getaway Escalade when Josie Fields was shot. I'm accusing Cayden, and he dumped her body. At this point, I've only uncovered Ignacio Vega working for him."

"He's suspected in several killings, but he's local," Preston said.

"My men are on top of things," Wilmington said. "They're watching Laurel and Daniel. We'd be fools not to figure Cayden's having all three of us watched."

"I'm concerned about the elder Hiltons." Laurel looked pale, but sleep deprivation attacked people in numerous ways. "I understand they have protection, but our guy has multiple reasons to eliminate them from the picture."

"I'm also keeping an eye on their hotel," Wilmington said.

She stiffened. "How do you know where they're being housed?"

"I have ways."

Daniel had no idea who Wilmington's men were. He hadn't seen anyone, but the man spent lots of time on the phone.

Preston turned to Thatcher. "Keep me posted with the updates in Miami. I'd like to know if Mrs. Cayden attempts to contact her husband or leave the country. Also keep me posted with her phone calls." He paused. "We haven't done our job or arrests would have been made. Let's get this job done."

The meeting adjourned, and Thatcher drove the waterway taxi back toward the docking point. Everyone remained quiet like Daniel, with only the sounds of nearby busy restaurants and the mall filtering through the night. Weary of the chase, he longed for simpler times when his biggest concern was arresting a speeder.

Preston and Wilmington joined Thatcher at the controls and Laurel remained with Daniel.

"How are you?"

He could write a dissertation on that question. "Okay. Be careful out there."

Her eyes softened. "I want this over as badly as you do."

A chill swept over him, a foreboding that he couldn't shake.

CHAPTER 53

Abby checked her watch again. Why hadn't Daniel returned her calls? It took her and Earl nearly twenty minutes to get to the Cafe Express at Uptown Park. Earl needed to make a pit stop. She'd done her best to rush him, but she couldn't fight nature. They sure had waited a long time. Maybe Daniel had given up and gone elsewhere for help. She fretted about the danger. If Earl hadn't threatened to leave without her, she would've made a few more calls. Worrying was like sitting in a rocking chair—all that work and no progress.

"Abby, we've been here a long time. Where do you suppose Jimmy went?"

"Honey, it's Daniel."

A car pulled up beside them on the passenger side, too close for her liking. She didn't want a single scrape on her Lexus. A man got out. He wore one of those nasty hoodies. He glared into Earl's open window.

She pushed the button to turn the car on, but the man slammed the barrel of a Sig into Earl's face.

"Don't say a word," he said softly. "Both of you get out of your car and into my backseat."

"Why?" Abby reached into her purse at her feet.

"Daniel has a surprise for you."

"How nice of him. And who are you?" Abby had encountered scary animals, those who thought she'd be their next meal. But they hadn't succeeded. And the steroid-using beast who had a gun on Earl wouldn't either.

"Doesn't matter, lady. Now get out before I pull the trigger."

"Where are we going? Someplace to collect on our life insurance policies?"

"Smart lady. Now."

"Of course. Earl, do as the man says." She slipped her gun to her side, opened the door, and stepped out. A light pole to the right gave her a better view of the kidnapper. She calculated the slight breeze. "Honey, you'll need your cane from the backseat."

When Earl took a step, she fired, sending the man flat against his car and sliding to the pavement.

"Abby, what did you do? Are you okay?"

"Hope he made his peace with God before I killed him." She trembled and drew in a breath to keep from passing out.

"What now?"

"I'm calling Daniel. If he doesn't answer this time, I'll contact Laurel."

CHAPTER 54

Tired but wired with an excess of adrenaline, Daniel waited for the waterway taxi to bring all of them to a stopping point.

"Hey, *amigos*," Wilmington said. "When this is over, I'm flipping for the best steak in town."

Daniel just wanted it to be over. "Until then—" His burner phone buzzed. Gran. He checked his watch, a bit past her normal bedtime. He saw she'd called earlier multiple times, but he'd set the phone on mute during the FBI meeting. Before then, it had been charging.

"Daniel?" Gran's high-pitched tone held her panic.

"What's wrong?"

"I've done something awful."

Daniel slid into mental alert. "Talk to me, Gran."

"Morton Wilmington called while I was in the shower. Earl answered. Mr. Wilmington said you were sick and needed us to pick you up at the Cafe Express in Uptown Park. We drove there but couldn't find you, and we've been waiting in the parking lot."

He flashed a look at Wilmington. "Why would I have him call you? Where is your bodyguard?" He attempted to shake off his emotions.

"He went to pick up his dinner and dessert for us, but I left a note for him to call you. Later I realized we'd been set up."

293

Daniel swallowed. They were in horrible danger. "Who's driving?"

"I was. But now we're parked. I haven't called the police yet." She sobbed. "Daniel, I killed a man."

"You hit him? What?"

"I shot him in the head. He tried to kidnap us."

Daniel sensed the blood draining from his face. He caught Laurel's attention. "You said the Cafe Express near Uptown Park? Stay put. I'll be on my way soon."

Laurel moved closer.

"I see a young couple walking our way. They shouldn't see the dead man, right?"

"Ask them to step back. Tell them it's a crime scene."

"Excuse me," Gran called out. "Please, stay back. This is a crime scene." She sighed. "Earl, honey, would you get the afghan out of the backseat and cover that poor man."

"Good job, Gran. Take a few deep breaths," Daniel said. "How's your heart?"

"I guess I'm okay. Can't believe I killed him. But he had a gun pointed at Earl."

"Are either of you hurt?"

"No."

"You killed a man in self-defense. I'll make the necessary calls to the authorities. Don't talk to anyone." He grabbed a slip of paper from his pocket and jotted down their license plate number, handing it to Laurel. "I'm switching you to speaker until I get there. Police officers will arrive before I do. Give them your phone and I'll talk to them. Meanwhile, you're going to hear everything I say to those around me, but I want to stay connected."

"Yes. I won't lose you," she said.

He wasn't losing them, either, not to a killer or anyone who tried to harm them. "Gran, I don't look like myself. Alert Gramps if necessary."

Wilmington placed his hand on Daniel's shoulder. "Did I hear right?" he whispered.

Daniel nodded. "SSA Preston, I just received an emergency call from my grandmother. Someone tried to nab them, and she shot him. Can we speed this thing up?"

"Thatcher," Preston said. "You heard Officer Hilton. Get a move on."

Daniel groaned. "I don't have a car."

"Take mine," Laurel said. "It's parked at Barnes & Noble. I'd like to ride along."

"Sure. I could use the company." The waterway taxi bumped to a docking point, and those on board stepped off.

"Call me when you can," Wilmington said as Daniel and Laurel raced toward the parking lot.

"I'll drive him home," Thatcher said.

What they'd feared about his grandparents was unfolding. No one had been able to stop the scamming and deaths. Not agents in five different states or police departments or one ex-con who claimed to be a good guy.

When they neared Laurel's vehicle, she unlocked it and tossed Daniel the keys before swinging around to the passenger side. Within moments, Daniel sped onto I-45 south and around the 610 loop to the Uptown Park shopping area on Post Oak near the Galleria. Traffic seemed thicker than usual for this time of night. A possible accident ahead. Not exactly conducive to speeding to a crime scene.

"Gran, I'm going to put my phone on mute so I can hear what's going on there with you. I'll pick up if you need me." He pushed Mute and set the phone on the console.

"Is the FBI on their way?" he said to Laurel.

"Yes. I'm sure someone has called HPD by now."

"Right." Daniel's mind zipped to his grandparents. "I used to laugh at my eccentric gran, the way she still goes to the shooting range. Her past escapades with her love of the outdoors. Her speeding tickets. But if she hadn't been packing and or didn't knew how to use it, she and Gramps might be dead."

"She's one special lady."

"Definitely. Gran hasn't driven at night in a couple of years. Poor night vision. I'm rambling. Need to get my investigative head on." He reached for her hand. "I feel better with you beside me."

"I've never left."

He smiled and pulled his phone from the console and unmuted it. "Talk to me, Gran." He heard sirens and recalled the last time he talked to her while waiting for an ambulance to help Pete.

"I'm praying to keep from hysterics. Earl is doing okay. The shot seemed to pull his mind to the present. He's blocking the view of the body. Oh, I told him not to say a word about how you look."

"Good. Tell him thanks." He swerved into the rightmost lane and then back to the left, leaving a car horn blaring in their wake.

"Daniel, get your foot off the gas. I know you."

The thought made him smile. "I can handle it. Remember to give the phone to the police officer and don't say a word about what happened."

Laurel's fingers entwined with his, and he lightly squeezed her hand. "Thanks for being here."

"We're in this together."

"You are the perfect woman. Gramps pointed that out the first time we met."

"He's quite the charmer. I saw your grandparents' wedding photo. He was a handsome man, and your grandmother looked like she walked off a magazine cover."

"They are amazing."

"Your grandmother is one of a kind."

"What does that mean?" Gran's voice came through, and Daniel realized he hadn't muted the phone again.

"That you'd be perfect backup—physically, mentally, or spiritually," Laurel said.

"Laurel, you're sweet, and you know I need to hear good things so I don't fall apart."

"Daniel, this is me." Gramps had obviously taken possession of the phone. "I've got this. I've been taking care of Abby for a long time."

"Thanks." Daniel heard shuffling.

"Oh, Daniel." Gran was back. "The police are here."

A moment later a voice spoke into Daniel's phone. "Yes, sir," a man said.

"I'm Officer Daniel Hilton and I'm en route to the crime scene. Ten minutes out. The FBI is also on their way."

"Is this their case?"

"Yes, sir. I've been assisting them. I'll explain when I get there. The couple with you are my grandparents. The dead man attempted to kill them."

"I'll keep the scene secured, sir."

The officer returned the phone to Gran. "I'm hanging up now. With HPD here, I'll be fine until you arrive."

He disconnected the call and reached for Laurel's hand again. Her silent support meant more than any words could convey. Breathing deeply, he grasped the wonder of the rest of their lives filled with this mental intimacy.

"I'm banking on the dead man opening up the case," Laurel said. "But if he's not Geoff Cayden, then who? Vega?"

Her burner rang. "It's Wilmington. Should I take it and spoil our time together?"

"This isn't exactly a date. Better see what he wants."

She pushed the Speaker button. "Yes."

"Are you at the crime scene?"

"Not yet. HPD is with Daniel's grandparents."

"Tell him I'm praying for them."

"He's listening."

"Great. Be strong, Daniel. Although tonight has been tragic, we could get solid answers."

"Hope so," he said. "Did Thatcher drive you home?"

"Sure did. Haven't been interrogated like that in years."

The call ended and Daniel shook his head. "If I find out Wilmington ordered this, keep me away from him."

"Calm down, Daniel. We'll have answers soon enough. What's the plan?"

"Until arrests are made, I'm sticking my grandparents someplace where only the FBI and I know where they are. New identities. All of it."

"A safe house in a rural area fits the bill."

Laurel's cell phone alerted her to another call. "This time it's Thatcher."

"Keep it on speaker."

"Laurel, we'll be at the crime scene in fifteen. I understand the officer who arrived first has called an ambulance for Mrs. Hilton."

Daniel's senses raced on alert. "She didn't say a word about being hurt."

"The officer stated the injury isn't too bad. Her shoulder is either dislocated or broken. Looks like she slipped moving around the car after the shooting. Why don't you head on over to Memorial Hospital. I'll meet you there. I'll make sure your grandfather rides in the ambulance."

"Good. Do you have an ID on the dead man?" Daniel said.

"Jack Breacher, and he failed his mission. Last known employer is Morton Wilmington. He claims the man was fired months ago. Makes our ex-con look real guilty."

CHAPTER 55

Daniel stayed with his grandparents at the hospital until Gran's minor cuts and bruises were treated, medical tests completed, and her dislocated shoulder placed in a sling. Gramps's mind had drifted in and out—perhaps oblivion was a better option than what they'd been through.

"Are you sure you don't hurt anywhere else?" Daniel noted a purplish-black bruise that extended from her right eye to her hairline.

"I'm good. Just embarrassed I fell."

Daniel wrapped his arm around her shoulders. "Gran, your quick thinking saved your and Gramps's lives."

"Are you talking about my Abby?" Gramps said. "She's the most courageous, smartest woman in the world."

She kissed his whiskered cheek. "I wasn't very smart today, and I owe so many people an apology. Gullible and clumsy. What a combo."

"The caller knew how to persuade me." Earl humphed. "I actually believed him."

"The officer shouldn't have left you unprotected." Daniel didn't have the heart to state their bodyguard had been found unconscious in the elevator. Not sure why his grandparents weren't

299

attacked in their hotel room, except it increased the likelihood of their deaths looking like murder instead of staging an accident. Gran and Gramps had used a back exit, and not even Wilmington's man had seen them leave.

"Don't blame him," Abby said. "If I hadn't asked for a hot chocolate dessert for all of us, he wouldn't have left us alone."

"I'm ready to get back to the hotel and climb into bed." Gramps's mind seemed to have returned to the present. "Going to tuck my girl in and let her sleep off this nightmare."

Daniel drew in a breath. "The FBI has suggested other arrangements. A nurse will escort you one at a time through the emergency exit. Two separate cars will transport you to Hobby Airport, where a private plane will fly you to a safe destination."

"You're not going with us?" Gran's eyes brimmed with tears.

He lifted her chin with his finger. "I'm going to help end this elderly scam. With you and Gramps in a safe house and FBI agents to protect you, I'm free to do whatever needs to be done. As soon as it's over, I'll be right there to bring you home."

"How long do you think it'll take, Jimmy?" Gramps said.

Daniel sighed. "Less than a week. We're close."

Gran's lips quivered. "You and Earl are my life. Promise me you'll take care of yourself."

"I'll do my best. You're my hero, Gran. Don't forget it."

He carefully embraced her, then gave Gramps a hug. They said their good-byes inside the hospital ER and exited according to the FBI's plan. Daniel and Laurel made their way to the parking lot.

"Where's your car?"

"At Wilmington's. Actually I'd like my truck. I want to stop by my house."

"Is your truck at the FBI office?"

"No, at a storage facility." He glanced around. "Can't tell if we're being followed. I think we'll pay Starbucks on Memorial a visit."

"Have you detected a tail?"

"No, just cautious. Once we're finished at Starbucks, I'll head for a parking garage across the street from the storage facility. You can have your little car back, and I'll retrieve my truck." Exhaustion fell on him like a dark fog, but he wanted to pick up his mail and check on his house.

After securing his truck and driving toward home, he attempted to make sense of what was happening. Wilmington stated Jack Breacher no longer worked for him. Was that the truth?

Another current of trouble flooded him. The figures from reported fraudulent services and products had escalated to several million dollars, and the estimated payout money on the life insurance policies amounted to millions. If Cayden panicked, he could take the money and run. Or would his arrogance keep him fixed on the fund-raiser? Something nudged at Daniel about the case, and he didn't think it was Wilmington double-crossing them.

Right now his thoughts jumbled together. In the darkness, the closer Daniel drove to home, the better his own bed looked. Pain anchored itself at the base of his skull, nothing a good night's rest wouldn't cure. He entered his subdivision to the whine of sirens and fire trucks whizzing by him. Normally curiosity would entice him to follow, but not tonight. He drove on, annoyed the emergency vehicles were in his way.

Smoke rose in the distance.

Too close to his brick, one-story home.

His headache grew worse.

The fire truck slowed a half block from his house. Daniel peered around it, praying it wasn't his house on fire. He gasped. Flames bellowed from the front windows of his ranch home. Firemen poured blasts of water through the windows.

Daniel gripped the steering wheel. How far would Cayden and his people go?

He parked his pickup and ran. Rage twisted inside him, kindling his own fire.

"Sir, stay clear of the area," a firefighter said.

"It's my house!"

"I'm sorry. But for your safety, please keep your distance."

Daniel refused to slow his pace. "Try to stop me."

"You'll get hurt." The firefighter stood in his path.

Daniel grasped his reasoning. What more could he do than the firefighters? "Do you know what caused it?"

"Found an empty gasoline can on the driveway."

"Arson," Daniel said, confirming what he expected. He stared at the white paint splotches on the end of his home opposite the blaze. In the darkness he couldn't quite make out the graffiti and walked closer.

"Sir. Please step back."

Two words clawed at his gut: *Loser Cop.*

CHAPTER 56

Laurel had been too tired to sleep well last night. She poured a glass of orange juice and popped an English muffin into the toaster. Snatching her cell phone, she scrolled through what had gone on while she slept. A headline captured her attention. An HPD police officer's home in the Memorial area had been set on fire. *"Officer Daniel Hilton . . ."*

Daniel's home set on fire! She shivered, reading every word of what happened. An online photo showed *Loser Cop* sprayed across the end of his brick home.

An empty gas can on the driveway was the arsonist's calling card. Using her burner phone, she pressed in Daniel's number. He answered on the third ring.

"Laurel? Are you all right?" His raspy voice indicated she'd wakened him from a deep sleep.

She regretted her impulsive call when he needed rest. "I'm sorry. I just now read about the fire. I'll talk to you later."

"I'm fine. Need to get up anyway."

"Sure?"

"Yep." He yawned.

"Are you at Wilmington's or your grandparents' home?"

"Wilmington's. Didn't want to take a chance on being barbecued at yet another Hilton residence."

"What did Wilmington say about last night?"

"Maintains Jack Breacher wasn't in his employ. No idea who roasted my house other than Cayden or his bodyguard."

"Any clues at the crime site?"

"A neighbor woman reported a yardman unloaded a lawn mower and gas can from a pickup early last evening. He wore a baseball cap and that's all she could remember. Neither did she pay attention to the license plate. The fire investigator's initial survey hasn't found anything substantial."

"Oh, Daniel, is there anything left of your home?"

"Yes. Last night investigators stopped me from going through what could be salvaged. Top of my list this morning." He yawned again. "I'm heading back over there in a bit."

"I'll join you. I have the wig from before."

"Doesn't Wilmington have all your time?"

"He'll have my attention at lunch."

"Have a good time."

"Gee, thanks." She ached for his loss, the memorabilia that could never be replaced. "I'll help for as long as I can."

"The arsonist ticked me off with his spray paint art."

"Cheap shot."

"Last night when I left the hospital, I realized arresting the scammer had become more than personal, almost an obsession. Then when I saw the fire, anger bubbled like a volcano eruption. Wanted to kill Cayden with my bare hands. And it's hard to continue being civil to Wilmington when his man attempted to kill my grandparents, and I can't figure out what side of the fence he's on. Had me a come-to-Jesus meeting to curb my temper."

"Did it work?"

"My head's more together this morning. I'm rational and angry."

"Instead of irrational and furious?"

He chuckled. "We're dynamite, Agent Evertson. Let me climb out of bed and meet you at my house. Investigators will be swarming the place, but it's still my property."

"And I'll have a huge Starbucks for you, with a little sugar. How about a scone to go with it? They have a fabulous triple berry."

"I love you."

She dropped her muffin.

"Laurel?"

"Yes."

"I meant I love you for bringing me breakfast."

She caught her breath. "I know what you meant. I'll see you in about an hour." The call ended. Laurel touched her heart, still pounding like a schoolgirl's with her first serious crush. After cleaning up the buttered muffin from the floor, she showered and dressed while his three little words replayed in her mind.

"Officer Hilton," she whispered, "I'd bring you coffee and a scone every day to hear those words." She was smitten, as Miss Kathryn used to say. But being with him was a dream.

At Daniel's home, HPD and fire investigators searched through rubble, storing possible evidence and tagging the containers. They knew what to look for while her expertise teetered between cryptology and violent crime. What a mix. Daniel waved and she headed his way, wearing a smile from the inside out.

He walked slowly. No doubt he'd gotten little sleep. She handed him the venti-size coffee and pastry sack.

His eyes emitted warmth. "Thanks. I could drink three of these."

"I added two extra shots of espresso."

He grinned. "A 'black eye'? Must have read my mind."

"Absolutely. Any new developments?" Ripples of embarrassment spread through her about his earlier comment.

"A fire investigator is in the back. The others are searching and prying, taking soil samples, and sorting through what's left of one end of my house."

"It takes time." She offered an encouraging smile. "But you know that. How's your own personal recovery process?"

"The fire started in the garage and spread to the kitchen and living room." He nodded at the fallen bricks and smoke. "The area there is totaled." He shrugged. "The sofa was on my list to be replaced anyway, and the dishes were from Target. The bedrooms have smoke damage, an easy fix."

"What about the irreplaceable items?"

He blew into the hot coffee. "Valuables and important documents are in a safety-deposit box. It's the old photos of Gran and Gramps I'll never see again, and my parents." He glanced back at the house, his jaw set.

Laurel followed his gaze and read the words spray-painted on the brick. Her stomach burned raw.

"I'd like to see whoever did this scrub off the paint with a toothbrush," Daniel said. "Cuff him and throw away the key. I heard this morning a video about the fire and message went viral."

"Not such a bad response. The city and various communities have their eyes open. There're two things the public won't tolerate: hurting children and victimizing the elderly. When this is over, your part in the investigation will prove you're a hero."

"I don't feel like anything but a 'loser cop.' But a neighbor approached me last night and said several of them would scrub off the paint," Daniel said. "Beginning late this afternoon."

"Proves the human race can be kind."

A man emerged from behind the house and called for Daniel. He wore a badge indicating his role as a fire investigator. "We've found a heel print near the back door of the garage."

Daniel and Laurel walked his way.

"I'm assuming you want to hear my findings?" the man said.

"Every word." Daniel introduced Laurel as a friend.

They approached the rear of his once-double garage, now smoldering embers. The stench filled her nostrils. This end of his house went up in flames while the other end with the spray paint had barely been touched. Several polyester bags had been filled and tagged.

The young man pointed to the remains and talked like he was conducting a class. "In my origin and cause investigation, I've collected enough from the ash and debris for the lab to perform a chemical analysis. But the gas can found in the driveway says it all. Mr. Hilton, you made someone angry."

"Looks that way."

"Any idea who would have set the fire?"

"If I did, he'd be under arrest or in the hospital."

The investigator stared at him. "Anger issues don't address the crime. I spoke to neighbors prior to your arrival, and all we have is the woman who saw a yardman."

"I do my own outside work."

The man jotted down Daniel's answers. "When were you last home?"

"I've been staying with a friend. It's in the report."

"This is my report. Would you normally have been home at the time of the fire?"

"Yes."

Laurel's mind drifted into investigative mode. The source didn't show any sophistication. Only an elementary mentality designed to inflict damage and attempt to control the victim. The arsonist could set fire to Daniel's house, so he did.

Shielding her eyes from the morning sun, she panned the backyard. A small metal object sparkled in the grass about ten feet from where she stood. Moving closer, she bent to examine it.

"Daniel, I found something."

He knelt beside her. "That's not mine. And I doubt a firefighter wears a diamond that size while battling a blaze."

A horseshoe ring lay on the burned grass.

CHAPTER 57

Wilmington and Laurel finished sharing a catered lunch in his dining room. She hated being there alone with him—all of it. What made matters worse—Jack Breacher had worked for him, the man who tried to kill Abby and Earl. Her mood had a foul stench, and she couldn't shake it. But she had a role to play.

"Laurel, you gave yourself away last night," Wilmington said.

Her thoughts slammed into reverse. "What do you mean?"

"Anyone watching you at the hospital with Daniel could see how you have feelings for him."

"I didn't say or do anything along those lines."

"You have no idea who was watching other than Cayden and Vega. Everyone's keeping tabs on our moves. To end this crime spree, we have to do our part."

He was right, but she hated to admit it. "I'll be more careful. What kind of advice did you give Jack Breacher? Or whoever torched Daniel's house?"

He blew out his response. "I had that coming. The fire last night can't be discussed with Cayden. Neither can I talk about the elder Hiltons except in generalities."

"Can't you ask him about Breacher?"

"No. He turned against me when I was in prison, but of course you have no reason to believe me."

"Bring on the violin."

"This is nearly over and when the arrests are made, your name will be at the top of the list of those who brought in Cayden and whoever else is involved. Your career will escalate."

"Fame isn't as important to me as it once was."

"It should be. You're the best."

Her heart froze. She played a game, but he followed his heart. He sucked in a breath.

"You're hurting," she said.

"Now and then."

She despised him, but her sympathies came out whenever anyone was in pain. "Take some meds and indulge in a nap."

His face paled and he pushed away a plate of uneaten food. "May need to. Are you going to stick around?"

"Can I use your computer?"

He chuckled. "Sure, go ahead. Can't get me into any more trouble than before. I no longer have a safe."

"Thanks for the heads-up. I have a few hours of research, which you can check later."

"Do you think you'll ever trust me?" he said.

She hesitated.

"That's okay. Someday you'll see I'm on God's side."

Not unless she was delusional. She'd copy his files this afternoon while researching her pet project: Natalie Ashton Cayden.

Thirty minutes later, she left Wilmington a text: Need to run a few errands b4 going 2 airport. Will be back later.

✳ ✳ ✳

2:00 P.M. MONDAY

Daniel met SSA Preston and Thatcher at the FBI office before changing and returning to Wilmington's condo. Laurel had texted him with her plans to work while Wilmington slept.

Now to find out what the men wanted done considering the fund-raiser in a few days.

Preston entered the interview room with Thatcher. "We're sorry to hear about the fire," Preston said. "But the arsonist made one big mistake."

"Or framed someone else and got away with it." Daniel frowned. "I'm tired and cynical."

"We're working all angles," he said. "In your position, I'd be cynical too. Probably out to slit a few throats."

Sympathy coated the SSA's words, but instead of appreciating the personal touch, Daniel wanted to explode. Definitely on overload. He prayed for clarity and a huge dose of patience. "The ring, sir. Who does it belong to?"

"Jack Breacher," Preston said.

"Can't question or prosecute a dead man." Daniel ran his hand over his face. "So he spread gasoline and then went after my grandparents. Who lit the match?"

"I understand your impatience. We're there too. Our path forward contains the work of several more agents."

"Path forward? Sounds like a course in leadership development." His head thumped with exasperation. He had to calm down, beginning by coaxing his blood pressure to a healthy level and steadying his breathing. "We're all under stress with the critical situation facing us on Thursday. Help me understand why I'm here this afternoon."

Thatcher glared at him. "You aren't the only one who's losing sleep with this case."

"And like you, I want those responsible behind bars."

"The FBI was on this case long before you were."

"Enough," Preston said. "We have work to do."

Daniel swallowed a nasty remark. "Did Breacher have a military background?"

"No," Preston said. "No connect with Wilmington or Cayden back then. Not sure about Vega, but it's doubtful."

"I haven't seen what Breacher looked like before my grandmother eliminated him from the equation."

Thatcher handed him his cell, but Daniel had never seen the man before. Grit stung his eyes. He toyed with a pen on the table, thoughts lining up like dominoes—if one fell, the scammers' whole operation collapsed.

"You two have a job to do tonight," Preston said. "Now's the time to put aside your personal differences." He stared at both men. "Wilmington used to be part owner of a club called the Instantaneous down on Washington."

Daniel knew the club.

"Jack Breacher used to work there. I want you to visit there tonight. Daniel, go as Wilmington's bodyguard. Express a little dissatisfaction with him. Possibly looking for a job. Thatcher, you're a friend looking for a good time."

"With all due respect, I think I could be of more value working in other areas," Thatcher said.

"You'll be at the Instantaneous at ten thirty tonight."

CHAPTER 58

Laurel stood in baggage claim at IAH by the escalator and waited for Geoff Cayden and his family to arrive. She was surrounded by limo drivers and corporate shuttle drivers, but she was the only one who carried red roses for Natalie and a gift card for Erin from the American Girl store. Courtesy of Morton Wilmington. She'd found Natalie's Facebook page and learned her daughter loved American Girl dolls.

While she waited, her thoughts raced with the insane idea that Wilmington could be trusted. Couldn't SSA Preston see Wilmington had connections to three henchmen who worked with Cayden?

Her misgivings were interrupted when she saw a familiar face. Dressed in jeans and a polo shirt, Cayden rode the escalator down with his arm around an attractive, tall blonde. A dark-haired little girl rode before them. Cayden tossed daggers her way. His problem.

She waved and gave her best theatrical smile. "Welcome to Houston! Morton asked me to greet you."

Cayden introduced her to his wife and daughter.

"It's a pleasure to meet you both." Laurel handed Natalie the roses and Erin the gift card. "We wanted you to have a little gift from us. The roses are in a plastic vase because I couldn't imagine your hotel room having one, and you could leave the vase behind."

"Thank you." Natalie inhaled the roses. "I love flowers. I haven't seen Morton in years. Is he doing okay since the accident?"

"Much better. Maybe we all could have dinner while you're here."

"Wonderful."

"Daddy, can we go shopping?" Erin looked familiar, but Laurel couldn't place her.

"We'll find time," he said. "Tell you what. I'll get our luggage, drive to the hotel, and then you and Mommy can go shopping. I'll put everything away."

"Thank you, Daddy." She hugged him. "You're the best daddy in the whole world."

"I'll take that, princess."

"Would you like for me to drive you to your hotel?" Laurel anticipated his response.

"No, thanks. I have a rental to pick up."

Once Cayden disappeared, she kept her smile intact. "I imagine your husband and Morton will be busy getting ready for the fundraiser. Would you like to have lunch tomorrow, just us three girls?"

Natalie, who towered over Laurel, placed her hand on her daughter's shoulder. "How nice for you to include Erin. Can I call you later to confirm?"

"Of course. Your husband has my number. Have you been to Houston before?"

"This is our first visit. So much to see and do in such a short time."

"If I can be of any assistance, don't hesitate to ask."

Cayden returned with their luggage, and the threesome disappeared to collect their rental.

Laurel hoped the tiny bug embedded in the stem of one of the roses picked up what she needed to hear. The transmitter was installed in the base of the vase. If Vega did a room sweep before they stepped foot inside the room, nothing would be detected.

✳ ✳ ✳

10:55 P.M. MONDAY

Daniel had no idea what he'd done to irritate Thatcher, but he had no intention of asking. They'd seated themselves at the bar of the

Instantaneous, where they could watch the door. Conversation between them occurred at two words a minute.

Daniel motioned to the bartender to order a Sprite. "Does Morton Wilmington still have ownership in the club?"

"No. He sold it once he got religion in prison."

"Who's the owner?"

"A woman from Florida. Natalie Ashton," the bartender said. "Never met her, though. She doesn't even sign the checks."

What else did Natalie have her hands into? If she was involved in the business, could be her husband was too. Or did Cayden use her name without her knowledge? "I was curious. We recently started working for Morton Wilmington and he hadn't mentioned the club."

"Heard he had a temper."

"I talked to a few who used to work for him. Haven't seen it yet."

The bartender laughed. "Maybe he did find religion. Been following him in the paper. Why he took that gal back is beyond me. I'd have filled her with holes."

"They seem to be happy, but—"

"Krestle, I'm here to socialize, not talk business," Thatcher said. "Maybe this guy can point me toward the right lady."

The bartender leaned on the counter. "You're on your own there, unless you want to pay."

Thatcher chuckled. "Not my style."

Daniel nodded to the dance floor. "I think Wilmington used to date that one."

"I wouldn't know," the bartender said. "See the brunette in red over there? He dated her before the gal who sent him to prison."

"Thanks," Thatcher said. "I'll see what I can do. Might get lucky." He made his way to the dance floor and the brunette.

Now was Daniel's chance. "I don't suppose you're looking for a bouncer," he said.

"Might be. Wilmington not pay well?"

"Not sure what he's into. Once did some time, and I don't want to head back there again."

"Don't blame you. Haven't seen him since before he went to prison. Word is he practically gave away the club."

"He's doing the good-guy walk, but the company he keeps is bad."

The bartender pulled an application from under the counter. "Bring it back tomorrow, and I'll see what I can do. One of his men used to work here."

Daniel raised a brow.

"Jack Breacher."

"He's dead. My point."

"What happened to your wrist?"

"I made it out alive."

CHAPTER 59

2:00 A.M. TUESDAY
TWO DAYS UNTIL OCTOBER 15

Laurel woke at her apartment to the phone ringing. She rolled over and grabbed her burner. Couldn't sleep with new information marching across her brain anyway.

"This is Daniel. Sorry to leave you alone with Wilmington."

"He slept a lot and I ran errands. Are you at the condo?"

"Yes." He explained the bartender's conversation at the Instantaneous. "Natalie Ashton's name has shown up twice. Is she helping her husband in the scam, or is he using her? Thatcher had little luck. The woman who used to date Wilmington hasn't heard from him in over six years. She despises him and has no idea who his current friends are. What about you?"

"I met Cayden and his family at the airport. Rather interesting."

"Hope you learned something we could use." Negativity crept into his tone.

"A strong possibility. I'm taking Natalie and her daughter to lunch tomorrow. But that's not the clincher. Erin Cayden doesn't look a thing like her parents. She's the spitting image of Josie Fields."

"Laurel, don't leave me hanging."

"I contacted SSA Preston to dig a little deeper. Our friend Cayden enjoys his family ties. Fields and Messner were half brother and sister. Natalie Cayden is a first cousin through their mother.

317

Eight years ago, Geoff and Natalie adopted an infant girl through an attorney."

"Are you saying Cayden killed his daughter's biological mother?"

"Are we surprised? The little girl's olive complexion in contrast to her parents' lighter skin hit me as unusual, and she looked so familiar."

"Let's talk this through. Geoff Cayden hired his wife's cousins to do his dirty work about the same time he adopted Fields's daughter."

Laurel was fully awake. "My question is where does this put Natalie? She has to know Fields and Messner are dead. How did Cayden explain that?"

"Good question. Did you mention this to Wilmington?"

"No."

"Think I'll wake up my friend. Doubt if it brings evidence to make an arrest, but it opens up the dynamics."

"Call me after you talk to him. I'm too wired to sleep."

*　*　*

2:15 A.M. TUESDAY

Common sense stopped Daniel from shining a flashlight into Wilmington's face, but he was furious. One more time it looked like the ex-con had kept vital information to himself. Instead he shook him gently until the man rolled over.

"We have to talk." Daniel flipped on the lamp.

"All right." He sat up, rather awkwardly since the wound in his back forced him to sleep on his stomach. "You aren't happy, so spill it."

Daniel pulled a chair to his bedside. "Why didn't you tell us the Instantaneous had been sold to Natalie Ashton?"

"When did that happen?"

"Since ownership was transferred from you to her."

He rubbed his face. "The club was sold to a corporation out of Florida."

"Right."

He shook his head as if he had no clue. "Cayden owns it?"

"His wife does and her name is on the offshore account holding your four mil."

"Daniel, my attorney took care of the sale. All I wanted was to unload it."

"Do you know how this looks?"

"Yeah, as though I'm on Cayden's side. Vega, Breacher, and now this. I'll talk to him first thing in the morning."

"Another tidbit of info to jog your memory. The Caydens adopted their daughter."

He shrugged. "Are you asking? Because I don't know."

"Have proof Erin is adopted, and the strange thing is she looks like Natalie's cousin, Josie Fields."

Wilmington startled. "Cayden built his operation after we separated." He paused. "Natalie has to know her cousins are dead."

"Exactly. Cayden can use her name on business dealings, but how does he explain family deaths? That's a stretch."

"Unless she doesn't have any idea until he plans to tell her. I'm getting up. Need to think this through. Brew the coffee, Daniel."

Daniel made his way to the kitchen. Sometimes he believed Wilmington, but tonight's findings shoved back the truth zone. The anger toward those who'd suffered under the hand of the scammer bubbled. Like Laurel, he pushed aside the reality of what they were doing to simply get the job done.

He texted Laurel and explained he and Wilmington would be up most of the night.

I'm on my way.

Daniel analyzed Wilmington, obviously tired, and from his stiffened back, he must be hurting. But Daniel and Laurel weren't much better off.

Daniel and Wilmington were working on their second cup of coffee when Laurel arrived. She had half moons under her eyes. They all did.

"Have a seat," Daniel said. "We waited for you to continue the discussion about Natalie Ashton Cayden."

She sank into a kitchen chair. "So what did you talk about?"

"Gun laws."

She cringed. "Go ahead. I'm ready."

Wilmington rubbed his face. "Geoff chose Natalie because she was in love with him and had no idea of his business dealings. She was his cover. A beautiful woman who believed every word he said."

"I met her," Laurel said. "Friendly. Protective of Erin. In fact, Cayden did a good job with the doting husband and father routine. But that's meaningless in light of what we've learned."

"I'm saying Cayden kept Fields's and Messner's deaths from her and used her name in his business dealings. He could be planning to . . ." Wilmington's words trailed off.

"Planning what?" Irritation rose in her voice.

"To leave her and cash in on those things in her name before she files for divorce."

Daniel raised a finger. "All the twists and turns lead to one question: How will he scam the four hundred guests and make himself look blameless? I have no reason to believe the plan he gave you and Laurel is legit. The public is going to scream for blood. And, ladies and gentlemen, that's you and Laurel."

"We were aware of that from the beginning." Laurel clenched her fist. "But it won't happen."

"Looks to me like he has a foolproof plan, originated eight years ago. You show me how he's scamming the group on Thursday, and then we can figure out how to catch him . . . or her . . . or both of them." Or all three. Daniel stood and reached for a coffee refill. "When you have those answers, we'll arrest him, or them, for murder and fraud too."

"You're hotter than I've ever seen you," Wilmington said.

"You weren't at the funeral of one of my grandparents' friends, a man who purchased a life insurance policy from Messner." Daniel's voice rose. "You weren't at the hospital when I learned Emma Dockson had died, and now that death is labeled murder. Your grandparents weren't almost kidnapped from an Uptown parking lot. And what about the other elderly either dead or in Cayden's database? Yeah, I'm hot. It's two days to a possible explosion time, and we aren't much better off than when this started."

Laurel stared at him, wide-eyed. "Daniel, I'm as angry as you are." Her voice whispered calm. "We're exhausted and frustrated. You're good with pencil and paper. We'll line up what to do next and do it."

Daniel grabbed pen and paper from the counter and sat at the dining room table. His face burned in the heat of fury. Wilmington wrapped an arm around his shoulders. "You saved my life. I'd do anything for you. Name it, and I'll get it done. My back's better, so don't cut me any slack."

Daniel nodded. "Thanks." He breathed in deeply and wrote Laurel's name first. He hadn't lost it for a long time. Actually the unloading felt good. His head cleared. "You're having lunch with Natalie and Erin tomorrow. Dive into family stuff. Pick her brain. Go shopping. Ask if anyone else close to Cayden will be at the fund-raiser. See if you can get her fingerprints."

"Got it, and I'll text Preston in a little while to see what he can find out. I know he thinks that's useless, but that was before the new info."

"Okay, Mr. Wilmington. Find out about Erin's adoption. Is his marriage solid?" Daniel lifted his pen. "He might have had his fill of the wife and her side of the family. Does he care for Erin? What did he mean when he used the word *explosion*? An explanation about his lack of fingerprints. Plans for future business ventures."

"I'm the ace when it comes to extracting information. Too bad I can't use some of my old tactics."

Daniel chuckled. "Laurel and I could hold him down." But what if this was all playing into Wilmington's strategy? He had a reputation for maneuvering people, and Daniel and Laurel could be dancing in tune to his strings. "Now my list. I want to walk around the Junior League. Place the guests, servers, FBI agents, host table, the stage, all of it. Pray for guidance." He didn't look at Laurel, but Wilmington offered an amen. He turned to the man. "I have a few loose ends to run down. Ignacio Vega isn't stupid, and I want to find out what he knows." He pushed the paper to the middle of the table for the other two to examine. "Can we check in with each other during the day and then regroup here tomorrow night, say seven?"

They all agreed. Soon after, Daniel walked Laurel to her car. "Text me when you get home."

"Sure. What are you really doing tomorrow?" she whispered.

He smiled in the darkness. "Just exactly what I said, and I intend to follow Wilmington."

"I have a secret too. I gave Natalie roses. Put a bug in one of the stems and the transmitter in the vase. Talked Preston into listening in."

"You really think she's in on it?"

"I'm covering all the bases."

He took her hand, craving the closeness of her. "I'd kiss you, but Wilmington or Cayden might be watching."

She opened her car door. "I'll take a rain check, Officer Hilton. Lots of them."

CHAPTER 60

Laurel texted SSA Preston regarding Natalie Cayden's bug. Nothing but family chatter. She asked him to continue monitoring, and he reluctantly agreed.

"Has she ever been in Houston before?"

"We have no flight record for Natalie Ashton or Natalie Cayden. Doesn't mean she hasn't been here."

"Don't think it's a rabbit trail to follow right now," she said.

A short while later, she grabbed her purse and drove to Truluck's on Westheimer, where she and Natalie had agreed to meet at eleven thirty. The meal went well. Erin talked freely, and her mother encouraged the little girl to be a part of the luncheon.

"How long have you and Geoff been married?"

"We celebrated our tenth anniversary in August. We wanted children, and Erin came along."

"Morton wants children soon, but I'm a little unsure. Did you have a hard pregnancy?"

"Not at all. Never had morning sickness, and the weight came off easily." She covered her mouth and laughed. "Erin is adopted."

"I was chosen," the little girl said.

Laurel's emotions sank. She'd been wrong about Natalie, a lovely woman who'd been used as Wilmington suggested. "You are one beautiful little girl."

"Thank you."

"Geoff has been smitten since the day she was placed in our arms. She's his princess, and while he's putty in her hands, he makes sure she behaves and is respectful. Schooling is a biggie, and we brought her assignments so she won't lag behind."

Laurel smiled at Erin. "What's your favorite subject?"

She touched her chin. "Science. What was yours, Miss Laurel?"

"Math."

"That's my number two favorite. And dance."

Laurel kept up appearances while she chastised herself for chasing a rabbit trail. Two days until the fund-raiser. Two days before four hundred people were scammed. Two days before a possible explosion. She shivered. Where were the answers?

✳ ✳ ✳

1:30 P.M. TUESDAY

Daniel had followed Wilmington. True to his word, he took a taxi to meet Cayden at a hotel at the Galleria. Stayed one hour and thirty-five minutes and took another taxi back to the condo. Nothing.

Now he felt like the carry-out king. Wilmington had called him and wanted to share what he'd learned from Cayden. Announced he was hungry. The man must have the metabolism of a lion. He put away more food than a football player in training, and none of it transferred to body fat.

Daniel entered the kitchen with a Sonic bag in one hand and a huge drink in the other.

"Thank you, my friend." Wilmington inhaled the aroma of burger and fries. "Sonic never made the prison menu. Did you bring anything for yourself?"

"It's all yours. Can't eat when I'm working hard on a case." He set the drink on the counter. "Here's your cherry slush. You're getting around pretty good with fifteen stitches in your back."

"Slept well before meeting Cayden and had an hour of prayer."

Daniel thought lightning would strike the man. Too many signs of deceit. He grabbed two bananas and set one beside Wilmington. "Want a potassium kick with your fries?"

With their food, they sat at a table overlooking the golf course. Wilmington said grace and dug into his double burger and fries. "I've learned a few things," he said between mouthfuls.

"I'm ready," Daniel said. "I learned nothing about Breacher, and Vega only comes out at night. I'll be on him later."

"Have you heard from Laurel?"

"She's bummed. Natalie told her Erin was adopted. Didn't read anything into her body language. Natalie asked her to do a little more shopping, and she went along with the idea in case something might slip. She also has a meeting with Thatcher."

"You don't like him."

"Thatcher has a chip on his shoulder the size of Mt. Everest."

"Needs the Lord." Wilmington took a long drink of his cherry slush. "You gave me a list, and I did my best. Cayden is bored with his trophy wife. Wandering eye. Found Josie more exciting but got tired of her not following orders. Kept her around because she was Natalie's cousin and the mother of his child." He lifted a brow. "Cayden and Josie are Erin's biological parents. When Josie was shot, he had to dispose of her."

"Sticky family situations."

"I told him my concern about my fingerprints and DNA following me the rest of my life. He laughed. Claimed he'd burned his off. Suggested I do the same. Said it helped in many instances, but he hadn't found a solution for rewriting DNA."

Wilmington's features rang true. Would Daniel ever be able to figure this man out before Thursday night? "How did you respond?"

"Said I'd look into it. Questioned him about future business ventures. Asked if the secret partner would be there. He refused to comment. Something's not right about this."

"Like he's taking orders from someone else?"

Wilmington nodded. "I texted Preston on the way back with what I learned. It looked like a book by the time I finished, but I didn't want to talk with the taxi driver listening."

"How'd you leave it?"

"Cayden will let me know in time for me and Laurel to get out of the way of the Feds. He's seen them snooping around the Junior League. The challenge intrigues him."

"What about the diversion he mentioned earlier?"

"Car bombs during the event."

"Doesn't it seem risky to involve his wife and daughter?"

Wilmington shook his head. "He cares about Erin, but Natalie has lost her worth. God help us. I hate to think I was at his level. I'm staying on him. I promise you this won't go down without a fight."

Where from here? Daniel prayed for wisdom like he'd never prayed before.

CHAPTER 61

Laurel finished her coffee and stared into Morton's face. They sat at his round dining table. Daniel had left a few minutes before to trail Vega, and Wilmington was waiting for a call from Cayden. The man had a business proposition to toss.

The awkwardness of once more being alone with Wilmington hovered over her, although he'd exhibited the attributes of a perfect gentleman. Fear snapped her attention. How long would he keep up the charade? The peacefulness in his face made him look younger. Yet if he'd planned her demise, it could happen at any moment. Her gaze swept to her purse and Glock.

His superficial caring for her and Daniel was such a marked polarity of the man she remembered.

She'd play every angle to find the truth.

"What's going on inside your head?" he said. "Hard to read a trained agent."

"This case and the countdown." A new tactic filtered into her thoughts. "By the way, thanks."

"For what? Not forcing you to play Monopoly?"

She smiled. "That too. I mean for having the guts to change."

"Is this part of the Laurel interrogation?"

"What do you want it to be?"

"The real deal." He glanced down, then back to her. "I've

decided money and power are not my gods. Neither are bad in and of themselves, but the way I used them was. Are you ready for the same lineup?"

"Don't think so. What puzzles me is why you're risking your neck to end an elderly crime. Daniel hasn't figured it out either."

"Like you, he has his doubts, especially with Vega and Breacher once on my payroll."

"Can you blame him?" she said.

"No. I vowed to help prevent crime when I became a Christian. I didn't think I'd be tested by having an old friend be the one to betray me."

The waters muddied, and she still second-guessed his alliance.

He folded a paper napkin in front of him. "The way I see it, you sacrificed everything to put me behind bars, and I deserved it. I was headed down a road of complete isolation. If I hated anyone, it was you. Then I found a God I could serve, and I figured if I could forgive you, I could forgive anyone. After all, God had done that for me." He paused. "Didn't mean to preach."

"It's okay." She'd heard it all before. Often wished she could believe.

He picked up the napkin and refolded it. "Then there's Daniel, a man dedicated to protecting his grandparents. A good man. Not sure how all of this will play out with us, but we're an unlikely three-some. I've stopped asking why and am trying to just be. However long I have left on this earth has to mean something. Starts with me doing my part to help you and Daniel stop Cayden's scam."

"Plans for tomorrow?"

"Prison ministry. Pastor Emerson McKee of Community Evangelical Church has the plans and funds. Who better to talk to criminals than an ex-con?"

"Crazy as it sounds, I believe you'll make a success of it."

"You think it's crazy? Imagine how I feel."

"I suppose so." *Please, Morton, don't say what's in your heart. It complicates the case even more.*

"Got a question for you," he said.

"All right." Her insides quivered. She stood and walked into the living room, processing what he'd probably ask.

"Was any of it real?"

Truth, Laurel. She swung to meet his scrutiny. "Remember the morning we saddled up Phantom and your horse and rode out early to see the sunrise? We watched it burst over the horizon together."

"I do. Had no idea the view would be so spectacular."

She swallowed the thickening in her throat. "That was the closest I ever felt to you as a friend. Mornings weren't your favorite time of the day, but the ride was your idea. Not once did you complain. Neither did you have bodyguards that morning."

"You thanked me." He joined her at the window.

"I liked you then, appreciated your gesture of making me happy."

He smiled. "I needed to know it wasn't all pretend."

She rubbed the chill bumps on her arms.

"We've come a long way, haven't we? From lovers to enemies to almost friends."

What could she say in light of all he'd done?

"Laurel, don't be afraid of giving your heart to Daniel. From what I've learned, he had a rough beginning. Like you."

Uneasiness inched through her. She'd thought Wilmington only knew she'd been orphaned at a young age, but he'd revealed more that day at the prison. He had means to discover a storehouse of info. "Do you know any more about me than what's in the records?"

He breathed in deeply. "No. It was a plan for after our wedding, to find out who'd murdered your parents."

She stared at him, a dangerous man and yet something else. *Change the subject.* "Are your men watching every angle of the building?"

"Yep. They follow us around like lost puppies."

"Armed puppies."

"I'm working on converting them."

She laughed, and it felt good. "Do you think Daniel is safe trailing Vega?"

"Daniel's smart, crafty. He's supposed to text both of us later." His phone sounded with an incoming text. "Might be sooner than I expected." He glanced at the phone. "We have—"

The shatter of the window's glass crackled the air.

"It's a grenade!" He lunged toward it.

✳ ✳ ✳

**12:15 A.M. WEDNESDAY
ONE DAY BEFORE OCTOBER 15**

Around midnight, Daniel had watched Vega disappear into the hotel where Cayden and his family stayed. He loathed the waiting part of his job. A text came in from Thatcher Graves on his iPhone. Good thing Daniel carried both phones.

Call me asap

He pressed in Thatcher's number. The agent responded on the first ring.

"What's going on?"

"Let me begin by saying Laurel is okay. Someone tossed a grenade inside Wilmington's condo while she was with him."

Stunned, he whipped into cop mode. "Who did it? Was she hurt? Is he okay?"

"Both escaped injuries. Wilmington tossed it back. Exploded on the way to the street."

"All that happened in four to five seconds." He shook his head. "Short of impossible."

"He claimed it was a God-thing."

Relief replaced Daniel's alarm. "Anyone hurt in the blast?"

"No, but two of Wilmington's men are dead. One man had his throat cut, and another man's undergoing surgery to repair a knife wound to his chest."

The dynamics of Laurel and Wilmington's escape from death hit him hard. "Wilmington took a huge chance with the grenade. Could have blown him and Laurel to bits."

"My thoughts too. Proves he might be on the level." With this case. With his faith.

Was Laurel convinced? For that matter, was Daniel? "Any clues?"

"Not yet. I'm at the hospital. Need to question the injured man when he wakes up from surgery. Providing he survives."

"Where's Laurel?"

"She's at her apartment. More upset than she lets on. Insisted on being alone."

"Wilmington's not with her?"

"Weren't you listening? By any chance have you heard from him?"

"No." Doubt about Wilmington rose.

"When the smoke cleared at Wilmington's place and I arrived, he took off."

Why would he leave the crime scene? "You're sure he's not at the hospital?"

Thatcher blew out exasperation. "Wouldn't I know that, Officer Hilton? He told Laurel he'd talk to her in the morning. Needed to visit the dead man's family and the other guy's girlfriend."

"Is the girlfriend there?"

"Yes. She told me Wilmington had already left. Said he'd be in touch. Look, call if you hear from him. I have important things to discuss with both of you."

"Why not now?"

"Just find Wilmington and call me."

Daniel knew exactly where Wilmington had gone. He was standing guard outside Laurel's apartment, and if Cayden wanted both of them dead, he wouldn't give up easily. But Vega had been with Cayden . . .

His gut told him Wilmington and Laurel were in the middle of a trap. One the FBI had created.

CHAPTER 62

After two calls to Wilmington rolled to voice mail, Daniel had three options—wait near the gate of Laurel's apartment until someone came in or out, use his police officer rank, or scale the gate. If Cayden had men on the inside of the property, they'd be watching the entrance for Wilmington to show up.

A sudden thought crossed his mind. What if Wilmington planted that grenade earlier?

Daniel pressed in Laurel's burner phone. "Are you okay?" he said.

"Sure. I wasn't hurt tonight. Why?"

"Because you're in danger. Cayden's men weren't successful, and they don't give up easily."

"I can take care of myself."

"Let's team forces. I'm right—"

"You do your job, and I'll do mine. I'll check in with you later." She ended the call.

Was Laurel sleep deprived?

After parking his BMW a block away from the rear of the property, Daniel grabbed his weapon and silently closed the car door. He hurried along a brick wall separating the apartment buildings from the street until he reached a rear gate. He silenced his phone and relied on its vibration to alert him.

Once inside the gate, he made his way between buildings until he found Laurel's apartment. Crouching behind bushes, he took in the grounds. Lights were on in her apartment, the drapes open. She wouldn't deliberately put herself out there for a clear shot.

Suspicion crept through him, and he didn't like where it was going.

Had Thatcher lied to him about where Laurel had gone?

Wilmington hid nearby. Daniel was sure of it. After what happened to Wilmington's men earlier, the man would not risk any more lives. He kept vigil of Laurel's apartment. Men like Cayden didn't take defeat lightly, and with his military training, he could easily mobilize as a lone sniper. Who else hid in the dark? Vega?

The residents had garages, but a parking area held a handful of vehicles. Two security Jeeps made their rounds on the property. Daniel stole around the empty vehicles while his thoughts stumbled over Thatcher Graves's instructions to call him when he'd located Wilmington. Anger clawed at his logic, and he dropped beside a car to regroup.

How stupid.

How trusting.

Thatcher knew Wilmington would head here. The agent was using the man to draw Cayden out.

Find Wilmington, then regroup.

An area several feet behind him contained a line of tall bushes that framed a swimming pool. That location was the only place Wilmington could conceal himself and keep an eye on Laurel's apartment. Love blinded the man . . . or his plan had led to her near demise tonight.

Daniel darted across the parking lot to where he believed Wilmington hid. The man stepped from behind a bush, but Daniel pushed him down.

"You knew I'd be here," Wilmington whispered. "Did the FBI send you to find me?"

"Not exactly." Sarcasm topped Daniel's words. "I think we've been sent as bait knowing Cayden and his men would follow us. I don't

think Laurel's here. She'd never keep her drapes open. The moment
we step out of these bushes, we'll be in the middle of a firefight."

"You mean they played us to draw out the bad boys?"

"If it walks like a duck and talks like a duck, then it's a duck."
Daniel pointed to the left. "One agent is posted behind the pool
hut. Two more are in a security Jeep. If I'm not mistaken, one
of Cayden's men is on the other side of that truck to our right.
Probably moves when the security Jeep drives by. Not sure about
any more." Daniel paused, watching his theory take action.

"I'm mad enough to switch sides."

Discouragement rose in Daniel too, but this wasn't the time to
point fingers. After all, he hadn't followed Thatcher's directions.
"No, you're not. We're dealing with people who have their own
agendas. We're the good guys. Thatcher had a plan, but I'd've liked
to have been told before walking into an inferno." He paused.
"I was supposed to call him when I located you."

"Was Laurel in on this?"

"I doubt it." She wouldn't have agreed. "I talked to her a few
minutes ago, and I think she's off on her own."

"What now?"

"Everyone's in place. All they need is a duck call."

Wilmington snorted. "I'm not walking out there to see who
has the best aim. Working to find the evidence to arrest Cayden is
one thing, but not this."

Daniel searched the area for every conceivable place someone
could take cover. "The bad guys are waiting for me to join you.
But they expected me to drive through the front gate. How did
you get inside?"

"Drove in when the gate opened."

"Were you followed?" Daniel said.

"No idea. Can't believe the FBI did this to us."

"We're just upset because we didn't think of it first. They have
eyes on us, and I'd like to think they'd prefer we leave in one piece."

"Body bags aren't my idea of evening attire."

Daniel chuckled. "I have an idea. Might not make the FBI happy, but I'm a little sour on Thatcher Graves right now."

✳ ✳ ✳

4:45 A.M. WEDNESDAY

"How could you have done this and not told me?" Laurel paced the floor of SSA Preston's office.

"We arranged the situation after you and Wilmington were nearly killed," he said.

"By the way, I don't have a scratch on me. No reason I shouldn't have been informed. When did you share the setup with Daniel and Wilmington?"

"Thatcher handled the details."

"Oh, really? Let me guess the conversation. 'Hey, guys, we're using you as targets to snag Cayden.'"

"They want the scammers stopped just like we do. Neither man would have argued."

Laurel spun around. Truth pierced needles into her heart. "'Would'? What does that mean?"

"Calm down. We have an operation in progress, and you can learn the details later."

She glared at him, the man she respected. Granted, her exhaustion spoke through her, but it didn't stop the words spitting from her mouth. "You put Daniel and Wilmington in danger so a couple of agents would look good."

"Of course not." His voice rose. "Thatcher proceeded because everyone involved agreed to the risks."

Laurel sank into a chair. "Then why haven't we heard anything?"

"You're paranoid about this case. You've let your feelings for Officer Hilton and your hatred for Wilmington override sound judgment."

Laurel gripped the sides of her chair. "Then go ahead. Get rid of me. If I'm not doing the job of an agent, I need to be relieved of duties."

His face reddened. "Excuse me?"

"You heard me. You don't have a clue about my real feelings for Daniel or how much I despise Wilmington or how the elderly scam is eating me alive. I will see this case to the end whether I have my badge or not." She grabbed her purse and phones.

Preston stared at her. "Laurel, you were and are the best agent to work with Morton Wilmington. Good judgment has always been your best trait. Fatigue and irrational emotions have robbed you of your best ability."

She headed to the door. "Never mind. I'm finished."

"You can't leave here," he said. "You don't have a car. It's dangerous to head to a potential crime scene alone. I order you to stand down."

"I arranged for my car to be brought here. Handled it long before you walked in. I'm not sitting around while more people are killed."

✳ ✳ ✳

5:10 A.M. WEDNESDAY

Daniel drew in a breath and filled his lungs.

"Glad I worked out in prison," Wilmington said, bending to grip his knees. "Not a twenty-year-old anymore. My back's killing me, but that was fun."

Daniel's wrist throbbed while Wilmington thrived on adrenaline. "You need to get out more if you thinking playing monkey over a gate is entertainment."

They hurried across the street away from the apartment complex, taking cover in the shadows.

"Were we seen?"

"The agent by the pool hut is Thatcher Graves." Daniel intended for Thatcher to see them. Later he'd approach the agent who forgot to mention the two awaited a trap.

"So the FBI knows we left the scene. Now they have to figure out who and how many of Cayden's men are there."

"Your car's inside the front gate, and you have your keys. Once we have my car, we'll park it between the two front main gates. You set off your car alarm at the front, then head to my car. I'll wait here. I'm hoping the sound brings them out of their holes."

"Then what?"

"It either works and this is over, or we help the FBI. Keep your phone on vibrate."

"We should go into the investigation business. Laurel too."

What an entrepreneur. "Not sure she'd leave the FBI. Or me, HPD."

"We could operate the business part-time. Work nights and days off."

"When did you get this idea?"

Wilmington shrugged. "My mind never shuts down. Now that I'm sure my old Army bud wants me dead and taking the blame for his crimes, I'm on overload."

"I've noticed. You don't sleep much either. Between the three of us, we have experience in almost every area."

"My point. Think about it, and we can talk later."

Wilmington lived from one high to another, but right now, the business proposal was on hold. Probably permanently. Once they parked several feet back from the main gate, Daniel stole to the rear. Wilmington made his way to the entrance and set off his car alarm. Flashing lights and the siren brought the early morning to life.

A few minutes later, Daniel's burner phone vibrated with Wilmington's call. "The shooter's still in place and the security Jeep is keeping its distance."

"Let me know the moment you see anything." He slipped the phone into his jacket pocket.

Wilmington's car alarm timed out.

No one exposed his position.

The longer time ticked away, the greater the likelihood of residents emerging from their homes to head to work, increasing the number of those who could get hurt. The muggy air didn't help his attitude, and neither did the sweat streaming down his face.

Headlights swung through the complex and toward the rear gate. He knelt in the bushes and pulled out his iPhone. When the driver pulled through, Daniel made sure his flash was off and snapped a pic of the license plate, but the woman behind the wheel had two small children with her.

What a waste.

Time passed and ushered in the dawn. A man dressed in black raced toward the gate. Not Cayden. Too muscular. Daniel pulled his Glock. Thatcher Graves sped behind the man, his size and gait giving him away.

"Stop. FBI!" Thatcher said.

The man spun around with his weapon aimed at Thatcher. Daniel fired at the neck, bringing him down.

Thatcher jogged to the body and examined it, feeling for a pulse. He glanced up. "He's dead. Thanks."

"Considering you set Wilmington and me up, you're welcome."

"You were supposed to call—"

"Now's not the time to discuss it. It is what it is."

"This is your fault, not mine."

"Right." Daniel reined in the anger. "Who's your friend?"

"No clue." He grabbed for his phone. "Calling this in."

"He wasn't alone."

Thatcher stood and walked to the iron gate. "We counted two."

Daniel lifted a brow. "Where?"

"A second man took out one of the security drivers after you left. I don't have a status."

"MO?"

"Broke the agent's neck. Trained."

Daniel's phone vibrated with a call from Wilmington. He answered. "I see a man scaling the top of the brick wall. Looks like he has a motorcycle a few yards away."

Daniel took off running toward the BMW, keeping his phone active. "Wilmington's spotted the other guy."

"I'm going with you," Thatcher said.

Daniel called over his shoulder. "You've got a body to handle, and I can't wait. I'll call you." He turned his attention to his phone. "What's happening?"

"You won't like this. Laurel's parked behind your Beamer."

CHAPTER 63

Daniel pressed the gas to keep up with the motorcycle, a Suzuki Hayabusa, one of the fastest made. The driver, dressed in black, flew toward the 249. He wore a helmet, making it impossible to ID him. Laurel stayed on Daniel's bumper. He hadn't called her yet. Better to take care of the mess in front of him, then deal with the woman on his rear.

"Told you we'd make a good team," Wilmington said. "She appeared out of nowhere while I watched the gate."

"Have you talked to her?"

"No. I'd probably demand she go home, and she'd turn her weapon on me." He sighed. "I'm afraid she'll get hurt. Unfortunately my protection detail is either dead or in the hospital. Most of the guys have left since I abandoned my old business practices. That leaves you and me and maybe the FBI."

"We'll sort it out later. Did your man pull through surgery?"

"Yes. He's in intensive care. His girlfriend's with him."

"I'm sorry."

"Thanks. Told me Vega tossed the grenade. Hey, I heard a shot back there."

"Bad guy dead. Brought him down before he could pump a bullet into Thatcher."

Wilmington whipped to him. "Now he owes you."

"He's okay. Personality differences." Daniel shook his head. "I'm mad. He wanted me to find you and then call him. I'm not an idiot. He knew where you'd gone from the hospital."

The Suzuki sped through a red light and whipped onto 249 north.

"I have to call Thatcher," Daniel said. "Deal with the other junk when this is over."

"Do I have a vote?"

"It's not about our egos. But it was a good thing he stood on the other side of the gate back there or I might have broken his jaw." He pressed in the agent's number. "We're now heading up 249 toward Tomball." He described the motorcycle. "I'll keep you posted." He laid the phone on his console. "If that's Cayden, he's done his homework. He'll know where he's going."

"Special ops. He planned for every scenario. Survival and outsmarting us."

Daniel wove into the right lane, ready to seize an opportunity to run him off the road. "At least we know he hasn't used the bank account numbers from the life insurance apps. That must be his grand finale along with the fund-raiser. Works to make the FBI look inept."

"Right. Gives him genius status."

"Good call. So if he hasn't programmed the withdrawals, then we need to keep him away from online activity." He added pressure to the gas.

The Suzuki darted to the left. Daniel crossed over behind him. Where to now?

✳ ✳ ✳

6:40 A.M. WEDNESDAY

Laurel kept up with the chase. She ignored a call from SSA Preston, still fuming with him not giving her all the information. Definitely her career ended. She took a call from Thatcher, who offered that he'd learned next to nothing about the chase in front of her. But when Daniel swerved into the right lane and she had a clear view of the motorcycle, she pressed in Wilmington's number.

"I need a little history," she said.

"She wants to know what's going on," he said, obviously to Daniel. "I've got the go-ahead, and we're on speaker," Wilmington said. "Where were you?"

"With SSA Preston."

"What are you not saying?" Daniel said. "Never mind. Why did you show up outside your apartment alone?"

"Because I realized Thatcher hadn't told you everything. Preston insisted he wouldn't have set you two up. But I had to see for myself."

Wilmington snorted. "Remains to be seen. Have you talked to Mr. T.?"

"Yes. Said Daniel saved his life. I asked why you were used as targets."

"And?"

"Claims he had no idea you'd show up there tonight. He found out Wilmington and I had reservations on a late-night flight to Paris. How very nice of Cayden to use our real names. Looks like we've been the scapegoats all along."

The motorcycle sped around a pickup. Daniel chased after him with Laurel in close pursuit. "He'll have another plan."

"He always does," Laurel said. "Roadblocks are in motion but with the rush-hour traffic going both ways, it'll be slow. For whatever it's worth, I learned something from Thatcher."

"Is this supposed to be the grace thing?

"Sorta. Some kind of family emergency. He's catching the first flight out Sunday morning, providing we have arrests made."

"Excuses that almost get people killed demand an apology," Wilmington said. "His ego's the size of Texas."

"Let's concentrate on keeping up with the motorcycle," Daniel said. "Laurel, you don't have a partner. Why don't you hold back until the FBI joins us?"

"Forget it. I had a choice of doing nothing or getting into trouble."

"What do you mean?"

"Preston's not happy with me."

Daniel gritted his teeth. "Laurel, please wait for Thatcher. You don't have anyone covering your back."

"I made my decision. Pay attention to the motorcycle. Not me. Run him off the road." Laurel ended the call and raced on behind Daniel.

Where was the rider going? He seemed to fly and knew how to control the motorcycle. He veered toward the shoulder.

Thatcher phoned. She hesitated to answer, but they needed backup.

"Yes."

"I'm ten to fifteen minutes out. Another car will be there in less time. Where's he headed?"

"Not sure. Wilmington gave me the motorcycle's license plate numbers." She recited them. "The rider's just run across the embankment to the feeder off the highway."

CHAPTER 64

Daniel bounced the BMW over the hilly embankment after the Suzuki. The rider sped in and around feeder traffic, swung a right, and raced down a side road. Daniel stayed on his tail, fearing a wide stretch of less-traveled road would leave him in the motorcycle's wake.

"If this guy is Cayden, what he did back at the complex is sufficient for bringing charges and we've managed to stop the scam. The FBI can detain him and cancel the fund-raiser," Wilmington said. "Won't have the secret partner, but I'm tired of dealing with him."

"What if it's not him?"

The Suzuki slowed behind the early morning vehicles pouring into a high school.

Daniel's mind swung to the worst possible scenario. "As much as I want him arrested, I want clear of those kids."

"He'll endanger every one of them." Wilmington pounded his fist on the dash. "Think about it, Daniel. If he hurts any of them, every parent will be out for blood."

"Let's hope he stays cool through this area." Cayden's past indicated his own agenda—body count held no meaning.

Traffic slowed further as kids turned into the student parking lot. Horns blared. The Suzuki wove in and out of the vehicles, no doubt entertaining kids. The rider looked like a dark hero or a comic strip character.

"Stay on him." Wilmington's words were uttered like a prayer. "If he'd just pass by the school."

A Honda rear-ended a truck.

A bicycle hit the ditch.

Two boys jumped a barbed-wire fence into a cow pasture.

The Suzuki turned right into the student parking lot. And Daniel followed. "I'm familiar with the layout of this school, and there's an entrance on the other side of the building," he said. "If he exits there, the kids and teachers will be safe."

Wilmington groaned. "He parked by the football stadium beside a Camry."

The car would shield him from law enforcement fire. "Is he calling us out? Or does he want to make a—?" Daniel's words were clipped off in midair. From under his leather jacket, the rider had produced an FN P90—an ultrashort "bullpup" submachine gun.

Oh, God, don't let him open fire on these kids.

Daniel quickly brought the BMW to a halt several dozen yards from the rider and waved to draw his attention away from the others. "I'll handle him. You and Laurel stay back. Looks like we need a SWAT team and a negotiator."

He pulled out his gun and jogged toward the Suzuki driver. They'd talk. Find out what he wanted and pray no one got hurt. He gestured for the kids to move away. Teachers and a security officer from the high school herded them like sheep toward the closest building. Sirens alerted him to other police officers en route. But the kids wanted to be in the center of the action, as though they were watching a movie shoot.

"Are you a one-man show?" The rider addressed Daniel. He had a Hispanic accent.

"I just want to discuss the situation."

"You mean stall until the FBI and HPD arrive?" He sneered.

Daniel ventured closer. "I don't want innocent people hurt. What can I do for you?"

He shifted his weapon. "Laurel Evertson. She comes with me, or I turn my rifle on these kids. Your choice."

No way would Laurel go with him. "That's not in any deal."

"Want to guess how many of those kids I can level?"

"I'll go." Laurel stood fifty feet to Daniel's right. She dropped her Glock on the pavement and raised her hands.

"No. That's crazy." Daniel refused to look at her, keeping his gaze fixed on the rider. One slip, and Daniel would drop him.

She moved toward the man, shoulders erect, steps determined.

"Laurel, listen to me," Daniel said. All the warnings about emotional involvement churned through him.

She ignored him, advancing toward the gunman.

"Take me instead," Wilmington said behind Daniel. "I'm worth more money than you can imagine."

The man laughed. "I'm no fool." As soon as Laurel stood near him, he grabbed her arm. "Get into the car." He opened the passenger side of the Camry's front seat. "Come to daddy, Laurel."

She obeyed. Not even a look back.

Daniel's senses froze. He calculated the timing of the man walking around the car to the driver's side. One second was all he needed. But the man kept his weapon aimed at Laurel while he made his way around the front to the other side.

Flashes of what Daniel could do pounded against his skull— sending fire into the car's tires, hopping onto the motorcycle and following, taking a shot with a prayer the man wouldn't squeeze the trigger first and kill Laurel.

No good options. From the corner of his eye, he saw that patrol cars, an ambulance, and a few unmarked vehicles had arrived. But they stayed back.

Daniel didn't have negotiator skills, and he needed them desperately.

"Gotcha," the man called out. "Never underestimate someone who is smarter than you. Better trained too."

"I'll remember that," Daniel said.

Laurel needed to act now if Daniel had a chance of bringing the man down. As if reading his mind, she opened the car door, diverting the rider's attention.

Daniel pulled the trigger, sending a bullet into his chest and leveling him to the ground. Laurel rushed to the body.

"He's gone," she said.

Daniel checked the rider's pulse and confirmed the man was dead. He lifted the helmet.

Ignacio Vega.

He pulled out Vega's phone. His last call had been to Natalie Cayden.

✳ ✳ ✳

8:45 A.M. WEDNESDAY

Laurel would never be able to figure out men. SSA Preston and Thatcher Graves were two of them. Although her career had been threatened, Preston responded to Vega's takedown as commendable. The FBI moved in on Cayden's hotel, but Natalie was gone, leaving Geoff and Erin wondering why and where.

How much of the operation had Natalie's name on it? Where had she gone?

Had Cayden arranged to have her disposed of like Fields?

She'd worked tough cases in the past. But none that tugged at her heart more than this one. Her mind flew to Abby and Earl, now out of harm's way. But what of the other victims? The families who'd lost everything and those who were deceased? The vendetta for Jesse's death clung to her like a parasite. At times, she thought it all would eat her alive before she helped arrest Cayden and Wilmington.

As sure as she breathed another breath, she'd not give up.

CHAPTER 65

Daniel hoped sitting with Wilmington and Cayden in a hotel room made the best use of his time, since it trickled away moment by moment. Cayden had asked his old Army bud to stay with him until Natalie returned or was found. He'd tossed out the roses in a fit of anger, destroying the bug. Not a whole lot Wilmington or Daniel could say with two FBI agents in the room.

"Did you two have an argument?" Wilmington said privately to Cayden when Erin left the suite's living room. "Tell me the truth."

"No. She went down to get a cup of coffee and didn't return. How many times do I have to repeat myself?"

Wilmington leaned in. "Why did she call Vega and talk to him for ten minutes?"

"Please do not whisper," an agent said.

Cayden's face hardened. "Why aren't you two out looking for my wife?"

"Sir, HPD received a tip that your life may be in danger too and requested our support. We're assigned to protect you."

"Do you think my wife is dead? What can you tell me?"

"Sir, we haven't been briefed. All we can do is follow orders, not issue them."

"Geoff, this will be sorted out soon," Wilmington said.

Cayden covered his face. "I don't know why Natalie called Vega, who is now dead for an unspeakable crime. I have no idea what he was doing or why he found it necessary to speak to my wife."

Erin burst into the room, tears streaming down her face.

He embraced her. "I'm sorry, baby."

"Has Mommy been hurt?"

"We just can't find her right now."

She crawled onto his lap and he held her tightly. "Is this like the last time?"

Daniel's ears perked.

"Sir, your wife has gone missing in the past?" the same agent said.

"She went shopping and forgot her phone. I panicked—guess it's my military training—and I thought the worst. Erin and I went looking for her. It was all a misunderstanding. Right, Erin?"

She nodded. "Mommy saw my aunt Josie and forgot the time."

Daniel wished he could explore that conversation.

"Geoff, what do you want me to do?" Wilmington said. "She's not been to the airport and HPD has a BOLO out on her. Security cameras filmed her leaving the hotel alone."

"I don't know." He sniffed. "We planned this trip around my medical leave and the nonprofit fund-raiser. Should I cancel it?"

Cayden and Wilmington should earn awards for this performance.

"Might need to," Wilmington said. "Are you even up to playing emcee tomorrow?"

Cayden's eyes watered. "My asthma has kicked into overtime. All we have now are questions with no answers. Is it selfish for me to abandon help for the elderly at the last minute?"

"No one would blame you under these circumstances," Wilmington said. "Donors will give regardless of a dinner and entertainment."

"Sir," the FBI agent said. "We know of your tireless efforts to assist the elderly afflicted with dementia. It would do those who support you a disservice to cancel your role at the fund-raiser."

Cayden gave the man a slight smile. "Thanks. I'll consider it. I know people give more generously to causes when they hear testimonies, and some of the out-of-town guests have already arrived." He kissed Erin on the cheek. "Perhaps I should go ahead as planned. Natalie could open the door and all this could be explained."

✳ ✳ ✳

9:45 P.M. MOUNTAIN TIME, WEDNESDAY

Abby rocked alone on the front porch of the northern Colorado cabin where she and Earl were staying. They'd fished all day in the Fall River, and she'd batter-fried rainbow trout just the way he liked them. Who cared about cholesterol? The FBI agent guarding them had eaten fish and hush puppies until she feared he'd be sick.

Inside the cabin, her dear, sweet husband slept, his mind in yesteryear. A tear trickled over her cheek, and she allowed it to flow until its saltiness ushered in prayers for those she loved.

Closing her eyes, she delighted in the cicadas' songs. An owl hooted as though adding a baritone to the chorus, and in the distance, she could make out the mating bugle call of an elk bull. How peaceful, as she rocked in rhythm to the night choir. Her memories flowed through the years spent with Earl.

When she met him at age fourteen, she never gave a moment of thought to how her heart would ache with love for him. Or how one day she'd look at him and still see the almost-man who saw a girl in trouble. Tears flowed but she didn't care. Liquid healing.

Her mind dwelled on the first few months of living with a loving family who attended Earl's church. Fear stalked her, along with shame for what she'd been forced to do.

"I'm so afraid he'll come after me," she'd said to Earl. "What if he told everyone in your church what I've done?"

"Abby, you were forced. I can't promise you he won't ever try to get you back. But I'll fight him with all I have. And I can promise this—you can always trust God."

"I'm trying hard to believe."

He laughed, that deep rumble she learned to treasure. "When we're old, our faith will be so much stronger."

Earl's words still lingered, caressing her ears and warming her heart.

Dear Daniel, are you being careful? Are you risking your life to stop the scam and murders on us old people? Are you holding on to God's hand tighter than ever before?

Daniel James Hilton, you're such a blessing, so different from Jimmy.

No, she wouldn't go there and beat herself up for mistakes made her first round of parenting. Tonight she focused on God, Earl, and Daniel. And Laurel too.

Keep them safe, Lord. Give them wisdom to end these crimes.

CHAPTER 66

Daniel, Laurel, and Wilmington sat in the FBI office with SSA Preston, Thatcher, and a dozen other agents who were working to find Natalie Cayden and enough evidence against Geoff Cayden to arrest him. Sleep was for those who relied on law enforcement to keep them safe. They'd learned Vega and Natalie had spent hours on the phone over the past year.

"We're pressed for time, but we're investigating Natalie," Preston said. "Did she handle the purchase of the Instantaneous? And who opened the offshore account in her name? Is she working for or against her husband?"

"Let's assume Natalie's dead." Daniel swirled the facts in his head. "Cayden or one of his men arranged it. The why could be anything from finding out she and Vega were having an affair to relieving his boredom. With her out of the picture, he has Erin and a whole lot of money."

"If this is part of the bigger picture, who will take the fall for tonight's scam?" Wilmington massaged his neck muscles. "Who will be left to eliminate the elderly who had the misfortune of purchasing life insurance policies? Others have to be on his payroll. Trouble is, I have no clue who they are. Word on the street is tight-lipped."

Preston stood and paced the floor. "We have footage of Natalie and Vega together in Miami, real cozy. But it doesn't bring us any closer to what we need. It's imperative that we find the silent partner and end the crime spree. Or I'd close down the fund-raiser."

"What's being done about the safety of the guests?" Daniel said.

"A leak to the media will happen in a few hours that will indicate the FBI is investigating reports of a bomb threat at Cayden's fundraiser. We have agents in place for tonight. Up until thirty minutes before the doors open, agents and K-9s will be searching for explosives. It's a risk we have to take. At that point, we're there on alert. Cayden has instructed Laurel to switch baskets with the credit card information and give that to a man waiting. One of our agents will be right there. Those guests will not lose a penny tonight."

"If I receive the credit card info, it's not going anywhere," Laurel said. "None of us trust Cayden, and he doesn't trust us. We must assume his plan is for Wilmington and me to take the fall, from start to finish. He's too smart to reveal to Wilmington how he's taking off with the credit card info. What's certain is that someone other than Cayden will take the fall. The wild card is Erin."

"From what I've seen, Cayden is devoted to his daughter." Daniel's mind sped with the few times he'd seen the man with Erin. Not an act. "I don't think he'd leave the event without her. This whole scam could be a catalyst to get what he really wants— his daughter and plenty of money to support them for the rest of his life."

"Unless we find Natalie Cayden dead and can bring Geoff in for questioning, all we can do is keep our noses to the grindstone," Preston said.

✳ ✳ ✳

6:30 P.M. THURSDAY

Laurel arrived at the Junior League with Daniel and Wilmington per Cayden's directions. All three were dressed in fashionable black. She chose a cocktail-length dress—to make running easier. FBI agents and two K-9s with handlers completed their building search. The banquet hall awaited guests and was filled with round tables for eight, spotless white tablecloths, white roses and candle centerpieces, exquisite china and crystal, and linen cards and envelopes for noting the donations.

Erin, in a long lavender gown, sat on the edge of the stage listening to the band tune up. She waved to her dad, and he returned the gesture.

Cayden motioned for Laurel, Daniel, and Wilmington to move back from the little girl to where they could see the guests as they entered. "The FBI told me they'd received a bomb threat for this evening." He chuckled and tugged on the jacket of his tux. "As if I'd walk into a trap. They can attempt whatever their policy and procedure book calls for. I won."

"No word from Natalie?" Wilmington said.

He frowned. "Don't know what she's doing. I can see where she might be upset about Vega's death, but leaving Erin is cruel. When tonight's over, I'll deal with my wife and her apparent affair with my bodyguard." Bitterness topped his words.

As if Geoff Cayden hadn't initiated enough deceit in his day. She glanced at Daniel and Wilmington. What a disparate bunch. No one trusted anyone, except her and Daniel.

"Last-minute changes," Cayden said. "Laurel, you and Wilmington leave with the credit card envelopes during the video. Everything else adheres to the original plan and schedule."

That sealed the blame on the ex-con and FBI agent.

Guests arrived in a parade of black ties and evening gowns from a list of who's who in the world of the incredibly wealthy with hearts for the needy. Without pause, they signed the guestbook. Cayden had done his homework. He greeted each one with a welcome.

Promptly at seven, the singer began, not too loud, entertaining the crowd with soothing melodies. At seven thirty, salads appeared on the tables and Cayden welcomed the group. Servers ushered in prime rib cooked to perfection, asparagus with hollandaise, wild rice, and three types of rolls. Dessert trays with an assortment of cheesecakes and pies sweetened the crowd.

Cayden took his spot and introduced Morton Wilmington, an old Army bud who'd found the Lord while in prison, a man Cayden loved like a brother. "In the past, he was called Robin Hood. Now he calls himself an honest man. He's also donated a hundred and fifty thousand dollars to aid our nonprofit for the care and advancement of research for those afflicted with dementia and Alzheimer's disease."

The crowd applauded and Wilmington took the mic from Cayden. "Honored guests, I'm humbled to be speaking to you tonight at this grand dinner. I confess it took me to age forty-three to walk the straight road, but no U-turns for me. God showed me . . ."

Laurel half listened as she concentrated on the guests. Two women from opposite sides of the room returned from a bathroom break. FBI agents stood in the room's shadows, earbuds in place. Daniel sat on the other side of Wilmington's chair.

When Wilmington completed his testimony and received a standing ovation, Cayden hugged him. "I'd like to take ten minutes and tell you about my grandmother," he said. "She lived with us because of dementia. My parents refused to place her in a memory care facility because they felt it was their duty to care for her. What I learned from my parents' example . . ." He completed his story and paused as though emotion had overcome him.

"At this time, I'm going to ask our lovely singer to grace us with another song, and I implore you to examine your hearts for the amount you can donate to our nonprofit. Cards, envelopes, and pens are on the tables, and our servers will gather them when you're ready."

The clock ticked closer to scam time. Laurel, Wilmington, and Daniel stood in the back of the hall opposite Cayden. The entertainment continued.

Once the envelopes were gathered, they were placed in a basket and set on the front of the stage. A server stuffed them into a larger envelope and laid it back in the basket. That wasn't the plan. Nerves on alert, Laurel checked in with agents and the two men beside her. She kept her eye on the basket and walked forward.

"I'd like for you to watch a brief video," Cayden said. "At the end, Morton Wilmington will close in prayer."

The houselights dimmed.

The video started.

Laurel kept half her focus on Erin and Cayden. They remained seated.

Five minutes into the presentation, the video came to a halt and complete darkness swept across the huge room. No emergency backup lights came on. This had to be Cayden's doing.

"Please excuse the delay," a man shouted. "Remain seated and calm while we rectify the situation. Thank you for your patience. Should take only a few—"

An explosion rocked the building. Screams pierced the air. Chairs crashed to the floor. Ten seconds later, another explosion burst the air.

"There's smoke coming from the front parking lot," an agent said over Laurel's earbuds. "Two car bombs."

Darkness and confusion imploded into a deafening roar.

Smartphones with flashlight apps looked like glowing candles. Laurel, Daniel, and Wilmington hurried to the front of the room. Cayden and Erin were gone.

Daniel bolted through an exit near the stage and on to the rear parking lot with Laurel and Wilmington on his heels. Outside, the three stopped cold.

Natalie held a .38 Special on her husband and daughter.

CHAPTER 67

In all the hours Daniel had spent on this case, he'd not imagined a child caught in the crosshairs of a violent crime. Cayden held Erin in his arms as though cradling a baby. The envelope with the donations lay atop her. They leaned against a car on the driver's side away from the light illuminating the small rear parking area.

"Put her down." Natalie aimed the revolver. "This is between you and me."

"Mommy, why are you pointing a gun at me and Daddy?"

"What are you doing? We're a team," Cayden said.

Erin sobbed against his chest.

"Let me take her," Laurel said. "She's an innocent child."

"She's my daughter!" Cayden shouted. "No one's taking her from me."

"Geoff, listen." Wilmington stepped closer. "Let me have her."

"You," Cayden said. "You owed me. You and Laurel were going to take the fall for all of it."

"Sure. Whatever you say. I do owe you. Let me start by taking Erin."

"Get away!" Natalie shouted. "Erin is mine."

"Then why let her see this?" Cayden said.

Wilmington took a few more steps forward. "You have an option here, Geoff. I know you love Erin. Give her to me so she'll be safe."

"I can't. She goes with me."

Only a handful of agents covered the area, since the majority of them worked the front parking lot explosion. Daniel had no doubt a SWAT team and negotiator were on their way. In his opinion, too late.

"I helped you every step of the way since before we were married." Natalie spit her words like venom. "I hacked into your brother's account and got what you deserved. All you had to do was eliminate them. Tell me, Geoff, who was the real brains behind this operation? Had it all worked out before mentioning it to you. All you are is a grunt man."

"Natalie, stop. We can talk about this later. Look around you. Cops everywhere."

"Do I care? You sent Ignacio on a hit that would get him killed. He loved me. Not like you."

"You were the one having an affair."

"Me? And where does Josie fit into your miserable excuse? Or Trey? I spent hours putting together impeccable databases that brought us millions of dollars. You were the idiot who didn't want to complete each segment and go dark until the time was right again."

"Natalie, shut up."

She laughed. "I'm such a good housewife. I stayed home and did the laundry. You have no idea the money I've stashed away."

Laurel inched closer. Daniel failed to secure her attention. She'd be killed. He moved toward Natalie.

"For you and Vega? Wasn't he a bit beneath your level?" Cayden shifted Erin in his arms. Was he going to let her go? Reach for his own weapon?

"The truth, Geoff. You and Josie. She told me the real story. No wonder you spoil Erin."

At least she hadn't revealed the man was Erin's father.

"Who designed the life insurance policies? Who gave you the list of rich old people? Who showed you who to eliminate, where, and when? Who gave you the idea of setting up Wilmington? You are nothing without me. Who arranged for the poisoned feed?"

"Please, Mommy. Daddy wants to take us someplace special."

Wilmington touched Cayden's shoulder. "Hey, Geoff. Let me take Erin before she gets hurt."

Laurel moved into Natalie's path. "We can keep her safe for you."

Natalie twisted and aimed at Laurel. "Don't think so."

"No!" Wilmington raced into the line of fire.

Natalie fired.

Wilmington fell back, his chest exploding in spurts of blood.

Laurel rushed to Erin and snatched her away from the scene.

Daniel wrestled the gun out of Natalie's hand.

Agents took over and apprehended Natalie and Cayden. Daniel rushed to Laurel.

She handed Erin to a female agent.

They'd all been wrong about Morton Wilmington. They'd believed he was part of the scam when all he wanted to do was help.

CHAPTER 68

Laurel dropped to her knees over Wilmington's body. Why had he taken the shot? Blood soaked his shirt from a gaping hole. Her stomach churned. "Morton, an ambulance is here. They'll get you to the hospital." It couldn't arrive soon enough.

He wet his lips. "I—"

"Please." Laurel took Daniel's tux jacket and covered the raw wound, applying pressure with one hand and clutching his hand with the other. Urgency whispered a deadly message. "I'm so sorry, Morton. I should have believed you."

Daniel knelt beside her, but she didn't acknowledge him. Couldn't.

Morton opened his mouth as though to speak, but she stopped him. "Save your strength. We can talk at the hospital."

He peered into her face, his own a mask of white. "It's okay," he whispered. "This is how it's supposed to be."

She breathed in regret. His eyes widened, the color draining from his face.

"Hey, buddy, we're right here," Daniel said. "The three musketeers, remember? We're going to form our own investigation business."

"Not in this life." His ragged breathing, the ebbing away of life, caused her to grip his hand even harder.

"Don't die on me, Morton." Tears slipped down her cheeks.

His eyes fixed on Daniel. "Take care of her."

"Sure. You can help me."

He opened his eyes. "Laurel, search for Jesus. You'll find Him." His hand went limp, and he breathed his last.

She jerked away the jacket and leaned over his blood-soaked body, weeping. How had she been so blind? "Morton, you were telling the truth all along, and I never saw it." She drew in a sob as though he might still hear her.

Daniel draped his arm around her shoulders. But she didn't want comfort. She wanted Morton alive so she could apologize again.

CHAPTER 69

Laurel and Daniel sat outside a small French café near Rice Village. Meeting him hadn't been a good idea. But she had to tell him what was on her heart. Neither had eaten much, although the restaurant served excellent food. The time neared Morton's two o'clock funeral, the final tribute to his life. She'd wept until one tear chased another. Dark circles under Daniel's eyes revealed the same stress of the past days. They both shared guilt over not trusting Morton.

Natalie and Geoff Cayden were in custody for a series of crimes, both willing to nail the other. Geoff's DNA testing linked him to two cold case murders seven years ago. Erin had been placed with social services. That part tormented Laurel, a glimpse of her own past that no child should have to endure.

"Daniel," she said, "who chose Pastor Emerson to officiate the funeral?"

"Morton. I met with him earlier. The pastor said he'd seen Morton a few times before his death. Wanted Pastor Emerson to officiate in the event of his death and me to do the eulogy. We discussed his conversion and how he wanted to make a difference."

"Did the pastor say anything else?" She'd learned over the past few weeks that Daniel was a processor. But her habits mirrored his. "I need to know, to help with closure." She swallowed the ever-present lump in her throat.

"The first place Morton visited upon his release was Pastor Emerson's office. He expressed a commitment to make up for past crimes and vowed to help the FBI in any way he could. No matter the cost. And—" his gaze captured hers—"to show you he'd changed and encourage you to find God."

"He became a man of his word." Her remorse surfaced through moistened eyes. Emotions were so hard for her to accept and dealing with them even more difficult. "Anything else?"

"He confessed to Pastor Emerson that he never stopped loving you. He attempted to hate you but couldn't. When he became a Christian, you were in the middle of his new faith as though he couldn't go forward unless he forgave you. Laurel, I believe he set out to give his life to a worthy cause, and you were it. He knew God had forgiven him, but he couldn't do the same for himself. He arranged for Jesse's family to be taken care of financially and established funds for the kids' college." He reached across the table and took her hand, entwining her fingers in his. "How can I help you?"

She pulled her hand back. "I have to figure this out." She blinked back the wetness while despising her weakness. "I've been better. I'm in a fog, reliving times with him since his prison release. Can't sleep. Can't concentrate in the day. He and I had a good conversation Thursday evening." She ushered in control. "When he tossed the grenade out the window, I realized I didn't despise him anymore. But I couldn't bring myself to trust him either. I reacted badly, pushed him away after he saved my life."

"I understand. We're trained to be smart, cautious. With Morton, I never believed anything he said. Always looked for an angle, telling myself he and I played a stupid game. He said he wanted you to have the credit for the takedown, but I thought he was lying."

"The *Chronicle* printed a beautiful article about his life since the conversion. His time was short but he accomplished much," she said. "Did you offer your perspective?"

"Some. Pastor Emerson contributed the most."

"I'm glad. Morton liked you." She paused for a beat. "Natalie Cayden was the one who surprised me. She was the mastermind behind it all."

He nodded. "She hacked into the users of dementia medications, obtained their health records, and accessed their bank information. The billing information was a gold mine. And that was only the beginning."

"I'm more aware of the real Morton every day. He suspected Cayden wasn't working alone, but he couldn't find the secret partner." She took a sip of water. "Natalie gained entry into the National Association of Insurance Commissioners, set up a fake ID to help others obtain a national producer number online, and went to work. Beginning in Florida, she worked through Blue Cross Blue Shield and learned over three hundred thousand people didn't have an NPN assigned to their health insurance applications. She assisted them in obtaining a number, and with a $25 per month fee for each application, that meant a nice monthly total of $7.5 million every month for the life of the policies. With insurance company red tape, it would take at least a year for the insurance company to flag why her NPN was receiving this incredible amount.

"By then she'd established other fake bank accounts to handle the influx of cash. She set up another alias account to be a navigator for those seeking insurance, and she brought in $5 for every individual she helped secure health insurance. Given the number of new policyholders, she was paid another hefty check. All deposited in offshore accounts under her maiden name." Laurel closed her eyes, weariness threatening to envelop her.

"Nothing in either of their backgrounds triggered an alarm to law enforcement," Daniel said. "Good thing no one was hurt in the car bombings. The vehicles belonged to guests, and one of Cayden's men wired explosives to two of them. At least he confessed his part in the operation and gave the FBI the name of the accomplice who cut the power at the Junior League and used his phone to set off the car bombs." He shook his head. "Who would have suspected that the bartender at the Instantaneous set off car bombs? And he also followed me to my grandparents' hotel, then escaped the FBI."

"Will Erin ever recover?" Laurel identified with her. "I hope the system identifies her need for long-term counseling."

"Are you going to see her?"

She nodded. "I have to. If I'm permitted."

The moments ticked by.

He glanced at his watch. "I told Gran and Gramps I'd meet them early at the church. Do you mind?"

"Of course not. How are they since returning home on Sunday?"

"Gramps is the same, and Gran will do all she can to fight the Alzheimer's battle. She wants to establish a relationship with Erin. At this point, there is no family to care for her."

She smiled. "Wonderful. Abby is a dear woman."

"My grandparents really like you. Looking forward to more visits."

The warm thoughts temporarily eased her troubled mind, and she basked in his family and their love for each other.

"Can I see you later on, after the funeral?"

Honesty held more importance than ever before. "Not yet, Daniel. I need space." Her pulse sped. "I need time to think through my past and the future."

"To decide if there's a future for us?"

She forced herself to look into his milk-chocolate eyes. Tears threatened, but she would not dissolve into them. "Morton

sacrificed his life for me and what he believed in. I've made a decision to honor him and search for the same truth."

He squeezed her hand, and she gently pulled it back. "After the
services, don't call or text." She thought of Abby and Earl and how
she'd miss them. "If we're ever going to build a relationship . . .
I need to go forward as a whole person. Right now I'm broken and
not good for myself."

He nodded slowly. "How long?"

She loved him, but the future was vague. "Maybe never. I don't
expect you to wait."

"But I will. You know that." Daniel smiled with a sweetness
she'd learned to treasure. But she also saw sadness. "Is this why you
wanted to attend the funeral separately?"

She nodded. "Don't you need to get to the church?"

He shrugged. "Guess so."

She trembled and reached deep inside for courage. "Then this
is good-bye."

EPILOGUE

Laurel checked her makeup for the umpteenth time. She strolled through her apartment, rearranging things, wiping invisible dust, listening to the clock tick the seconds.

Daniel might have changed his mind.

He might have decided her baggage wasn't worth the investment.

His feelings could have been the emotional high of two people working together and experiencing danger.

He could have found someone else.

But he wouldn't have accepted her invitation to dinner if he hadn't wanted to see her.

She'd missed him from the moment he walked out of the restaurant on the day of Morton's funeral. Not a day passed she didn't long to hear his voice. Abby had become her lifeline, and they talked several times a week. Laurel drew strength from the woman as she'd done with Miss Kathryn. Several times they'd visited Erin at her foster home, where a wonderful couple who were childless had come to love her. She continued dance lessons and proudly showed Laurel and Abby new steps.

Laurel sank onto her sofa, smoothing out the blue knit dress purchased yesterday for this occasion. Modest yet feminine. Her rehearsed speech would never work. Only the truth. He deserved to know where her exploration had taken her. Brought her. Pushed her to look deep where denial reigned for so many years.

The doorbell rang and she startled as if she didn't know who was calling. The scent of dinner wafted through her home. Daniel's favorite, per Abby: pork chops simmering in gravy, scalloped corn with peppers, Caesar salad, rye bread, and apple cobbler with cinnamon ice cream.

Standing on legs that threatened to give way, she made purposeful strides across the room.

Lord, don't let me fall apart.

She opened the door. Daniel balanced pink roses, a foot-long Snickers bar, and a miniature white stallion. Dressed in jeans, a dark-brown sports jacket, and a button-down shirt, open at the collar, he simply stole her breath. Especially his milk-chocolate eyes.

"Do you need help?" She laughed.

"Is this the woman of the house?"

"It is. Are you the gentleman coming for dinner?" When he grinned, she melted into a pool of giddiness. "Come in."

"You are gorgeous," he whispered.

The sparkle in his eyes gave her hope. "Thank you. You look pretty incredible yourself." She took the roses and inhaled deeply, smiling her appreciation. She touched the Snickers bar. "It's frozen."

"I wanted dinner to be special."

"You made it special by accepting my invitation." His presence spoke louder than anything she could have prepared. She pointed to the white horse. "Looks like my Phantom."

"My intent." He set the steed on the table. "Those smells are making my stomach growl. But can I give you a proper hello first?"

She laid the roses on the kitchen counter and placed their dessert in the freezer.

His gaze captured hers. "It's been a long time."

She stepped into his arms, and his kiss set her tingling all the way to her toes. Dinner slipped her mind. Only the two of them together mattered. "Hey," she finally said. "The food will get cold."

"There's always the microwave." He stepped back. "Let me help you—to keep my hands busy."

She laughed. Did he have any idea how nervousness raced through her body? Once seated, she asked him to say grace and thanked him. A first. He claimed the meal was the best he'd ever tasted.

"I've prepared it three times to make sure it would turn out." She caught the merriment on his face. "I've never been a good cook."

"It's wonderful. I searched four flower shops before I could find pink roses. We're a mess."

Her face seemed to be a permanent smile, and she couldn't taste any of the food. "How's everything on the police force?"

"Good. I've applied to law school," he said. "Should know soon."

He'd never mentioned this. "Wonderful. I can see you as a lawyer, defending the innocent." How she'd missed him. "Thatcher said you two were meeting once a week? How wild is that?"

He laughed. "We haven't killed each other yet. He contacted me after Morton's funeral. Depressed. He faced discipline for not informing us about the setup at your apartment. Then his dad passed after suffering a stroke. Wanted to get together. I agreed. So we've been having breakfast on Saturday mornings. Early. I bring my Bible."

"He's always been a private person. Guilty there too. Friendships can do wonders in a person's life."

"Su-Min?"

"She's now working in Chicago. Contacted me after the arrests. A lot of issues between us. Not sure they'll ever be resolved. But I'm trying."

He reached across the table for her hand. She touched his fingers, and electricity flowed. "Where have you been?"

"Around the world and back."

"An adventure?"

"At times it was not smooth sailing."

"Are you back to me?"

"I hope so." She must curb her emotions. "I'd like to tell you where I've been during the past four months. Do you mind?" She hesitated. "I tried to memorize this but gave up."

He squeezed her hand and she remembered the night at his grandparents' home when she confessed her past. This wouldn't be any easier.

"I wanted to honor Morton and see if I could find the same truths as he did—and you. So I asked Abby if she'd help me, and she has been a remarkable mentor."

The look on his face told her he had no idea the two had spent time together.

"She gave me Bible passages to read and answered my questions. Learned her middle name is Grace." She smiled. Couldn't help it. "I had to face my anger at Morton for the night Jesse was killed. In my rage, I blamed him instead of myself and the circumstances. In my heart, I was no better than him. Hard—very hard—for me to accept. May take years to deal with it."

"We all have regrets, Laurel. My life is filled with them too."

"I realize it's a part of life, growing and changing us into better people. I also spent time with Pastor Emerson. Christmas Eve was the day I became a Christian. I waited to contact you because I needed time to work through more regrettable things." She offered a slight smile. "It may take a lifetime."

"We can do that together," he said.

"Are you sure? There are so many things I've done. Things you should know. Things I'm embarrassed to discuss."

"We could start with my perfectionism and need to save the world, then move on to yours in fifty years or so. I need you in my life, Laurel. Beginning right now."

"Okay." She nodded.

He startled. "No argument?"

"Nope. I'm ready."

"So am I."

A NOTE FROM THE AUTHOR

DEAR READER,

I hope you've enjoyed *Double Cross* and the characters who played leading roles in the story. What I value from writing this story is what the characters learned from each other.

Laurel couldn't shake her past, the psychological repercussions drawing her slowly away from the world where she believed the hurt would no longer torment her. She had her home with her antiques, a career in the FBI, and Phantom. Laurel could have continued her downward spiral without Abby's, Daniel's, and Morton's impressions on her life.

Daniel thought he could save the world. His role as a police officer helped him step toward that goal, an impossible one. When he faced the truth about his mother and later Morton Wilmington, he discovered freedom and purpose.

Abby believed in doing everything possible to keep her body, mind, and spirit in good shape. She understood the meaning of survival and the joy of living every day to its fullest. But when life zoomed out of control, she accepted assistance from those who could rectify the situation.

Morton showed the characters how they could step into the waters of life and be clean.

I think we all have a few traits of each character in *Double*

Cross. The question is whether we can learn from those around us to grow our relationship with Jesus. I hope so. I know I'm trying.

Sincerely,

DiAnn

Expect an Adventure
DiAnn Mills
www.diannmills.com
www.facebook.com/diannmills

CHAPTER 1

Taryn's perfect day melted in the heat of an early morning bottleneck. Houston traffic was a war zone during rush hour. Six lanes of bumper-to-bumper vehicles slowed to a crawl with a road construction crew flashing warning lights ahead. Six lanes narrowed to five, then four, then three, then two.

Shep touched her arm, his gold-brown eyes expressing tenderness. "Babe, the driver will get us to the airport in plenty of time."

"I hate traffic." She pulled her iPad from her purse, a habit when she needed to keep her mind occupied.

"Taryn, our honeymoon starts today." He smiled. "Do your new husband a favor and put away your gadgets. Didn't the VP tell you to forget about work and concentrate on your husband?"

"He did, and you have all my attention."

"Better yet, let me have all your toys, and I'll keep them safe. The one thing I plan to do for the rest of my life is take care of you."

Oh, this wonderful man. And he was all hers. "You're right. My life's no longer a solo project. I've been single for so long—"

"And a workaholic. Don't worry. I have room right here in my backpack." He chuckled, the rich sound reminding her of a thundering waterfall. "I'll keep them for you, Mrs. Shepherd. But I doubt you'll have time to use them."

She blushed, remembering last night. How could she argue with such devotion? "Can I at least keep my phone?"

"I suppose." He brushed a kiss across her lips. "I love the blush in your cheeks."

Would she always grow warm with his touch? "Comes with the hair."

"A gorgeous match." He twirled a tendril of her hair around his fingers and let it fall against her neck, causing a shiver from far too many sources.

Taryn knew what he was thinking, but she couldn't respond with the limo driver listening to every word. She handed Shep her iPad, hoping he understood that until she met him, her first love had been designing software. Now, with bittersweet regret, she watched him tuck her technological lifeline into his leather backpack.

"We'll be at the airport in twenty minutes." He took her hand into his. "Then we're off to our San Juan paradise. We might never come back. Live in Puerto Rico forever."

She snuggled close to him. For the first time in years, she wouldn't miss work—no software development projects or unrealistic deadlines. And to think she'd spend the rest of her life with this delicious man. Had it only been three months since they'd met and fallen in love? From the moment he walked into her life, he'd become her prince. They'd been inseparable, just the two of them, realizing they were meant for a lifetime. She'd dreamed of a man like Shep since she was a little girl, a man who wouldn't care that she kept her nose in books. His entrance into her heart was like a golden path to a fairy-tale future.

After checking in at the airport, she stared at her boarding pass and wished it held her married name: Mrs. Francis Shepherd. Their next trip would show them as husband and wife.

Security moved like the traffic they'd left behind. In the crowd, everyone's personal space was invaded, and some people responded with hostility. Taryn stepped into a long, winding line, and Shep wrapped an arm around her waist. Oh, she loved her new life. He blew her a kiss while loading his shoes and personal belongings into a bin. If cravings like these occupied her mind for the next fifty years, how would she ever get any work done again?

Once they walked through the body scanner and gathered their things, they wove through the crowd and on toward the gate. The predawn coffee caught up with her. With the urgency, she pointed to the women's restroom. "Do I have time for a quick stop?"

"Sure. My fault since I filled your cup twice to wake you. Let me have your carry-on, and I'll wait here." His smoldering look could have melted the wings off a jumbo jet.

"I'll hurry."

"No problem. The future's ours."

Rushing inside, she noted six women ahead of her, one with two children. Shep had a tendency to be impatient with time constraints, but she'd be miserable on the plane if she didn't wait her turn. Her iPhone notified her that she had fifteen minutes before boarding time.

Finally a stall opened and she hurried in. While she was drying her hands, a thunderous explosion shook the floor. A crack snaked up the wall. Then another. The mirror shattered, breaking her image into shards of glass.

She screamed and swung toward the entrance. Before she could take a step, the ceiling collapsed. Amid dirt and fallen tile, moans filled the air like a nightmare that refused to end. The walls creaked, metal and concrete shifting . . . falling.

Muffled groans alerted Taryn to her impaired hearing from the blast. Trembling, she bent to check on a young woman sprawled at her feet. Blood seeped from a head wound, and Taryn couldn't detect a pulse.

Debris rained on her. Something crashed against her head, sending her spiraling into darkness.

DISCUSSION QUESTIONS

1. Laurel has been trying to let go of the guilt she feels over what happened when she put Morton Wilmington in prison five years ago. Does Laurel ever release her guilt? How? Can guilt be a good thing or lead to a good consequence? If you were in Laurel's shoes, what steps would you take to turn the guilt into something good?

2. As a police officer, Daniel is used to taking charge and finding the answers himself. Why is he so reluctant to work with the FBI? Is his attitude justified? Why or why not? What makes him change his mind about interagency cooperation?

3. Daniel's grandfather, Earl Hilton, lives with Alzheimer's, a disease that affects more than 5 million Americans and their caregivers. Is there someone in your life who has received this diagnosis? What sort of day-to-day challenges do caregivers face? How can you show love and compassion to dementia patients and their families?

4. In this novel, the FBI has spent years investigating a scam targeting the elderly, and Laurel feels desperate enough to bargain with a criminal, even offering to shorten his sentence if he cooperates. What's behind her motivation for

making such a plea? Is this a reasonable risk for her to take? What are the potential pitfalls in her plan?

5. Have you or someone you love ever been robbed or taken advantage of in some way? How did it change your life or theirs? What precautions can you take, or advise your loved ones to take, to avoid a scam like the one in the story?

6. Morton Wilmington claims to have turned his life around since being imprisoned. Would you have trusted him initially? Is there a point where your feelings toward him begin to change?

7. Abby Hilton is a woman of action, facing challenges with faith and resolve. But "the more she trusted [God], the more the devil tossed her way." Have you found this to be true in your own life? What do you do when the circumstances before you threaten to overwhelm you?

8. From an early age, Laurel was told that one day she would have to surrender to her need for God. What are some of the false gods people hold on to before reaching their breaking points? What have you held on to in your life and what was your breaking point?

9. After years of silence, Daniel comes to a crossroads in his relationship with his mom. Does his conversation with her go the way you expected it to? How does Daniel honor God in what he says?

10. As a teenager, Abby ran away from home and straight into a horrible situation. Eventually she had the courage to escape from her living nightmare. What lessons does Laurel take away from Abby's past? Are you living with the consequences of a bad choice, or do you know someone who is? What encouragement can you find in Abby's story?

11. In chapter 44, Daniel dismisses the idea that he should be working as a detective. He says, "Right now this is what God wants me to do. . . . My significance is in being available for whatever's needed." Describe a time when you could say this about your life. Have you ever said no to an opportunity that, to an outsider, seemed like a no-brainer? What did you learn from that experience?

12. At the climax of the story, Laurel is caught in the crosshairs of a showdown. Were you surprised by what happened next? Do you believe the motives behind the actions were genuine?

ABOUT THE AUTHOR

DiAnn Mills is a bestselling author who believes her readers should expect an adventure. She currently has more than fifty-five books published.

Her titles have appeared on the CBA and ECPA bestseller lists; won two Christy Awards; and been finalists for the RITA, Daphne Du Maurier, Inspirational Readers' Choice, and Carol Award contests. DiAnn is a founding board member of the American Christian Fiction Writers; the 2014 president of the Romance Writers of America's Faith, Hope, & Love chapter; and a member of Inspirational Writers Alive, Advanced Writers and Speakers Association, and International Thriller Writers. She speaks to various groups and teaches writing workshops around the country. DiAnn is also a craftsman mentor for the Jerry B. Jenkins Christian Writers Guild.

She and her husband live in sunny Houston, Texas. Visit her website at www.diannmills.com and connect with her on Facebook (www.facebook.com/DiAnnMills), Twitter (@DiAnnMills), Pinterest (www.pinterest.com/DiAnnMills), and Goodreads (www.goodreads.com/DiAnnMills).

4-15